# *DREAMS OF PASSION*

In the shade of a towering oak, Lysette lay back on the velvety grass. There was beauty all around but she saw none of it. Her mind was far away, lost in the mists of time. She was drawn back to a night three years before when a stranger she now knew as Nicholas Callaway had taken her into his arms and given her her first taste of womanhood.

She had thought never to see the man again, but now he had reentered her life. She was at his mercy, much as she had been that night when he had taken her into his arms and kissed her as she had never even dreamed of being kissed—touched her where she had never dared hope to be touched—awakened emotions she had never known slumbered within her.

Nicholas Callaway would be arriving soon. Why did the thought send her pulses leaping? He was a cad; he was callous, ruthless. He was everything she detested. Why, then, did her senses seem to spring to life at the thought of spending time in his presence? The man was very likely coming to foreclose on everything she owned in the world and all she could think of was the sensual grace that marked all his movements, the glimmer in his black eyes that bespoke some dark, secret knowledge only he possessed, the firm, fully sculpted mouth that had evoked such a shocking reaction in her.

Lying in the dappled shade, Lysette plucked five big petals from the hibiscus blossom in her hand and dropped them one by one onto the grass. It was not until she cast aside the bedraggled remains that her heretofore unnoticed observer spoke.

"Well? Does he love you or doesn't he?"

Lysette sat up and watched, mortified, as Nicholas Callaway appeared from behind the thick trunk of a gnarled live oak.

Other Leisure books by Sandra DuBay:

FLAME OF FIDELITY
FIDELITY'S FLIGHT
CRIMSON CONQUEST
WHISPERS OF PASSION
IN PASSION'S SHADOW
WHERE PASSION DWELLS
BURN ON, SWEET FIRE
SCARLET SURRENDER
WILDER SHORES OF LOVE
TEMPEST

# By Love Beguiled

Sandra
DuBay

*For Joe*
*who gave me friendship and encouragement*
*when I needed both the most.*

Book Margins, Inc.

A BMI Edition

Published by special arrangement with Dorchester Publishing



Printed in the United States of America.

# PROLOGUE

*July—1842*
*New Orleans*

In the soft light cast by the shaded candles of the crystal chandeliers, the emerald and diamond necklace encircling Lysette Ravaisson's slender white throat glittered with a savage fire all its own. It drew the envious glances of the women she passed who noticed, with more than one pang of spiteful jealousy, that she also possessed the waterfall ear-drops and bracelet that completed the set. It drew as well the admiring glances of the gentlemen whose eyes were first drawn to its sparkle then lingered on the delicate young beauty upon whose creamy skin the jewels shimmered. For the women who envied her her treasures, the lone consolation was that the husband whose money had purchased the gems was two score years her senior, an aging sixty to her youthful twenty. Those ladies whose husbands were younger, handsomer, more virile, compressed their lips in smug satisfaction and tsked-tsked behind their fans over the lengths some women will go to for wealth. For the men who admired her, her husband was no less a source of interest; the thoughtful gaze of more than one gentleman present in the ballroom of Christopher Bishop's New Orleans mansion that night masked speculation of how well, if at all, old Jules Ravaisson could satisfy his exquisite young wife and of how much better they could accomplish the task if given the opportunity.

To both the disdainful women and the covetous men, the fact that Lysette's flawless oval face wore an expression of serene contentment as her hand rested snugly in the crook of her husband's arm was a bitter thought to swallow.

Halfway along the darkly paneled room, Jules stopped and shook hands with a tall, grey-haired man whose chiseled face was no less startlingly handsome for its advanced years. Jules drew Lysette forward proudly.

"Cherie, this is Monsieur Callaway. You have heard me speak of him."

Lysette smiled shyly. "Certainement," she murmured, extending her hand. She blushed charmingly. "Forgive me, monsieur. I am not so accustomed to English. At Saint-Cloud, you see, we speak only French."

"Of course, madame." Mr. Callaway lifted Lysette's gloved hand to his lips. "And how is the work on your home progressing?"

Lysette's wide eyes, not so very different in color from the rich, glowing chestnut of her hair, sparkled. "The house is nearly finished. Ah, it is so beautiful! You must visit us and see it, monsieur, since you had such a great part in making Jules's dream a reality."

"I should be happy to see it when it is

finished, madame. And though I cannot claim to have had more than a financial part in its becoming a reality, I am more than happy to accept such pretty thanks from such a lovely lady."

Lysette flushed, unused to such compliments. Occasions such as this were rare for her—Jules generally left her at home on their plantation halfway between New Orleans and Natchez while he went to conduct his business. It was seldom that she accompanied him on his trips and rarer still that they accepted any of the many invitations extended to them. In her four years of marriage to Jules Ravaisson, she had met scarcely a fraction of the men with whom he conducted the business of building a great plantation. For the rest she was merely a rumor. All that was generally known of Madame Ravaisson was that she was very beautiful and very young.

As her husband and his financier friend delved further into their discussion, Lysette accepted a glass of champagne from a passing servant and sipped it gratefully. Though the night was not as warm as might be expected of midsummer in New Orleans and the line of French doors had been thrown open along the garden veranda, the air in the crowded room was sultry and oppressive. Over the hum of conversation, the music of a string quartet was barely audible. In an adjoining room a sumptuous buffet was being served by liveried servants.

Lysette watched the milling crowd with interest. Now and then she intercepted a glance—envious, friendly, hostile, flirtatious. The first and third she ignored, the second she aknowledged only if the other party was a woman or a gentleman to whom she had been previously introduced, with the last she invariably dropped her gaze demurely, turning her attention to the smoothing of a wrinkle in her emerald silk gown or the fall of the wide lace bertha collar that encircled her bare shoulders.

She had no interest in a flirtation, however innocent. She had married Jules Ravaisson at sixteen, on the day her father had taken her from the French convent in which she had thought poverty would force her to spend her life, and had been scrupulously faithful to him ever since. It had been an arranged marriage, to be sure. Jules was a long-time friend of her father's, but she was fond of him. She had, in fact, known him since her earliest childhood and was not adverse to wedding a man who had never shown her ought but kindness.

There were those who said that her faithfulness to a man thrice her age stemmed from the fact that Jules never let her out of his sight but this was not so. There were many men employed at Saint-Cloud—young Frenchmen who had come as apprentices to the craftsmen Jules had imported to construct for him a manor in the tradition of his homeland. Some of them were handsome, most more than a little enamoured of their employer's wife. Jules left her alone there for days and nights at a time while he traveled to New Orleans to conduct his business. There was more than ample opportunity had Lysette been interested in an affair. She was not.

She drained her glass and relinquished it to a servant who offered her another which she declined with a little shake of her gleaming curls.

"Jules?" she said softly, smiling apologetically at Mr. Callaway for intruding on their conversation. "Jules, I am going out onto the veranda."

Her husband raised her hand and kissed her fingers. "Do not take a chill, minette."

Making her way through the crowd, Lysette at last found herself standing in one of the arches that formed a colonnade along the rear of the mansion. Looking out over the moonlit gardens, she found it hard to realize that she was, in fact, in the center of a large city. The gardens were lush, the shrubberies and trees were bowed beneath the weight of their blossoms and fruit. Nightbirds called in the darkness and the whirring of insects seemed a miniscule echo of the unceasing din from the ballroom that intruded so rudely upon the garden's hushed serenity.

Her rustling skirts whispered as they trailed over the black and white checkered marble floor of the night-shrouded veranda. The blue-white light of an enormous moon cast the arching shadows of the colonnade across the floor. The contrast between the overcrowded ballroom and the cool darkness sent a delicious chill coursing through Lysette as the night air caressed her shoulders and the pale flesh of her neck where her upswept curls laid bare the delicate nape. She smiled and sighed contentedly as she strolled along.

It was not until she saw the cigar's red glow that she realized she was not alone. She paused, framed in a marble arch, and strained her eyes into the darkness.

"I beg your pardon, monsieur," she said to a man the shadows kept hidden from her. "I did not mean to disturb you."

Turning, she retraced her steps. She did not look back when she heard the tapping of the man's footsteps on the marble; she did not see the man leave the shadows and flick his half smoked cigar away into the darkness of the garden.

"Wait," a deep voice commanded from behind her.

Lysette hesitated. A timid little voice within told her to flee back to the safety of the ballroom, back to the security of Jules's arm. Good manners dictated that, having intruded upon him, she owed it to the man to see what it was he wanted.

She turned and the breath seemed suddenly to leave her in a dizzying rush as her eyes beheld the most extraordinarily handsome man she'd ever seen.

He moved toward her fluidly, alternately swallowed by the darkness and bathed in the moonlight. His stark black and white evening dress was tailored to perfection and the wide-shouldered frock coat with its pinched-in waist and the tapered trousers which current fashion dictated seemed created with him in mind. His white cravat gleamed in the moonglow which shone off the black satin revers of his coat. Diamond studs winked in his white shirt. The same moonlight that sparkled in his shirtstuds disappeared into the ebony depths of his thick, waving hair. His eyes were deeply set and shaded by arching brows. His face was sharply planed and just as barbarically, as incredibly, perfect as the rest of him. There was about him an air of ruthless, unrelenting arrogance; everything about him proclaimed to the world that here was a man who knew precisely what he wanted of life—and one who would stop at nothing to have it.

Instinctively, Lysette feared him. She glanced toward the row of French doors that seemed suddenly so distant. Why had she wandered so far from the ballroom? Where was Jules? Surely he would come looking for her soon.

"You dropped this," the man said, stopping scarcely two feet from her.

Lysette saw her fan lying dwarfed in the man's outstretched hand. The delicate, pierced ivory sticks looked like fragile lace in the silvery light.

Cursing herself for a suspicious coward, Lysette smiled gratefully, if somewhat sheepishly, as she took the fan from him.

"Merci, monsieur," she whispered.

"You should be more careful of where you stroll," he told her gravely. "Even though this is private property, intruders are not unknown."

"You are quite correct, monsieur," Lysette admitted, wondering why his every word seemed to touch some hidden chord inside her. "I shall be more careful in future."

He was not ready to let her go though her desire to be gone was apparent.

"I wonder that your father let you go off on your own like this."

"My father?"

A mocking smile touched the man's firmly sculpted mouth. He gave a small nod toward the shafts of light spilling from the open doors.

"Old Ravaisson."

Lysette's eyes blazed. It was exactly the sort of remark that she knew caused Jules no end of chagrin. Moreover, she strongly suspected he knew perfectly well that Jules was her husband. Loyalty demanded a rebuke. She lifted her chin and threw him a scathing glare.

"You are insulting my husband, monsieur, and I shall hear no more of it!"

With a swish of her skirts, she turned to go. In an instant her wrist was imprisoned in his iron grasp—the emeralds and diamonds of her bracelet dug painfully into her wrist through the thin silk of her gloves.

"Let me go!" Lysette ordered, the tremor in her voice betraying her fear. "I demand it!"

"First you must allow me to tender my apologies."

Though his words were polite, there was, in his eyes, and in the fierceness with which he held her wrist imprisoned, a chilling ruthlessness that terrified Lysette.

"It is not necessary," she breathed. She tried to yank her wrist free but the jewels of her bracelet bit more deeply into her flesh.

"I insist," he hissed.

His arm snaked about her waist and he dragged her toward him. Lysette gasped as her body was crushed against his. Her wrist freed, she pummeled his shoulders. She arched away but he pulled her closer still; she felt the icy touch of one of his diamond studs against her breast. His face loomed above hers, hard, dark, uncompromising. His black eyes glittered and narrowed; they captured Lysette, wove a spell about her in the way that a spider weaves a silken cage about its prey.

She quivered helplessly within the unyielding circle of his arm. "No," she pleaded softly even as his head came down and his lips slanted across hers.

His mouth was hard, savage, demanding; he tasted of champagne and fine cigars. With no small measure of satisfaction, he felt Lysette's struggles cease. She stiffened, then a soft, almost anguished moan escaped her. One arm still imprisoning her, the man brought his other hand up slowly, lingeringly, over her satin bodice until it found her breast. He heard her little cry and felt the shudder that tore through her but still he would not free her.

For Lysette, it seemed that only the man's arm, so tight about her waist, kept her on her feet. From the first instant she'd realized that he meant to kiss her, her senses had been hopelessly muddled. It was wrong! the voice of propriety cried inside her. No man had the right to kiss her except her husband—no man had ever kissed her but Jules. But merciful heavens! She had never dreamed of a kiss like this.

It was the touch of his hand on her breast that shocked her back to her senses. She flailed at him with her tiny fists and at last he released her, so abruptly that she stumbled backward nearly falling.

She stared at him, one hand raised to her lips. She was confused, appalled, furious. Her arm slashed through the air and her closed fan caught his cheek. The antique ivory sticks snapped and the fragile, painted silk mount tore into ragged shreds.

She snatched up her skirts and fled back toward the ballroom convinced that to remain would be to put herself in peril. But from the shadows behind her she heard only the low, infuriating sounds of his mocking laughter.

She blinked in the ballroom's glowing light. A voice behind her made her start violently.

"Here you are, cherie." Jules was beside her smiling. Dear, kind Jules! She wanted to throw her arms about him and weep her relief. A tiny frown drew his grey brows together. "What is it, ma chere? You are flushed. You're trembling."

"I think I have taken a chill," she lied, guiltily avoiding his concerned blue eyes. "May we go now?"

"But of course." Signalling to a servant, he ordered Lysette's wrap and their carriage. "Come, ma petite, we will bid Monsieur and Madame Bishop adieu."

Her hand clasping her husband's arm, Lysette followed Jules across the room to say goodnight to Christopher and Louisa Bishop. Though she did not hazard a glance, she could feel a pair of ice cold ebony eyes piercing to her very heart.

Lysette's bedroom in the Ravaisson's suite was lit only by the flickering light of the lamps on her dressing table. Clad in the high necked, long sleeved linen gown that was her habitual night attire, Lysette absently stroked her brush through the thick chestnut curls which, freed from their pins, cascaded heavily down her back to curl about her narrow waist.

The door of the adjoining room opened and Jules appeared. His bare calves stuck out from beneath his voluminous nightshirt and his grey hair was covered by a long tasseled cap. To some he might have presented a ridiculous picture; to Lysette, who bore for her husband a genuine if less than passionate love, the effect was endearing. She smiled up at him as he came to stand beside her.

"I was very proud of you tonight, *mon ange*," he told her. "You make me proud to be your husband."

Turning her head, Lysette kissed the hand that rested on her shoulder.

Jules drew a sharp breath. He pulled his hand away with an almost guilty air. Bending, he gave her a chaste peck on the cheek before leaving her to return to his own room.

Lysette sighed as she turned back to her mirror. His reaction came as no surprise. It was not lack of desire that prompted Jules Ravaisson to turn away from his exquisite young wife. In fact, the opposite was true. But Lysette was the daughter of his closest friend, Fabrice Segur. He had seen her as a mewling babe, her tiny rosebud mouth tugging hungrily at her mother's breast. He had watched her toddle across the floor on her chubby baby's legs, had seen her sitting at a table, her long sausage curls hanging in her custard. He had dandled her on his knee.

When her mother died, he had gone with her father to place her with the nuns at the Ursuline convent outside of Paris. She had been eight then. He did not see her again for eight years.

By then, Fabrice was dying. There was little money to leave his only child—not enough to give her a worthy dowry, not even enough to allow her to remain as a boarder in the convent. She had no vocation for the religious life, he knew. What, then, would become of her?

When he'd heard that his old friend Jules, himself now a widower, was leaving France to begin anew in America, he had called upon him and arranged a marriage between his sixteen year old daughter and the then fifty-six year old Jules. Lysette, schooled to obedience by the sisters and genuinely fond of Jules Ravaisson, had bowed without question to her father's wishes. She had seen many of her friends sent off to marriages with men older and far less kindly than the man she had always called "Uncle Jules."

From the first, while they traveled to America and founded Saint-Cloud, theirs was a marriage in name only. That Jules wanted her was never in question but he was heartily ashamed of his desire for the woman "petite Lysette" had become.

Lysette gazed at herself in the mirror. She loved her husband; she was, and would always be, faithful to him. But she was twenty—four years a wife—and still as innocent of life as she had been on the morning of her wedding.

Well, she mused, brushing the rose-patterned silver brush across her lips, perhaps not quite that innocent. She could not help remembering the wickedly exciting feeling of being held in that evil man's arms. His kiss had been so different from Jules's guilty pecks; his embrace was so strong, his caress. . .

"Mon Dieu!" she breathed as a cloying warmth flooded her. Even now she could feel the dizzying thrill of his hand on her breast. With hesitant fingers, she touched her breast through the fine linen of her gown; the pale pink crest was a tight, aching rosebud that tingled beneath her tentative touch.

"Damn him!" she hissed. "What has that bastard done to me! For the first time I have been disloyal to my husband and for what? A stolen kiss? An illicit caress? If this is what passion does to a person, I am better off without it!"

She slammed the heavy brush down onto the satinwood tabletop.

"Cherie?" Jules had awakened.

"I'm sorry," Lysette called back, swiveling on the striped satin stool toward the half-opened door. "I dropped my hairbrush."

Twice! her conscience reminded her. That was the second time she had lied to him tonight—the second time in the entire four years of their marriage.

"You should be asleep, minette," he admonished gently. "We leave for Saint-Cloud very early tomorrow."

"I am going to bed right now, mon cher."

Rising, she extinguished the lamps and climbed into the lace netted bed. But sleep eluded her long into the night for images of a savagely handsome man with flashing black eyes and a cruel, sensuous mouth filled her mind, and longings she didn't fully understand seemed to ache in the very soul of her.

# CHAPTER 1

*August—1845*
*Saint-Cloud*

Lysette sighed as she felt a trickle of perspiration sliding down between her breasts. The heat was oppressive, even in the shade of the little white gazebo at the end of the garden, and the black silk of her gown seemed determined to absorb every last tortuous degree of it.

It had been two weeks since Jule's death. At twenty-three, Lysette was a widow without ever having been truly a wife. Frowning, she pushed those disloyal thoughts resolutely from her mind. Jules had been a good husband to her until the day he died.

And he had left her Saint-Cloud. Her russet-hued eyes skimmed the magnificent garden and golden stone mansion in the distance which sat majestically on the top of a man-made hill. Both the mansion and the intricately fashioned gardens that surrounded it looked as though they had been plucked from the beautiful Loire valley of Jules's native France.

Lost in her reverie, Lysette did not hear the silken swish of her housekeeper's skirts as the woman approached on the flagstone path.

"Oh, Tess!" She started as the short, compact, grey-haired woman stepped before her. "You gave me such a fright!"

"Forgive me, madame. There is a gentleman asking to see you."

"A gentleman? C'est impossible. I am in mourning. I can receive no one."

Tess lifted her sturdy shoulders. "I told him that, madame. He insists."

"Insists? Who is he?"

A card was placed in Lysette's hand. "Mayford Wyatt," she read. "He is an attorney from New Orleans." She frowned. "Jules's attorneys assured me that everything was being seen to. They assured me I would not be disturbed."

"I can call some of the men and have him thrown out," Tess offered.

Lysette tapped the card with one pink nail. "Did he say anything that would give you any notion of his business here?"

"He said it concerned the immediate future of Saint-Cloud."

"How so?" She saw the blank look on Tess's face. "Oh, I suppose it will do no harm to see him but I want you to stay with me."

"But of course, madame!" The thought of any other arrangement scandalized Tess. She had seen Lysette through seven years of marriage—she was not about to see her reputation besmirched after only two weeks of widowhood.

Together the women entered the elegant rococo parlor with its gilt-trimmed ivory walls and frescoed ceiling which made the room seem to soar into the clouds. On a gilded Louis Quinze sofa, a man in grey and black awaited them.

He stood politely as they entered and Lysette was more than a little surprised at the air of respectability that surrounded him. He was well-dressed, well-groomed, and altogether presentable. He looked like precisely what he was—a successful attorney whose clients were themselves successful in their chosen fields.

"Madame Ravaisson." His voice was low, carefully modulated. "Permit me to convey my sympathies."

"Thank you, Mr. . . ." She glanced down at the card. "Wyatt?"

"That's right." He nodded and Lysette noticed the speckling of grey in his dark brown hair. "Mayford Wyatt."

"Please sit down, Mr. Wyatt. You will not, of course, object to my housekeeper remaining with us?"

"Of course not, madame."

He resumed his seat and took up a leather portfolio while Lysette took a seat opposite him. Tess hovered protectively behind her.

"You are not one of my husband's attorneys, are you, sir?"

"No indeed, madame. I represent Mr. Nicholas Callaway. He is a financier in New Orleans."

"I have met Monsieur Callaway." Lysette remembered the handsome grey-haired man she'd met three years before.

"Ah, indeed. Well, then, you know that your late husband had dealings with Mr. Callaway's firm. It was from that firm that he received several substantial loans with which to build Saint-Cloud."

Lysette shifted uncomfortably in her chair. Why did she feel as though her world were about to fall apart?

"I did not know that," she admitted softly. "Jules seldom mentioned finances to me."

"I see. That is unfortunate. There are, I am sorry to say, payments on these loans which are far in arrears. I have been dispatched to discover what arrangements you wish to make to repay the monies owed my client."

Leaving her chair, Lysette moved nervously across the floor while Tess shot a withering glare at the man who had caused her lady such distress.

"How much . . . that is to say . . . what exactly is the amount Jules owed to Monsieur Callaway?" Not daring to look at the lawyer, Lysette gazed vacantly into an ormulu framed mirror which had once hung in the Brighton Pavilion of the late King George IV.

"Let me see." Mr. Wyatt shuffled through what seemed a mountain of ominously official looking documents. "The total debt amounts to just slightly over—" He glanced toward Tess and she, taking the hint, moved to Lysette's side. "Two hundred thousand dollars."

"Two hundred thou—" The blood drained from Lysette's face. She reached out blindly and Tess clasped her cold and trembling hand and guided her to a chair. "There must be some mistake!"

Mayford Wyatt cleared his throat. The woman before him seemed so young, so vulnerable. He'd been told that Jules Ravaisson's wife was beautiful but nothing had prepared him for such delicate loveliness. Suddenly he hated Nicholas Callaway for delegating him as the bearer of such devastating news.

"I'm sorry, madame, but there is no mistake."

Lysette lifted her chin and blinked back the tears of fear and desperation that threatened to spill from her wide, haunted eyes.

"What sort of arrangements did Monsieur Callaway suggest with regard to repayment, monsieur?" she asked, fighting to remain calm.

The lawyer clenched his teeth. It was all he could do to keep from packing away his papers and taking the boat back to New Orleans. He wanted to dump the whole matter back in Nicholas Callaway's lap. For his part, he had no taste for throwing widows out into the streets.

"He is willing to allow you one month, madame."

"One month!" Lysette felt faint but resolutely pushed aside the vinaigrette Tess scurried to fetch from the desk. She couldn't sit still. She wanted to scream or cry or break something—preferably Nicholas Callaway's head!

Thrusting herself out of her chair, she

paced the floor nervously twisting her wedding band on her finger.

"Why don't you simply be honest with me, monsieur?" she demanded at last. "Nicholas Callaway wants Saint-Cloud. He wants to take it from me and Jules's death has given him the perfect opportunity. Do you deny this is true?"

"No, madame," he answered honestly. "In all candor, I do believe that that is his reason for demanding payment in full."

Lysette's russet eyes met the lawyer's blue ones and she found there a pity she did not want.

"Do not feel sorry for me yet, monsieur," she told him gravely. "I still have my home, my beloved Saint-Cloud, and I do not intend to give her up so easily."

"Mr. Callaway is a stubborn man, madame."

"And I am a stubborn woman. I will go to New Orleans and talk to him. I will make him see how much Saint-Cloud means to me."

"He will not change his mind."

Lysette smiled, forcing a bravado she was far from feeling. "Neither will I, Monsieur Wyatt." She turned to Tess. "Pack for us, s'il vous plait, Tess. We are going to New Orleans."

"But, madame! You are in mourning!"

"I will mourn more if I find myself sleeping in the road at month's end!" Lysette pointed out with no little exasperation. "Now do as I say! Vite! Vite!"

She turned back to Mayford Wyatt. "I will speak to your Monsieur Callaway. And then we will see what is to become of Saint-Cloud."

Mayford smiled as he gathered his papers. He was definitely going to hurry back to New Orleans. His client was a hard man, ruthless and domineering, but Madame Ravaisson was like an exquisite little Napoleon going off to battle an arch-enemy. Their confrontation was one he wouldn't miss for the world.

Head held high, Lysette marched into the elegantly appointed offices of "Callaway and Callaway." Her black silk skirts hissed as she stormed up to the young clerk who labored behind his high desk.

"Madam!" His dark eyes were wide with indignation. Ladies did not present themselves in offices. It was simply not done. A scandal could result and scandal could easily prove the death blow to a firm whose stock in trade was its respectability.

"I wish to see Monsieur Nicholas Callaway," Lysette announced, ignoring the whispers of the gentlemen seated in the tufted leather wing chairs. The outer office served as a waiting room for Nicholas Callaway's lesser clients. It taught them humility, he liked to say.

Taken aback, the clerk stared at Lysette and at the grim-faced woman dressed similarly in black who glared ferociously at anyone with the temerity to mind her mistress's business.

"Well?" Lysette prompted after several moments had passed.

The clerk brushed back the maddening lock of lank blond hair that fell over his forehead. He swallowed hard and tried to decide which was the more daunting prospect—turning away this determined little female who clearly meant to have her way, or admitting to his master's presence such an unorthodox caller fully knowing Nicholas's volatile temper. Nor was there any comfort in being cognizant of the fact that he was Nicholas's twentieth clerk in as many months.

"Have you an appointment?" he managed at last, pretending to skim the morocco-bound appointment book which governed the office's hours.

"No, I have not," Lysette admitted haughtily. "But then Monsieur Mayford Wyatt did not have an appointment either when he forced his way into my home with the news that Monsieur Callaway intended to steal everything that belongs to me!"

The murmur of voices had risen to a steady buzz. As Lysette's words settled in, a tall, red-haired man in a threadbare coat and checked trousers suddenly bolted from the room. The clerk groaned; the man was a reporter who had been granted an interview with Nicholas Callaway. Doubtless he judged this little contretemps more worthy of his editor's ear.

"Please wait a moment, madame," the clerk begged at last.

He disappeared into the adjoining office only to reappear a moment later.

"This way, madame, if you please. Ah, Mr. Callaway asks that your companion wait out here."

"I will not!" Tess protested. "Madame is a lady and. . ."

"It's all right, Tess," Lysette assured her.

"But, madame!"

Lysette waved her back and Tess, still sputtering, stalked to an unoccupied chair. Noticing the gentlemen's eyes upon her, she scowled at them and sent their noses back into the pages of their afternoon papers.

The clerk, relieved to find that his master had not only welcomed the lady but had been expecting her, showed Lysette into an oak paneled office. He seated her in an armchair before a leather-topped desk of intimidating size. To her left, damask-draped windows framed a picturesque view of the city. To her right, a fireplace of grey marble stood below a gilt-framed portrait by Boucher, the great artist of eighteenth-century France. His style was unmistakable, Lysette reflected, more than a little shocked to find such a work in a public office. No other artist she knew could portray the nude female body with such an air of utter sensual abandon.

"Do you like it?" a low, male voice purred from the far corner of the room.

Lysette turned toward the voice expecting

to see the kind, handsome man Jules had introduced her to three years before. Instead, she found herself gazing into a pair of glittering ebony eyes which she had seen all too often in her dreams since that same night on Christopher Bishop's veranda.

# CHAPTER 2

"You!" Lysette tried to stand but the strength seemed to have ebbed from her body.

The sensual lips she remembered all too well curved into a faintly mocking smile.

"Bonjour, Madame Ravaisson. We meet again. But then, of course, I always knew we would."

He strode forward with the same unique fluid grace that made Lysette feel as though she were being stalked by some beautiful, dangerous beast.

"I am not here to see you," she hissed. "I am here to see Monsieur Callaway."

"But I am Monsieur Callaway," he insisted, imitating her accent.

"You are not! I met Monsieur Callaway at the Bishop's ball. My husband introduced me to him."

"You met James Callaway, my father." He lifted his broad shoulders. "Alas, his health is not good these days. I have assumed the lion's share of our business. Permit me to introduce myself, madame—a belated courtesy, I grant you, but there you are—I am Nicholas Callaway." His sable eyes missed nothing of her stark widow's garb. "Allow me to extend my condolences on your loss."

"Bah!" Fury reviving her, Lysette leapt out of her chair. "You are a hypocrite and a liar! Your condolences indeed! You're glad Jules is dead because you want Saint-Cloud! Admit it! That is why you helped him drive himself further and further into debt—so you could take Saint-Cloud when he died!"

"That's not true," Nicholas stated quietly.

"It is true!" Lysette stormed. "It is! I hate you!"

Rounding his desk, Nicholas seized her shoulders and shook her. "Be quiet, you little fool! You don't know what you're talking about!"

"I do know!" she shouted. Her little fists in their black lace gloves pummeled his chest. "You're trying to steal Saint-Cloud! You cheated my husband and now you're trying to—"

"Lysette!" He shook her hard. "Shut up! Stop acting like a hysterical woman and listen to me!"

Furious, she tore herself from his grasp. "Well, I am a hysterical woman! I have a right to be!"

"If you would stop ranting like a fishwife for five minutes and listen, I'll explain the situation."

Lysette stared at him, astonished. Never had Jules spoken to her in such a callous manner. Never had he lain violent hands upon her. She had been his little cherie, his minette.

"A fishwife!" she screeched. "How dare you!"

"I'm not going to spare your delicate feelings," he told her flatly. "You had the gumption to barge in here knowing full well it was a place of business. Very well, then, if you want to conduct a man's business, you can't hide behind your feminine sensibilities."

He went to a cabinet and took out a thick sheaf of papers. Returning to his desk, he patted the thickly tufted, blood-red leather chair.

"Come here, Lysette, I'm going to explain this to you." When she hesitated, he shot her an exasperated look. "Come!" he commanded.

"I'm not a dog to be ordered to and fro at your command!" she snapped even as she went to the chair and was seated and pushed up close to the desk. "Next you'll be telling me to heel and fetch!"

Nicholas's grin was dazzling. "Delightful as that prospect is, madame, we have other matters to attend to just now."

For the next hour, Nicholas went through the papers with Lysette. The amounts staggered her and yet at the bottom of each was the irrefutable signature, "Jules Ravaisson." At length, Nicholas tucked the last paper into its folder. He sat on the edge of the desk and stretched one long leg out before him.

"It's all there, Lysette," he told her, his tone more gentle than before. "If I hadn't loaned him the money, he could have gotten it elsewhere."

"Perhaps not," Lysette disagreed. "Perhaps if you had refused him, the other financiers in the city would have followed your example."

Nicholas shrugged. "He could have gone elsewhere. With the collateral he offered—Saint-Cloud, its furnishings, your jewels—he could have gotten money anywhere. There are many unscrupulous men in my profession. Many would simply cast you into the street without a backward glance."

"And you?"

"I've been thinking." Rising, he moved across the room and stood at the window, his hands clasped behind his back.

"And?" Lysette prompted, breathless. Leaving the chair, she moved toward him but did not dare go to his side.

Abruptly, he turned away from the window. He shook his head. "I haven't decided." He smiled at her sigh of exasperation. "Let me take you to dinner tonight. New Orleans is famous for its food, you know. You have been too infrequent a visitor."

"I am in mourning," she reminded him sharply.

"Even mourners must eat."

"Have I a choice?"

The humor faded from his swarthy face. "You will always have a choice, Lysette."

"And if I say no?"

"Then no it is."

"In that case, no, Monsieur Callaway, I will

not dine with you. I will return to Saint-Cloud while you ponder my fate."

Nicholas flashed a gleaming smile as he conducted her to the door. "As you wish, madame, but I would ask one favor of you."

Lysette eyed him suspiciously. "And that is?"

"I want to visit Saint-Cloud. I've never seen it although my father told me it's quite beautiful. Like its mistress, I believe he said. No, I'm wrong. Its mistress, he said, was breathtaking." His black gaze slid over her then returned to her pinkening face. "I must say, I concur."

Swallowing hard, Lysette fumbled with the ribbons on her black silk bonnet. "If you wish to visit, you may do so," she managed with just the right degree of indifference. "When shall I expect you?"

She watched as he went back to his desk and turned several pages in an appointment book very like the one the clerk possessed in the outer office.

"In two weeks?" he suggested. "I have clients to see to until then but I should be able to get away by, shall we say, September first?"

"Fine." Lysette brushed out a wrinkle in her glove hoping he would not see the way her hands trembled. "I'll have Tess see to the preparations. Good day, Monsieur Callaway."

"Good day, Madame Ravaisson." Opening the door, he stepped back to let her pass. But as she did, he touched her arm. "I am genuinely sorry about Jules's death," he said softly, his eyes warm with sincerity.

"Merci," Lysette murmured. Then she and Tess were gone leaving Nicholas to gaze after them with a curiously enigmatic smile playing at the corners of his full, sculpted mouth.

Lysette passed the fortnight before Nicholas's visit in a constant state of turmoil. She alternated between confidence that he would play the gentleman and allow her to repay Jules's debts with the revenues of Saint-Cloud's bountiful cotton crop and despairing certainty that he would order them off the land with scarce the clothes on their backs to call their own.

When the first of September at last arrived, she awoke with the dawn and spent the morning pacing a track in the magnificent rose and azure Savonnerie carpet of the morning room.

"What time is it, Tess?" she asked as the housekeeper bustled into the room.

Tess glanced wearily at the ormulu and ebony French clock in the corner. "Half past one, madame."

Lysette's smile was sheepish. "I'm sorry. I've asked you every hour, haven't I?"

"Every half hour, more like." Tess watched grimly as Lysette gazed at her reflection in the gilt-framed mirror over the sofa. "I don't see why you're fussing so about the way you look. You've no need to impress this villain."

Lysette smoothed back a curl and straightened the bodice of her high-necked, long-sleeved black silk gown. She wore mourning out of respect for Jules and that was as it should be, Tess reflected, but no one could fail to notice how the stark color and cut of her gown drew attention to her delicate figure, how it emphasized the creamy flawlessness of her skin, or how the severe chignon into which her chestnut curls had been confined made her beautiful red-brown eyes look enormous in her fine oval face. No, no one could fail to notice those things—particularly not a wicked scoundrel like Nicholas Callaway.

"But we do have to impress him," Lysette disagreed. "We are all of us at his mercy."

"At his mercy, indeed!" Tess was the very picture of indignance. "If I had my way, I'd meet him at the door with Monsieur's gun!"

"You cannot order a man from his own property, Tess."

"His own—! Madame!"

Lysette lifted her slender shoulders in a little, philosophical shrug. "To all intents and purposes, Saint-Cloud belongs to Nicholas Callaway. If he chose, he could send us packing without a sou."

Tess compressed her lips into a thin, disapproving line. "When I think of Monsieur Ravaisson committing such a folly! Leaving you unable to call your soul your own!"

Lysette fingered the mourning brooch with

Jules's initials worked in diamonds. "He had a dream, Tess. It sustained him through all his years of hardship and struggle. He believed in it." She caressed a magnificent marquetry roll-top desk which had once belonged to the Comte de Provence. "He made it come true. It is not for us to judge the wisdom of what he did."

Tess ground her teeth in exasperation. "But, madame! To leave you so far in debt!"

"He did not die deliberately," Lysette chided gently. "I'm sure he meant to pay the debts. He simply ran out of time."

She saw the housekeeper's mouth working, framing yet another protest, and stilled it by saying, "I'm going outside. Send for me if Monsieur Callaway arrives. Merci, Tess."

Lysette wandered through the sun-bathed gardens where the elaborate formal beds with their floral borders and carefully manicured box tree arabesques surrounded a fountain that played day and night. Beyond lay a shady grove, ostensibly nature's own handiwork but in fact as carefully planted and tended as any of the intricate designs of the flower beds.

In the shade of a towering oak, Lysette lay back on the velvety grass. As she gazed up through the lush, interlaced branches of the ancient tree with its grey festoons of Spanish moss, she twirled a pink hibiscus blossom in her hand. There was beauty all around but she saw none of it. She heard neither the gentle murmuring of the wind in the treetops nor the calls of the birds flitting among the leaves. Her mind was far away, lost in the mists of time. She was drawn back to a night three years before when a stranger she now knew as Nicholas Callaway had taken her into his arms and given her her first taste of womanhood.

She had thought never to see the man again but now he had reentered her life. She was at his mercy, much as she had been that night when he had taken her into his arms and kissed her as she had never even dreamed of being kissed—touched her as she had never dared hope to be touched—awakened emotions she had never known slumbered within her.

Unconsciously she brushed the soft flower against her lips. Nicholas Callaway would be arriving soon. Why did the thought send her pulses leaping? He was a cad; he was callous, ruthless. He was everything she detested. Why, then, did her senses seem to spring to life at the thought of spending time in his presence?

Her mouth curved into a smile that was rife with self-mockery. The man was very likely coming to foreclose on everything she owned in the world and all she could think of was the sensual grace that marked all his movements, the glimmer in his black eyes that bespoke some dark, secret knowledge only he possessed, the firm, fully sculpted mouth that had evoked such a shocking reaction in her.

She remembered her astonishment when

she'd found him waiting for her in his New Orleans office. How could she have known who he was? She should have been furious but all she could remember was noticing the flecks of grey in the lush black waves at his temples and how they added a certain, indefinable dash to his already elegant mane.

Lying in the dappled shade, Lysette plucked the five big petals from the blossom and dropped them one by one onto the grass. It was not until she cast aside the bedraggled remains that her heretofore unnoticed observer spoke.

"Well? Does he love you or doesn't he?"

Lysette sat up and watched, mortified, as Nicholas Callaway appeared from behind the thick trunk of a gnarled live oak.

"Do you always spy on people, monsieur?" she demanded coldly. In spite of herself, she noticed how handsome he looked. His suit was dove grey, his vest and cravat charcoal. His only ornaments were a gold stickpin and watchchain.

"When it suits me," he answered truthfully. He offered her his hand and pulled her to her feet. "You can't imagine the picture you made lying in the grass."

Lysette felt the hot flush creeping into her cheeks. The glimmer that so disconcerted her was back in his ebony eyes.

"You wanted to see Saint-Cloud," she reminded him. "There is much to see and we had better start immediately if you want to see it all before you leave."

Nicholas grinned. "I'm in no hurry to leave, madame. In fact, I have cancelled all my appointments for the next week."

"A week! Saint-Cloud is large, monsieur, but I assure you there is nothing here that will occupy you for an entire week."

"I could argue that point."

He reached toward her and Lysette jumped back.

"What are you doing?" she demanded.

He plucked a leaf from her hair, then another and another. "Your hair is full of them," he told her. "If you wear them back to the house, that dragoness you call a housekeeper is likely to think I had something to do with their being there. I don't like the fond glances she gives the sabers crossed on the walls of the entrance hall. Somehow I think she'd like to skewer me with one of them."

Lysette smothered a smile. "Tess is very protective of me. She had been Jules's housekeeper for many years before he left France. She came to America with us. I was a new bride, young and inexperienced. She took me under her wing."

They started back toward the formal garden. Nicholas shortened his normally long strides to accommodate Lysette's shorter legs. Looking down at her, he noticed one last leaf clinging to a curl that had strayed from her chignon.

"How old were you when you married Jules?" he asked.

"Sixteen. We left France almost immediately. Jules was eager to begin work on his dream."

"I'm glad I didn't know you then."

Lysette glanced up at him quizzically. "Why do you say that?"

"I would very likely have dismissed you as a pretty little girl then."

"And you don't like pretty little girls?"

He smiled roguishly. "I much prefer beautiful women."

Lysette looked away quickly. The look on his face was too disturbing—it was a hungry look, wanting and yet somehow already triumphant. It reminded her of the look a wolf gives its prey after it has been captured but just before it is devoured.

To mask her discomfiture, Lysette began a long, rambling monologue on the many and varied features that made Saint-Cloud unique among the plantations of the Mississippi River region. Her tour took them through the gardens and the sumptuous house.

They ended in a salon that was one of Lysette's favorites. It was a lofty oval room whose ungilded white paneling alternated with tall, arched mirrors whose draping valances were of sky blue and silver figured silk.

"Well?" she prompted as Nicholas sat in an armchair with his legs stretched out before him.

"You've seen what you came to see. What now?"

He pondered the matter. "A brandy would be nice."

"Oh! You are the rudest man I have ever met!"

"How so?" His tone was wounded.

She jammed her fists into her hips and glared at him. "My life rests on your whim and you expect me to entertain you!"

He sighed dramatically. "Oh, very well. Sit down. And stop glaring at me. You do a very credible imitation of— What is her name?"

"Tess."

"Yes. I'm not sure she's a good influence on you, Lysette."

"Tess is none of your business. She is my friend. When you take Saint-Cloud away from me, she will come with me."

"Have I said I would take Saint-Cloud away from you?" he inquired. "Now sit down, as I asked, and listen to me."

Rising, he seated Lysette in the chair he had just vacated and stood before her, hands clasped behind his back.

"I am prepared to dismiss all Jules's debts, Lysette. It will be as though they never existed. Saint-Cloud, and you, will be completely unencumbered."

"Monsieur!" Lysette breathed.

"However," he went on, raising a hand to stifle her premature excitement, "I would expect something of you in return. It is something I have been thinking of for some time. In fact, I suppose the thought first entered my mind on the night of Christopher Bishop's ball."

Lysette leapt to her feet, eyes blazing. Her slender body shook with the force of her outrage.

"You bastard!" she screamed. "You unspeakable, odious bastard! How dare you come into my house and suggest that I become your mistress!"

She balled her fist and brought it slashing through the air but he caught her wrist before the blow connected. When he spoke, his face was scant inches from hers.

"I'm not asking you to be my mistress, my exquisite little spitfire, I am asking you to be my wife."

# CHAPTER 3

"Your—" Lysette sank slowly back down into her chair. The angry flush faded from her cheeks leaving her an alarming chalk white. "Your wife?" She shook her head trying in vain to clear away the jumble whirling inside it. "But . . . but . . ."

Nicholas waved a dismissing hand. "Come now, there is no need for such fuss. What I am proposing is a simple business arrangement. A merger, if you will."

"A merger?" Lysette repeated, stunned.

He frowned. "Perhaps I'm not explaining this well."

He went to the cabinet where Jules kept his liquor and poured himself a healthy draught of whiskey.

"Perhaps not," Lysette agreed, dazed. "Monsieur Callaway, before you go any further, I must tell you that I have no desire to marry—"

"Nor have I," he assured her, too emphatically for politeness, as he came back to sit opposite her.

"Then why have you made such an astonishing offer? I cannot flatter myself that it is because you have been madly in love with me for the past three years."

"No, no. Let us understand from the outset that love has nothing whatsoever to do with this. We wouldn't want to get all mixed up with that nonsense."

"Certainly not," Lysette assented, but her tone was far less certain than his.

He sipped his whiskey and leaned toward her. "Let me try to sort all this out for you, shall I?"

Taking the glass from his hand, Lysette took a swig of the liquor. It burned its way down her throat and her eyes teared as she managed a strangled: "Please do."

Retrieving his drink, Nicholas leaned back in his chair. He stretched out his legs and the tips of his boots touched the hem of Lysette's spreading skirts.

"I am thirty-eight years old, Lysette. I was an only child. My father, whom I love and greatly respect, is seventy-three. His dearest wish, and that of my mother, who is equally precious to me, is to see me settled as a husband and a father.

"I confess I had never given the matter much thought. It always seemed that there was all the time in the world. But my father's health has begun failing rapidly in the past year. Twice he has suffered attacks and only the mercy of the good Lord has seen him through them. I know he has only a few years left to him. I see suddenly that the time is long past when I should have settled myself and become the son he wished me to be."

"But you really have no desire to wed?"

The empty crystal glass in his hands sparkled in the afternoon sunshine as he toyed with it.

"To be perfectly honest, I cannot say it has ever been my life's ambition, no."

"And yet you would do this to please your father?"

His grin took her by surprise. "There is also the matter of business, you know. Financiers such as myself seem somehow more trustworthy when they are married."

"That seems terriby cold-blooded, monsieur."

The grin faded and a hint of steel glinted in his black eyes. "I am a cold-hearted man, madame. It's what makes me so good at what I do."

A chill coursed down Lysette's spine. Remembering the way he had possessed her so completely in the garden three years before, she could certainly believe that he was a man who did as he pleased and the Devil take the consequences. His willingness to go against his own wishes for his father's sake surprised her. She would have sworn that he was a man who cared not a whit for any other living creature.

"I understand your reasons, monsieur," she said at last. "What I do not understand is why you have chosen me. Is it because this—" With a sweeping gesture she encompassed the splendor that surrounded them. "—also holds some attraction for you?"

His look and his sigh were filled with exasperation. "Lysette, magnificent as Saint-Cloud is, I could tear up Jules's letters of credit and not miss a cent of it."

"Then why don't you?"

"Because I have decided that you are the woman I want for my wife."

"And Saint-Cloud is the weapon you will use to force me to agree?"

His eyes glinted with a devilish glow. "Say rather it is the bait in my trap."

Trying desperately to conceal her rising agitation, Lysette went to a tall vase of flowers standing before the window and began rearranging the blossoms. In a few minutes the once-lovely arrangement had been reduced to a shambles. She swung toward Nicholas setting her silken skirts to swaying.

"Why me!"

Her obvious vexation affected Nicholas not in the least. He set his glass aside and regarded her dispassionately.

"If I must marry," he replied with exaggerated patience, "I prefer a woman with some knowledge of the world. A woman of some experience. And yet, if we are to have a child, she should be some years younger than I. Though looks are not a primary consideration, I would naturally prefer that the woman appeal to me physically." His dark gaze swept appreciatively over her causing the delicate color to flood into her cheeks. "You would seem to fit the bill admirably."

"Surely there are women of your acquaintance who—"

He shook his head impatiently. "The only eligible women in New Orleans are prattling, coy maidens who are paraded before me at every social function I attend. They are, without exception, silly creatures whose only thoughts—if, indeed, they have any thoughts at all—are of marrying some love-struck fool and spending the rest of their lives in a state of romantic bliss.

"I have no patience with such notions. I want a woman like you who, having been married, is past all that."

"Oh!" Lysette's eyes were round with indignation.

His sable brows drew downward. "There was one matter that concerned me. You were married to Jules for seven years and yet there were no children."

Lysette stiffened. The hot color crept up to her cheeks. "How dare you . .!" she began.

He waved her outrage aside as though it were but a pesky gnat buzzing about his leonine head. "After a bit of research, however, I discovered that Jules was married before and had no children with his first wife either. It seems likely that the fault lay with him. It need not concern us."

"You, sir, are rude in the extreme!"

"I suppose I am," he agreed blandly. "Nevertheless, it was a question which required an answer. We are discussing business, madame, not courting. Let me lay out the rest of my proposal for you."

Lysette returned to her chair. "First I want to ask one question. If I say no, will you turn me out of Saint-Cloud?"

His expression lost all hint of levity. "Regrettably, yes. I will, however, allow you to take your personal belongings, including your jewels. I am not completely devoid of conscience, you know."

Only of feeling, Lysette thought.

"It seems to me, monsieur, that this arrangement you propose is very much to your benefit but very little to mine. What would I gain from it save the dubious pleasure of being trapped in a marriage I do not desire?"

"Please, madame. I am in no way seeking to trap you in anything. This marriage is purely one of convenience for both of us. You will have the protection marriage affords a woman. You must see that this world is a difficult place for a young, beautiful woman to be alone."

"A marriage of convenience," Lysette murmured, "but still a marriage in every respect."

"Ah, I see what you mean. Well, of course if we are to beget a child, we must be husband and wife in that sense. But let me assure you that once you have conceived my child, we need have nothing to do with one another physically. I have a mistress, of course."

He seemed so blithely unconcerned at the thought of leaving her bed once he'd accomplished his task that Lysette felt almost insulted.

"How comforting to know," she murmured.

"In fact, if you like, I will have that put into the agreement."

"Agreement," she repeated, bemused.

"Marital agreement. I like to have things in writing. The rest of my proposition is as follows: On the day you bear our child, I will sign over to you the deed to Saint-Cloud, its surrounding lands, and all its contents. They will be yours and yours alone. At that time you may, if you wish, choose to live there. I will not interfere in your running of the plantation although I will, of course, manage all its finances. I hope you will agree that you are hardly qualified in such matters."

"Hardly," Lysette agreed, dazed.

"And so, Madame Ravaisson, what is your answer? Will you marry me?"

Lysette wished she could force back the emotions warring within her and think rationally. But it was impossible. The situation was so completely unexpected.

"I must consider the matter," she murmured at long last.

"As you wish," he agreed easily. Standing, he came to her and lifted her hand to his lips. "I will give you until tomorrow morning."

Lysette watched him stride from the room. The door closed behind him and the lofty, sumptuous chamber seemed suddenly empty, as though the life had been taken away with Nicholas's departure.

"Until tomorrow morning," she whispered shakily. "Sacre coeur! What am I going to do!"

* * *

The night was fast turning into morning and still Lysette lay awake in the wide bed with its blue damask hangings.

"What will I do?" she asked the night yet again, but the darkness had no answers for her. The decision was hers alone.

Climbing out of bed, she padded down the staircase into whose wrought iron balustrade Jules Ravaisson's monogram had been worked. Eschewing the grander chambers, she took refuge in a small parlor whose unadorned cream-silk walls and gold-bordered cream draperies Jules had ridiculed when first Lysette had suggested them. She had given way only enough to allow the installation of a magnificent Aubusson carpet in shades of lavender, pink, and blue. Otherwise the simple, elegant room had been decorated to her dictates. It was, and had always been, her favorite chamber in the whole, ostentatious manse.

With the skill she'd learned at the convent, she kindled a fire in the white marble fireplace. Sitting cross-legged on the carpet before it, she stared into the flames and pondered her dilemma.

She had no illusions as to the nature of any marriage she might contract with Nicholas Callaway. It would be far, far different than her union with Jules. Nicholas was not the kind of man who would be content to have a wife who was merely a fitting mistress for his home and a dazzling ornament for his arm when they ventured forth into society. Oh, no. He wanted a child. Even Lysette in her innocence, knew that there was only one way of begetting them.

Still, if she rejected him and left Saint-Cloud, she knew she would not go alone. Many of the household servants had come with Jules and his young bride from France. If Lysette left, they would follow. Nicholas had said he would allow her to take her jewels—generous, since she knew they formed a not inconsiderable portion of the collateral Jules had used to secure his loans—but even so, how long could she provide for a band of a dozen and more homeless people?

She heard the door swing open and looked up expecting to see Tess. Instead she found Nicholas crossing the room silently, his tall, broad-shouldered, narrow-hipped body sheathed in a flowing robe of rich burgundy damask. The deep vee at the throat revealed an expanse of tanned, black-haired flesh and the rippling hem allowed glimpses of long, muscular legs. With a start, Lysette realized that beneath the sumptuous garment, he was totally and obviously unashamedly naked.

The knowledge gave birth to an odd quivering somewhere in the pit of her stomach. She hoped passionately that the orange glow of the flames would mask the flaming crimson of her cheeks.

"Monsieur, I thought you would be asleep," she breathed, not daring to look at him as he sat down beside her lest his robe—

fastened only by the sash at his waist—reveal to her certain facts of life of which she had thus far managed to remain ignorant.

"I was reading," he told her softly. "I heard someone pass my door. When I looked out, I saw you going down the stairs. I thought perhaps you had come to a decision."

Lysette gazed into the flames completely unaware of the way the fire's glow lent a radiance to her delicate profile. Nicholas, in turn, watched her, marveling in the air of innocence that surrounded her. With her lush chestnut curls tumbling about her face and the high-necked, demure linen nightrail she wore, he found it hard to believe she was twenty-three and had been a wife for seven years. Looking at her, he believed he could see the virginal sixteen year old Jules Ravaisson had wed in the chapel of the Ursuline convent.

He felt the sweet ache of urgent desire growing inside him and leaned toward her, longing for her reply.

"I have," she whispered to the fire after a breathtaking tense silence. "I will marry you, monsieur."

Nicholas felt the pent-up breath he hadn't realized he was holding leave his lungs in a rush. The sense of elation that suffused him took him by surprise.

"Tomorrow?" he asked, his voice seeming unnaturally loud in the room.

"Tomorrow?"

For the first time, Lysette looked directly

into his face. Nicholas was startled, for her dark eyes were huge and haunted, filled with a fear he could not begin to understand.

"Why not?" he demanded. "We can send for a clergyman. He can be here by mid-afternoon."

"Tomorrow," Lysette repeated tonelessly.

"I have a week, Lysette, before I have to return to my business in New Orleans. If we were married tomorrow, we would have a week alone. A honeymoon, if you like. I know it's not much, but I don't know how long it will be before I can get away again."

"A honeymoon," she breathed. Her heart lurched in her chest. A honeymoon. Which would naturally follow a wedding night. A real wedding night, not like the fond hug and chaste kiss Jules had given her before leaving her to be tucked alone into her bridal bed by Tess while he went off to his own bed in another chamber.

She ventured a glance toward Nicholas and found him studying her; his sharply-planed, handsome face was set in an expression of unmistakable desire. Here was not a man to be sent off to his lonely rest while his nubile young bride slept alone.

She shivered and looked away. "Tomorrow, then," she agreed shakily.

She gasped as his fingertips traced her jaw. He was bending toward her but she dared not move. She felt the hot caress of his breath on her cheek, then his lips were against her throat.

"I want you, Lysette," he rasped against her ear. "How I want you!"

"No," she managed. "Nicholas, no!"

"What difference can it make?" he demanded.

She felt his hands stealing to the high-buttoned throat of her gown. His fingers moved over the buttons parting them as if by magic. His lips were warm on her cheek as they made their stealthy, enticing way toward her trembling mouth.

Lysette gasped as one of his hands found its way inside her gown. For the first time she knew the touch of a man's hand on her breast. It formed a warm cup about the soft, satiny mound—his thumb brushed the silky tip until it tautened.

A thrill tore through her taking her breath away, sending her senses scattering to the ends of the earth. She moaned softly but even that sound was muffled as Nicholas's mouth found and possessed hers.

He kissed her slowly, lingeringly, but no less passionately than he had on that night three years before. Lysette's hands moved on his shoulders, unable to decide whether to push him away or pull him closer.

His hand left her breast and she sighed unconsciously at the loss. But it was soon replaced as Nicholas bent his dark head and kissed the taut, pink crest that peeked so impudently from the opened front of her gown.

"Mon Dieu!" Lysette cried softly, and the vibrations of his answering chuckle seemed to rumble in the heart of her. She felt his hand stroke her back through her gown then it moved to her hip and the long curve of her thigh. Without her realizing it, the gown was tugged aside and his hand found the smooth flesh of her knee.

She shivered as he caressed the tender place at the back of her knee then stroked upward over the agonizingly sensitive flesh of her thigh. For a moment the questing fingers seemed to hesitate then they touched her there, in that dark, hot, secret place of which the good Ursulines had warned their students it was a sin to even think.

It was this last touch that brought Lysette hurtling back to reality. If she allowed this to happen, he would learn the truth! He would find that his 'woman of some experience' was in fact as innocent as the prattling young girls of whom he spoke so disparagingly. Perhaps he would change his mind—perhaps he would turn her out of Saint-Cloud to fend for herself and for the people who would follow her out of loyalty. She could not let that happen.

She struggled against him. "Let me go! Nicholas! Let me go!"

She thrashed in Nicholas's arms and he, surprised, released her. Scrambling to her feet, she clutched her nightgown about her.

"What is it, Lysette?" he demanded.

"We must not," she managed, backing toward the door. "We are not yet married."

"Don't be ridiculous." Pushing himself to

his feet, Nicholas glared at her. Desire was still rampant within him; its hot urgency still burned through his veins.

"We must wait." She saw the exasperation, the frustration etched on his face. The sheer intensity of his emotions frightened her.

"Come back to me, Lysette," he urged, holding out a hand to her.

Shaking her head, she moved away from him. "I'm afraid," she whispered.

"Afraid?" He was astonished. "Of me?"

Lysette stared at him. Dare she admit that he terrified her? That the thought of giving herself to him made her want to bolt to some locked chamber where she could hide? No, she did not want him to know. She could not imagine what the reaction of such a worldly, cynical man would be upon learning that she was truly innocent.

"It's wrong," she stated simply. Then, without waiting for his reply, she turned and ran out the door.

Nicholas stood in the darkened room, brow furled in puzzlement. Wrong, she had said. What could be wrong in their desiring one another?

Shrugging, he knelt and banked the fire for the night. Lysette had not been raised with the same values as the women he knew, he reminded himself. She had been raised in a convent then married to a man older than her own father. It was hardly surprising that her morals should be more than a little outdated for a woman her age. Still, he had hoped for a wife whose sensuality might allow her to overcome such old-fashioned scruples. After all, she was a widow, he a bachelor; within twenty-four hours they would be man and wife. What was to prevent their enjoying one another?

"Ah, well," he sighed as he retied the sash of his robe. "By tomorrow night she will be a wife and all her prudish notions will be cast aside."

The prospect cheered him as he climbed the curving stairs to return to his room. He had never imagined that he could actually be eager for his own wedding day to dawn.

# CHAPTER 4

Tess wept as Lysette and Nicholas were married in the tiny chapel of Saint-Cloud. Her tears might well have added a moving touch to the ceremony but the heart-rending, obviously agonized sobs with which they were punctuated were hardly calculated to please the groom who knew beyond all doubt that he was the cause of her distress.

"Why does she despise me so?" he demanded of Lysette as he watched the housekeeper lay aside her fork at the wedding supper and rummage in her pocket for yet another handkerchief.

"She does not despise you, monsieur," Lysette whispered back. "It is only that she was very, very fond of Jules."

"Well, damnit, Jules is dead!"

A silence fell about the long ballroom in which a small reception for the servants was being held. Nicholas felt thirty pairs of reproachful eyes being trained upon him. He scowled and Lysette thought how terribly stern he looked.

"And don't call me 'monsieur'," he finished lamely.

Lysette's chin quivered. Her nerves were

stretched to the breaking point and beyond. Tess had insisted upon dressing her that morning in the unadorned gown of lavender silk she'd chosen as her wedding dress. Though no doubt her intentions had been of the best, the housekeeper's monologue had done nothing to allay her young mistress's fears.

"To think what my poor cherie will go through tonight!" Tess had wailed, slapping away the hands of Mimette, Lysette's maid, as she tried to help with the dressing of Lysette's hair.

"Please, Tess," Lysette had begged. "Let us speak of something else—anything else."

"He will hurt you, cherie," Tess had continued, as though Lysette had never spoken. "On my wedding night I prayed to faint. I cried out to the Holy Virgin to save me!"

"Tess!"

"It is the curse of being a woman. It is the price we must pay to bear children."

Lysette's hands shook as she reached for the single strand of pearls she would wear. "There are many women who enjoy—"

"Harlots!" Tess spat. "Only harlots!" She closed her eyes and clenched her hands until her knuckles were strained and bloodless. "If only Monsieur Jules were still alive! You would not be at the mercy of this monster!"

"He is not a monster," Lysette defended, a little too uncertainly to be convincing.

"All men are monsters when their base appetites are indulged. I have seen the way this Nicholas Callaway looks at you. He rapes you with his eyes. He cannot wait to force himself upon you and—"

"Stop it!" Lysette clapped her hands over her ears. "Stop it! Go away and leave me alone!"

The picture of self-righteous indignation, Tess stalked out of the room leaving Mimette to try and erase the outward evidence of Lysette's terror.

The memories of the morning still coursing relentlessly through her mind, Lysette's hand shook as she lifted her goblet. Several drops of the sparkling wine splashed onto the rich tablecloth. Nicholas reached out to keep her from spilling the lot.

"What is it, Lysette?" he asked, seeing her bite her lower lip.

"Nothing, mon. . . I mean, Nicholas," she breathed.

He touched her cheek and found it alarmingly cool. "Only a little longer. Then we will have the rest of the night to ourselves."

Lysette looked up into his dark eyes. Yes, the look in them was hungry, almost predatory. She heard Tess's voice inside her head:

"He will hurt you, cherie. On my wedding night I prayed to faint."

Nicholas was startled to see her wide brown eyes filling with tears. She was so pale. She was trembling. Come to think of it, she had not ceased to tremble since the moment he had come to her room to fetch her down for the ceremony.

He took her arm. "Come, darling. We have played the genial hosts long enough. Let's go upstairs."

"No!" She yanked her arm from his grasp and pushed herself to her feet.

"Lysette!" he barked, both alarmed and confused by her reaction.

"I . . . I . . ." She swayed on her feet. As her eyes rolled slowly back in her head, Tess sprang from her chair. But before she could cross half the distance to her mistress's side, Nicholas had swept his bride into his arms.

"I'll come up and take care of her," the housekeeper stated, wishing she could snatch her mistress's limp body from the tall, commanding man who held her.

"She won't be needing you," Nicholas snarled. "See to the others. Lysette won't need you until morning."

Restraining herself from physically attacking Nicholas as he disappeared in the direction of the grand marble staircase, Tess finally collapsed into a chair and dissolved into mournful tears. The others clustered around offering their sympathies and calling down maledictions upon the shoulders of the man who was now their master.

They knew little of him at first-hand—the greater part of their information having come by way of the highly-colored reports of the housekeeper. Like her, they were convinced that their dear little mistress had fallen into the clutches of a beast.

Nicholas carried Lysette into the room he

had chosen for them to share. It was neither Lysette's room nor the sumptuous chamber that had been Jules's. Rather, it was a cozy, elegant room that overlooked the garden.

After laying her across the bed which settled in an alcove, he drew the gold-fringed, lilac draperies over the windows dimming the evening light. The orange glow of the setting sun shone through the silk lighting the room with its muted brilliance and eliminating the need to light a lamp.

He returned to the bed and gazed down at Lysette just as she stirred. Her heavily-lashed lids fluttered and lifted. She found herself gazing up at him as he towered over her.

"Nicholas," she whispered, a plea in her voice.

"Hush." He touched her cheek gently, calming her as he might a small child. At that moment, she seemed very young and very dear to him.

"How did I get here?" She frowned, puzzled, as her eyes scanned the darkened room.

"You fainted. Are you ill? How do you feel?"

The very real concern in his voice soothed Lysette more than his words could. Sitting up, she shook her head.

"I'm all right," she assured him. "It was only—" Blushing, she looked away. "Only the excitement, I suppose."

He tugged playfully at one of her tumbled curls. "I hope it is not your habit to faint at moments of excitement, madame. Although I have heard of women who do. 'Le petite mort.' "

"The little death," Lysette breathed, awed. "They die?"

Nicholas laughed, but his humor faded when he saw that she was not only serious, she was quite obviously appalled.

"Of course they don't die, sweetheart," he hastened to assure her. "They are merely overcome with passion."

"Overcome with passion," she repeated softly. It sounded delicious but then, considering Nicholas's purported extensive experience, these were very likely less than respectable women.

She glanced at the clock. It was nearly half past seven.

"It is early," she told him. "Everyone will think it odd that we have retired so soon."

"No one will think it odd," he contradicted fondly. "Most, in fact, would think it very odd if we wasted any more time than we had to."

Lysette's insides roiled with nervous anticipation. She cast about for some way to distract him but there was nothing. The moment had come. He was her husband; he would be obeyed.

"I will call Mimette to help me change," she murmured, sliding off the bed.

Nicholas caught her skirt and pulled her back between his knees as he sat on the edge of the bed.

"Can you manage alone if I unhook your gown?"

"Yes," she admitted softly.

She felt his fingers working swiftly over the concealed hooks in the back of her gown. How knowledgeable he is with the intricacies of feminine apparel, she thought. It made her feel all the more awkward and ignorant.

When the hooks were opened, Lysette caught the loose bodice against her breasts. She gazed at Nicholas in mute appeal and he, more than a little surprised, rose.

"I'll leave you alone to change, shall I?" he asked.

"Please." She heard the curiosity in his tone but kept her eyes studiously downcast. It was not until she heard his retreating footsteps followed by the closing of the door that she scurried behind the shirred silk screen in the corner and changed into one of her nightgowns.

She was sitting on the bed's edge brushing her hair when Nicholas returned. He paused in the doorway and watched, mesmerized by the flash of the silver brush and the soft, rich cascade of her curls which gleamed in the light of the lamp she'd lit against the gathering darkness.

Without a word, he went to the screen and stepped behind. Though Lysette did not look up, she knew he was undressing. The thought prompted the start of a dull ache of apprehension in the pit of her stomach.

She felt rather than heard him approach the bed. It gave as he sat behind her. She held her breath. His fingers were warm and strong on hers as he took the brush from her hand.

"Nicholas," she breathed.

"Shhh," he hushed. "Let me."

There was a moment of killing suspense then, to her wonderment, Lysette felt the brush begin to stroke through her curls once more. His touch was tender, far more gentle than even Mimette who often brushed her mistress's hair to soothe her.

Lysette shivered. It had never occurred to her in her wildest dreams that the simple act of brushing one's hair could be so pleasurable. His every stroke seemed a caress. Her lids fluttered shut and her head fell back as the rhythmic stroking of the brush calmed her even as the warmth of Nicholas's body, so close to her own, tapped some heretofore unplumbed well-spring of emotion within her innocent breast.

"Good?" Nicholas asked, hearing her soft sigh of contentment.

"Ummm," she murmured. She was fast losing her fear. Nicholas Callaway, ruthless businessman though he might be, cold-hearted and callous though general concensus named him, was no monster, no defiler. He had not seized her the moment they had found themselves alone and forced himself upon her as Tess had intimated that he might.

She saw the flash of the lamplight on the brush as he laid it aside. She stiffened as his hands encircled her slender shoulders but he only drew her against him, cushioning her against his chest, supporting her head on his shoulder. She felt the sharpness of his jaw against her temple and smelled the clean scent of his soap. His arms were about her but she felt no fear at finding herself so completely in his power. There was only anticipation, perhaps more than a little tempered by uncertainty of the unknown, and, even though it shocked Lysette herself, a hint of eagerness to sample all of life's experiences.

Shifting her in his arms, Nicholas lay her down across the lilac silk counterpane. He reclined on his side gazing down at her. In her eyes he saw all of her warring emotions and he could not but wonder anew at the enigmatic little beauty he now found himself wedded to.

"What are you about, petite Lysette?" he asked softly, his fingers playing with the shimmering curls that pooled about her small head.

"About?" she asked, wanting, yet not daring, to touch him. Her eyes found a smooth, tanned place in his throat where a vein throbbed. She felt a giddy longing to press her lips to it.

A tiny giggle escaped her as she recalled the horrors Tess had vowed lay in wait for her here, in her marriage bed.

"You're like a beautiful, innocent child." His voice was low and husky; his eyes glowed with the smoky light of desire.

Lowering his head, he kissed the dimple in her cheek, the soft curve at the corner of her dainty mouth. Lysette held her breath waiting . . .waiting. Then his lips found hers and she discovered once more, after three long, barren years, the thrill of her fast awakening sensuality.

His hand worked at the small pearl buttons of her gown but, as he would have drawn the garment from her shoulders, Lysette pulled away.

"Nicholas," she breathed, her mouth pink and trembling, "the light."

He glanced toward the lamp that still burned on the table across the softly-lit chamber.

"I want to look at you, cherie," he told her. "I want to look into your eyes and see. . ."

"Please."

His expression turned to one of surprise. "Did Jules never make love to you in the light?"

Lysette's cheeks flamed. "Never," she whispered.

It was the truth if not, perhaps, the entire truth.

"He should have. You are far too beautiful to be hidden from your lover's sight."

"My lover," Lysette repeated wonderingly. From this marriage Nicholas Callaway had forced upon her, she had thought to gain a husband at best, a master at worst, but never, never had she thought to find a lover.

"Lysette."

With the brush of one hand, he swept her gown aside and bent his head to her breasts.

Lysette squirmed, suddenly frightened by her own quickening desire. But Nicholas only kissed her again, hungrily, as his fingers tugged impatiently at the long, trailing skirt of her gown.

She felt his touch on her thigh, her hip. She grew taut and still, dreading, yet painfully eager for his next touch. It came, and she moaned softly, the sound muffled beneath the bruising onslaught of his mouth.

His touch was gentle, tender, but each caress was a revelation to her. She wanted . . . wanted. . .

She felt herself being lifted as Nicholas pulled away her twisted gown. It joined his robe on the floor as he moved over her.

She reached up to touch his cheek, a tremulous, bemused smile playing at the corners of her mouth. But the smile vanished, the small hand froze, as a searing pain tore through her.

She screamed. It was a jarring sound whose origins were equally rooted in her pain and her fear. This, then, was what Tess had meant, her mind raged. This was the darker side of desire.

Through tear-filled eyes she looked up at Nicholas and saw in his face the shock of realization. Her head tossed, she writhed, trying to escape from him—from the pain he was so callously inflicting upon her.

Then the pain began to ebb. Nicholas held her, his arms beneath her holding her small, trembling body closer to his.

"Let me go," she sobbed brokenly, realizing with no little sense of bewilderment, that he had not left her even though the pain of a moment before was fast disappearing.

"It won't hurt anymore," he told her, his lips soft against her ear.

Lysette clung to him as he moved against her. The pain was gone and in its place a burgeoning pleasure that was far beyond anything she'd ever imagined in her virginal daydreams of love.

The feeling grew inside her, the pleasure heightened, expanded, until Lysette felt herself falling into a sweet oblivion from which no true lover ever completely escapes.

Her feathery lashes fluttered. A little shudder coursed through her. She opened her eyes to find Nicholas holding her, his fingers smoothing the damp baby curls back from her forehead.

"Le petit mort," she whispered shyly, not quite daring to meet his dark eyes.

"Did you die, my love?" he asked playfully, his eyes alight with tenderness.

"Oh, yes," she sighed, her lids veiling her eyes once more. "I died, Nicholas, and went to heaven!"

# CHAPTER 5

It was long after dawn by the time Lysette awoke. Her first conscious thought was of how warm, how deliciously warm she was. Her next was of a prickling sensation on her temple.

She reached up to brush away whatever was prickling her and felt the soft back of her hand against the hard, stubbly edge of a man's jaw.

Gasping, she realized that the warmth that felt so heavenly was in fact the heat of Nicholas's body. He lay curled protectively, possessively, and so, so intimately about her.

Shocked, she turned her face away but in his sleep Nicholas rubbed his cheek against the fragrant masses of her hair. A tremor coursed down Lysette's spine. Against her will, she remembered what had passed between them the night before.

"Sweet heavens," she murmured, recalling, with a blush of shame, the delights Nicholas had shown her—the paradise to which he had taken her—and, once he had overcome her fear and natural reticence, her own eagerness to return to his arms.

Her mind was a hodgepodge of warring

emotions. In one moment she wanted to wrench herself from his embrace and flee. In the next, she wished nothing more than to cuddle as close to him as his own skin. Then, after still another moment, she wished he would awaken and love her yet again.

"How easy it would be," she whispered, feeling his arm tighten about her waist. "How terribly, how dreadfully easy it would be to fall in love with this man."

But did she dare? He was her husband, after all. Should he not, then, be the very man to whom she should look for the fulfillment of all her dreams of life and love?

She remembered the cold, ruthless gleam in his eyes when he had so bluntly set down the terms of their marriage. A love match was the last thing he'd had in mind. He had ridiculed the young girls of New Orleans for harboring precisely those same notions which were even then running through Lysette's befuddled mind.

Easing her way out of his arms, she slipped from the bed. The cool morning air chilled her and she snatched up her nightgown from where it lay in a creamy pool on the floor. She had never in her life slept in such a state. With what frightening ease had Nicholas Callaway overcome her long held scruples!

Reaching for her robe, she pulled it over her gown and the long, loosely-twisted coil of her hair. As she would have turned from the bed, the sight of Nicholas arrested her. He was so handsome, so heartbreakingly, breathtakingly handsome. But so cold. Oh, not cold-blooded, to be sure. He was by far more passionate than any man had a right to be. But cold-hearted, cynical. She wondered if any woman had ever found a heart within him much less touched it. Certainly no woman could ever have captured it.

Unless— She remembered the words he had said to her two days (could it really have been only two days?) before. He'd meant them as a comfort to her; now they came back to haunt her.

"I have," he had said in that blunt, piercing way of his, "a mistress, of course."

At the time, the words had evoked no emotion in her breast save a certain annoyance. Now each syllable seemed to tear at her reminding her of just how little this marriage meant to him. And, in consequence, of just how little she, as his wife, meant to him.

She saw those firm, sculpted lips which had taught her to kiss curve into a lazy, sensual smile.

He's thinking of her, she thought suddenly, furiously. He's dreaming of her, his mistress. I hate her!

"What is happening to me?" she hissed, appalled at the ferocity of her own emotions. Her haunted eyes caressed his face. "What have you done to me, you wicked, pitiless man!"

Stalking out of the bedroom, she went to the dressing room where a basin of warm water had been left for her.

"Dear Tess, so thoughtful," she murmured.

She felt an inexplicable, overpowering desire to weep. Even as she washed away the last traces of Nicholas's lovemaking and dressed in a simple daygown from one of the armoires that lined the walls, she wished she need never again give herself up to the raptures, and tortures, of Nicholas Callaway's loving.

Leaving the dressing room, she descended the grand, curving staircase and went to the restful morning room where she had accepted Nicholas's proposal. Outside the blue and silver silk-hung windows the sunbathed gardens were just as they had been. Not a blossom, not a leaf seemed to have been disturbed. Inside, the chamber had not changed—indeed, it seemed as permanent as the very earth upon which Saint-Cloud's mighty foundations rested. It was she—only she—who had changed.

She would never be the same. A part of her would always and for ever belong to Nicholas Callaway now. This realization struck her without warning. This knowledge, which, she supposed, had had its beginnings when first Nicholas had kissed her three long years before, dawned fully upon her at that moment.

Her knees buckling beneath her, she sank into an armchair and began, bitterly, to weep.

A floor above in the wide, canopied bed, Nicholas stirred. Stretching, he pulled himself up and glanced about for his wife.

"Lysette?" There was no response. He swung his long legs over the side of the bed and rose. Almost as an afterthought, he picked up the robe he'd discarded the night before and draped it about him. Being married now, he supposed he'd have to be more careful about the state he wandered about his rooms in. There would be maids in and out now and. . .

As if to illustrate his thoughts, a noise from the dressing room caught his attention. Upon investigation, he discovered a pair of maids who had come to leave fresh water for his morning ablutions.

"I shall want a bath later and water for shaving," he told them, grinning as they giggled behind their hands. "But this will suffice for now. Is your mistress downstairs already?"

The two girls continued to stare and continued to giggle until Nicholas finally realized that they didn't understand him. He rephrased the question in French and this time managed to elicit a confirming nod from one of the girls before the pair fled the room amidst gales of shrill laughter.

Nicholas smiled as he shed his robe. Who would have imagined—who could possibly have foretold—what surprises this marriage held in store for him? He would never, in all his wildest fantasies, have believed that Lysette Ravaisson—Lysette Callaway, he reminded himself with a smile that held not a little self-satisfaction—could have been married for seven years to a man who so obviously adored her and yet have been still a virgin on her second wedding night.

He hummed softly to himself while he washed and dressed. The night replayed itself in his memory like some hauntingly seductive melody. He'd been stunned when first he'd realized the reason for Lysette's fear; he'd cursed himself for his own blindness. Then again, Jules Ravaisson had always doted on his beautiful young wife—would any rational man have imagined that he could have lived with such a delicate, enticing creature for seven years without touching her?

As he left the dressing room and descended the stairs, Nicholas counted his blessings. Not the least of those was the beautiful wife who had given him far more than he'd had any sane reason to expect.

"A letter for you, m'sieur," a servant announced.

Taking the missive, Nicholas went to the breakfast room.

Seemingly from nowhere, Tess appeared. It was as if she had been hovering nearby awaiting some sign that someone had stirred. Her face, as she saw that it was Nicholas and not Lysette, left no doubt as to her opinion of her new master.

"Monsieur?" she said coldly, her eyes icy with loathing.

Ignoring her insolence, Nicholas ordered

his breakfast. Without bothering to acknowledge her sketchy curtsy, he broke the seal of the letter.

"My own darling Nicholas," he read. There was no need for him to glance toward the bottom of the page for the signature. He had recognized the handwriting on the envelope. The letter was from Rosalyn D'Everaux—beautiful Rosalyn—his mistress.

Tess entered the room but her appearance seemed to make no impression on Nicholas as his black eyes skimmed over the page. He did not appear to notice that his breakfast was being set before him. Nor did he seem aware that Tess was busying herself behind him ostensibly going about her business but in reality reading her master's private correspondence.

The passionate tone of the letter shocked her as did the explicit terms in which the woman called her lover's memory back to intimate moments they had shared. That a woman, any woman, could possibly write such a letter to a man not her husband scandalized the old housekeeper. That she should write it to a man she knew (and she had to know, didn't she? Tess reasoned) to be newly married was so far removed from her realm of understanding as to be totally incomprehensible.

". . . I know, mon amour," the letter continued, confirming Tess's suspicions, "that your marriage to Madame Ravaisson is one of convenience alone. Trust me to realize that it need prove no more an obstacle to our love than does my own marriage to Edouard. Come back soon to your Rosalyn, mon cher. . ."

Fairly shaking with shocked fury, Tess moved to Nicholas's side and cleared her throat noisily to gain his attention.

"Well?" he asked, not bothering to take his eyes from the page before him.

"With the m'sieur's permission, I will attend to my mistress."

"Haven't you seen her this morning?" He scowled at the blank look on the woman's face. "Lysette was already gone when I awoke."

Alarmed, Tess fled the room without waiting for his permission. Nicholas stared after her wondering if her concern was justified. Then, deciding that the old biddy was simply over-protective, he returned to his letter.

Poor Rosalyn, he thought as he reread the passionate lines she'd repeated to him too many times already. Did she really imagine that he was duped by her? Oh, doubtless she cared for him in her fashion but Rosalyn D'Everaux was too cold-blooded to love for love's sake alone. She chose her lovers with an eye toward New Orleans society. Would the other women secretly envy her? Was her lover a man respected by his peers? Feared by his enemies? Admired by the ladies? She could never, he knew full well, love any man who did not add to her own status. Let her lover fall from grace with the society of New

Orleans and he would soon find himself unwelcomed in her bed as well.

Still, she was beautiful and could be charming and amusing. What more had he ever expected to get from a woman? Trust? His mouth twisted bitterly. He had learned long ago not to trust a woman. He had thought to find comfort with Rosalyn after his marriage with Lysette. Now, he wasn't so sure their liaison would survive the delights he had found in—of all places—his marriage bed.

Where was Lysette? His dark brows furled. If even Tess, that old watchdog, hadn't seen her, she must have hidden herself somewhere. But where? Why?

Leaving his breakfast untouched, he left the table and went to look for her.

Tess held Lysette as she wept her endless tears. They were bathed in the morning light that streamed through the windows and yet even its penetrating warmth could not ease the chill of apprehension that gnawed at Lysette's heart.

"Pauvre petite," Tess comforted. "He was brutal to you, that evil man. Did he hurt you, ma cherie?"

Lysette did not answer—she could not. But it was not disgust over her wedding night that prompted her tears. In fact, just the opposite was true. In her heart she knew that, no matter what emotions Nicholas felt for her, she would never, never be completely her own again.

"Listen to me, sweeting," Tess said. "You

must not despair. I know for certain that it will not be long before that ame de boue leaves you alone!"

Lysette wiped her wet cheeks with the back of her hand. "What do you mean, Tess?"

"There was a letter this morning." Tess's lips were pinched with disapproval; her tone was one of utter disdain. "I read it over his shoulder at the breakfast table."

Lysette's sense of propriety rebelled from hearing information garnered in such an underhanded fashion, but she could not help saying, "And?"

"It was from a woman. Rosalyn D'Everaux —Madame Edouard D'Everaux. Pardon, madame, but there was no mistaking the tone of the letter. Madame D'Everaux and your . . . your. . ." She could not force herself to say the word 'husband' when referring to Nicholas. ". . . and that man have been intimate."

Lysette supported herself against the tufted back of the loveseat. "What did she say?" she asked weakly.

"Really, madame, it was not fit for your ears."

"Then she intends for their liaison to continue?"

"Without doubt." Tess's lip curled in disgust. "The lorette!"

Lysette felt sick at heart. "And Nicholas," she could scarcely bear to ask. "How did he seem when he was reading it?"

"Interested," Tess spat. "Very interested."

A sudden knifing pain seemed to spring to life, throbbing behind Lysette's eyes. She saw herself in the future role that seemed destined to be hers. Loving a man who saw in her only the means of achieving his goals—the accumulation of wealth, the begetting of an heir. She saw herself alone, unloved, neglected.

How many nights, she wondered miserably, will I spend alone, wanting him, all the while knowing that he is somewhere else, in another woman's bed, in another woman's arms. . .

And yet, even as those thoughts filled her mind with their dark and melancholy images, she knew that the moment he deigned to come home she would fly into his arms at the merest beckoning crook of his finger.

He had bound her to him with his love and she knew that each time he loved her he would forge yet another link in the chain that bound her to his side.

Outside the chamber, Nicholas, attracted by the sound of voices, approached the parlor door. He lifted a hand to knock but the gesture was stayed as he heard Lysette's anguished cry:

"Oh, Tess! How I wish I never had to let him touch me again!"

Hearing Tess's shocked gasp, Lysette let her hands fall from her face. She found herself gazing up into the dark, stormy face of her husband.

"Get out," he snarled to Tess who seemed unsure of whether to throw herself between husband and wife or run to safety. "I said get out!"

Tess fled, pulling the door shut behind her with a deafening crash.

"I would not have believed this of you, madame," Nicholas ground out when they were alone. "I should have thought that a natural sense of discretion would have prevented you from discussing the intimate details of our marriage with anyone! I would no more confide such particulars to a servant than I would to—"

"Madame D'Everaux?" Lysette hissed. "So the old bitch was reading over my shoulder!"

"Tess is concerned for my welfare!"

"Tess is a meddlesome biddy and if she persists in her meddling she'll find herself looking for a new home!"

Lysette rose, appalled at the thought of his turning Tess out. "You wouldn't!"

"Try me, madame!"

"Jules would never have—"

"Goddammit, Lysette, Jules is dead! I am your husband now!"

Lysette turned away, desperately trying to hold back her tears. Nicholas reached out a hand toward her shaking shoulders but he couldn't bring himself to touch her for fear she would recoil from him.

She was, he could see, far too closely linked with the past at Saint-Cloud. Its memories of

Jules, of the prolonged childhood that had been her first marriage, would keep her from growing, from blossoming into the woman he knew she could become. He'd glimpsed that woman the night before—he'd seen her born in his arms. He couldn't allow Saint-Cloud and its ever-present shadows to hinder that growth.

"I've reconsidered my decision to remain at Saint-Cloud, Lysette," he told her. "We will leave for New Orleans as soon as possible."

Lysette swung toward him. Her eyes were huge and haunted in her ashen face. "Please, monsieur, say we may stay. Only a little longer."

Nicholas hardened himself against her pleading gaze. "As soon as possible, madame," he repeated.

Are you so hungry for your Madame D'Everaux? Lysette's tortured heart cried out. She said only, "It will take some time to prepare, monsieur. You know one cannot simply leave the servants to close the house."

Nicholas searched her face longing for her to lift her downcast eyes. Had she, then, been so repelled by what had been between them the night before that she wished for him to leave her here, amidst the memories of her life that had been?

Still, there was some truth to what she said. He himself did not believe in leaving the servants to do their master's work.

"Very well," he said at last, his voice gentler—and sadder—than she had ever heard it. "I will leave. You may stay long enough to close the mansion." He reached out and lifted her chin with his forefinger. She did not dare pull away. "And then you will join me in New Orleans. Do you understand?"

Though her face was tilted toward his, Lysette refused to look into his eyes. "Oui, monsieur," she whispered.

Nicholas sighed. Perhaps he had been too hasty in counting the blessings of his new situation. Turning away from her, he left the room.

It was only a moment later that Tess reappeared.

"Nicholas is leaving for New Orleans," Lysette told her, her voice quivering with unexpected emotion. "He will require his belongings to be packed."

"Grace a Dieu!" Tess rejoiced. "His mistress is welcome to him!"

"His mistress," Lysette murmured dully.

Ignoring Tess's continued mumblings, she wandered from the room and up the stairs to her long-delayed bath.

# CHAPTER 6

From opposite ends of the long, triple pedestaled dining table, Nicholas and Lysette covertly eyed one another.

Do I dare ask him to stay? Lysette wondered. She winced as he took out his pocket watch and checked the time. Was he really so anxious for the hour to arrive when he descended to Saint-Cloud's docks to board the boat for New Orleans? Perhaps if I. . . She frowned into her soup. No, he longs to be gone. He cannot wait to leave me—he cannot wait to return to Rosalyn D'Everaux's welcoming arms.

The thought of Nicholas with another woman wrenched at Lysette's heart. The knowledge that another woman knew him so much better than she thought she ever could or would gnawed at her like a festering canker.

He did not bargain upon my innocence, she reminded herself. He thought himself to be gaining a bride already well-versed in the more intimate matters of marriage and my ignorance has made me distasteful to him. Tess is right! His mistress is welcome to him!

But that thought brought the stinging salt

tears welling into her eyes. She scowled ferociously to hold them at bay.

Glancing up, Nicholas found his bride looking daggers at him from the far end of the gleaming table. With a puzzled lift of his brows, he returned his attention to his meal.

Foul-tempered little termagant, he thought. What's gotten her French blood boiling now? What had happened the night before had been as much her fault as his—no, it had been more hers. Why hadn't she told him that her marriage to Jules had been in name only? She hadn't given him a clue that she was innocent until it had been far too late. Surely she could have told him; would that have been so difficult? He would have been more patient with her, taken more time, more care.

With a life-weary sigh he pushed aside the remainder of his soup. Taking out his watch, he checked the time yet again.

"It is nearing your hour of departure?" Lysette asked dispassionately.

"It won't be much longer," he replied, matching her tone.

Cold-hearted little bitch, he thought viciously. You can't wait to bid me a hearty adieu and send me on my way, can you? Well, you've no need to worry. I won't darken your door much longer. But don't think you've had done with me, my beauty. You've agreed to give me a child and you will!

The thought brought a sly knowing smile creeping across his sculpted lips. His black eyes sparkled as he regarded his wife who stared back at him with obvious, growing unease.

Rising, he circled the long table and held out a beckoning hand to Lysette. Her eyes widened, the pale roses in her cheeks faded leaving her with a pallor that all too clearly conveyed her emotions.

"Aren't you going to accompany me to the dock, madame?" he asked sardonically.

Lysette's audible sigh of relief was no balm for his injured pride. Laying her hand in his, she rose and left the dining room with him.

"Did you imagine that I would insist upon my husbandly rights one last time, cherie?" he asked sotto voce as they moved toward the front door.

"Truly, monsieur, I did not know," Lysette replied primly as her heart beat a wild tattoo.

And what if I had, my priggish bride? he thought. Would you have screamed and fought? Would you have called out for your loyal servants to protect you from me?

The budding blossom of Nicholas's love for Lysette which had been born in the heat of his passion withered on the vine in the face of her distaste for him. He wanted an heir and she would give him one—he would see to that. But once she had conceived his child, he would leave her bed and seek his pleasures in the arms of women with a right to the name.

But even as these vindictive thoughts coursed through his brain, Nicholas could not stay his gaze from straying to the exquisite woman-child who walked so stiffly at his side. Her full, tempting mouth was pursed ever so slightly, ever so invitingly, and her little, tip-tilted nose was raised haughtily. From this angle he could see the lush arch of her lashes and he could not help remembering the way those lashes had lain in silky crescents across her porcelain cheeks the night before.

She had responded to his lovemaking—she had! He was no benighted stripling. He knew how to please a woman. Why, then, had she changed so in a matter of a few hours?

Tess! The housekeeper's pinched, unpalatable countenance appeared in his mind's eye. It had to be. Who knew what tales the old harpy stood at Lysette's shoulder and spun like an evil siren. And Lysette, though a grown woman in years, was still such an innocent in mind, in emotion, that she believed whatever cock-and-bull story the woman elected to tell her. He'd be damned if he'd tolerate the woman in his home in New Orleans.

They had reached the docks. In the distance the billowing smoke spewed from the twin stacks of the riverboat, the Claiborne, which was even then being signaled to stop and receive another passenger.

Nicholas took Lysette's arm and drew her away from the servants who waited near the stack of his baggage.

"Don't tarry here too long," he admonished sternly. "I expect to see you in New Orleans within a reasonable length of time."

Lysette nodded, saying nothing, biting back with no little difficulty the bitter retort that sprang to her lips.

"And Lysette. . ."

She did not look up. He took her chin between his thumb and forefinger and tipped her face toward his.

"Listen to me," he ordered. "Under no circumstances are you to bring Tess with you."

A protest leapt to the tip of Lysette's tongue but a wiser voice from the back of her mind prevailed.

"Just as you say, mon . . ." She colored prettily. ". . . Nicholas."

Nicholas freed her chin and his hand softly caressed her cheek. Lysette shivered and felt a sudden, almost uncontrollable urge to kiss that warm, stroking hand. Their eyes met, held, and as one they stepped apart.

Nicholas clasped his hands behind his back and stared off toward the approaching boat.

"You will be good, won't you, mon enfant," he said, not looking at her. It was a statement, not a question.

Mon enfant! Lysette's cheeks colored again, this time in anger. How dare he call her a child! She had been woman enough for him the night be— Another unwelcome thought quelled that one. Had she been woman enough for him? Apparently not, else why was he in such a hurry to run off to his mistress—the bitch, Rosalyn!

Her eyes widened at the venom in her

thoughts. What was wrong with her? She had never, never thought of another woman in such harsh terms. She was jealous—much as she hated to admit it, there it was. And if she were, wouldn't that mean that she was well on the way to falling in love with her husband?

"No!" she cried sharply.

Nicholas glanced down at her, brows upraised. "You won't be good?"

"Pardon? Oh! Yes, of course I will."

The riverboat had drawn up to the dock. It was immense, looking like nothing so much as a double-storied mansion afloat on the rippling water. Nicholas watched as his bags were hoisted aboard. If he seemed reluctant to leave, Lysette did not notice so great was the turmoil of her own emotions.

"Kiss me, my love," he murmured, and Lysette, not sure she had heard him correctly, gaped up at him in wonderment.

He drew a finger gently across the velvet softness of her cheek and twined it in the downy soft curl just in front of her ear. Lysette's heart hammered in her breast as he bent toward her. His lips grazed her ear, her cheek, then brushed her lips so tenderly that she could not repress a sigh of such longing that it seemed to emanate from her very soul.

She wanted to throw her arms about him and beg him to stay with her—plead with him to love her.

"A bientôt, chere Lysette," Nicholas murmured against her ear.

"A bientôt," she replied, her voice barely above a whisper.

It was impossible. She could not make a move to stay his departure. She was still too new to the ways of men and women; still too in awe of the man who was now her husband; still too unsure of her place in his life and in his affections.

She stood, hands clasped to still their trembling, and watched as Nicholas boarded the Claiborne. He climbed to the upper deck and stood at the railing as the enormous paddle wheel began to turn.

Lysette lifted her hand in a wan farewell. She was a mass of conflicting emotions. But all those seething feelings were suddenly coalesced into a single, heart-wrenching jolt as she noticed the woman who suddenly appeared at Nicholas's shoulder.

The woman was no taller than Lysette. Her figure was no daintier, no more voluptuous, her hair, though golden rather than the dark chestnut of Lysette's, was no more beautiful, and yet there was about her such an air of full-blown femininity that beside her Lysette felt gauche as a schoolgirl.

As Lysette watched with stricken eyes, the woman laid a gloved hand on Nicholas's sleeve. The simple gesture held within it more possessiveness than a hundred more intimate actions possibly could. As Lysette watched, Nicholas turned and gazed down at the woman. Though his bride could not hear his voice, his lips formed the single, unmistakable word: Rosalyn.

Astonished, Nicholas stared down into the once-adored face that somehow seemed infinitely less attractive to him now. Rosalyn's golden lashes fell demurely then lifted as she smiled up at him.

"What the hell are you doing here?" he demanded.

"I went to visit my sister, Rebecca, in Baton Rouge," she explained softly. "Poor Becca, she's so bored at Fairhaven. And that dreadful husband of hers cares nothing for her." She sighed ostentatiously. "Husbands! I ask you, are there any more useless creatures on. . ." Her pale green eyes widened. "Oh, darling, I am sorry. I'd almost forgotten. You are a husband yourself now, aren't you?" She turned her attention toward the dock. "Where is your little bride? Surely that can't be her. Why, she's charging across the lawn like a regular little hoyden!"

Nicholas scowled across the widening expanse of water that separated him from the docks of Saint-Cloud. There, just as Rosalyn had said, was Lysette, skirts in her hands, running at full tilt toward the mansion in the distance.

"Damn!" he hissed beneath his breath.

"What is it, darling?" Rosalyn asked, all innocence.

"Nothing." Nicholas watched as Lysette disappeared from view. "Nothing at all."

At the crest of the hill upon which the mansion stood, Lysette pressed herself against the comforting gnarled trunk of an ancient oak. Nails digging into the weathered bark, she closed her eyes and tried to will away the crushing pain that filled her delicate frame.

"Damn him!" she muttered. "Damn him! Damn him! Damn him! I hope the boat explodes!"

The sudden, shrill whistle tore a gasp from her aching lungs.

"I didn't mean it," she amended hastily, lest the Almighty take her at her word. She frowned, confused by the painful intensity of the emotions that were so new to her. "Maybe I did mean it," she mused aloud. "Maybe I . . . oh, I don't know what I mean anymore."

"So," a voice purred from behind her. "He could not even wait to reach New Orleans. His harlot was waiting for him."

Lysette shot Tess a scathing glare. "Shut up!" she snarled. With a twitch of her skirts, she stalked past the astonished housekeeper and into the mansion. But though she was determined to put on a brave face, nothing and no one would ever convince her that Nicholas had not known Rosalyn would be awaiting him aboard the Claiborne.

The days, passing so slowly, began to meld one into another until Lysette began to lose track of their passage. It was not until a tersely worded letter arrived from Nicholas demanding to know how she was progressing on closing the mansion that Lysette noticed that nearly a month had gone by since his departure.

"I cannot wait much longer, Tess," she said as she unconsciously fondled the thick writing paper upon which Nicholas's message was written in his bold, flowing hand. "But I do not relish the prospect of joining him."

"Nor should you," Tess agreed, her thin lips pursed with distaste.

Lysette gazed at Nicholas's letter. He demanded that she join him. But to what purpose? Surely he had everything he wanted. A wife and a mistress. A magnificent plantation. A child . . .

She closed her eyes and tried to pretend that that last thought had never entered her mind. And yet the first symptoms had already made themselves undeniably apparent. Still, she could be proved wrong—it had happened to other women aplenty. She must hold on to that thought and hope for the best.

"No, nor should I," she echoed Tess's words. "Why should I be eager to go to his side knowing as I do that he sees me simply as a convenience? How will I pretend not to care when he chooses his mistress over me?"

"Do you care?" Tess was clearly astonished at the mere thought that Nicholas's comings and goings should be of the slightest interest to Lysette.

Lysette did not answer but her eyes were drawn to the wide, gleaming band that encircled her finger. Yes, she had to admit, though she loathed herself for her own weakness of will, she did care. Far too much.

Another week passed, then another. Lysette was in her sewing room one rainy morning in early October when a caller was announced.

"A messenger," Tess anounced tightly, "from the Monsieur."

With unseemly eagerness, Lysette swept from the room and down to the parlor where the gentleman had been bade to wait for the mistress of the house.

The young fair-haired man stood as Lysette entered the room.

"You have a message from my husband?" she demanded, slightly breathless.

"You're to sign these documents, Mrs. Callaway, and I am to return them to New Orleans as soon as possible."

"Sign them?" Curious, Lysette tore open the envelope and pulled out a sheaf of papers. As she skimmed the tightly-worded documents once, then again, she realized that they comprised the marital agreement Nicholas had spoken of on the night he had proposed to her. Her heart sank within her breast. So he had meant every word of it. On these pages he had lain down the terms of their marriage, those hateful, cold-blooded terms, and she had no recourse but to agree to them.

With a feigned air of calm, she began to read the pages slowly, carefully. There was no doubt that Nicholas had written it himself. He had effectively, ruthlessly, sealed off her every avenue of escape.

With a truly herculean effort, Lysette hid

her inner turmoil. But for a slight shaking of her hands, she seemed perfectly at ease. Until, that is, she came to the clause in which Nicholas boldly stated that once she proved with child, their physical relationship would end for good and all.

Nothing could have more clearly conveyed his feelings to her. Nothing could have told her more of how little he cared for her as a woman. Tears filled her eyes. In the past fortnight she had come to be more and more certain that her suspicions were correct. That single night with Nicholas—those few precious hours when no one and nothing had stood between them, had borne fruit. She was to bear Nicholas Callaway his longed-for heir and, in so doing, she was marking the end of their marriage in any sense but name.

Blinking back her tears, she went to a desk and signed the hateful compact. Thrusting the pages back into the uneasy messenger's hands, she fled the room.

"What did you say to her?" Tess demanded, descending upon the young man like the wrath of Heaven itself.

"Nothing, ma'am," the gangly youth protested. "Mr. Callaway said I was to have this signed. I did. Mrs. Callaway didn't even wait for the note he sent with it."

"I'll take the note." Tess snatched the flimsy missive from his hands. "You can go."

The boy lifted his peach-fuzzed chin. "Mr. Callaway said I was to wait for an answer."

Tess glared at him. "Very well, wait if you must."

Tess found Lysette lying on her bed staring up at the silk canopy above. Tears ran unheeded down her face to spot the apricot silk of the coverlet.

"Cherie! Cherie! What is it?"

"Nothing," Lysette mumbled. "Nothing at all."

Tess felt a pang of jealousy. Since *he* had come—that man, that wicked man—Lysette had not been the same. No longer did she confide in her beloved Tess. No longer was Tess her closest friend. For a moment she thought of destroying the note and telling the messenger downstairs that there was no reply. She quickly thought better of such a rash action.

"There was a note for you, cherie," she said grudgingly. "You didn't wait to get it."

Sitting up, Lysette took the note and tore it open. Inside she found only a harshly-worded demand that she come immediately. 'Stop shilly-shallying' Nicholas demanded. There was to be a reception given on the fifteenth and she would—she *would*—be there!

This was the end, Lysette knew. She must bow to the inevitable. And why not? Could the reality be any worse than her painful imaginings? Far better to face the pain and then, perhaps, see it fade with time. If Nicholas could not love her as a woman, perhaps he could at least respect her as the mother of his child.

"Tell the messenger," she instructed Tess wearily, "to tell Nicholas that I will come to New Orleans on the fourteenth."

"The fourteenth! That's barely a week from now!"

"The fourteenth, Tess," Lysette repeated dully. "My husband demands it and I must obey."

# CHAPTER 7

The days which had previously seemed to drag by at a funereal pace now quickened. The final week of Lysette's self-imposed immurment passed in what seemed the breadth of an hour until she found herself standing in her bedchamber watching as her trunks were packed for her journey to New Orleans.

"Are you certain," Tess asked, "that there is not something you can do that would allow us to remain here?"

"Nothing," Lysette insisted. She drew a deep, fortifying breath and took the housekeeper's arm. "Come with me, Tess, there is something I must speak to you about."

Leaving the bedchamber, the two women went to the adjoining sitting room. With its precious furnishings swathed in protective sheeting, it seemed barren, cold, and lifeless, as though long bereft of human habitation.

"Tess," she began. "Dear Tess. You know that you are my dearest friend. You know, don't you, that I cherish our friendship—that I am forever grateful for the years you have devoted to Jules and to me and for the loyalty and help you have always provided."

"Oui, madame," Tess acknowledged, suddenly wary.

"I don't want to hurt you." Lysette shook her head, sorely troubled. "I don't know how to tell you this except to simply blurt it out. The truth of it is, Tess, that you are to remain here at Saint-Cloud."

The housekeeper's narrow face lost all hint of color. In the space of a second, her thin body seemed to shudder and wilt. Her shock was painful for Lysette to witness. But then, as quickly as she had lost control she regained it, straightening and stiffening, coming back to herself.

"The monsieur decrees it?" she asked coldly, her tone clearly conveying her contempt for her master.

"He thinks it best, yes," Lysette admitted.

When Tess would have gone on, Lysette lifted her chin imperiously.

"You are to remain here, Tess, and it is not for either of us to question Nicholas's decision."

"You wish it as well?"

Lysette winced at the pain in Tess's voice, the hurt in her eyes. Still, guilty though it made her feel, she had to admit that yes, she did want Tess to remain at Saint-Cloud. Though in her heart she feared she had nothing to look forward to from Nicholas but the pain of being an uncared for, neglected wife, she wanted to be free of the shadow Tess's resentment cast over her. She wanted to bear her pain in private without Tess constantly reminding her that she loved a man who cared not a whit for her except for the child she was going to provide for him.

"I do think it best. At least for the present," she admitted softly. "Perhaps later—"

For the first time in all the years she'd spent with Jules and Lysette, Tess sank into a stiff curtsy before her mistress.

"Just as you say, madame," she ground out. "With your permission, I will see to your packing."

Lysette raised a comforting hand toward her friend but the ice in Tess's blue eyes refused to thaw. "You may go," she murmured at last.

With a swish of her midnight skirts, the housekeeper returned to Lysette's room and coldly went about packing her mistress's belongings.

The dreaded fourteenth dawned overcast and windy. The morning passed and afternoon commenced to find Lysette standing at the front parlor windows vacillating between eagerness for the hour of her departure to arrive and dread as she watched the hands of the clock moving inexorably closer to the appointed hour.

When at last the time arrived, Lysette, with Mimette in tow, went down to the docks where Lysette's baggage was piled beneath a tarpaulin.

Lysette glanced toward the assembled servants who had come to bid their mistress adieu. Tess was not among them. In fact, she had scarcely seen her since the moment when she had told her she was to be left behind. It pained Lysette to have caused the woman such anguish but she felt in some strange way liberated, like a child venturing forth from behind the sheltering skirts of her mother.

Her heart skipped a beat as the sound of the whistle reached her ears and the billowing plumes of smoke that rose above the riverboats appeared above the trees at the next bend in the river.

"It is the Bienville?" Lysette asked one of the men who stood at the end of the dock.

"Oui, madame, it is," he called back.

"It won't be long now, Mimette," Lysette whispered to her maid who stood nearby. "Soon we will be on our way to Ni—" She blushed, realizing she had been about to say 'to Nicholas.' "New Orleans," she finished lamely.

"Yes, madame," Mimette agreed, pretending not to have noticed her mistress's slip of the tongue.

In short order the riverboat had drawn to a halt and a gangplank had been laid down. Lysette stepped daintily across and was met by a blue-coated steward.

"This way, if you will, madame," he beckoned.

Followed by Mimette, Lysette and the steward left the gallery and entered the magnificently opulent salon of the Bienville. Decorated in the style of the great French chateaux of the days of Louis XV, the salon was a showcase of gilding and tapestries and fine French carpets.

Though she managed to suppress her own astonishment, Lysette heard Mimette's awed sigh and secretly shared the maid's feelings. Saint-Cloud had been one of the most ostentatious of the river plantations but even its sumptuous chambers paled in comparison to this floating palace.

"Madame Callaway?" a voice said at her shoulder.

"Oui?"

"Your suite will be ready in a moment, madame. If you would care to wait here." He indicated a circular ottoman upholstered in royal blue tufted velvet fringed with gold.

"Merci." Taking a seat, Lysette smiled at the steward whose showy uniform was his badge of authority. She watched as he bowed to her and then moved away through the throng. As he disappeared, her attention was captured by the overheard conversation of two elegant ladies who were partially hidden by a pair of blue velvet portieres artfully draped across one of the salons trio of soaring arches.

"Did he say Madame Callaway?" the tall, languid blonde asked her more petite, darker companion.

"I do believe he did."

Though she did not dare look up, Lysette could feel their combined stares upon her as they peered around the fringed draperies.

"So," the deeper-pitched voice of the

darker lady purred. "That is Nicholas's bride. She's pretty enough, I suppose. She has that air of innocence about her that men like Nicholas seem so to admire."

"Ummm. It is always the rakes who want their brides to be milk-and-water virgins. Still, she is a delicate little thing. Perhaps it was a love match after all."

"Love match!" The brunette lowered her voice in response to the blonde's urgent 'Shhh!' "Come now, Phyllis, Nicholas left her after their wedding night! Everyone in New Orleans knows it."

Had the women peeked again at the subject of their conversation, they would have realized by the flush of her porcelain cheeks that she could hear every word. But they were mercifully too engrossed in their scandal-mongering to notice.

The brunette continued. "That is hardly the action of a man madly in love. In any case, he's been seen all over New Orleans with Rosalyn D'Everaux this past month."

"Well," Phyllis conceeded, "perhaps she will put Rosalyn in her place. Heavens knows someone should!"

Her companion's laugh was insultingly rife with disdain. "Rosalyn will eat that little girl alive."

Averting her face so that the brim of her bonnet hid her crimsoned cheeks, Lysette fought to conceal the pain their cruelty caused her. When the steward who had bade her wait for her suite returned and bowed before her, she rose gratefully and followed him away from her unknowing informants. But their words echoed and re-echoed in her ears.

"He's been seen all over New Orleans with Rosalyn D'Everaux this past month."

Tess was right about him, a small, pained voice whispered inside her. He is a heartless roue. The sooner I come to my senses about him the better. It was folly for me to imagine I could ever mean anything to him. All he wants of me is a child. Well, so be it! The moment I see him, I will tell him that we are to have a child. That will force him to seek his pleasures elsewhere. Her mouth twisted bitterly. Not that he will not do so anyway; but perhaps banishing him from my bed will be the first step toward banishing him from my heart.

The steward stopped before a white-painted door. "Here we are, madame."

Opening the door, he stood back and allowed Lysette and her maid to enter what proved to be a sitting room whose pale blue walls and furnishings in shades of ivory and blue were considerably less taxing on the senses than the rococo splendor of the salon.

Bowing, the steward left and Lysette heaved a sigh of relief at being away from prying eyes and gossiping tongues.

"Oh, madame," Mimette breathed, "the boat is so beautiful. May we not go and look at the rest?"

Lysette frowned. She would not, could not,

face another round of hearing her husband's philandering discussed by total strangers.

"I think not," she said after a lengthy pause. Her scowl eased in the face of Mimette's sulky pout. "Why don't you go?"

The maid's piquant face brightened but her delighted smile quickly faded. "Oh, madame, I couldn't leave you here alone."

"Go on, Mimette," Lysette urged. "I shall lock the door behind you. Really, I had thought to leave my duegne at Saint-Cloud but you are as much a clucking mother hen as Tess ever was."

"Well—" The maid feigned the reluctance she imagined Lysette wished to see but she was too eager to explore the magnificent vessel to hold out for long. "I shan't be long," she promised, already half way out the door.

Lysette closed the door behind her grateful for any moment of solitude she could manage to steal. Unfastening her coat, she pulled it off and draped it over the spindle-back settee.

"Aren't you going to lock the door?"

With a sharp, frightened cry, Lysette whirled toward the voice. Nicholas leaned casually against the jamb of the door connecting the parlor with the bedroom. His black eyes held in their ebon depths some unfathomable emotion as they moved lingeringly over the wife he had not seen in well over a month.

For Lysette's part, the breath had seemed to leave her body in a dizzying rush the instant her eyes met his. If possible, he seemed even more devastatingly handsome than when she'd seen him last. In the breadth of a second, all the bittersweet memories of the single, rapturous night they'd spent together came back to her. But the emotions those memories evoked in her were quickly quelled by the newer, rawer pain of what she had overheard in the Bienville's salon only minutes before.

She lifted her chin in a gesture that was pure braggadocio.

"What are you doing here, Nicholas?"

Had she not averted her eyes, she might well have seen the mixture of anger and dismay that flitted across his face. His tone, when he replied, was as full of icy indifference as her own.

"Do you think I would let my wife travel alone?"

"Mimette is with me."

"Mimette is hardly protection. Where is she now, madame? She left you here alone not knowing that there was someone here, in your suite, waiting for you."

"Surely the steward knew you were here."

A muscle flexed in Nicholas's lean jaw. He would rather she had attacked him—screamed and played the shrew—this damned frigid apathy of hers filled him with a hot, black fury.

"That is not the point."

Lysette gazed at him. How could his mere presence arouse such a furor within her? She cast down her eyes before her emotions could be read in them.

"And what is the point?" she asked defiantly.

"The point, my dear, is that there are men plying this river who prey upon rich women."

In the face of his concern the ice in Lysette's heart thawed a little. But the chill returned as soon as his next words left his lips:

"I should not like to see you spirited away and held for an exorbitant ransom."

Is it only the ransom you care about, Nicholas? her heart ached to ask. But she didn't dare. Instead, she turned away and her fingers worked clumsily at the ribbons of her bonnet as she said, "There is something I must tell you, Nicholas."

"Can't it wait?"

There was a huskiness in his voice that reminded her of . . . of . . . She swung toward him eyes wide with astonishment.

"Pardon?"

His hands cupped her chin. The bonnet slipped unheeded from her fingers. His lips were but a kiss away from her own.

"Mimette is gone. We are alone." The spark in his black eyes flickered and caught fire. "I have missed you, Lysette."

As his lips touched her own, brushing them softly, teasingly, a rebellious voice inside her incited her to refuse him—to curse him for his dalliance with Rosalyn. Her lips parted, trying in vain to form the words that alone had the power to shatter the spell his lips, his hands, were fast weaving about her. But as she would have told him her news—told him that she carried the child whose conception would mean the end of their physical relationship, she felt Nicholas's fingers in her hair, loosing the fine net that held her heavy curls demurely imprisoned.

A tiny, half-smothered murmur of protest forced its way between her small curved lips and the strong, forceful mouth that had captured them was, even at that moment, plundering the sweetness that lay within.

Lysette felt her resolve slipping away, melting under the heat of Nicholas's passion as easily as the buttons fastening the front of her gown slipped through their holes beneath Nicholas's nimble fingers.

His lips found her throat, the first, delicate curve of her breast, and Lysette's fingers sank into his ebony curls. A soft moan that was half-delight and half-dismay broke free from her throat. The world seemed to be slipping from beneath her feet as Nicholas swept her into his arms and carried her through the half-open door to the bedroom.

"Nicholas, no," she whispered as he began quickly, and expertly, to divest her of the intricate layers of clothing that was every fashionable woman's armor.

He nuzzled her neck; nipped softly at the tender lobe of her ear. "Do you really mean that?" he murmured.

"I . . ." His tongue traced the contours of

her ear. "Yes, I . . ." His hands trimphed over the lacings of her corselet and found the softness of her breasts. "Nicholas, I. . ." He drew her against him and she felt the undeniable proof of his desire for her.

"Do you, Lysette?" he asked again, his hands caressing her through the tissue-thin silk of her camisole and pantelets.

"No," she conceded weakly. "Oh, no."

Embracing, they sank together onto the crimson silk coverlet. The voice of conscience sounded an alarm in Lysette's mind but it went unheeded as Nicholas reawakened in her all the scarcely-reined passions with an almost frightening ease.

He was a devil, surely, diabolically endowed with the power to seduce her. But as Lysette held him, as her hands relearned all the superb contours of the magnificent man fate had joined her to, she didn't care if he were an angel or a demon. All that mattered was that, at that moment, for those precious hours, he was hers and hers alone.

# CHAPTER 8

Lysette stepped out of the carriage and stood in the curving drive before the elegant New Orleans townhouse of which she was now mistress.

The mansion itself was ringed with square columns. Double galleried, matching balustrades encircled both the upper gallery and the flat roof. It had once been the 'big house' of a great plantation but as New Orleans had grown out beyond its boundaries the plantations owners had found that subdividing and selling their land was far more profitable than cultivating crops.

Nicholas offered her his arm and she took it but she could not lift her eyes to his as they started toward her new home. She was troubled, deeply, lamentably troubled. Not, as she might have expected, over her violation of the terms of Nicholas's marriage contract, but rather over her own actions the night before in the chamber they had shared aboard the Bienville.

She had been like a woman possessed. Had that really been her, that uninhibited, passionate woman in whose tender body a flame had been lit that had burned out of control until dawn—and exhaustion—had overtaken her? Her cheeks flamed as she remembered awakening Nicholas in the night with her bold caresses. She had been as brazen as the tawdrily-dressed whores who had hailed Nicholas with unblushing exuberance. It did not ease her mortification to recall the unmistakably exultant glow in Nicholas's eyes as he gave her the love she so shamelessly demanded.

But even as she cursed herself for her shocking lack of self-control—for the hitherto undiscovered sensuality that seemed so easily brought to the boiling point within her—Lysette could not suppress the thrill that coursed up her spine at the memory of Nicholas's lovemaking. She trembled as she recalled those exquisite moments when first he possessed her—when his body and hers had become one.

To her astonishment, the fire she'd thought quenched flickered and throbbed into life within her once more.

"Sacre coeur!" she breathed.

"What was that?" Nicholas asked as he opened the door and stepped back to allow her to enter.

"Nothing," Nicholas," she murmured quickly. "Nothing at all."

But in her heart of hearts she realized that the battle for her heart, her soul, would not be fought against Nicholas Callaway but against her own treacherous senses. With a few carefully chosen phrases she knew she could rid herself of Nicholas's presence in her bed. He was already so cynical, so mistrusting of women, it would not take a great deal to convince him of what she believed he already thought—that she was as scheming and cruel as all of the other women of his acquaintance. The real struggle lay in convincing herself that she actually wanted him out of her bed in the first place.

The entrance hall into which Nicholas led her was graced by an elegant staircase in which twin flights rose to a landing before merging to soar to the second floor. In the alcove between them a japanned tall case clock ticked loudly. Through an open set of doors to her left, Lysette saw the white-trimmed, pale green wall of a parlor. Opposite, another door opened on a far more dramatic chamber done in rich burgundy and cream.

"It's lovely, Nicholas," Lysette murmured. She wondered if Rosalyn had helped him decorate it. But no sooner had that troublesome thought entered her mind than she banished it, chiding herself for allowing that woman's name to even enter her thoughts. Foolish as she knew it was, she wondered if she couldn't dismiss Rosalyn from her life and Nicholas's by simply dismissing her from her thoughts.

"I'm glad you like it, my dear," Nicholas was saying. "Although, of course, you are free to make any changes you'd like. I will ask, however, that you not turn it into a little Versailles like Saint-Cloud."

Lysette's temper flared at his unwarranted attack on the home she already missed.

"If you dislike Saint-Cloud, why did you go to such lengths to possess it?"

Nicholas's smug smile was maddening. "You forget what I told you, cherie. It was not so much Saint-Cloud I longed to possess as her mistress."

"Let's not discuss that again, shall we?"

"Just as you say, my love," Nicholas acquiesced, a teasing smile still lurking at the corners of his mouth.

He was fast discovering that he rather enjoyed baiting the exquisite little spitfire he had married. He liked seeing that temper flare in her beautiful eyes, enjoyed watching as her proud little chin came up haughtily. But neither of those could compare with watching her passion overcome the reserve she tried so hard and so vainly to maintain when he took her into his arms.

He saw her again as she had been the night before, lying in his arms, flushed, yielding, soft and unbelievably feminine, pushed to exhaustion but not quite—never quite, he thought wonderingly—sated. How such a passion as Lysette possessed had lain unawakened until her twenty-third year was a mystery he believed he would never solve. Not that it mattered—all that fire, all that rampant sensuality responded to his touch alone.

He felt a tug on his sleeve and looked down to find Lysette gazing up at him with a questioning expression. She threw a pointed look across the foyer and he found his housekeeper, Anne Jonelle, eyeing him with a similar look.

"Ah, Mrs. Jonelle, here you are. I trust you will help my wife become acquainted with the house?"

"Of course, monsieur," the housekeeper concurred.

She was a plump woman with a rosy face and a ready smile. She could not, Lysette reflected, have possibly been any more different from Tess. It was more fortunate than she had imagined that Nicholas had decreed that Tess remain at Saint-Cloud. There was no doubt in Lysette's mind that the two of them could not have peacefully coexisted beneath Nicholas's roof.

"Lysette's maid has already taken her mistress's personal belongings upstairs. Her trunks are being brought up the backstairs, I presume?" He waited for the housekeeper's nod. "Good." He smiled down at Lysette. "Mrs. Jonelle will show you to our rooms, sweet. Perhaps you should rest. We may have a late night tonight."

"The reception," Lysette murmured. "I had forgotten."

"Give the gown you'll be wearing to Mrs. Jonelle, darling. She'll see that it is pressed. I should be back in plenty of time to get ready."

"Back?" Lysette echoed. "Where are you going?"

"I have business to attend to, mon enfant. I have been away, remember?" Leaning down, he gave her a peck on the temple. "I shan't be any longer than I must."

Lysette watched as he turned and strode out the door to the carriage still waiting in the drive. Climbing in, he gave an address to the driver, then the vehicle disappeared down the curving drive.

Is he going to Rosalyn? Lysette couldn't help wondering. Has he missed her so during the past few days that he cannot keep away from her for another moment? Did those hours, those glorious, cherished hours they'd spent in one another's arms count for nothing beside the incomparable enticements of his mistress?

Swallowing the bitter taste that seemed to fill her mouth, Lysette turned away from the door. Nicholas's housekeeper was watching her with what looked suspiciously like pity and Lysette wondered, mortified, how much of her emotion had been there to see in her face.

"Will you show me to my rooms, Mrs. Jonelle?" she asked, as coolly as she could manage.

The housekeeper's round face was carefully composed. If she had seen Lysette's dismay, her expression at that moment gave no hint of it.

"But of course, madame," she agreed pleasantly, her smile at once friendly and reassuring. "This way, if you please."

Lysette followed Mrs. Jonelle up the buff-carpeted stairs to the wide upstairs corridor. After passing but a few doors, the housekeeper opened one of a pair.

"This is the master suite, madame," she said.

Lysette entered and found herself in a long, high-ceilinged room whose white-trimmed emerald green walls set the tone which reflected the more masculine tastes of its inhabitant. The draperies both at the windows and decorating the massive canopy bed with its tall, gracefully tapering, reeded posts, were white with an elaborate embroidered edge of green. Both were drawn back with emerald silk, tasseled cords.

At the far end of the room, a pleasant sitting area had been formed around the fireplace. A tall escritoire stood near the window and the late morning sunshine shone across the papers scattered on its desk-top.

"Your belongings will have been stored in the dressing room, madame," Mrs. Jonelle told her. "It's just through there." She nodded toward one of two doors flanking the fireplace. "Perhaps I should see how the maids are progressing."

She disappeared into the adjoining chamber and Lysette wandered about the room. This, then, was Nicholas's lair. Each and every item that made up its furnishings had an unmistakable air of having been selected specifically for the place it now occupied.

No doubt Nicholas loves this room, Lysette reflected. When at last he learns the truth, that there is to be a child, it will be I who finds herself banished to some distant chamber to breed while he goes on in the manner he has always done.

She found herself standing before the escritoire. Unbidden, her eyes fell on the papers strewn there. All bore at least Nicholas's signature, many were completely written in that bold, flowing hand she had come to recognize as his. Lysette bit her lip. This was obviously Nicholas's private correspondence. She had no right even glancing at it. And yet . . . She could not help wondering if there, among those official looking missives, might not lurk a billet-doux from his mistress.

With one reluctant finger, she reached out and lifted a letter aside; then another. It was not until she had shifted one entire pile of papers from one side of the desk to the other that she heard the rustling of Mrs. Jonelle's silk skirts.

Shamefaced, she buried her hands in the folds of her gown but she could not as easily hide the flush of her pinkened cheeks.

"Is the unpacking progressing well?" she asked, her eyes not quite meeting the piercing blue gaze of her husband's housekeeper.

Whatever Mrs. Jonelle's feelings toward what she had seen, she maintained an air of insouciance that was a credit to her position.

"Quite well, madame. Is there anything else you require just now?"

"Perhaps you could locate Mimette, my maid, for me. I should like to undress and rest for a while."

"Of course, madame. She is in the dressing room with the other maids."

In short order Mimette was summoned and Lysette was freed, with no little sense of relief, from the boned embrace of her corset and the dragging weight of her gown and petticoats. In her fine cotton, lace-frothed camisole and pantalets, she climbed into the big bed as Mimette drew down the net baire.

Lying there beneath the soft coverlets, Lysette toyed with the embroidered edge of the sheet. This was Nicholas's bed. How strange to find herself here; how ironic to know that she didn't really belong here. To know that, according to the terms of that cursed marriage contract, she should have been put into some other room. To know that she, Nicholas's wife, the mother of his child, really had no business being in his bed.

A tiny line formed between her tawny brows as she frowned. It was still there some hours later when Mimette shook her gently by the shoulder.

"Madame. Madame! You must wake up."

"What do you want," Lysette muttered crossly, refusing to open her eyes.

"It is time to get up if you want to be ready when the Monsieur gets home."

The comforting mantle of slumber fell

away with shocking suddenness.

"Nicholas hasn't returned?" She felt a sickening certainty that his 'business' was with a certain woman whose name she didn't even want to repeat in her own mind.

"No, madame, his business. . ." The direction of Lysette's thoughts dawned on the maid. "Oh, madame, you don't think. . !"

"Don't I?" Lysette scowled. "Damn him to hell!"

"Madame!"

"Damn him to hell for the whoring lecher he is! I hope—hope—" She ground her teeth, frustrated at not being able to think of a fate horrible enough to satisfy the jealous rage burning within her.

In the end she was forced to content herself with flinging his pillow across the room but even in that she was foiled for it caught the edge of the baire and fell harmlessly to the floor.

"Perhaps the Monsieur will allow you to return to Saint-Cloud," Mimette offered by way of comfort.

"No!" Lysette cried, but whether it was in denial of Mimette's statement or in fear that he would do just that even she didn't know.

"Once you tell him about the child. . ." the maid persisted.

"I am not certain when that will happen," Lysette admitted. It seemed she fluctuated constantly between a determination to tell Nicholas her news the moment he walked through the door and a desire to postpone telling him for as long as possible and thus delay the inevitable separation she knew he desired.

"You must tell him eventually," Mimette went on. "There will come a time when the bébé will make itself apparent. One cannot conceal these things forever."

"Don't you think I know that?" Lysette snarled, the truth making her increasingly cross with Mimette in particular and with the world in general.

"The monsieur will think it strange that you did not tell him of the bébé before and . . ."

"Will you be quiet!" Lysette demanded. "What if someone should overhear? You can be certain they would scurry to their precious master the moment his feet touched the drive outside."

"What will you do, madame?" Mimette asked, endearingly full of sympathy.

Lysette heaved a great sigh. "Truly, Mimette, I do not know."

There was a brief tap on the door followed immediately by the unheralded appearance of Mrs. Jonelle.

"Pardon me, madame. I thought I should ask if you would be wanting your gown pressed for the reception tonight."

"Oui, merci," Lysette answered. "Quelle heure est-il, s'il vous plaît?"

"I'm sorry, madame, I do not speak French."

"Oh, I thought... Well, your name is French."

"My husband was of French descent. My maiden name was Squires."

"I see. Well, I merely asked the time."

Mrs. Jonelle consulted a large pocket watch which depended from a gold chatelaine at her ample waist.

"It is half after five, madame."

"Then you will please order me a bath. And I would like my pink gown pressed. Mimette will show you the one." She glanced at the maid. "The one I wear with the pink topazes, Mimette."

The housekeeper curtsied and Mimette led the way to the dressing room to point out the gown Lysette wanted.

Behind, still sheltered beneath the draping net of the baire, Lysette wondered, with a little quiver of dread, how much of what had passed between Mimette and herself had reached the listening ears of Nicholas's housekeeper.

# CHAPTER 9

Coiffed and dressed, Lysette paced restlessly to and fro across the shaded burgundy carpet of the downstairs parlor. She tossed her head impatiently setting the carefully arranged cascade of chestnut curls to bouncing. The rise and fall of her bosom made the diamond brooch with its three-pendant pink topazes sparkle. Above her fists, which rode amidst the folds of pink silk at her hips, matching bracelets glimmered in the light of the lamps lit to dispel the gathering darkness of evening.

"Where is he?" she muttered. "He demands that I be ready for this damned reception but he cannot tear himself out of his paramour's arms long enough to follow his own advice!"

Once more the determination to put an end to this farce of a marriage rose up inside her. The moment—the very moment Nicholas stepped through the door, she would tell him the truth—fling her news into his teeth. If Rosalyn D'Everaux's charms were so alluring to Nicholas let him have them and only them!

From outside the wine silk draped windows came the sound of carriage wheels and horses' hooves on the graveled drive. Turning, Lysette saw the glow of the carriage lanterns as the vehicle drew up to the wrought-iron carriage step. Resolved, she marched into the foyer and stood, poised and prepared to put her errant husband in his place.

Nicholas burst through the door. His white teeth flashed in a blinding smile as he saw her there. The pink silk of her gown gave a heightened color to the porcelain skin of her bared shoulders. The graceful sweep of her throat unencumbered by jewels. The enticing swell of her bosom was enhanced by the strategic placing of her brooch. The lamplight shone softly in her dark curls as they lay, a gleaming mass, over one shoulder. In all, she was as beguiling a confection as he could ever remember having beheld. Truly, she was utterly feminine—he could have asked for nothing more in a woman.

"You look very beautiful, enfant," he murmured, his lips brushing a butterfly kiss across her cheek.

"I must speak to you, Nicholas," Lysette said swiftly, trying hard to ignore the little thrill that even such a tiny kiss evoked in her.

"Not now." He was already past her and moving toward the stairs. "We're already late. I hope Anne had the foresight to have a bath waiting."

"But, Nicholas," Lysette protested, watching him bound up the stairs.

He disappeared around the landing but his

deep voice echoed down the stairwell to her. "Later, enfant."

She slapped her skirts in frustration. "Later! Later!" She didn't want to wait until later. She wanted to tell him now. Now! When she was filled with the self-righteous wrath that would give her the strength to tell him, knowing all the while what such a disclosure would mean.

Steeling herself, she snatched up her skirts and followed him.

At the bedroom door her courage flagged but she forced herself to go on. A bathroom, built to Nicholas's demanding specifications, adjoined both the bedchamber and the dressing room. Pushing wide the door, Lysette found a steaming tub awaiting her husband. But no Nicholas. Rounding the tub, she moved toward the dressing room door. It opened before she could reach it.

Nicholas entered. Seeing her, he grinned, his black eyes sparkling, amused by the round-eyed shock on her face as she became aware of his nudity.

"Well, enfant? Come to scrub my back?"

"N-n-no," she managed, locking her eyes to his to avoid their traveling any lower. "I only . . . only. . ."

Brows arched, mouth etching a mocking smile, he strolled to the tub and stepped into the water.

"Only?" he prompted. When she could say no more, he held out a hand. "The soap, cherie, if you don't mind."

Dazed, Lysette dutifully passed him the cake of soap that lay in a porcelain dish. Taking it, Nicholas began a leisurely bath apparently unconcerned that his bride was standing beside the tub looking as though she'd been struck. The only indication that the situation was anything out of the ordinary was the faint, amused smile twitching at the corners of his mouth.

It was not until Lysette suddenly whirled, with a mad rustling of skirts and petticoats, and stalked out of the room that he allowed the laughter aching inside him to rumble forth.

Through the door Lysette could hear his merriment. She ground her teeth. "Damn him!" The words seemed to have become almost a litany to her now.

She stormed back down the stairs and sank into a sofa. The minutes, marked by the sonorous ticking of the tall case clock in the foyer, passed. Lysette scowled. What would Nicholas do if their positions were reversed—if it were she who lolled upstairs in a steaming bath while he waited down here for her to make her belated appearance.

Still, she reminded herself, she hadn't particularly wanted to attend this reception in the first place. It had been Nicholas's doing from the beginning. It was he who had first decreed that they would attend—hadn't he told her so in the last letter she'd received at Saint-Cloud? Placated, she sat back against the striped silk cushions. Perhaps if they were late enough, he'd decide to forget the reception entirely. Then she'd have him at her mercy—her lips curved into a complaisant smile—she'd tell him about the baby and watch his face. He wouldn't look so smug then, she'd wager!

So pleasant were her musings that she was not aware of Nicholas's presence in the room until her thoughts were abruptly cut off by a gentle kiss on her still-smiling lips.

"Stop that!" she hissed, pushing herself to her feet.

"Ah, ma petite chatte is showing her claws," Nicholas mocked. "I don't blame you, cherie. I have often felt peckish when I've had to wait for a lady to finish her toilette."

Lysette scowled at him, infuriated by his ever mocking sense of humor. Still, a grudging admiration forced itself to the fore. There had never been a man whose looks showed to such advantage in evening dress. Over one arm he carried the shell-pink, hooded cloak that completed Lysette's ensemble. Diamond studs winked in his shirt front and the glow of the lamplight on his shining ebony curls was echoed by the gleam of the satin revers of his coat.

Furious with herself, Lysette forced her mind back to matters at hand.

"I must speak to you, Nicholas," she insisted.

"I know, my love, you've said so. But not now."

"Nicholas!"

He swirled her cloak about her and fastened the clasp at her throat even as he was drawing her toward the door.

"Later, my sweet," he murmured. "We are very late."

Sputtering, Lysette allowed herself to be propelled out the door and to the waiting carriage. The ride to Nicholas's parents' home on Chartres Street in the Vieux Carre was made in silence. For Lysette's part, she assumed that Nicholas's silence was a sign that he was preoccupied with other thoughts no doubt centering on his highly suspect absence earlier in the day. Nicholas, on the other hand, attributed Lysette's lack of conversation to a fit of pique he was certain stemmed from his not arriving home soon enough to allow them to reach the reception in time to stand in a receiving line playing the center of attention.

"You were very secluded during your marriage to Jules, weren't you?" he asked suddenly.

Lysette glanced up at his face, half-hidden in the shadows cast by the carriage lanterns. "I suppose you could say that," she admitted. A glint of rebellion sparkled in her eyes. "Perhaps Jules was afraid that if he brought me to balls and receptions some roue would accost me on a deserted veranda."

Nicholas chuckled. "Touché, cherie. But the point I was making was simply this: You must have longed to play the social butterfly, flitting to and fro in society, being courted and admired."

"Truly, monsieur, I cannot say that I did." She shrugged. "Before my marriage I had spent half my life in a convent. Not a place, you will admit, in which one acquires a taste for la beau monde."

"Perhaps not. But now, when you have the opportunity, you must be eager to sample—"

Bristling, Lysette glared at him. "I wonder that you are willing to be seen with me in polite society, Nicholas, since you believe me such a . . . a . . . bumpkin!"

"I never said you were—"

"How impressed you must be," she interrupted, imitating his tone with biting accuracy. "How eager. How you must have longed for society."

"Lysette—"

"My life did not begin with our marriage, you know!"

"Didn't it?" Nicholas countered tightly.

"You overbearing, insufferable. . ."

The rumble of the carriage wheels and clatter of the horses' hooves drowned out the rest of Lysette's epithets as the carriage rolled through a stone archway and into a courtyard.

As it drew up before a stone staircase, Nicholas scowled blackly at his bride while she met his furious glance with an icy disdain he was beginning to find infuriatingly familiar.

"We've arrived," he announced grimly. "Try to behave as befits a lady, madame. Not for my sake but for my father's and my mother's. They, at least, must be innocent of whatever grudge it is you bear against me."

Without waiting for an answer, he stepped down into the courtyard and swept Lysette down beside him. After none-too-gently clapping her hand into the crook of his arm, he led her up the stairs and into the house.

The long front hall was walled in hand-painted French wallpaper in soothing, delicate pastels. It was there, beneath the brass and crystal chandelier that Nicholas relieved Lysette of her cloak and waited while she tidied her tousled curls in a gilt-framed girandole.

Not a word passed between them as they moved with stately grace along the hall toward the two adjoining parlors whose connecting doors had been thrown open to accommodate the Callaways' guests. The hum of conversation swelled as they approached, then died as they entered. Beaming, James and Elizabeth Callaway came to them.

Lysette was shocked by her first sight of James Callaway in three years. When last she'd seen him, on the night of Christopher Bishop's ball—on the night, an unbidden voice inside her reminded her, that she'd first encountered Nicholas—he'd been a vigorous, handsome man fairly radiating strength. Now he seemed so frail and small, so much smaller.

Swiftly, to veil her shock, Lysette turned her attention to Nicholas's mother.

Though well past middle age and the mother of a forty year old son, Elizabeth

Pilkington Callaway still retained much of the beauty that had made her the belle of Charleston society. At eighteen she could have had her choice of any scion of any one of the proud Low Country families. At sixty, she still turned heads whenever she appeared in public. Her raven hair was only lightly dusted with grey, her snowy, porcelain skin marked only with the lines that a lifetime of living life to the fullest had etched at the corners of her almond-shaped, robin's-egg blue eyes. Her figure, encased in exquisite scarlet moire, was the envy of many a girl less than a third her age.

Nicholas performed the introductions and Lysette was moved by the warmth of her new in-laws' welcome. Was it possible, she wondered, watching James Callaway congratulating Nicholas so effusively, that they did not know their son's marriage was but a sham—a union contracted solely to please an ill old man? Surely they did not imagine that Nicholas had been but biding his time until the woman he loved was left a young widow. They could not believe that she and Nicholas were actually in love with one another.

And yet Elizabeth's next words seemed to indicate precisely that:

"My dear," she said, taking Lysette's hands into her own, "you cannot imagine how happy we are that Nicholas has at last found the woman he wishes to spend the rest of his life with."

Lysette ventured a look askance at her husband. He was watching her, his black eyes daring her to disillusion the two people who mattered most in the world to him.

"Thank you, madame," she murmured dutifully.

"Please, not so formal. You must call me your belle-mère."

The amenities observed, Nicholas and Lysette were formally presented to the assembled guests. A glass of champagne was pressed into Lysette's hand and she smiled mechanically as a toast was proposed and drunk celebrating her marriage.

She lifted her glass to her lips but the cool crystal never touched her skin. Over the rim of the glass her eyes met the cold, appraising stare of a pair of spring green eyes that held in their golden-lashed depths a wealth of unveiled malice.

The breath seemed to leave Lysette's body in a heart-stopping rush. She felt giddy, sick with shame as she remembered that this woman, her husband's mistress, knew the truth about her marriage.

She ventured another glance in Rosalyn's direction. The woman's eyes glittered, her rosy, all too enticing mouth curved into a superior smile that told Lysette in no uncertain terms that she considered her no threat to her liaison with Nicholas.

Even as Lysette watched, Rosalyn's eyes left her and moved to Nicholas. The expression in them changed, growing less haughty, less disdainful. There was, in her eyes, in her beautiful face, such a look of pride, such a feeling of ownership, that Lysette felt suddenly like the intruder, the other woman, the interloper.

Something stirred sickly in the pit of her stomach. If Rosalyn felt secure enough in Nicholas's affections to appear at this reception knowing full well his wife would be at his side, what chance did she, Lysette, have of winning a place in his heart? Wouldn't it be better for all concerned to simply end the farce that was her marriage? Wouldn't it be more sensible to simply tell Nicholas of the child and be done with it for good and all?

Unexpected tears welled into her eyes. Fool! she cursed herself. What did you imagine would happen? Didn't he tell you precisely what he wanted and did not want from this union? Didn't he warn you that he had no patience with notions of love and romance? Why, then, should you be so chagrined to find that he is only as good as his word?

"My dear?" Elizabeth Callaway was at her elbow, a steadying hand on her arm. "Are you ill?"

Lysette blinked. The hum of conversation had begun again in the long double room but more than one curious gaze rested squarely upon Nicholas's alarmingly pale young bride.

"Not at all," Lysette assured her.

"Perhaps Nicholas should take you home."

"No, no, really, it's not necessary."

"Let me see, where has he gone . . . oh!"

Hearing the dismay that was plain in her mother-in-law's voice, Lysette followed Elizabeth's gaze. Across the room she saw Nicholas deep in conversation with Rosalyn. The woman whose angelic blonde beauty was enhanced by a magnificent Parisian gown of rich azure, stood too close for propriety. But if that had not proclaimed her relationship with Nicholas, the proprietary hand she laid on his forearm as they talked, his dark head so close to her fair one, would have laid the greatest skeptic's doubts to rest.

Feigning an indifference she did not feel, Lysette turned her attention away from the scandalous display.

"Really, madame," she assured Elizabeth. "I'm quite all right."

"Lysette." Elizabeth's tone was conspiratorial as she drew her apart from the milling crowd. "I imagine you know of Nicholas's . . . what I mean to say is that Nicholas has been a bachelor for a long time and . . ." She sighed, "Oh, dear, I knew I'd make a muddle of this."

Lysette squeezed her hand. "I know about Nicholas and Madame D'Everaux."

"Ah." Relieved, Elizabeth smiled wanly. "Well, then, I must explain her presence here tonight."

"It is not necessary," Lysette told her tightly.

"But it is; it is not what you think. Nicholas did not ask to have Rosalyn and Edouard included."

"No?" She could not hide her astonishment.

"Of course not. Whatever Nicholas may be, my dear, he is not so insensitive as to invite his former mistress to his wife's wedding reception."

Former mistress, Lysette thought wryly. Little does she know!

Elizabeth was continuing. "The guest list for tonight was drawn from among the firm's more important clients and associates. Edouard D'Everaux is very influential among the Creole society here in New Orleans. To have snubbed him would have been a serious breach of manners."

"But doesn't he know that Nicholas and Rosalyn. . ."

"Of course he knows, darling. But his marriage to Rosalyn was one of convenience. And she and Nicholas have been discreet."

Lysette remembered the two women aboard the Bienville who spoke of Nicholas and Rosalyn's having been seen all over New Orleans in the month between their marriage and Lysette's leaving Saint-Cloud. Apparently the lovers had not been quite as discreet as Elizabeth chose to believe.

"Marriages of convenience seem to be the fashion," she commented, more than a hint of bitterness in her tone.

"You're quite right," Elizabeth agreed. "In that, we two may consider ourselves fortunate. We married for love."

Lysette opened her mouth, intending to dissuade Elizabeth of her mistaken impression. But she could not tell her. She could not bring herself to be the one to shatter her illusions about the sort of man her son had become.

She was distracted for some time as guests approached seeking introductions. Many had known Jules, most had known that he'd been married to a much younger woman, only a few had actually met her. And now here she was, scarcely two months after Jules's death, married to a man who'd long eluded the best matchmakers in the city. Combined with a beauty that outshone most of the women in the room that night, the mystique surrounding Lysette's marriage promised to make her one of the chief ornaments of New Orleans society.

With Elizabeth called away to settle some dispute between the chef and the butler, Lysette was left on her own. Nicholas was nowhere to be seen and neither, she noticed with an unwelcome pang of jealousy, was Rosalyn D'Everaux.

"Discreet, indeed!" she groused.

"I beg your pardon, madame?"

Coloring prettily, Lysette glanced up at the man she had not realized stood beside her.

"Nothing, monsieur," she assured him quickly.

"Permit me to introduce myself, madame," he said, obviously glad for the opportunity to speak to her. "I had intended to ask Madame Elizabeth for an introduction but she seems to have vanished." He smiled charmingly in apology for his small breech of good manners. "In any case, I am Christopher Stratton—Kit, to my friends."

"Monsieur Stratton." She smiled warily up into clear blue eyes set in a long, oval face that, if not precisely handsome, had a certain boyish charm.

Kit Stratton was not tall, nor was he really short. His limbs were long but his movements were graceful; he was slender but not to the point of being thin. He had none of Nicholas's overpowering masculinity but there was about him some indefinable quality, a sort of decadent elegance, that intrigued Lysette.

"You are involved in finance, monsieur?" she asked. He did not seem in the least like the other gentlemen in the room. They were, nearly to a man, sober, serious men who found it hard to leave their business in the paneled confines of their offices. Even as she spoke, Lysette saw several groups of two or three or four of those men clustered about the room deep in their discussions while their wives stood about with little to do but pray for a pause they knew perfectly well was unlikely to come.

Kit Stratton, on the other hand, exuded an air of joie de vivre that suggested he spent little time preoccupied with such ponderous subjects as business and finance. What, Lysette could not but wonder, was such a blithe spirit doing among such an august group?

"No, madame, I am a painter. A portrait

artist, to be precise."

Lysette did not bother to hide her surprise. "I had no idea that the Callaways were patrons of the arts."

"I am painting Madame Elizabeth's portrait."

"Indeed? I shall look forward to seeing it."

"Perhaps you would like to see it now. It is unfinished, of course, but still . . ."

"It is here, in the house?"

"But of course. I would never ask a lady to attend me in my studio."

"Of course not. I should like very much to see it, sir."

"This way, then. It is in the library."

With Kit's guiding hand at the small of Lysette's back, they made their way through the crowd to the front hall. Across the hall, near the foot of the stairs, a pair of double doors stood closed. Without bothering to knock, Kit depressed the gleaming brass latch and opened one door for Lysette.

Lysette smiled her thanks and took a step forward but her foot never crossed the threshold.

The oak-paneled room was filled with shadows for the gold brocade draperies had been drawn across the windows and only a single lamp burned to dispel the darkness. But that dusky glow was enough to reveal the chamber's secrets to Lysette.

Near a white marble fireplace a couple embraced. The woman, far smaller than the man who held her, pressed close to him; her skirts swirled about his legs as they kissed. In his blue-black hair the lamplight gleamed—it sparkled in the blonde tresses of the woman in his arms.

Frozen in the doorway, Lysette felt a wave of dizziness. Man and woman, large and small, fair and dark—Nicholas and Rosalyn.

Smothering the moan of despair that sprang to her lips, she turned away. A single glance into the room revealed to Kit his mistake. Soundlessly, never alerting the unsuspecting couple of their discovery, he drew the door closed.

Unseeing, Lysette stumbled away. Her legs seemed made of jelly, her head whirled. To find them there, together, was a nightmare she'd never thought to encounter. Was Nicholas really so indifferent to her feelings that he would risk a tryst with his mistress while his wife was beneath the same roof? It seemed so.

Unable to go further, Lysette sank onto the brocade cushions of the Chippendale settee in the hall. She was trembling uncontrollably and Kit, alarmed by her pallor, was torn between trying to calm her and running for Elizabeth.

The far more alarming prospect of trying to explain to Elizabeth the cause of Lysette's condition, decided the question for him. He sat down beside Lysette and took one of her cold, trembling hands between his two warm ones.

"Please forgive me," he entreated. "Had I known—"

"It is not your fault," she assured him,

taking pity upon him in his obvious distress. "You couldn't know."

"There must have been something I—"

Lysette gazed into his eyes. "Nothing. You mustn't blame yourself."

"Tonight, of all nights," he breathed.

"Please, monsieur—Kit," she amended. "It is not your fault that my husband is a . . . a . . . roue."

Kit shook his tawny head, miserable. "Still, if I had not suggested that you see the portrait—"

"Hush. We will speak of it no more, you and I. D'accord?"

"You are too kind, madame," he whispered fervently. "You are an angel."

"Nonsense, monsieur."

"An angel," he repeated. Clasping one of her hands with one of his, he raised the other to his lips and pressed a reverent kiss into her palm.

Lysette smiled into Kit's blue eyes. The sting of Nicholas's betrayal eased a little in the face of the young painter's admiration.

He raised her other hand to his lips and kissed it. He was still kissing it when Nicholas's massive shadow fell across them.

# CHAPTER 10

In the carriage on the long ride home the air was charged with tension. Lysette, burrowed deeply into the caressing silk of her cloak, stared straight ahead refusing to look up at Nicholas who glared at her.

"Well?" he snapped when he could stand no more of her stubborn silence.

"Well?" she countered, matching his tone with biting accuracy.

"Are you going to explain what I found in the hall?"

Not yet meeting his eyes, she tilted her chin haughtily. "What is it you think you found, monsieur?"

"Damn it, Lysette, look at me!" He waited until she raised defiant eyes to meet his furious stare. "You know exactly what I'm talking about!"

"Do I?"

His fists clenched. In that instant, for the first time in his life, he felt as though he were capable of striking a woman.

"Goddammit, Lysette, you were with Kit Stratton! The bastard was making love to you!"

Lysette laughed disdainfully. "Hardly that!

If you must know, he was comforting me."

"Comforting you! And just why in the hell should you run to him for comfort? I am your husband?"

"How good of you to remember."

"What does that mean?"

"You were the reason I needed comforting!" She saw the flicker of unease in his black eyes. "Ah, you remember, don't you? Perhaps you heard the door open? The sound of voices? If, that is, there was any room for any perception beyond the charms of your mistress!"

"That was nothing." His voice was cold, his manner insultingly aloof.

"Nothing!" Lysette hissed. "Come now, monsieur, give me credit for some modicum of intelligence."

"Rosalyn is not my mistress any longer."

"Sweet Jesus!" she exploded. "Betray me if you wish, Nicholas; hurt me if you must. But please, I beg of you, do not lie to me! I can abide any cruelty from you but that!"

"I am not lying to you," he insisted. "But Rosalyn is not the issue here. The issue is you—you and Kit Stratton. You are my wife, I will not tolerate your welcoming the attentions of other men."

Lysette's look was glacial. "A pity Edouard D'Everaux does not feel the same way. But—" She held up a silencing hand when he would have protested further. "But I shall object no further to your liaison with Madame D'Everaux. In fact, I wish you the joy of her bed, monsieur, since you shall find no joy in mine."

Nicholas stared at her in stunned silence. His eyes glittered with wicked malice, the swarthy skin drew taut over the high bones of his cheeks, his full lips tightened menacingly.

"Listen to me, you high-nosed little hoyden. If you think you can back out of our agreement that easily, you're deluding yourself. I'm not a man to be dismissed from my wife's bed with an airy wave of her perfumed hand."

"I do not seek to back out of our agreement, as you put it, monsieur," she informed him haughtily. "In fact, I intend to fulfill my part of the bargain to the very letter of our contract."

"If that is the case, madame, you must realize that I must have the right to your bed whenever I wish it."

She held up a finger. "Until, monsieur, until I prove with child. Well, congratulations, Nicholas, you are to be a father."

For a long time Nicholas merely stared at her, aghast. Then the muscles at the corners of his mouth twitched and suddenly his rich, booming laughter filled the carriage.

"By God, enfant, you had me there for a moment. Now, let's not have any more of your joking, shall we? I'd like to have this matter settled by. . ."

"I'm not joking, Nicholas," she contradicted softly. "I am with child. According to our marriage contract—the contract you insisted upon and wrote, I might remind you—henceforth our marriage is to be in name only."

"Is that what you want?"

"Yes!"

His lip curled mockingly. "You weren't so adamant about it last night."

Lysette drew back into the shadows to hide her pinkening cheeks. "You hardly gave me a chance to protest," she reminded him tremulously.

"I didn't force you."

She turned her face away. "Really, Nicholas, if you were a gentleman. . ."

"Perhaps I'm not." Cupping her chin, he forced her to face him. "Why didn't you tell me this last night?"

"I wasn't sure last night," she lied unconvincingly.

"Sure about. . ?"

"The baby."

"But you are sure tonight."

"Yes, I am."

Nicholas scowled but there was little he could do. He wasn't sure he believed her but he couldn't imagine that she'd be so foolish as to try and deceive him when a simple examination could have exposed any lies.

Damn! Other men prayed for a son; other women lived their whole lives in quiet desperation, miserable because they could not give their husband a child. But not him—oh, no. He had to marry a little French hellion who made love like an angel and bred like a rabbit!

The rest of the ride was made in grudging silence. Nicholas was furious but whether at Lysette, himself, or the world in general he couldn't be sure. It was true, what he had told Lysette. He had told Rosalyn in the library that their affair was over. The kiss—that damned kiss—had been their last, a gesture of desperation on her part, of gallantry on his. Why, oh why, did Kit Stratton have to choose that moment to bring Lysette to the library?

For Lysette's part, she had won what she'd set out to win. In all good faith, Nicholas could not insist upon the husbandly rights he had forfeited in the marriage contract of his own forging. Why, then, did she feel like crying? She stole a glance at him. Dieu! But he was handsome! She felt a glimmering of desire for him deep inside her. What had she done? Had she been too hasty, foolish, perhaps? But no, wasn't this what he wanted? Wasn't it what they both wanted? She had been so sure before. Why wasn't she sure now?

The lamplight gleamed softly on the loosened waves of Lysette's hair as she sat at her dressing table. Mimette had been summoned to help her mistress undress and thus far they had removed Lysette's jewels and freed the curls that now cascaded over her shoulders.

Reflected in the mirror, she could see the long room that had been Nicholas's. For tonight he was sleeping in a guest room across the hall. Come the morning, Lysette's things would be moved to a bedroom which adjoined the dressing room in which both their clothes were stored. Only this morning she had seen this room for the first time. She had thought how much it reminded her of Nicholas. She had tried to imagine what it would be like sharing it with him as a proper wife to a proper husband. But that would never happen. Not now. The break had been made. Who knew? Perhaps it was for the best. Nicholas did not love her—why, then, prolong the farce that was their marriage?

While Lysette sat before her dressing table, Mimette went to the dressing room to fetch one of her nightdresses. A magnificent Coromandel screen stood across the room and behind it, the maid laid out the nightdress her mistress would wear.

Lysette stood as the maid moved behind her to unfasten her gown. She felt first one button then another being opened and ached to be freed of the constricting embrace of the boned bodice and the corset within.

She sighed as the rapping at the door stayed Mimette's efforts.

"Entrez!" she called impatiently.

The door swung open and Nicholas appeared. Having discarded his coat and the diamond studs of his shirt, he looked far less formidable but no less devastating. His ebony curls were in disarray, as though he had run his fingers through them, but to Lysette's enchanted eyes, that only lent him a rakish air she found heart-stoppingly alluring.

His eyes captured Lysette's and held them. They issued an unspoken command and she was powerless to disobey.

"That will be all, Mimette," she said softly.

With an uneasy glance from her mistress to the master of whom she stood in awe, Mimette bobbed a little curtsy then scampered out of the room.

Swirling a snifter of brandy in one hand, Nicholas entered the chamber and kicked the door closed behind him.

Tearing her eyes from his, Lysette reached back and tried to unfasten her own gown.

Nicholas drained his glass and set it aside. Sitting on a chair, he beckoned her to him.

"Let me do that for you."

Warily, Lysette turned in front of him and let him draw her back between his knees. She felt his fingers moving over the buttons with a certainty that said nothing for his moral character.

A man, she decided rather priggishly, should not be so familiar with the intricacies of women's apparel. Particularly not a man who has been married for such a short time. I wonder if he does this for. . .

She gasped as he told her he'd finished with a sharp slap on the rump. She shot him a vicious glare but he only gazed at her with that faintly amused, mocking look she found so unfuriating. Lifting her sagging gown, she stalked to the screen and slipped behind.

"You do intend to keep your word, don't you, Nicholas?" she asked, stepping out of the gown which pooled at her feet.

She was invisible to him, the six-foot screen hiding her completely. But as he lounged in his chair, one black booted ankle resting on the opposite knee, a movement caught Nicholas's eye. Glancing toward the dressing table he discovered, to his delight, that the mirror offered him an unrestricted view of his wife in delicious dishabille. As he watched, tantalized, her little fingers worked at the fastenings of her petticoats and they too fell into a tangle of lace around her silk slippered feet.

Having gotten no reply, she peeked around the screen. "Nicholas?"

He was the very picture of innocent attention. "My love?"

"I asked if you intend to keep your word."

"Absolutely."

She eyed him suspiciously. He was up to something—she'd spent too much time in his presence not to recognize that devilish gleam in his eyes. Troubled, she went back to her undressing.

Mercifully, her corselet fastened in front and proved no obstacle. When it, too, was discarded, Lysette sighed and, in so doing, did not hear Nicholas's murmur of appreciation at the sight of his wife in her high heeled slippers, pink stockings, and the short, wispy chemise that her constricting corselet had molded to her.

"I thought, perhaps, you might change your mind."

Nicholas shifted in his chair. Having kicked off her slippers, Lysette bent to unfasten her garters. The loose neck of her chemise gaped away offering Nicholas a ravishingly unhindered view of her breasts.

"Have you?" She scowled around the screen.

"My sweet?" Only the faint beading of perspiration on his forehead betrayed the havoc she was wreaking upon him.

"Changed your mind. You haven't?"

"Of course not."

"Good."

Returning to her preparations, Lysette rolled the fine silk stockings down her legs. She heard Nicholas clear his throat and wondered what it was he had come to speak to her about in the first place.

Untying the satin ribbon that fastened the neck of her chemise, she let it slip from her shoulders.

"Was there some reason you came in here, Nicholas?" she asked as the diaphanous garment slid down over her hips.

"Oh, God, no."

Lysette frowned, puzzled. He was certainly the most unpredictable man she'd ever met. Yawning, she stretched sensuously, delighting in the unencumbered freedom of her nudity. She reached for the nightdress which had slipped from the stool to the floor asking as she did:

"When are you going to tell your parents about the baby, Nicholas?"

In the way of an answer, there was only the sound of footsteps muffled by the carpet and the slamming of the chamber door.

Lysette peeked from behind the screen. She was alone. Nicholas had fled.

Pulling the nightdress over her head, she emerged from behind the screen.

"What a rude man!" she complained to the empty room. "He could at least have said good night!"

Shrugging, resigned to marriage with a totally incomprehensible man, she went around the room extinguishing the lamps for the night.

# CHAPTER 11

As the days following the Callaways' reception grew into weeks and the weeks became months, Nicholas and Lysette's marriage settled into a discouraging pattern. They seldom saw one another in the morning. Lysette, beset by the trials of early pregnancy and a listlessness which grew, though she would have been the last to admit it, of a despondency over Nicholas's neglect, fell into the habit of lying abed until well past the time when Nicholas had driven off to attend to his never-ending round of business meetings. In the evenings they habitually dined together at home (Lysette's pregnancy providing them with a convenient excuse for avoiding the social occasions when they would have been expected to put on a show of marital bliss neither felt capable of feigning). They were cordial, pleasant even, but there was always that undercurrent of tension flowing between them.

I hate him, Lysette thought to herself one evening in early December. I loathe him. I despise him. She pushed her spoon around in the strawberry sorbet which had, until that night, been her reigning passion. Now, for some mysterious reason, it had ceased to appeal to her as so many dishes had in the past two months. She wondered if she should eat it just to please Cook who was, not unreasonably, at her wit's end. The woman was French, a marvelous cook who had had several offers from families in the Vieux Carre. Were it not that she had a weakness for 'la petite madame' and that she put Lysette's disagreeability down to the strains of her first pregnancy, the Callaways would have found themselves lacking a cook long ago.

Her eyes never leaving Nicholas, Lysette forced a spoonful of the sorbet past her lips.

He's a beast. She savored that thought far more than the sweet concoction she forced herself to swallow. He's a demon. He's worse than the Devil himself.

Her eyes gleamed with malice. Nicholas, glancing up, found her malevolent stare as exasperating as always. Forcing his full lips into some semblance of a smile, he nodded cordially to her. But his own thoughts were scarcely more pleasant than hers.

Little bitch, he thought. If there was a knife within reach she'd plunge it into my heart with pleasure.

With a disgusted sigh, he wiped his mouth and cast away his napkin.

"Dinner was not to your liking, monsieur?" Lysette asked, her voice fairly dripping sweetness. "I thought it marvelous. Particularly this delicious sorbet." Scooping up the last, heaping spoonful of the dessert, she shoved it into her mouth and swallowed it with exaggerated relish.

"Dinner was perfectly fine."

It was the opening Lysette wanted. "Then perhaps the company was not to your liking. I hope you do not feel you must deprive yourself of more appealing companions merely to keep me company. After all, we have an understanding, do we not?"

Nicholas's black eyes flashed. He had been truthful when he had told Lysette that his affair with Rosalyn D'Everaux was at an end. He had not been with her—nor, indeed, with any woman—since the night Lysette had told him of her pregnancy. He wished to God Rosalyn was still his mistress—celibacy was not in the least to his liking and after two months of it he was more than a little touchy on the subject of women. Still, he knew that Rosalyn would take him back. Doubtless she would consider it a personal triumph to think he had deserted his wife's bed for hers. But the truth of the matter, much as it rankled, was that he did not desire Rosalyn, nor any other woman come to that. It was Lysette he wanted. Only Lysette. His wife, damn it all. The one woman he could not have.

"Indeed we have, madame," he answered at last. "And I do thank you for your concern. Let me assure you, however, that I do not mind in the least dining with you. I really have nothing better to do at this hour."

Lysette's spoon rattled against the crystal

sorbet dish. Nothing better to do! What a boor! How could she ever have thought him gallant! How could she have ever thought him anything but the rude, conceited fool that he was!

He rose and circled the long mahogany table. Lysette stiffened as he approached. Much as she despised herself for it, his nearness affected her. He had awakened her senses in those few, blissful times when their marriage had been in more than merely name and those damned stubborn senses were not easily put back to sleep.

A shiver ran through her as his hands came to rest on white shoulders laid bare by her off-shoulder gown and upswept curls.

"What do you want?" she demanded, laying down her spoon lest he see the trembling of her hand and know how his touch stirred her.

Nicholas smiled down at the gleaming crown of her head. He had felt her shiver, had noted her trembling. Only the knowledge that had he wished to, he could have forced her senses to betray her, salved his pride.

"Want, my love?" he asked. "Why nothing at all. Haven't you already given me everything I asked you for?"

"I have," Lysette affirmed defensively.

"Indeed you have, and far more quickly than I dared hope. You've finished playing with your dessert, I presume? Come into the parlor."

Rising, Lysette allowed her hand to remain

where he had placed it on his arm as he led her from the dining room into the pale green parlor. But when she made as if to sit on the cushioned settee, Nicholas held her near with an arm draped tightly about her waist.

That single, powerful hand forced her to turn within the circle of his arm until she faced him, their bodies scant inches apart.

Lysette gazed up into his swarthy, cynical face. The rebellious defiance of a moment ago had been replaced by a wariness which shone like a beacon from her wide, haunted eyes.

"What do you want?" she repeated, breathless.

"Only to put you on notice, madame. My parents have invited us to keep Christmas with them at Montcalm and I have accepted. They must not suspect that ours is anything but the blissful love match they have been led to believe it is. Our visit will last a fortnight or more. We will not take our own staff save for Mimette and so will find ourselves in close association with my parents' servants. Fooling them will necessitate drastic measures on both our parts." His eyes glittered with malicious satisfaction terrifying Lysette. "We will have to be pleasant to one another at all times, madame. We will have to bill and coo like two lovebirds in a gilded cage for we will be on display. We will have to walk together, talk together, eat together. . ." His hands closed about her waist; he bent his head so that his lips nearly brushed her ear. ". . . sleep together."

"No!" Lysette recoiled but his strong hands held her in an almost painful embrace. She struggled. "No!"

"Listen to me!" He shook her. "Damn it, hear me! I didn't say I would touch you." His lips curled with contempt. "You over-estimate your attractions, madame, if you think I would brave your claws and venom for the dubious pleasure of coupling with you."

"You bastard!"

Nicholas laughed. "You can't bear for me to touch you but you can't stand the thought that I might not even want to, is that it? Would you like to lie up in your prim, un-sullied bed and imagine that I am across the hall writhing in a paroxysm of longing? I am sorry to disillusion you, madame. I fear it is you who does most of the longing in this house."

"It's not true!" she hissed. "I hate you. I loathed your touching me!"

A thick, ebony brow arched skeptically. "Did you? Do you still?"

"Yes! More than ever!"

"I wonder." His laugh was cruel, mocking them both. "Truly, I wonder. It might be worth the testing were you not carrying so precious a burden. Even for the satisfaction that would come with proving you wrong, I will not risk you so enraging yourself that you lose my child." The disdainful smirk left his lips. "Do as you will, madame. Please yourself. But remember, we are keeping Christmas with my parents and I would risk anything—anything—to prevent their disillusionment."

"Even your child?" Lysette asked archly.

A muscle ticked in his lean cheek. "Even my child," he confirmed, adding, with more than a touch of threat. "Even you."

He released Lysette and, with a scornful half-bow, left her to stare after him. She was still standing there when he walked out the door and climbed into a waiting carriage that took him off into the New Orleans night.

Montcalm, a superb brick and stucco mansion, stood in the center of rolling lawns overlooking an oak-lined stream. The side of the mansion facing the bayou boasted an open loggia. A stairway rose from it to the upper gallery which was protected from the weather by shutters called jalousies. All around the mansion cypress and willows competed for space; their festoons of grey-green Spanish moss intertwined as the breeze off the bayou played among their branches.

Nicholas and Lysette arrived at Montcalm a week before Christmas. They had made the long journey from New Orleans in almost total silence for each still cherished their private grudge as dearly as a miser guards his gold. Neither trusted the other, neither believed that the other bore for them anything but the bitterest contempt, and yet each longed to find in their counterfeit marriage some measure of the passion they had known in those few precious hours when they had managed to banish the mistrust and suspicion that seemed now to be the lifeblood of their union.

Within its elegant walls the mansion had been decorated for the holiday. Boughs of boxwood and holly draped the mantles and the balustrade of the grand staircase which rose to the top of the three story mansion in a lazy, oval spiral. Elizabeth Callaway appeared on the first landing as Nicholas and Lysette stood poised beneath the archway in the stairway.

"Here you are at last," she smiled, descending the stairs in a rustle of emerald silk. "We had nearly given you up until tomorrow."

"We got a late start," Nicholas explained, bending to receive his mother's kiss. His black eyes scanned the room worriedly. "Father isn't ill?"

"Oh, no," she assured him, touching his sleeve. "But he does occasionally lie down before dinner. He's fine, really, dear."

She kissed Lysette's cheek fondly. Since Nicholas had told his delighted parents that they were to be grandparents at long last, their fondness for their daughter-in-law had grown by leaps and bounds. Though the emotions shamed him, Nicholas occasionally knew a pang of resentment when he witnessed his parents' adoration for a woman he felt was completely unworthy of their smallest regard. She was fulfilling her role as his wife—her role as a woman—but in his biased eyes that did not begin to atone for her faults as a human being.

"I've had your things sent up to the west guest suite," Elizabeth told him. "Your old room is far too small for the two of you."

Lysette cast a look askance and found Nicholas's black eyes flashing a warning. She forced a smile to her lips as he said:

"I'm sure whatever rooms you choose for us will be delightful, Mother."

Elizabeth laughed her merry, infectious laugh. "How tractable you've become, darling." She patted Lysette's cheek. "You're a good influence on him, child."

"That must be it," Lysette agreed, enjoying the angry tic that had begun in Nicholas's cheek. "Though he does have his difficult moments."

"They all do," her mother-in-law assured her. "He's exactly like his father. Hopefully, fatherhood will mellow him."

"Do you think that's likely, madame?"

Elizabeth's sigh was wistful. "Not very. But we can hope, can't we?"

Nicholas scowled. "If you two insist upon discussing me as though I weren't here, I might as well not be." He made them a shallow, mocking bow. "You'll excuse me."

Elizabeth and Lysette watched him stride into the nearest parlor where he knew he could find some of his father's prize bourbon.

The women exchanged a conspiratorial glance, then Elizabeth took Lysette's arm.

"Come along, child, let me show you around a bit then I'll take you upstairs to change for dinner. Travel always did make Nicholas hard to get along with."

The two laughed and Nicholas, hearing them, bolted down his drink in a single, throat-burning swallow.

"Damned women," he muttered. "They stick together like bees in a hive!"

Dressed in heliotrope velvet, Lysette covertly studied her husband in the glimmering light of the candles which were adorned with tiny wreaths of holly. From the moment Elizabeth had shown her to the suite she and Nicholas would share—from the moment she had seen the silk-draped Empire bed—it had seemed she could think of nothing else save the coming night when they would be alone together.

Would he want to make love to her? If he did, could she resist him? More to the point, did she even want to? Her eyes caressed the sculpted planes of his face as he spoke to his father at the head of the table. Her gaze seemed drawn to a tanned, smooth place at his throat above the white collar of his shirt. She felt a sudden, insane desire to press her lips to that impossibly tantalizing spot. She wanted to kiss it, caress it with her lips, feel its living warmth.

Dieu! Flushing, she dragged her eyes back

to her scarcely-touched meal. What was wrong with her? Was she mad? How could the thought of sleeping with a man she hated give rise to such unashamedly lascivious thoughts?

She glanced discreetly to the left and right wondering if either James or Elizabeth had noticed her look and fathomed the shocking direction of her thoughts. To her relief they either had not or they had seen nothing wrong in a wife's casting such looks toward the husband she'd wed only three months before.

Still, to avoid a repetition, she forced herself to concentrate on her meal, on the conversation, the decor of the elegant room, anything, anything at all, except Nicholas.

In doing so, she missed noticing that his gazes were, if anything, more covetous, more heated, than her own. His ebon eyes feasted on her bosom as it swelled daringly above the neckline of her purple gown. They devoured the tender flesh of her throat, lingered on the shadowed curve of her shoulder.

Unlike Lysette, his attention did not go unnoticed. More than once his mother addressed him and received no reply. A single glance at his face told her that his thoughts were elsewhere—in the silk-draped bed a floor above.

Lowering her eyes, Elizabeth smiled. She was delighted that the dashing, handsome son she so doted upon had at last found a woman with whom he was so obviously in love. And Lysette had conceived their child so quickly. Perhaps her long-harbored dream of hearing the lofty chambers of Montcalm ring with the laughter of grandchildren was not so far-fetched as they had seemed only a few short months ago.

"Lysette," she said, drawing her daughter-in-law's attention away from the plate she studied with curious intensity. "Have you and Nicholas discussed names for the baby?"

Lysette's cheeks pinkened. She wondered what her mother-in-law would think if she knew just how little time she and Nicholas spent in discussion of any topic.

"No, we haven't," she answered truthfully. "I thought Nicholas would want to decide."

Nicholas spoke up. "He will be named James; after Father."

"And if it's a girl?"

He shrugged his wide shoulders; his black eyes bore into Lysette. "If it's a girl, we'll simply have to try again as quickly as possible."

Lysette stiffened. A child, that had been their bargain. Of course, in that overbearingly arrogant mind of his there would be no room for doubt that any child he sired would be a male child. They would have to try again. The prospect left her with mixed emotions. She knew that Nicholas had planned on their leading separate lies once their child had been born. But now, since he was so determined to have a son. . .

Memories of her life at the French convent

stirred within her. She remembered the girl who had shared the bare little room which had been her home for eight years. Adrienne de Furneaux, daughter of the Comte de Furneaux. Pretty Adrienne, the eldest of seven daughters.

"Why are there so many children in your family?" Lysette remembered whispering to Adrienne as they lay one night in their hard, narrow cots.

Adrienne's voice had replied in the darkness: "Because my father wanted a son."

Biting her lips, Lysette barely stiffled a giggle. Her eyes sparkled as she glanced at Nicholas and not even the glowering frown that told her plainly he suspected he was the butt of some private joke could not help her stifle her mirth.

Elizabeth sensed the tension flowing between the two but put it down to the insensitivity of a man talking so casually about having a second child when his wife was not nearly ready to deliver the first.

She decided to change the subject.

"By the bye, Lysette," she said lightly. "You seem to have made quite an impression on Kit Stratton. I sat for him just before we left Montcalm and he could scarcely speak of anything else."

Nicholas made a sound of disgust. "Kit Stratton! Why do you waste your time sitting for that incompetent clod?"

Elizabeth lifted her black brows. "As to his being incompetent, dear, he is by far the most fashionable portrait artist in New Orleans. As to his being a clod, I can tell you that his attentions are highly prized by more than one lady of our acquaintance—ladies, I might add, of indisputably discriminating tastes. As to why I waste my time, let me remind you that it was you who commissioned the portrait in the first place."

A giggle bubbled out of Lysette's throat and Nicholas scowled. Damn it all! he thought furiously, no man is a match for a pair of scheming women!

A noise from the head of the table caught their attention. A glance revealed that James Callaway had nodded into a doze over his dessert.

"Poor darling," Elizabeth murmured. "Help him to bed, won't you, Nicholas?"

While Nicholas complied with his mother's wishes, Lysette remained behind. She was struck by the tender concern in Elizabeth's beautiful eyes, the signs of strain and worry etched into her classically lovely face.

She loves him, she thought, not without a little pang of envy. She knows she will not have him with her much longer and the thought of losing him agonizes her.

They had, Nicholas had once told her, been married forty-two years. And yet, when Elizabeth looked at her husband, there was in her eyes the undimmed adoration of a young girl in the first blush of infatuation.

What must it be, she wondered, to love so long and so deeply? To feel that there is another who is like the other half of yourself? What would it be like to share such a love with someone who felt the same way about you?

The pang of envy inside her grew, giving birth to a resentment that she had not been so fortunate. She watched Nicholas help his father up the stairs. He was so gentle, so loving with the elderly man. It was a side of him he did not show to many people—a side she believed she could never hope to see shown to her.

Why, her jealous heart raged, am I so unworthy of his affection? He was the one who laid down the rules by which we must abide. He was the one who made it clear from the first that he desired nothing of love from me.

She remembered the first time she saw him—the first time he kissed her. It had been the stuff of fantasies. In the three years that followed that night she had often found herself daydreaming of the dark stranger on the veranda. Sometimes she caught herself wishing she knew who he was, wishing she could see him again, envying the woman he loved. Now she knew him—perhaps she should have contented herself with her fantasies.

Tears welled into her eyes. She could have loved Nicholas. If only . . . if only . . . No, it was no use. He had not married her because he wanted her—he had married her because she fit a set of criteria he had established as the necessary attributes of a wife. Of Lysette herself, what did she matter to him?

Noticing her daughter-in-law's tears, Elizabeth was instantly concerned.

"What is it, dear? What's wrong?"

"Nothing," Lysette lied.

"Nonsense, you're weeping."

"Really, madame, I. . ."

"Come into the parlor with me, sweeting. and tell me what is wrong."

Unable to resist, Lysette allowed Elizabeth to lead her into the mahogany-walled formal parlor and settle her on an ivory-brocade sofa.

"Now tell me, darling, what can possibly be worrying that pretty head of yours? You're young, beautiful, carrying your first child. Your husband is handsome, rich, and so very much in love with. . ."

Lysette's chin quivered and the tears began to flow unchecked down her satiny cheeks. She covered her face with her hands and wept.

Elizabeth patted her gently but her mind was awhirl.

"Hush, dear, please, you mustn't upset yourself so. Surely you cannot believe that Nicholas does not. . ."

"He hates me," Lysette whimpered. "He loathes me."

"No, no, sweeting, hush. Of course he loves you. You must remember that he was a bachelor for so many years. The adjustment is difficult, I'm sure. But remember, you are the woman he chose as his wife. Many women have set their caps for him, you know. None came near to winning his heart."

"He has no heart!"

"Lysette!"

Nicholas's voice cut the air like the slash of a saber. He filled the doorway, his swarthy face dark with anger. Lysette drew swiftly away from Elizabeth and rose from the sofa. She pressed her fingers to her treacherous lips.

"Nicholas," Elizabeth breathed. She could not fathom the reason for his anger. Nor could she understand Lysette's fear. Rising, she approached her son; in so doing, she missed seeing Lysette snatch up her skirts and retreat through the hall door.

Upstairs, in her room, Lysette snapped at Mimette as she undressed her and readied her for bed. Seeing the hurt in the maid's eyes, she felt sorry but there was nothing she could do. She was too aware of the fact that Nicholas would appear at any moment breathing fire over the fact that she had allowed his mother to know all was not sweetness and light between them.

When she was dressed for the night, she sat at the dressing table and brushed her hair for want of anything else to still her restless hands.

But the brush wavered as she heard the click of the latch and the creak of the door as it was opened.

On the tufted silk of the dressing stool, Lysette froze. In the mirror she could see

Nicholas framed in the doorway. He watched her, black eyes narrowed, not moving a muscle. In turn Lysette watched him, her red-brown eyes wide and wary, waiting for him to show her the depth of his fury.

# CHAPTER 12

Without a word Nicholas entered the room. Lysette watched him as he crossed the floor and disappeared into the dressing room where one of the elder Callaways' menservants waited to play valet to him.

Lysette lay the silver and ivory brush onto the polished tulipwood tabletop. His reaction was so completely unexpected; it made her all the more nervous. What had Elizabeth said to him? How much of what she had said to Elizabeth had he heard? As always, her mind was filled with questions and, like always, there seemed to be no ready answers.

Leaving her dressing table, she climbed into the big bed and huddled close to the edge furthest from the dressing room door. One part of her wished Nicholas had stormed into the room eyes blazing, ready for a fight. Then, perhaps, she might have been goaded into demanding answers to all the questions that plagued her. The other part of her prayed that he would choose not to raise the subject between them. There were too many of her questions whose answers she feared would only send her deeper into despair.

She heard the door open and close and

Nicholas reentered the room. One by one the lamps were extinquished as he blew out their flickering flames. At last the only light in the room came from a low, smoldering fire in the grate that burned to dispel the winter's damp chill and the glowing tip of the cheroot he held as he climbed into the bed and plumped the pillows behind his head.

Whether he believed her already asleep or not, he did not touch her but only lay silently, one arm folded behind his head, smoking in the shadowy darkness. Beside him, Lysette lay motionless, unwilling to draw his attention by the slightest movement. His mood was strangely thoughtful and she thought it best not to intrude upon whatever ponderings were keeping him from sleeping and from taking her to task for revealing any part of the truth about their marriage to his mother.

But Nicholas had no intention of taking Lysette to task. Indeed, he was not in the least angry with her. He was troubled, confused, uncertain. He had been stunned to find her there, weeping, in the parlor. Hers were not simply the overwrought tears of a young woman whose delicate condition brought with it an imbalance of her nerves. No, it had been something else. He had been the cause of her distress.

"He hates me," she had wept. "He loathes me. He has no heart!"

His little termagant. His hellcat. His French shrew. He had thought her beyond hurting. He had never imagined she cared a whit whether he loved her or loathed her. He had never considered whether or not she could be hurt by anything he did, for it had never occurred to him that she considered his feelings any more than he did hers. And yet, she had said those things; with his own ears he had heard her.

He glanced toward her. In the dim, orange glow given off by the dying fire, he could see her dark head on the snowy pillow. Her long, loose chestnut curls fanned out over the lacy linen. He remembered his mother's words after Lysette had left the parlor.

"She loves you, Nicholas," his mother had told him. "I know it's difficult for you to believe, to trust her, to accept her love, but you must try. Consider Lysette now. Remember, in the space of a few months she has not only become a widow, but a new bride and now a mother. Pregnancy can do strange things to a woman. Be patient with her. Give her what she needs."

"I give her everything, Mother," he had replied tightly.

Elizabeth's raven brows had drawn downward. "Don't fence with me, Nicholas. You know perfectly well I do not mean material objects. Patience, kindness, and love mean more—to any woman—than anything your money can buy. Your gold will not comfort her when she is lonely or soothe her when she is frightened. I know that you love her." She smiled triumphantly at the surprise in his face. "Oh, yes, you thought you were hiding it so well, didn't you? And so you do, from Lysette, but she does not know you as well as I. I can see it. Why don't you show it to her?"

Blowing out a last, billowing stream of silver-grey smoke, Nicholas stubbed out his cheroot in a porcelain dish on the bedside table.

'Show it to her,' his mother had said. But how? And why? Did he truly love Lysette? After all, theirs was not a marriage in the true sense, only a business arrangement entered into for their mutual benefit. He scowled. Damn it all, he had never meant for anything like this to happen. He had thought Lysette mature enough to accept the marriage in the sense he had proposed it. As for himself, he could not begin to explain the feelings that seemed to have taken root inside him. Why, when he had been pursued by some of the most beautiful, most sophisticated women in Louisiana, should a hot-tempered little innocent ensnare him? It was past all understanding.

Leaning up on one elbow, he gazed down at her. She lay still, having turned onto her back, and he wondered if she were merely feigning sleep. Damnation but she was beautiful! Lying there, eyes closed, lashes fanning across her pale cheeks, she looked young as a girl and just as innocent. Fragile, even. His eyes traveled the length of her body which scarcely raised the coverlet. Soon enough their child would make its presence known. But for now, she was as petite as ever, delicate, and yes, he had to admit it, precious to him.

Desire for her filled him, the visions in his brain of her as she had been on their wedding night served as the kindling for the fire that burst into life inside him. A tiny moan of frustration wormed its way between his clenched teeth.

Closing his eyes, he shook his head even as a smirk rife with self-mockery curved his lips. You fool, he taunted himself, you stupid, ridiculous fool. Here you lie beside your lawful wife wanting her, needing her, afire for her, and yet forbidden her by your own doing. Was there ever such a ninny in all the world?

Filled with self-loathing, Nicholas rolled onto his side carefully facing away from Lysette. With a herculean effort, he willed away the desire that only moments before had threatened to make him cast aside his pride, his self-control, and make love to the wife he himself had set beyond his own reach.

All throughout the following day, Lysette watched Nicholas warily as a mouse watches the cat who lurks just without its lair. Everytime they encountered one another she tensed, expecting the worst, and yet he was unfailingly courteous to her. What was even more puzzling, there were several occasions when he was positively pleasant.

When he brought her a kitten born to the mouser who patrolled the stables, he presented it to her as shyly as a boy bringing a gift to a girl of whose affections he is not yet sure.

"Oh, Nicholas!" she cooed, clutching the squirming bundle of orange and white fur to her breast. "May I keep her? May I take her back to New Orleans?"

"Of course, enfant." He smiled, hands clasped behind his back, inordinately pleased by her obvious delight in his simple gift.

Lysette stretched up on tiptoe and pressed a kiss to his cheek. The surprise in his dark eyes reminded her that such gestures of affection were rare between them and she blushed and stepped back.

Nicholas sighed for the loss of the brief moment's intimacy. Reaching out, he stroked the tiny striped head nestled against the peach silk bodice of Lysette's gown.

"What will you name her, enfant?" he asked softly.

She smiled shyly. "I shall have to consider."

"And we shall have to consider names for the baby, shan't we? I confess, my mother made me pause and think yesterday. It is a matter we should discuss."

"James for a boy," she reminded him.

"And for a girl?"

She nuzzled the kitten. "Will you be terribly disappointed if the child is a girl, Nicholas?"

She held her breath as he reached out and stroked the glossy baby curl near her ear. His voice had a strange, husky quality as he replied:

"Not if she is as beautiful as her mother, cherie."

Lysette gazed at him, nonplussed, but the spell was shattered by the arrival of a manservant.

" 'Scuse me, sir. You said to tell you when Mist' Michael had come."

"Thank you, Eleazar. I'll be along directly." He smiled at Lysette. "Try to think of some names that appeal to you, sweet. We'll discuss it later."

He bent and kissed her cheek, then turned and strode from the room leaving Lysette to gaze after him completely and totally bewildered. What could have wrought this change in him? Was he up to something? There was always that possibility but what could it be?

Her kitten nibbled her chin and she absently scratched its ears but her mind was wholly preoccupied with thoughts of Nicholas.

"Lysette?" Elizabeth's voice, coming unexpectedly, startled her.

"Oui?" The kitten squirmed and she let it down to play with the fringed edge of the parlor carpet.

"Darling, here is someone I want you to meet. This is Leigh Scofield. Her husband, Michael, was Nicholas's boyhood companion.

You will meet him if the two of them can ever manage to drag themselves in from the stables."

Turning, Lysette found before her a young woman some five years older than herself. Slightly shorter, Leigh Scofield was all curves and circles. Strawberry blonde curls surrounded a pretty, pixieish face. She was no ravishing beauty—there was about her the undeniable look of an Irish elf—but she was possessed of an intriguing gamin charm that would have made her stand out as special in a room filled with belles.

"How do you do," Lysette said politely.

Impulsively, as she did almost everything, Leigh kissed Lysette's cheek.

"How pretty you are," she trilled. "But then, I've always known that no ordinary woman would ever capture Nicholas."

Lysette's cheeks pinkened prettily. "Please, madame."

"Leigh, please," the other corrected. "After all, Nicholas and Michael have been friends forever. We must follow their example, mustn't we?"

"Of course," Lysette agreed, her tone less than enthusiastic.

Her hesitancy stemmed not from any reservations about Leigh herself. On the contrary, she felt a real kinship with the wife of Nicholas's best friend. Rather, it was simply that she had never had occasion to have a close woman friend before. At the convent she had had playmates but once her school days had ended so had those tenuous connections.

"Why don't the two of you get to know one another?" Elizabeth suggested. "Leigh and Michael will be staying tonight and I must see to the preparations."

"Don't go to any trouble, Elizabeth," Leigh urged.

"It's no trouble at all," Elizabeth assured her, giving her a quick hug. "You know how delighted we always are to see the two of you."

She was gone then with a whisper of russet velvet leaving Lysette and Leigh to smile uncertainly at one another.

"Michael and Nicholas grew up together?" Lysette finally asked more to break the silence than anything else.

"We all did," Leigh answered gaily. "Nicholas here at Montcalm and Michael and I at Buckland." She giggled at Lysette's obvious bewilderment.

"My parents, you see, were lost at sea when I was a child. Michael's father was my guardian." Her azure eyes took on a distant gleam. "I can still remember my first sight of Buckland." She pressed Lysette's hand. "You must visit, of course. Oh, I know you're likely biased toward Montcalm but I consider Buckland the most beautiful home I've ever seen."

"How old were you when you came there?"

"Nine. Michael was eighteen. Nicholas was nineteen. I worshipped them; they were so old and wise. Not to mention handsome, of course, though I didn't really notice that until I was a few years older. I followed them like a puppy." She rolled her eyes, remembering. "I made such a nuisance of myself. I'm sure Michael would have banished me from his presence had it not been for Nicholas's kindness."

"Nicholas's?" Lysette did not bother to hide her surprise. Nicholas was not the sort of man she would think of as overly tolerant of a bothersome child.

"Of course. He took pity on me, poor, besotted moppet that I was. He made Michael let me come when they rode and hunted." She smiled a little sheepishly. "He even made toys for me. Naturally, I was madly in love with him. I was devastated when he left to study the law."

"He didn't return your feelings?"

Leigh's musical laugh bubbled forth. "Not at all. I was only a child. And I was destined to marry Michael, though I didn't know it at the time. Michael knew it, though, his father told him. Perhaps that's why he resented me when I first came to live at Buckland." She waved a delicate hand in dismissal. "It doesn't matter now, really, we're very happy."

"You're fortunate," Lysette murmured.

Leigh squeezed her hand. "No, my dear, it is you who are fortunate. After all, you are Mrs. Nicholas Callaway, aren't you? I envy you."

Lysette was astonished. "But why?"

"Oh, I suppose because no woman ever truly gets over her first love. Even if she knows it is hopeless; and I did know it was hopeless. But here I am boring you. This is all too familiar to you, I'm sure. No doubt Nicholas has told you all about his youth here on Bayou Teche."

Lysette averted her eyes. Everyone assumed that Nicholas confided in her. How could she tell them that she was merely a partner in Nicholas's latest business venture?

"No. Quite honestly, he hasn't."

"Really?" Leigh frowned, puzzled. "He's always been so open with those he loves."

An awkward silence fell between them until a timely ruckus from the entrance hall shattered the stillness. Their silken skirts swayed in unison as the women went out to find their husbands who had just come in from the stables.

Michael Scofield's chocolate brown eyes lit with admiration as they came to rest on his best friend's wife. Having seen Nicholas through a score of flirtations and half a dozen mistresses, he had been delighted to hear that his friend had at last found a woman who'd inspired him to settle down. He'd been beset by curiosity to see this wonder and now, faced with Lysette's delicate beauty, he thought he could see what it was that had captivated Nicholas's fickle senses.

Running his fingers through the thick, brown hair which, despite his best efforts, remained in its perpetual state of gleaming disarray, he flashed Lysette a smile that radiated charm.

"So!" His voice, like everything else about him, seemed larger than life. It fairly boomed in the long, oval hall and echoed up the soaring stairwell. "You are Nick's lady. I should have known he'd never take the plunge until he'd found the prettiest girl in all Louisiana."

Lysette blushed and dropped her eyes demurely and Michael grinned with delight at Nicholas over her head. To his astonishment, Nicholas did not return his smile. Indeed, he did not even see it. Instead his black, appraising gaze was fixed securely upon the slender shoulders of his wife. It seemed, though Michael immediately dismissed the thought as absurd, that Nicholas was waiting to gauge his wife's reaction to his bluff, handsome friend.

"Nick cheated me out of standing for him at his wedding," he told Lysette with a broad wink, "but he won't cheat me of the chance to kiss the bride."

Before Lysette knew what was happening, Michael had enfolded her in his smothering embrace. He kissed her, in full view of his wife and her husband, with far more gusto than was called for—far more, in fact, than either of their two spectators considered strictly necessary.

When he released her, Lysette stared up at

him in amazement. Her gaze flew from his smiling, obviously self-satisfied face to her husband's dark, unsmiling countenance.

Nicholas's eyes were boring into her and in their bottomless ebon depths she read an accusation she could not begin to understand.

"Let's go into the parlor," he suggested abruptly. "I don't know about the rest of you, but I'm damned thirsty."

Turning on his heel, Nicholas led Michael into the parlor from which Leigh and Lysette had just emerged. Leigh followed, trailing the men as she had from her earliest days at Buckland and Montcalm. Behind them, Lysette hesitated. Of what crime had Nicholas judged her guilty? Should she have slapped Michael's ruddy, smiling face? Certainly she would have had he been anyone other than her husband's best friend. But if she had chastized him for his boldness, might Nicholas not have found equal fault in her for prudishness and rudeness toward his bosom companion?

Her senses reeled; her emotions were hopelessly muddled. As much as she wanted to please Nicholas—as desperately as she wanted to win his affection—he was proving as changeable as the wind and as impossible to predict. She felt like the lonely sapling whipped to and fro by the destructive force of the storm. How long could she bend to Nicholas's whims before she was snapped like a fragile twig?

# CHAPTER 13

Leigh and Michael Scofield readily accepted Elizabeth's invitation to remain at Montcalm throughout the Christmas holidays. Although Lysette thought they should surely prefer to be in their own home, they seemed not in the least disappointed to be spending the time with Nicholas's family. It was, she supposed, the fact that they had both grown up almost as members of the Callaway family that made them so at home in their midst.

Though the presence of the Scofields meant that Nicholas spent more time out riding and hunting with Michael and less time with her, Lysette was glad for Leigh's company. She loved Nicholas's mother but it made her uncomfortable to hear Elizabeth rhapsodizing over her pleasure in seeing Nicholas in love at last when she knew all too well that was hardly the case. With Leigh, however, it was different. She could be more open, more honest with Leigh for it was apparent that Leigh and Michael's marriage, while in no danger of collapse, had survived many difficult times and was fully expected to survive many more as they arose. With

Leigh, Lysette could voice some of her fears, allude to some of her problems with Nicholas.

The air was crisp and the morning frost had not yet left the ground when Lysette and Leigh left the mansion and wandered down toward the winding bayou at the bottom of the garden. In the distance they heard the baying of the hounds at whose heels Nicholas and Michael followed.

"They're like boys again when they're together," Leigh commented, hearing Michael's challenging shout as Nicholas apparently fell behind.

"Nicholas seems contented here," Lysette observed. "Somehow more relaxed. He loves Montcalm."

"He always has. It's home, after all."

Lysette pulled her cloak closer. "I should think he would prefer New Orleans. The society, you know. The balls, the eternal business, the. . ." Her voice trailed off to nothing.

"The women?" Leigh asked. She saw the hurt in Lysette's face. "Forgive me," she begged, contrite. "That was a thoughtless thing to say. What went before should be forgotten. All that is in the past now and. . ." She frowned, confused, as Lysette threw her an agonized look.

"My dear." She took Lysette's arm and pulled her to a halt. "Surely you can't mean that Nicholas is still. . . Oh, Lysette."

Lysette averted her face hoping the brim of

her bonnet would hide her emotion. "It doesn't matter—"

"Doesn't matter! How can you say that? If you love Nicholas, and I know you do. . ."

"Please, Leigh, listen to me." Lysette took the other woman's hand and led her to an iron bench beneath a moss-draped oak. For a few minutes they sat in silence then Lysette gathered her courage and said:

"I must beg you, Leigh, to say nothing of what I am about to tell you. Elizabeth knows nothing; neither does James." She lifted a hand to her forehead. "Dieu! It would kill James if he knew."

"Knew what?" Leigh prompted, mystified.

Lysette sighed. "First promise, Leigh. Promise me that you will say nothing."

"I swear it. Not even to Michael if that is what you wish."

"No. Not even to Michael."

Lysette bit her lip wondering if she should confide in Leigh. But there was a need inside her—a desperate aching need to tell the truth to someone, anyone. She needed to have one friend with whom it was unnecessary to pretend. It would have to be Leigh or no one.

Somewhere inside her a dam burst and all the pain, all the uncertainty and indecision which had been her constant companions in the months past gushed forth. By the time she was finished, she felt drained, exhausted, as if the sheer emotional energy that had sustained her had been expended in that single, violent outburst.

With the release came the tears and the two women huddled together on the bench. Leigh held Lysette tightly, urging her to free the hurt she'd harbored for so long, and Lysette wept in great, wracking sobs.

"What will you do?" Leigh asked, offering Lysette a fresh handkerchief to replace the shredded wreck wadded in her hand.

"Nothing," Lysette admitted. "I agreed to Nicholas's terms. I must—I will—abide by them."

"But how, if you love Nicholas, can you hope to live out your life in this fashion?"

"I do love him. Oh, Leigh, I do! And it is precisely because of that that I must live my life according to the dictates he has imposed upon it. Don't you see? I agreed to his terms. I accepted them. I knew before we were married that he never intended for us to be man and wife in the usual sense."

"But you didn't love him then."

"No," Lysette admitted miserably. "I didn't. Or perhaps. . ." She thought of that night, so long before, on Christopher Bishop's veranda. "Perhaps the seed had been planted and I simply didn't realize. . ." She forced a wan smile. "It doesn't really matter. There's nothing I can do to change it. If I want to be a part of Nicholas's life I must remain true to our agreement. He would be within his rights, you know, to send me away to Saint-Cloud once our child is born."

"He wouldn't!"

"Hopefully not, but to ensure my remaining with him I must not try to change him." She pressed Leigh's hand. "Don't look so worried. As long as I am near Nicholas, I can endure the rest."

"Are you sure?"

Moved by Leigh's concern, Lysette hugged her. "Quite sure."

From the forest on the opposite side of the bayou they heard Nicholas calling to Michael. The two women shared a wan smile before they went to the stables to greet their returning husbands.

"You seem quite at ease with Michael," Nicholas commented as he fastened Lysette's necklace of diamond flowers.

Lysette glanced at his reflection in the mirror. The remark had seemed casual but there had been an underlying hardness, almost a bitterness, to it that bewildered her.

"I feel quite at ease with him," she agreed. She turned toward her husband. "Would you rather I didn't?"

"Why should I?" Stepping around her, he examined the knot of his cravat in the mirror.

"I don't know. You're the one who brought it up."

"I only mentioned it. There's no need to start a quarrel."

"A quarrel? Who was trying to start a quarrel?"

Nicholas arched a questioning brow at his exasperated wife. "Certainly not I." His gaze swept over her. "Are you ready?"

She took up her brush. "Not quite."

"Well, come down when you are." He went to the door. As he stepped out, he turned; his eyes bore into her. "Perhaps Michael will escort you."

The door closed behind him as Lysette gaped.

"What does that mean?" she demanded, but he was already out of earshot.

With a little scream of pure frustration, she slammed the brush onto the inlaid tabletop and stalked out of the room.

In the corridor she nearly collided with Michael. Perversely, her first thought was that he cut a far less dashing figure in evening clothes than Nicholas.

He made her a comically exaggerated bow. "Ah, madame, will you allow me to escort you to dinner?"

The unstinting admiration in his eyes heartened Lysette. With a piquant little curtsy she laid her hand on his outstretched arm.

"By all means, monsieur," she purred.

Together they descended the spiralling stairs. Lysette smiled up at her companion. Michael's infectious charm, his constant air of bonhomie, had won her completely. Though no other man could compare, in her eyes, with Nicholas, she thought Leigh fortunate to have married such a good-humored man.

He was looking up and Lysette glanced in the direction of his gaze. Suspended from the archway at the foot of the stairs was a red-ribboned ball of mistletoe.

"A kissing ball," Michael whispered, brows waggling ludicrously.

Lysette giggled. What might have been considered salacious in another man was merely charming in Michael Scofield.

Her entire face cupped in one of his great fists, Michael tipped Lysette's head back to accommodate his height. His kiss was brief, fleeting, a friend's kiss. But even so, they parted to find Nicholas regarding them with a venomous glare.

"If you are finished, madame," he snarled. He held out a hand to her and Lysette had no recourse but to go to him.

"It was nothing, Nicholas," she began, though she loathed herself for feeling she owed him an explanation for such an innocent offense.

"Did I accuse you of anything, Lysette?" he asked sternly.

"No, but your look. . ."

"Ah, my look. I beg your pardon. I must exercise more control over my looks, mustn't I?"

Wounded by his stinging sarcasm, Lysette dropped her gaze and meekly accompanied him into the parlor where Elizabeth, James, and Leigh awaited them. It was Christmas Eve and dinner was to be a sumptuous affair, but for Lysette the joy of the occasion was marred by the waves of disdain and mistrust that seemed to emanate from Nicholas.

Lysette retired early. Though she'd expected Nicholas to remain downstairs long into the night, she had not yet even blown out the last lamp when he appeared.

"Is something wrong?" she asked, wondering at his presence with her when he could have been with his friends.

"There is something I want to ask you," he said seriously.

Lysette knew a moment's trepidation. Nicholas seemed so unpredictable to her; she never knew what to expect.

"What is it?" she asked warily.

He sat on the edge of the bed. For lack of other occupation, he fondled the heavy coil of chestnut hair that hung to the coverlet Lysette had drawn up to her waist. Had anyone asked, he would have dismissed the gesture as meaningless but the truth was that he simply had to touch her. His need for her weighed heavily upon him and he was helpless to prevent himself from reaching out to her if only in such an innocuous fashion.

"Nicholas?" Lysette prompted when he remained silent.

He frowned and tossed the heavy curl back over her shoulder. "I was speaking to Michael earlier about Leigh. The two of you are becoming friends, aren't you?"

Lysette's smile was soft with affection. "Oh, yes. I like her very much."

Nicholas wondered, with a twinge of jealousy, if she had confided her feelings for him to the other woman. Surely she had; she couldn't have resisted regaling Leigh with the epic tale of his myriad cruelties, could she? No wonder Leigh had treated him coldly all evening.

He forced his mind back to the matter at hand.

"Michael will be leaving soon. He's going to Washington on business. He'd rather not leave Leigh at Buckland all alone and I wondered if you would like for me to invite her to come home with us to New Orleans. I thought you might enjoy having another woman with you during these next mon. . ."

His last word was cut off as Lysette threw her arms about his neck and hugged him.

"Oh, yes!" she cried, her face buried in the warm hollow of his throat. "Oh, Nicholas, thank you!"

None too gently, he put her away from him. Her body, beneath the thin fabric of her nightdress, was too soft, too alluring, and his need for her was too great to allow him to accept this manner of thanking him.

Lysette took his action as rejection. She caught her lip between her teeth as he moved toward the door. Her pride steeled her against the temptation to call out to him but for once her heart triumphed over her head.

"Nicholas!"

At the door he turned and looked back at her. Kneeling among the rumpled bedclothes, the light of the single lamp gleaming in her tousled curls, she seemed the most beautiful, the most desirable creature he'd ever seen.

"What is it?" he asked tightly.

"What have I done?" Her tone was plaintive, her enormous eyes pleaded with him for a moment's gentleness.

"Lysette. . ." He paused, at a loss for something to tell her. "I can't. . . Dammit, Lysette, I'm only a man. Don't you see that. . ." But from the bewilderment in her eyes, he could see it was hopeless. With a growl that had its beginnings in the frustrated desire that had sorely nettled him for longer than he cared to remember, he glared at her. "You wouldn't understand."

Lysette slumped against the pillows as he slammed out of the room. What had she done? One moment he was offering her a friend and the next he was snarling as though she had committed some grievous crime. There was no pleasing him—none at all.

Christmas dawned and the Callaways and Scofields gathered in the holly-bedecked front parlor to exchange their gifts. For Lysette, Nicholas had selected a set of opals and diamonds. For Nicholas, Lysette had a gold toilette set fitted into a brass-bound rosewood case. For them both, a pair of magnificent sorrel horses waited in the stables, the gifts of Nicholas's parents.

It was early afternoon when Nicholas and Lysette went out to the stables. The suggestion to go riding had been Nicholas's and Lysette, after recovering from her initial surprise, was delighted.

The towering stallion and dainty mare had been saddled and Nicholas himself lifted her carefully onto the mare's back and guided her knee into place on the exquisitely tooled sidesaddle. Then he swung himself up onto his own mount and they were off following the bayou, riding among the moss-draped oaks and cypress.

Steeped in legends dating from the dawn of time, the eerily beautiful Bayou Teche wound its sluggish way across more than a hundred miles of Louisiana. Though the day was bright, the tall trees with their gently waving draperies of grey-green Spanish moss trapped the light far above throwing the ground into a state of perpetual twilight.

Together Lysette and Nicholas rode, silent as the lush forest around them. Lost in thought, they scarcely noticed the splash of the turtles or the great egret who stood on the rotting log of a once-proud cypress, its snowy plummage so startingly white against the shadowy forest backdrop.

The gunshot that spooked Lysette's mare came out of nowhere. That the person who fired the shot was trespassing on Callaway land would not occur to Nicholas until later. At that moment all he could see was the plunging mare carrying a terrified Lysette deeper and deeper into the forest.

Unable to slow her panicking mare, Lysette clung to the reins. Her leg ached as she wound it tighter about the leather-covered pommel. Beneath her the ground flashed by, churned by the mare's hooves—hooves which before had looked so dainty, so charming, but which, with their iron shoes, could easily have killed Lysette had she fallen.

From behind came the sound of Nicholas's

voice but she could not understand him. Not that it mattered. The best intentioned instructions could not have halted the mare's headlong flight into the forest.

The thundering of pursuing hooves drew nearer. Lysette's mare, frightened into recklessness first by the shot and now by the stallion, lengthened her strides but she was no match for Nicholas's horse. Even as Nicholas reached the reins clutched in Lysette's blood-drained hands, he called out to encourage her. But in her panicked, pleading eyes he saw no sign that she had heard.

Urging his horse forward, he seized the mare's bridle. For a long, tense time the two horses raced side by side and then, gradually, he succeeded in bringing the mare to a panting halt.

Still holding the bridle, Nicholas slid from his stallion. He held up an arm toward Lysette. In a single, breathless movement, she threw her arms about him and leapt from the horse's back. Her toes scarcely touching the ground, she clung to him desperately. Her arms were locked about his neck; her face, ghastly white with fear, was buried in the hollow of his throat. Nicholas's heart melted as he felt the violent trembling that shook her.

He released his hold on the mare not caring that she took immediately to her heels once more, and held Lysette as close as he could.

"Are you hurt?" he asked softly. "Lysette, are you hurt?"

She said nothing but he felt the shake of her head against his shoulder and neck. Slipping a hand behind her knees, he carried her to the base of an ancient oak and laid her on the ground. Gently he unwound her arms from about his neck and stroked her ashen cheeks as he murmured soft, unintelligible words of comfort.

"Are you sure you're all right?" he persisted.

"Yes, I'm sure," she managed shakily.

He scowled toward the forest, his black eyes searching in the direction from which they'd come. "I'm going to find out who the hell is behind this. Stay here."

He made as though to rise but Lysette clutched at his hand.

"Don't leave me," she begged. "Please, Nicholas, stay with me."

Returning to her, Nicholas gathered her [illegible]is arms. She nestled against him like a [illegible]rightened, trusting, vulnerable. He [illegible] close, enchanted by her softness, by [illegible] fragrance of her perfume. It was at [illegible]this, when their mutual grievances [illegible]ions were temporarily laid to rest, [illegible]holas had a glimpse of his life that [illegible]be—of the love he'd believed would al[illegible]ays be denied him. How desperately he wanted to love Lysette; how much he wished to have with her the sort of marriage his parents had.

But that was impossible, wasn't it? He looked down at Lysette in his arms. Her trembling had ceased and when she gazed up at him he saw that the fear had left her eyes. Her mouth—oh, why, a small, pained voice asked from the depths of his mind, did that delicate, cupid's bow mouth wreak such havoc on him?—curved into a little reassuring smile.

"Better now?" he asked.

She nodded. "You saved my life, Nicholas."

Her unabashed admiration was a balm to his masculine pride which had taken a beating in the past few months. He grinned. "My pleasure, madame."

Stretching up, she kissed his cheek timidly, her lips like the fluttering wings of a passing butterfly. Nicholas held his breath then, bending, he returned her kiss at the tempting corner of that bewitching mouth. Lysette sighed. Emboldened, he caressed her waist which had broadened with her pregnancy but remained winsomely curved, seemingly formed expressly to accommodate his [illegible]

"Nicholas," Lysette murmured, an[illegible] the shiver that coursed through her[illegible]

A flare of hope shot through hi[illegible] tightened about her, his han[illegible] upward from her waist until it fou[illegible] curve of her breast beneath the soft [illegible] her habit.

"Sweet Jesus," Lysette breathed. She [illegible] her arms about his neck and drew his head down. Her mouth found his, possessed his, her passion, her desire, equalled his, exceeded it, inflamed it. She arched against him helplessly as he lowered her to the ground.

From beyond a stand of young willows, Michael Scofield's booming voice bellowed Nicholas's name.

"Oh, Christ," Nicholas moaned.

He made no move to stop Lysette as she pushed herself out of his arms. His ardor considerably cooled, he got to his feet.

"Here, Scofield!" he called back. "Damn your hide!" he muttered.

The thundering of hooves shattered the idyllic calm of the clearing. Michael appeared astride a sable stallion as massive as he himself.

"Lysette's mare showed up at the stables," he explained. "I thought, perhaps. . ." His brown eyes scanned Lysette's crimson cheeks and the sheen of perspiration that bedewed Nicholas's brow. "Oh, damn," he swore softly. "Nick, I'm sorry, I didn't know . . . I thought. . ."

"[illegible] ite all right," Nicholas assured him [illegible] ly, though the tension, the embarrass- [illegible] g heavily in the air. "Lysette's mare [illegible] were just starting for home."

[illegible] Lysette in his saddle, Nicholas [illegible] behind her. With Michael trailing [illegible] a great abashed child, they set out [illegible] ontcalm.

Once they reached the mansion nothing would do but that Lysette should retire to her room and rest. Neither James nor Elizabeth were willing to risk their grandchild, and both were so chagrined at having given her a horse who had proven skittish, that Lysette agreed to their wishes if only to reassure them.

She hummed softly to herself as Mimette undressed her and tucked her into bed. Nicholas had wanted her; had desired her. In that moment she had been the only woman his magnificent ebony eyes could see. The only woman in his thoughts—his heart. She saw again the flame of passion in his eyes, felt again the burning of his lips against hers. Snuggling into the soft down pillows, she went to sleep dreaming of him.

She was fast asleep by the time Nicholas let himself into their room. For a long time he stood beside the bed watching her. The heat of his desire for her stunned him; the magnitude of his need for her astonished him. It was madness, surely, to want a woman so desperately. What was wrong with him?

Scowling, he forced aside all thought
Lysette as anything but simply an
woman. That was it, he told himself by
comfort. He had deprived hims
woman for far too long. After all,
nothing in their marriage con
bound him to her once their chil
conceived.

Turning on his heel, he strode fr
chamber and down the stairs, his stride in
with a new purposefulness.

Carefully attired in her most becoming gown of rose pink moire, her chestnut curls cascading over one porcelain shoulder, Nicholas's Christmas opals banding her throat and dangling from her ears, Lysette descended the elegant spiralling stairs. There was a movement at the bottom and Lysette's hopes soared but it was Elizabeth who appeared, watching as her daughter-in-law neared her.

"Darling, how very pretty you look. Enceinte women are always lovely but you positively glow. If only Nicholas could see you."

"Where is he?" Lysette asked, glancing toward the front parlor.

Elizabeth's beautiful face clouded. "That, my sweet, is what Nicholas asked me to explain to you."

Lysette's smile faded. "Explain?"

"Business," Elizabeth sighed, investing the word with all the tediousness it had come to represent during the years of her marriage to James. "That infernal, eternal business of his. It was the same with James; everything else pales before the allure of business."

"But Nicholas. . ."

"He had to go, darling. Apparently it was some sort of an emergency although no messenger arrived that I know of." She smiled brilliantly. "But he said you should stay here with us until we go back. Never mind, darling. We'll go to Buckland and help Leigh pack. We'll keep you so busy you won't have time to miss him. Come along, let's go into the parlor."

Lysette allowed her mother-in-law to take her arm and lead her toward the parlor door but she heard none of her chattering. All she knew—the only agonizing thought that kept coursing through her brain—was that Nicholas had left her, abandoned her, to return to New Orleans. And, waiting in New Orleans, like one of the poisonous black and white fishing spiders who lurked on the water-lettuce leaves in the bayou, was Rosalyn D'Everaux.

# CHAPTER 14

Rosalyn D'Everaux's boudoir in her husband's elegant Vieux Carre house was a study in luxury. The oval room was lit by a chandelier dripping with diamond-faceted crystals that hung by a golden chain from a domed ceiling painted to resemble a cloud-bespeckled sky. Panels of handpainted wallpaper alternated with mirrors around the room and the gilded, Louis Quinze furniture stood on priceless Oriental carpets.

In the midst of it all, her pink and white and golden beauty not the least overwhelmed by the splendor surrounding her, Rosalyn D'Everaux reclined on a black-lacquered chaise that stood on clawed lion's feet. Though to the casual observer she was the epitome of soft femininity, there was a hardness in her spring green eyes that would have disconcerted the most fearless of men. At that moment, those eyes were trained on the gentleman caller who roamed restlessly about the sumptuous chamber.

"Tell me once more, cousin," she asked softly. Her voice was as sweet as honey with all the warmth of a cobra.

The man silently pondered a painting

hanging over the fireplace. "I've already told you everything," he replied, his tone at once bored, disdainful, and containing more than a hint of remorse.

Pale green eyes flashed in a flawless face of incomparable beauty. "Tell me again!"

With a sigh of profound ennui, Kit Stratton turned from the painting he himself had done of Rosalyn. It had been his first commission; his cousin's way of introducing him to New Orleans society.

"I sent the man to Montcalm. From one of the Callaways' stablemen he learned that James and Elizabeth were going to present Nicholas and Lysette with matched hunters as a Christmas gift. On Christmas day he saw them ride out alone. He followed them. He fired and shot to spook Lysette's horse. Nicholas caught her and stopped the horse." He spread his hands. "La fin."

"What happened next?" she persisted.

"He carried her to the base of a tree. I've no doubt he was concerned about her well being."

"About the child!" Rosalyn corrected waspishly. "How many times must I tell you that it is the child he cares for, not that stupid little bitch."

"If that is the case, ma cousine, why should he desire her even after she is enceinte?"

"You don't know that he does."

"Don't I?"

Rosalyn's eyes narrowed; her body, beneath the elegant, shimmering drapery of her aqua silk dressing gown, stiffened.

"Precisely what is it you are trying to say, cousin?"

Kit sighed and casually brushed an imaginary speck of dust from his immaculately tailored black trousers. "I can tell you no more; my man didn't stay to see the rest. He's no voyeur, Ros."

Trembling with rage, Rosalyn thrust herself to her feet. Her dressing gown whipped about her legs as she paced the floor of the beautiful salon.

"I don't believe it!" she stormed. "You're lying!" Stopping before her cousin, she shook a pointed finger in his handsome face. "I could kill you for this, Kit!"

His only reply was an eloquent shrug but she could see by the smirk lurking at the corners of his mouth that he was vastly amused by her discomfiture.

Rosalyn resumed her pacing. "No! I won't believe it! Their marriage is one of convenience! It is in name only! Nicholas would never touch that little fool now that she's managed to get herself with child!"

"Who is the fool now, Ros?" Kit asked caustically. "Why don't you open your eyes to the facts of the matter. Lysette Callaway is a beauty. She's sweet, unspoiled, young. . . Any man would want—"

"Good God!" Rosalyn broke in with a harsh, disdainful laugh. "You sound as though you're in love with her yourself!"

Kit drew himself up defensively. "She's a charming girl, Rosalyn. I wouldn't want to see her hurt."

"Her hurt! Hah! What about me? Nicholas told me this marriage was one of convenience!" With sheer force of will she calmed herself. "Once their brat is born he'll pack her off to old Ravaisson's plantation. Then he'll come back to me."

"Perhaps not," Kit suggested quietly, almost pitying her.

"I tell you he will!" she screamed. "I'll see to it!"

"Don't hurt her, Ros."

She sneered at the tautness in his voice, the stony determination in his stance. "Are you threatening me, Kit?" she asked sweetly. "Let us not forget that you are the one who hired someone to fire that shot. Had your precious Lysette fallen from that horse, she would most likely have been killed and who would have shared the blame?"

"Don't remind me. I'd never have forgiven myself—or you." His blue eyes were filled with black loathing. "I wouldn't have done it if you hadn't blackmailed me."

"Oh-ho! How very honorable we've become. A pity you didn't have such high principles three years ago in Saint-Louis."

"Rosalyn. . ." Kit snarled.

"Let me see," she went on, blithely ignoring him. "What was her name? Violet . . . Violet Winston . . . Winsom . . . Winslow . . . Yes! That was it! Violet Winslow!"

"You know damned well it was," he snapped.

"Well, really, Kit! It was too, too, scandalous! The girl was only fifteen, after all. And you were engaged to paint her, not to seduce her." She laughed at the shame that had crept into his eyes. "I can't imagine what would happen to your career if word got about."

"I can," Kit admitted miserably.

"Yes, perhaps I can too. You'd be finished. No decent family in New Orleans would open their doors to you."

Kit winced at the all too apparent relish with which his cousin pondered that wholly unappetizing prospect.

"You wouldn't tell anyone?"

She ran a hand through his soft ash-brown hair. "Not if you agree to help me," she said gently.

"Help you come between Callaway and Lysette!" he spat. Rising, he moved out of her reach as though she were something loathsome whose touch was beyond his bearing.

"Precisely."

"I don't want to be a part of any scheme to harm her. When I think of what could have happened. . ."

"You will do as I ask if you want to remain New Orleans's most fashionable portraitist," she insisted harshly.

"Dammit, Ros, I said I. . ."

He cut himself off as the boudoir door flew open and Nanine, Rosalyn's maid, appeared.

"Pardon, madame, monsieur, but . . . but . . . oh, madame, Monsieur Callaway is below!"

Rosalyn's hands flew to her tousled hair. "Nicholas! My God! Quickly, Nanine, bring me a fresh dressing gown. Show Monsieur Stratton down the back. . ."

"Good afternoon, Rosalyn."

All three heads turned to find Nicholas lounging in the doorway. Rosalyn's green eyes slid over him greedily. She hadn't seen him since that night at his parents' home almost three months before. Lord, but he was a magnificent man! How could she have thought him merely another in a long line of lovers she'd taken to assuage her boredom and enhance her status. There was no one, she'd soon found, who could take her to the heights of rapture or plunge her to the depths of despair like Nicholas Callaway.

"Nicholas," she whispered. An inkling of dread stirred inside her. Had she been betrayed? Had he somehow discovered it had been she who had masterminded the attempt on the lives of his wife and child? But no, she assured herself, relaxing. Nicholas was possessed of a quick-silver temper. He was no man to play cat and mouse games with an enemy. Had he known who had been behind his wife's near tragedy, he would not have appeared so gently nor would he even then be gazing at her as he had months before when her passion for him had been reciprocated in full.

"Nicholas," she said again, this time less in awe and more in question.

By way of reply, his black gaze slid slowly over her before returning to meet her eyes.

Watching, Kit felt a rush of hatred for his

cousin and her lover. Rosalyn he knew, and had always known, was a selfish, scheming bitch neither above nor beneath any action that would accomplish whatever task she had set for herself. As for Nicholas Callaway, he had held no real opinion of him before. He was simply another of Rosalyn's men. And, to give the man his due, he had recommended Kit to Elizabeth as an artist thus providing him with an important commission that went far toward establishing him as New Orleans's premier portraitist.

But now, now he loathed Nicholas. He loathed him for his betrayal of Lysette. Kit forced himself to shake Nicholas's hand and exchange a civil greeting but he seethed inside. Since that night at the Callaways'—that night when he had inadvertently shown Lysette her husband's perfidy—he had come to regard her as a paragon of all that was sweet, all that was good. He longed to paint her, indeed, his other commissions, including Elizabeth's, were suffering because Lysette's face filled his mind blinding him to the face of whatever New Orleans belle might be sitting before him at the moment. He tried to force himself to complete Elizabeth's portrait, if only that one, because he believed that if Nicholas were satisfied with his mother's likeness he might commission one of his wife as well.

His wife! How Kit hated him for having married Lysette. He had forgiven men for greater sins, after all, as Rosalyn was so fond of reminding him, he himself was hardly blameless. But to marry such an innocent; to marry her and then so callously hurt her. . . By his actions, Kit thought in a burst of chivalry, Nicholas Callaway had forfeited any and all right to be called a gentleman.

"I know you will excuse me," he said tightly, already chafing to be gone. "I hope, Mr. Callaway, that you will remember me to Madame Elizabeth and to your charming wife as well."

Nicholas's black eyes flashed a warning; his temper flared. If there was one person in the world he did not wish to think of at that moment, it was Lysette.

"I will," he snapped.

"Good day, then, monsieur. Cousine."

Bowing, Kit followed Nanine out of the boudoir but his mind was filled with thoughts of Lysette. His heart went out to her.

As he left the elegant Vieux Carre residence and strolled up the street intending to visit the gallery of Collier Shaw, the dealer who had first offered his work for sale upon his arrival in New Orleans, he thought of Lysette as she had been on that night when first he'd met her.

Even though she had been married to Jules Ravaisson and he knew her to be three and twenty, she seemed to him the essence of innocence.

That was it! Stopping in the middle of the walk, oblivious to the stares of the passersby, Kit was struck with a profound inspiration.

All the passion, all the joy of life that his art had once brought to him but which had, for far too long, lain dormant, apparently gone forever, came rushing back to him. He would paint Lysette! No, he would paint the Essence of Innocence and Lysette would be his inspiration.

He laughed aloud and several ladies drew in their skirts as they passed, convinced that he was a lunatic or a drunkard. Perhaps he was at that—he was mad with the desire to pick up his pallet and his brushes, drunk with the sheer joy of having found once more the well-spring within from which his art flowed.

"To hell with portraits!" he muttered, hands shoved deeply into his pockets as he strode toward his studio filled with new purpose. "To hell with the commissions, with the horse-faced dowagers and their poxy daughters all wanting to be transformed into some vision they can only find in their musty looking glasses. To hell with them all!"

For once he would paint his ideal—he would paint the beauty he saw in his mind, in his heart, and not the illusions he was forced by others to translate onto canvas.

In the beautiful boudoir of the house Kit had just left, Nicholas Callaway was at that moment none-too-gently pushing his mistress down across the tufted velvet of her chaise-longue. Rosalyn trembled as she watched him pull off his clothes. His black eyes fairly burned with the heat of his passion. He frightened her as he had never done before—as no man had ever done before. Her pale green eyes went to the door, then to the embroidered bell pull hanging just out of her reach. For all that she had cursed the fates that kept Nicholas from her—for all that she had beseeched the powers that be to send him back to her—now that he was here, she almost wished he had never returned.

She cried out as he ruthlessly pushed aside the ruffled skirts of her dressing gown and took her without the least show of affection, of consideration. Her fists pummeled his broad shoulders; he seemed not to notice. She pleaded with him for tenderness, for mercy; he had none to give. For the first time in more years than it was her custom to count, Rosalyn D'Everaux wept. Tears blurred her eyes as Nicholas drew away from her. His face was moist, his eyes narrowed, his mouth tight with bitterness.

Ignoring her sobs, he left her lying there and began to dress. Rosalyn watched, longing for some word from him; something that would explain his behavior. In amazement, she saw him adjust his cravat in the looking glass then stride toward the door.

"Nicholas!" Her own voice sounded foreign to them both—plaintive, begging for something he could no longer give to her.

Hand poised over the latch, Nicholas turned back to her. "I'm sorry," he muttered thickly. "I shouldn't have come here. I won't be back."

"Don't go!"

He already had.

Rising from the couch, Rosalyn went to the window and watched him climb into his carriage and drive away.

"I love you," she whispered, her tears trickling in diamond paths down the bevelled panes. "Oh, Nicholas, I love you."

It did not occur to her at that moment that now, the first time a man had ever left her, was also the first time she had ever spoken those words with sincerity.

Sunk deeply into the velvet squabs of his carriage, Nicholas cursed himself for a fool and worse. Oh, to be sure, the physical ache which had plagued him for weeks was assuaged, if only temporarily, but he had lost none of his desire for Lysette. Not the smallest fraction of the yearning that dogged him day and night had been banished by the ugly reunion with a woman for whom he no longer felt anything. What was more, he loathed himself for what he had just done. There had been nothing of love in it; nothing of tenderness or even passion. The beasts of the field felt more for their mates than he had just felt for the woman beneath him.

Filled with self-disgust he did not notice when his carriage passed the high, iron-grilled windows of Kit Stratton's studio—windows behind which a young artist was even then feverishly preparing a canvas upon which he would create a vision that throbbed with life in his brain.

It would, no doubt, have surprised both men had they but known that the images that danced in their minds' eyes at that moment shared the same cupid's bow mouth, wide russet eyes, and tumbled chestnut curls.

# CHAPTER 15

Much as she would have liked to deny it, Lysette hungered for the sight of Nicholas. As they neared New Orleans on their journey home from Montcalm, it seemed she could almost feel herself drawing closer and closer to him.

The child within her stirred and she unconsciously caressed the place, smiling softly. Noticing, Elizabeth sighed and remembered the blissful days when she was carrying Nicholas, the child of a husband she adored. Surely, she told herself, Lysette must be feeling the same emotions she herself had felt.

Leigh shattered the idyllic moment. For an instant Elizabeth could have sworn she had done it by design but that notion she quickly abandoned as foolish. Of course Leigh adored Lysette—she was one of Nicholas's best friends. Like her husband, Michael, she must be delighted to find that he'd at last found the woman to make his life complete.

"Do you remember when Nicholas was courting Barbara Waverly?" Leigh asked Elizabeth. "Everyone expected them to marry." She smiled at Lysette. "Barbara was so beautiful. Her father was very rich, of course, but even if he hadn't been, her beauty alone would have been an adequate dowry."

"What happened?" Lysette asked listlessly. She was beginning to feel dowdy and bloated. Just that morning she had discovered that most of her gowns now refused to close about her expanding waist. The last thing she needed or wanted to hear at that moment was an accounting of the beauty of Nicholas's former amours.

"Oh, I don't know. It seems he escorted her to a ball and met another girl there. Who came next, Elizabeth?" Deep in thought, Leigh pondered the matter oblivious to Elizabeth's disapproving frown and Lysette's exasperated sigh. "I know!" She snapped her fingers. That was Vivienne Peverelle. Lord! She was magnificent. Of course no one knew it as well as she. She led Nicholas a merry chase. I think he might have married her, too, had she not netted the Comte de Colville. It seems she wanted to be a Comtesse more than she wanted to be Mrs. Nicholas Callaway." She shrugged. "Ah, well, I suppose it doesn't matter how many times a man falls in love so long as. . ."

"Leigh," Elizabeth said softly. She nodded in the direction of James who had dozed off in the corner of the carriage.

Obeying the older woman's look, Leigh lapsed into silence. Snuggled into the soft folds of her fox-lined mantle, Lysette shot Elizabeth a grateful glance. She had heard quite enough about the loves of Nicholas Callaway. Why Leigh should take it upon herself to enlighten her as to Nicholas's romantic past was beyond her, particularly in view of the fact that she knew how it pained Lysette to love him when he did not return her love.

She's thoughtless, Lysette told herself, anxious to forgive a friend she'd grown fond of. She doesn't realize how it hurts me to know that Nicholas is not only capable of loving a woman but has been in love on several occasions.

Glancing out the window, she longed ever more for the miles to pass swiftly hastening their arrival in New Orleans—hastening her return to the exquisite torment of life at Nicholas's side.

Not so very many miles away, Nicholas sat in his office gazing at the portrait above the fireplace—the portrait that had so shocked Lysette when first she'd come to New Orleans to plead Saint-Cloud's case after Jules's death.

Concentration on the demanding business before him had proven impossible. With a disgusted groan, he shoved a sheaf of papers across the desktop. He had never, in all the years since joining his father's firm, accomplished so little in so much time. It seemed that in the weeks since his precipitate departure from Montcalm, he had not managed to complete a single task. Thoughts of Lysette plagued him—her face swam before his eyes. In the streets he found his gaze drawn to women who in some way, however small, resembled her. He wanted her, needed her, yearned beyond imagining to hear her voice, touch her skin, drown in the russet depths of her beautiful eyes.

And then there was Rosalyn. Propping his elbows on his desk, he dropped his head into his hands and cursed himself for having been so stupid as to believe he could exorcise Lysette from his heart by returning to Rosalyn's arms. What a fool he had been. What an asinine, ridiculous fool.

A rapping at his door drew him out of his orgy of self-castigation.

"Come," he called wearily.

His clerk appeared. "A lady to see you, sir."

A desperate hope sprang up inside him. "A lady?"

The clerk stepped back and allowed Rosalyn D'Everaux to enter. With a scandalized look at his employer, he closed the door leaving them alone.

Nicholas leaned back in his great leather chair and regarded Rosalyn with a mixture of pity and expasperation.

"What are you doing here?" he demanded. "What if you were seen?"

"I wasn't." She drew off her veiled bonnet and self-consciously smoothed the bodice of her apple-green gown. "But it wouldn't matter if I had been."

"I think it would," he disagreed. "You're being needlessly indiscreet."

His apathy shook Rosalyn's confidence to its very foundation. She was used to holding the upper hand in her love affairs. Dealing with a man who no longer cared for her was simply not in her realm of experience.

"I had to see you, Nicholas," she said quickly, hoping to get the words she'd prepared out before she lost her nerve. "I have to make you see your mistake before it's too late."

"My mistake?" he repeated skeptically. "And precisely what was that?"

"Marrying that. . ." She saw the cautioning glimmer in his black eyes. "Marrying Lysette," she amended hastily.

"Rosalyn," he warned.

She rushed to the desk. "You don't love her, Nicholas. You know you don't! The longer you stay with her the worse it will be. Don't you see? Leave her. Leave her now. Give her Saint-Cloud. Surely its revenues will provide for her and her child."

"You're behaving foolishly," Nicholas muttered, disgusted with the scene she was creating and not a little saddened to see what had once been a delightful affair de coeur come to this sorry state. "Why don't you go and we will pretend this discussion never occurred."

"I don't want to pretend it never occurred!" she cried, desperately afraid that he was lost beyond redemption. "Nicholas! I love you! Don't you believe that?"

"I believe you think so," he told her with

brutal honesty. "I also believe you did not come to this astonishing realization until I ended our liaison."

Rosalyn trembled, teetering on the brink of hysteria. "That's not true! I've always loved you! Leave Lysette. Leave her and I'll divorce Edouard." She saw the repugnance in his handsome face and panicked. "I could divorce him, you know. He is impotent; has been for years. That is grounds for a divorce."

Thoroughly disgusted, Nicholas thrust himself out of his chair. "I do not want to hear this, madame. If nothing else, I always gave you credit for having the manners which good breeding usually imparts. I beg you not to disillusion me further."

"But Nicholas, I tell you—"

"No!" The word was like the cracking of a whip. Nicholas's great body sagged with fatigue. He ran a distracted hand through his ebony hair. "Listen to me, Rosalyn. I cannot, I will not, leave Lysette."

"But why! The child is yours. No matter the state of your marriage, the child is your heir."

"It is not the child," he said softly.

"Then why, Nicholas? Why!"

His black eyes shimmered with a fire she had never seen there as his stare seemed to bore through her.

"I love her," he said simply.

A scream rose into Rosalyn's throat and died there behind the strangling constriction that took her breath away.

"No!" she croaked. "You can't. You can't!"

"It's true." He pitied her at that moment and loathed her in equal measure. "It is true."

Walking to the door, he summoned his clerk. "Collect yourself, madame, you are leaving."

"I don't want to go," she whispered, her beautiful face the picture of anguish.

"Leave with dignity, Rosalyn," he told her gently. "At least let us part as befits sensible adults. Don't force me to call the doorman from downstairs and have you ejected. Remember, some of those men in the outer office are also associates of Edouard's."

Tying the ribbons of her bonnet, Rosalyn drew down its concealing veil. Scorning the proffered arm of the clerk, she lifted her chin and took her leave with the haughty dignity of a queen. If nothing else, Nicholas thought wryly, watching the door close behind her, the woman was a consummate actress.

As she left the elegant building in which Nicholas kept his offices, Rosalyn paused and threw back her veil. She gazed up at the windows she knew to be his.

"You will come back to me, Nicholas," she vowed. "One day, when at last your eyes have been opened and you see your precious Lysette for what she is, you will be mine again."

Turning to climb into her carriage, she did not notice the dark blue brougham that was passing. But one of the occupants of that carriage saw her.

Lysette felt weak with shock as she noticed Rosalyn climbing into Edouard D'Everaux's burgundy and black town carriage. She had been with Nicholas! No doubt she had been his constant companion since his return from Montcalm.

She glanced quickly at her companions but James slept and Elizabeth was concentrating on the embroidering of an impossibly small gown for her grandchild. Leigh, delighted to be once more in the city she loved, was busily perusing the opposite side of the street.

Thank Heaven for that, Lysette thought irreverently. At least I am spared my shame for the moment. Soon enough they will discover that even now Nicholas prefers his mistress to me. For now I have been spared my dignity. For now I have that, if nothing else. Unconsciously, her hand went to the place beneath which her child rested. For now, she thought gloomily. But how long is now?

Unable to face the all too familiar confines of her home, Rosalyn directed her coachman to take her to Kit Stratton's studio.

Situated on the upper floor of a former plantation house in a less than fashionable neighborhood, Kit's studio was cluttered with canvases, both finished and abandoned. The once-elegant paneling bristled with sketches and studies. Empty bottles and half-eaten meals lay on paint spattered tables. Only one chamber was free of the debris that filled the kitchen, parlor, and bedroom. In that pristine room a threadbare Louis XV sofa stood on a platform before tall bowed windows. An easel stood waiting as did a table of paints and brushes.

Rosalyn entered without knocking. Kit never locked his door. Unlike many of his calling, he was not plagued by bill collectors—he was New Orleans's favorite painter of the moment. Had he wished to, had he had the ambition, he could have lived in a style nearly equal to that of his finest patrons.

As always, his cousin was appalled by the litter that seemed to accumulate around her cousin. Where Kit went, it seemed to follow. Where he paused, it inevitably began to collect. But that familiar emotion was banished by another as she searched him out in the shadowy bedchamber that was dominated by an immense, grotesquely carved four-poster he had purchased chiefly because some obscure French painter no one but Kit seemed ever to have heard of had committed suicide in it.

On this day, however, even that morbid knowledge was overshadowed in Rosalyn's mind. Her eyes, having grown accustomed to the dim light filtering through the midnight blue velvet draperies which remained always drawn across the windows, left the inert form of Kit sprawled across the bed, one elegantly tapering hand wrapped around a wine bottle, and went to the sketches that seemed to paper the walls. Pinned to the walls, to the armoire, even to the carved gargoyles that clung to the bedposts, the sketches had a single theme—a single face:—Lysette Callaway.

"My God," Rosalyn breathed. In every imaginable attitude, in every possible setting, Lysette's face stared out from pages torn from innumerable sketchbooks.

"Welcome, cousine," Kit muttered from the depths of the three feather matresses he claimed he needed to soothe him to sleep at night.

"What is all this?" she demanded. Storming over to the bed, she snatched the half-empty bottle from him and sent it crashing into a corner. "What in Heaven's name are you doing?"

"The Essence of Innocence," he sighed drunkenly. "My masterpiece."

"Lysette Callaway," she spat.

"Yes." A beatific smile crept over his boyishly handsome face. "Lysette." The smile faded and was replaced by a look of abject sorrow. "It's impossible, coz. I try to paint her—I sketch her again and again—but I can't get the image out. I can't get it right. I've seen her only once, you see. The night of the reception. I need to see her again."

An idea was born in Rosalyn's mind, a notion born of equal parts hatred and desperation.

"How would you like to paint your chere Lysette, Kit?"

He pushed himself to a sitting position. "Paint her?" he repeated, awed by the mere prospect. "From life?"

"Of course. Tell me, what are you doing about your other commissions? The portrait of Elizabeth Callaway, for example?"

He waved a dismissing hand. "I can't," he whimpered. "I want to paint Lysette."

Rosalyn's lip curled in disgust but she squelched a harsh rejoinder. "Elizabeth and James are returning soon if they haven't already. My advice to you, dear Kit, is to finish Elizabeth's portrait and drop a few hints about how lovely Lysette is and how much you would like to paint her. I think Elizabeth will take the suggestion well."

She rose and made to leave the room. Turning back to the figure which once more lay inert in the center of the enormous, ugly bed, she warned, "And leave the cheap wine alone, dear, so you can do a decent job. Elizabeth will not commission you to paint Lysette if you botch her portrait, you know."

She waited for a reply but Kit was lost in his dreams of one day setting up an easel before the woman he was fast convincing himself he loved more than any creature on earth.

"Lysette," he whispered rapturously. "Belle Lysette."

With a disgusted snort, Rosalyn stormed out of the apartment and down to her carriage. She had heard quite enough of the perfection of Lysette for one day!

[illegible]

# CHAPTER 16

Though shopping was not and had never been one of Lysette's abiding passions, Leigh, too long sequestered in the depths of the Bayou Teche, delighted in the seemingly inexhaustible variety of shops to be found in New Orleans. Bored with hours of trying on bonnets and admiring fabrics and gowns, Lysette's interest was piqued by the sight of Collier Shaw's art gallery in the French Quarter.

"Let's go in," she suggested.

Leigh pouted. "What is the point? If you want a painting, commission one."

"I want to look," Lysette insisted. Without waiting for any further objection Leigh might care to make, she marched into the airy shop where the art of New Orleans hopefuls, as well as established artists from all over the world, hung on creamy walls.

"Look at this," she told Leigh, who lingered just within the door as though bored to distraction already. "Leigh, look at it. I know the artist."

Grudgingly, Leigh came to her side and gazed dispassionately at a pretty, if somewhat tame, pastoral scene. She looked at the ornate signature scrawled in the bottom left-hand corner.

"K. Stratton?" she read.

"Kit," Lysette explained. "He's painting Elizabeth's portrait. I didn't know he did anything but portraits but I must say this is really very pretty."

"You must allow me to make a gift of it to you, madame," a soft, masculine voice called from the far end of the long, narrow gallery.

Lysette and Leigh turned to find Kit standing in the doorway. Beside him, soberly dressed in dove gray that nearly matched the color of his carefully barbered hair, stood Collier Shaw himself.

Kit stolled toward them and once more Lysette was struck by his lightness of spirit. There was a zest about him that somehow lightened Lysette's sagging spirits.

"Who is he?" Leigh hissed in Lysette's ear. "He's delightful!"

Kit reached them and lifted Lysette's hand to his lips. "Madame Callaway. I understood that you were spending some time at Montcalm."

"As you can see, sir," Lysette rejoined. "I have returned. This lady is Mrs. Leigh Scofield. Her husband, Michael Scofield, is a great friend of Nicholas's. He is master of Buckland near Montcalm. Leigh will be spending some time as a guest of my husband and myself. Leigh? Kit Stratton."

Gallantly, Kit kissed Leigh's hand though there was noticeably less enthusiasm in this second salutation.

"Mrs. Scofield," he murmured.

Leigh dimpled prettily. "I find your painting an absolute marvel, Mr. Stratton."

"Kit, please," Kit corrected. "Your praise is a balm to my beleaguered soul, madame."

"Why beleagured?" Lysette wanted to know.

"An occupational hazard," he explained arily. "We artists are expected to suffer. Our patrons would think less of us if we did not seem tortured by the burdens of our calling."

"But you are very successful. I understand that you are to have a sitting with my mother-in-law this afternoon."

"I am," he agreed. "Madame Elizabeth has agreed to resume her sittings."

"The portrait is beautiful," Leigh chimed in. "I saw it last night."

"With so lovely a subject, how can the portrait help its beauty?" Kit's cerulean eyes sparkled, bringing roses into Leigh's round cheeks.

Even Lysette was not immune to his infectious charm but she thought it best to comment, "Leigh and I are planning to call on Elizabeth this afternoon, sir. Will our presence disturb you?"

"Not at all. I fear that most ladies find sittings exceedingly boring. Perhaps the company of two such engaging ladies will make a tedious task bearable."

"Then we will see you there," Lysette promised. "For now, we are expected at home for luncheon. Goodbye, monsieur."

Kit kissed her hand once more and for a long, lingering moment his eyes gazed into hers with more than proper intensity. Feeling the color rush into her cheeks, Lysette drew her hand out of his and left the shop so quickly that Leigh had to scurry to catch up.

"He's in love with you!" Leigh cried the moment they were ensconced in the privacy of their carriage.

Lysette glanced quickly at Leigh wondering if she had actually heard the note of jealousy that had seemed to be present in the woman's tone. Then, deciding she must have been mistaken, she laughed lightly.

"Really, Leigh, you take Kit's charm too much to heart. It is his stock in trade, if you think of it. True, he is talented—his work speaks for itself. But if he were disagreeable, the ladies of New Orleans would be less eager to commission portraits of him. He flatters them, smiles, fawns, and of course they wish to have him immortalize them on canvas."

Leigh did not disagree but neither was she in the least convinced. There had been, in Kit's eyes, in his tone, in the very attitude of his body as he stood near Lysette, every indication that here was a man who, if not actually in love, was seriously infatuated with a woman who belonged to another.

Leigh was still turning the matter over in her mind as she and Lysette sat down to lunch in the smaller, family dining room at the back of the house.

"I think you're wrong about Kit Stratton,"

she told Lysette as a servant set their plates before them.

Lysette sighed, wishing she had never suggested they enter Collier Shaw's gallery. "Really, Leigh. He's a born charmer, that's all." She smiled wryly. "It runs in the family."

"What do you mean?"

Lysette stirred her soup idly. "His cousin is Rosalyn D'Everaux."

"Nicholas's mistress?" She missed Lysette's wince. "Well, perhaps Kit has it in mind to be your lover."

"Leigh! You mustn't say such things, even in jest!"

"What things?" Nicholas asked from the doorway.

Lysette's eyes grew round with apprehension as she watched him hand his overcoat and hat to a waiting servant.

"Nothing," Leigh said hastily.

"Keeping secrets?" he asked lightly as he sat between the two women and waited for a servant to set a place before him.

"Isn't that what ladies are supposed to do?" Lysette asked demurely.

He spread his napkin across his lap. "Perhaps, providing the secrets they share do not concern matters touching upon the honor of one or the other of the ladies' husbands."

Lysette's hand shook betrayingly as she lifted her goblet to her mouth which had suddenly seemed to go dry. She could feel the hot color rising into her cheeks. It was unfair that he should be able to see through her defenses so easily. Before those piercing black eyes of his she felt transparent as the finest glass.

"Where did you go this morning, Lysette?" he asked quietly.

"Shopping," she answered shortly.

"And?"

She forced herself to look into those black, devil's eyes of his. "And we stopped at Collier Shaw's art gallery. Kit Stratton was there."

"Ah, your gallant swain."

Lysette bridled before the unconcealed contempt in his tone. "I find him charming. I don't see why you object to him so, Nicholas. You seem to have a predilection for his family. Or, I should say, certain members of his family."

Apart from the heightened color in his face, Nicholas seemed unaffected by her jibe. He took a long, leisurely sip of his wine before he said, "I'm not surprised that you find him charming, madame. So, I'm told, did Miss Violet Winslow of Saint-Louis."

"Am I supposed to know who this person might be?"

"No, but I will tell you. Miss Violet Winslow is the fifteen-year old girl your fine cavalier servent seduced after her father commissioned him to paint her portrait."

"I don't believe you," Lysette whispered over Leigh's shocked gasp.

"Don't you? How loyal of you. Nevertheless, it is the truth. He ruined the girl, madame, heartlessly, shamelessly, then fled the city before her father could take his revenge."

"And yet you recommended this man to paint your mother's portrait?"

"My mother is no naive schoolgirl to be smitten by his puerile charms. Unfortunately, I fear the same cannot be said for you since you are so quick to leap to his defense."

Furious, Lysette crumpled her napkin and threw it aside. "You'll excuse me, monsieur, but Leigh and I are due at your mother's. Had you told me you were coming home, I would have refused your mother's invitation."

Nicholas waved a dismissing hand. "Go along, my dear, enjoy yourself."

"I shall," she snapped. "Particularly so since we are to keep her company while she sits for her portrait. Shall I say hello to Kit for you?"

"I would tell you what you could say to Kit Stratton for me, my love," he replied with exaggerated sweetness. "But I shouldn't like to think of such words leaving my wife's lips."

"How gallant of you. Leigh, are you coming?"

Daubing hastily at her lips with her napkin, Leigh abandoned her half-eaten lunch and hurried after Lysette. At the door a servant scurried to fetch their wraps and bonnets. Once outside, Lysette happily climbed into the carriage waiting to take Nicholas back to his office. She took a malicious pleasure in the knowledge that he would have to wait while another was harnessed and brought from the stables.

"Do you and Nicholas always argue that way?" Leigh asked bluntly. She had felt the tension that flowed so freely between them and believed it came from the mutual attraction each sought so desperately to hide from the other. But this cattish bickering was something new.

Lysette sighed. "Only, it seems, when Kit Stratton's name enters the conversation." She shrugged. "Oh, Leigh, it all began quite a while ago. I was upset and Kit comforted me. Nicholas found us together and jumped immediately to the wrong conclusion."

"Surely he doesn't believe that you are interested in having Kit as a lover."

"No, no, I'm quite sure he knows better than that. But I think he believes that, given encouragement, Kit might try to seduce me."

Leigh smiled slyly. "And will you give him any encouragement?"

"Leigh!" Lysette was truly shocked. She had honestly never even considered the possibility of taking a lover—any lover. There was no man she'd ever met save Nicholas for whom she had even thought of having touch her.

Leigh's eyes sparkled with mischief. "Well? He is quite charming and very handsome. Oh, I know, not handsome in the way Nicholas is handsome. Nicholas devastates a woman from her first glance. Still, you must admit that Kit is a devilishly attractive man."

"I admit it freely," Lysette replied honestly. "Kit is a very attractive man. But, as you said, Nicholas is devastating."

"You love him, don't you?"

"Kit?" Lysette asked playfully. Her smile grew wistful. "Yes, I can admit it to you. I do love Nicholas. Hopelessly."

"Why don't you tell him?"

"Oh, no." Her laugh was melancholy, filled with poignant misgivings. "He would only mock me and call me a foolish schoolgirl filled with childish notions of romance and starlight. He has no patience with such things, you know."

They lapsed into silence from which they did not emerge until they reached the parlor of the elder Callaways', where they found Elizabeth pouring tea for Kit Stratton.

He rose as they entered the room.

"Mesdames." One after the other he lifted their hands to his lips and once more Leigh noted, with a pang of envy, that he lingered longer over Lysette's.

"Nicholas sends his love, belle-mère," Lysette said, bending to kiss Elizabeth's cheek.

"Give him mine, darling," she replied. She stood. "If you young people will excuse me, I will go upstairs and change. Kit is painting my gown today so I must wear my best."

Gliding out of the room, she left Lysette to serve tea to Leigh and herself.

"The portrait is almost finished?" she asked Kit as she refilled his cup.

"Almost," he admitted, his cerulean eyes lovingly tracing the contours of her face. He sighed. "Madame, what I wouldn't give to paint you."

Roses bloomed in Lysette's cheeks. She was unused to such flattery as Kit served up in heaping portions.

"Really, monsieur. . ." She bowed to his unspoken request. "Very well, then, Kit," she amended. "In any case, the commission would have to come from Nicholas."

"I've always wanted to have my portrait painted," Leigh interjected hopefully.

"You should," Kit replied shortly, not even taking his eyes from Lysette long enough to glance at the other woman. "I could paint you so easily," he breathed, his attention once more wholly centered on Lysette. "It would be my masterpiece."

"As I said," Lysette demurred modestly, "the commission would have to come from my husband." She stressed the last two words. "I could hardly arrange such a thing without his permission."

"Permission?" Elizabeth appeared in a ravishing gown of stark black silk unrelieved save for a magnificent rope of flawless pearls that banded her beautiful, bare shoulders. Her raven hair with its elegant dusting of grey, had been drawn up to reveal the ivory perfection of her throat and the beauty of her classic features. She was breathtaking—as beautiful a woman as her son was a handsome man. Though Lysette had always assumed that Nicholas got his looks from his father, she could see now that the true source was the Pilkington bloodlines from the hallowed shores of Charleston. "What do you need permission for, my dear?"

"Kit would like to paint my portrait, bellemère," Lysette told her.

Kit lifted Lysette's chin with one forefinger bringing it into the sunlight that spilled through the windows.

"Her face is perfection, Madame Elizabeth," he said, as though stating a fact rather than being outrageously bold. "It should be immortalized on canvas."

Elizabeth smiled indulgently. "I think it's a fine idea. You must speak to Nicholas about it, darling."

"I don't think I should," Lysette hedged.

"But why not?" she persisted.

"Yes," Kit argued, taking offense that anyone should be less than delighted at the prospect of having their portrait painted by the most fashionable artist in New Orleans and soon, he was convinced, in America. "Why not?"

"Nicholas may not approve." She shot Elizabeth a look that was instantly comprehended.

"Well, I'll work on him, shall I?" her mother-in-law asked serenely as she took her place in a gilded chair supported on the tails of four dolphins.

The discussion ended as Kit slipped out of his coat and into the smock that protected his clothing. Lysette and Leigh arranged themselves so that they had a clear view of both the artist at work and his ravishing subject. While Kit painted and flirted with Lysette, Leigh sat quietly nurturing a kernel of resentment that Lysette should not only have Nicholas, whom she had adored from childhood, but now this delightful young man as well.

It's not fair, she groused to herself. She cursed the elfin looks she blamed as the reason she'd never enjoyed the privileges of being a beauty. Her marriage with Michael Scofield had been arranged. He didn't love her; she didn't love him. But they were comfortable with one another as those who grow up together often are. Still, she would have welcomed a flirtation; welcomed the outrageously bold advances of a fashionable, well-connected, if slightly less than respectable artist with such an enchanting smile and sparkling, mischievous eyes.

But he wanted Lysette, not her. Any fool could see that. He was mad for Lysette. And so was Nicholas—her Nicholas! One could almost feel the yearning in him whenever Lysette was near.

Well, she can't have them both, Leigh decided suddenly. One or the other—Nicholas or Kit—but not both!

# CHAPTER 17

Elizabeth Callaway's eyes were soft with love as she looked up at her son. She clasped his arm with both her hands as they strolled along the iron-railed balcony overlooking the courtyard of the elder Callaways' townhouse.

"Please reconsider," she asked as they passed out of the shadows and into the silvery shower of moonlight.

"Why is it that you are so enthused over the notion of my commissioning Stratton to paint Lysette?" Nicholas demanded.

"I am enthused, dear, over the thought of Lysette being painted. In case you hadn't noticed, Nicholas, you are married to an extraordinarily beautiful woman."

A wry smile curved the corners of Nicholas's mouth. "Believe me, mother, I am very much aware of Lysette's beauty." Too aware! he thought to himself, unwillingly remembering the sleepless nights which were growing more and more frequent.

"Well, then, don't you think such beauty should be painted?"

"As you wish," he relented reluctantly, knowing his mother well enough to realize that he would get not a moment's peace until he agreed. "I will commission the portrait. But not by Stratton."

Elizabeth nearly stamped her foot in frustration. "Nicholas! Kit is the finest painter in New Orleans!"

He was frankly skeptical. "There are others equally as talented."

"Are you dissatisfied with my portrait?" she challenged. The painting had been unveiled a few evenings before to unanimous praise.

"Not at all. It's a marvelous likeness. I do not fault Stratton's talents, Mother. I merely say that there are others who could have produced one as good. Hire one of those men—any one of them—and I will happily commission the portrait."

"It's only Kit you object to."

"That is what I've said all along. I do not like the man."

"Lysette likes him," Elizabeth murmured, carefully watching for his reaction.

Nicholas's face hardened growing taut and hawkish. "He flatters her; flirts with her."

"Shamelessly," Elizabeth acknowledged blithely. "Surely you must know that that is part of his stock in trade as a society portraitist."

Nicholas gazed out into the darkness toward the lanterns that burned on either side of the iron-gated archway on the opposite side of the courtyard. In the night-shrouded city beyond the wall a carriage passed. A woman laughed. Within the walls, time seemed to have come to a standstill.

At last he spoke. "Does she encourage him?"

Elizabeth gaped. "Is that what you believe?" she demanded, dumbfounded. "Do you sincerely believe that Lysette— That she— My God, Nicholas! She's carrying your child! She adores you."

Nicholas closed his eyes and drew a deep breath. You're wrong, Mother, he thought wistfully. If you only knew how wrong you are. He said: "Does she?"

"I shouldn't dignify that question with a reply but if you must know, yes, she does, I'm sure of it. As to your other ridiculous question, no, Lysette does not encourage Kit. She makes it clear that she is a married woman and defers to her husband in all matters."

Deference and love are two entirely different emotions, he reflected bitterly. Of course she deferred to him—she had been raised to believe that a wife was subservient to her husband. How he wished her loyalty sprang from love. But that was a pipe dream. He shook his head. He was beginning to sound like one of the foolish, romantic girls he had so scorned in his bachelor days.

Taking his silence for refusal, Elizabeth took his arm once more and propelled him on along the balcony. "Darling," she murmured, her voice soft, her tone the same cajoling one that had never failed her in her dealings with Nicholas's father, "you had no such compunctions about Kit when you recommended him to me last summer."

"Well, damnation, Mother, that was last summer. I wanted to help Stratton because. . ."

"Because he is Rosalyn's cousin. Yes, dear, I know. The fact remains, however, that he has proven himself a fine painter. Please, please, reconsider."

Nicholas scowled but he was, and had always been, putty in the soft, perfumed hands of the mother he adored. It she desired him to commission Stratton to paint Lysette's portrait, he supposed no harm could come of it. Still, he didn't want to be seen to give in too easily. His male pride, which had taken quite a beating in the past few months, simply would not bear that blow.

"I will consider the matter," he allowed grudgingly.

Though inwardly she considered her case won, Elizabeth knew the sound of a man salving his battered ego when she heard one.

"Thank you, dear," she cooed. "I'm certain your decision will be the right one."

Nicholas's black eyes met the ebony gaze of his mother. She was a butterfly, fragile like exquisitely colored spun glass. But that fine, delicate glass was mounted on a frame of pure, tempered steel.

"Let's go inside, madame," he said, his eyes and his voice filled with admiration.

"Just as you wish, darling," Elizabeth purred, the very epitome of femininity.

They reentered the parlor where Lysette

sat reading to James who seemed remarkably alert considering the lateness of the hour. Leigh sat nearby, embroidering on a tiny nightshirt that was part of the layette she was making as a christening gift for Nicholas and Lysette's child.

"Lysette, dear, may I speak to you?" Elizabeth asked.

Lysette's eyes went from Nicholas to his mother and back again. She knew that Elizabeth had intended to broach the subject of the painting tonight but neither her husband's face nor her mother-in-law's gave her any hint as to what decision, or compromise, had been reached.

"Of course," Lysette replied automatically, rising. She gave the book to Leigh who laid aside her sewing and took up the story where Lysette had left off.

Lysette followed Elizabeth out onto the balcony. The cool night air bit at the exposed flesh above the heart-shaped neck of her champagne velvet gown.

"Good news," Elizabeth told her. "Though of course he hasn't said it in so many words, Nicholas has all but agreed to let Kit paint you."

"How wonderful!"

"Now you mustn't say anything just yet. The final permission must come from Nicholas. You understand how men are, don't you, darling? They want to be the arbiters of every decision."

"I won't say a word," Lysette promised.

"Oh, but Elizabeth, I am glad! I like Kit so much! I'd adore having him paint me!"

"You do know, don't you, sweet, that he's Rosalyn D'Everaux's cousin."

Lysette rolled her eyes. "Yes, I'd heard. Well, I'll try not to hold that against him."

Lysette and Elizabeth laughed not knowing that just inside the partly opened French doors Nicholas stood, a brandy in hand. A picture of Kit comforting Lysette down in the hallway of this very house flashed in his memory and a sharp, stinging pang of jealousy pierced him. Had he given in too easily? Was he wrong to allow Lysette to spend so much time in Kit's company?

An uneasy uncertainty blossomed inside him and the evidence of it was plain to see on his face. A hesitation in the rhythm of Leigh's reading caught his ear and he glanced up to find her watching him, a quizzical expression on her pretty, pixie's face.

Bolting down his drink, he strode from the room looking to find a private place to exorcise his insecurities without the prying eyes of others upon him.

Sitting between Leigh and Lysette on the ride home, Nicholas was frustratingly silent. More than once Lysette gazed up at him expectantly, but apart from a faint, teasing smile, she had no inkling that he had come to any decision affecting her. At last her patience came to an abrupt end.

"Have you decided, Nicholas?" she demanded petulantly.

"Decided what, enfant?" he asked innocently.

"Ohhh!" she doubled her little fists. "You know perfectly well what I mean! About the portrait!"

"Ah, yes, the portrait." He sighed. "I suppose you won't be fit to live with if I refuse."

"I shall be a perfect shrew," she promised solemnly.

"Then I suppose I will have to agree."

"Yes, you will!" She tilted a defiant nose at him and it was some time before she realized that he was simply teasing her. "You have, haven't you?" she demanded, not quite believing she had gotten her way so easily. "You will allow Kit to paint me?"

"Yes, enfant, if you wish it so earnestly."

"Oh, Nicholas!"

Delighted, she snuggled against him and he laughed as he wrapped his arms about her. For the remainder of the ride home they held one another. Neither quite knew why it felt so very right, so almost sinfully good.

By the time the carriage drew to a halt in front of the lantern lit door, they were sorry to part. Stepping down first, Nicholas helped Leigh descend, then swung Lysette gently to the graveled drive. His hands lingered on her waist—a wave of tenderness swept over him as he noted its expansion and thought of the child she carried. His eyes seemed unable to leave hers until her lush lashes came down demurely veiling her gaze which seemed dangerously near to revealing far too many of her turbulent emotions.

Together they followed Leigh into the house and up the stairs. She disappeared into her room and Nicholas and Lysette halted at Lysette's door.

"Good night, ma petite," he said softly. His hands ached to caress her; his lips longed to kiss her. The mere thought of watching her take down those primly pinned curls and letting them cascade in a gleaming mass down her back was unbearably stimulating to his long-deprived senses.

Stretching on tiptoe, Lysette kissed his cheek. The caress, soft, elusive as a butterfly, sent a shiver down his spine.

"Thank you again, Nicholas," she murmured shyly.

They stood there in the glimmering light of a single candle burning in a wall sconce and each longed for what neither could dare ask to receive. The words died on their lips before either could gather the courage to utter a syllable. In the end, Lysette simply gave him a tremulous half-smile and slipped into her bedchamber.

It was only later, after Mimette had dressed her for the night and been dismissed that Lysette laid restlessly in her bed cursing herself for her cowardice.

"You want him," she hissed to her own foolish heart. "You love him. He wanted you tonight; you could see it in his eyes, feel it charging the very air around you." Angrily she kicked away the stifling bedclothes.

"Damn my cursed pride! If I'm right, I'm only punishing myself by playing the untouchable to him. If I'm wrong—what difference will it make? My pride's been hurt before; I've lived to tell the tale. What harm can another blow do to something so battered?

Feeling around in the darkness for her robe, she drew it over her nightdress and padded barefoot from her room.

The candle in the wall sconce was on the verge of guttering out as she made her way to the door of Nicholas's room. A voice inside her urged her to retreat but she forced herself to knock on the white-painted panels.

There was no reply. She knew that Nicholas seldom went right to sleep upon retiring. He usually spent the better part of an hour reading papers, preparing for the next day's appointments, pondering the best way to deal with some client's problem. She opened the door and stuck her head inside.

"Nicholas?" She squinted down the length of the long, emerald-walled room. A pang of longing assailed her for she remembered her brief tenure as an occupant of this room—a tenure which had ended on the day after she'd told Nicholas of their child. "Nicholas?"

The room was empty. Her courage sadly deflated, Lysette retreated up the corridor toward her own door. Her hand was poised above the latch when she heard a noise from downstairs.

Perhaps this was better, she told herself as

she carefully descended the stairs, the trailing skirts of her gown and robe held in one hand. It might seem overbold if she were to beard Nicholas in his bedroom, but she was still mistress of the house and as such perfectly within her rights to appear in any chamber downstairs. If Nicholas happened to be there as well, well c'est la vie!

Her foot sank into the soft carpet at the bottom of the staircase and she paused as Nicholas's low, rumbling laughter echoed from the twin parlors off the entrance hall.

Curious, Lysette padded silently into the first of the adjoining rooms. It was dark; the only sources of light were a twin-branched candelabra burning on a table in the second parlor and a tall ormulu torchere in the entrance hall. She picked her way carefully through the shadowy room until she reached the velvet portiered archway that separated the two parlors.

From her place in the shadows, Lysette could see Nicholas and Leigh sitting side by side on the silk-cushioned settee before the black marble fireplace. Leigh, her strawberry curls spilling over her shoulders, gazed up with rapt admiration at Nicholas who was telling her some story in tones too low for Lysette to hear. Lysette's eyes drank in the sight of him. Though in his evening attire she always found Nicholas elegant beyond description, the negligence of his scarlet brocade robe brought out an almost barbaric side to his looks that frightened her as much as it attracted her. His was a dangerous, savage masculinity that appealed to some scarcely unleashed emotion deep within her.

As she watched, Nicholas finished his story. Leigh laughed delightedly then murmured something and Nicholas threw back his head and laughed. Alone in the shadows Lysette felt like an outsider. The kinship that so many years of friendship had formed between Leigh and Nicholas had never made itself so painfully apparent to Lysette as it was at that moment.

Gathering her skirts, she turned and fled back up the stairs to her room. She wished she had never left it; she felt foolish, gauche. Throwing off her robe, she climbed back into her bed and dissolved into tears.

Below, Nicholas and Leigh wearily climbed the stairs. At Leigh's door, Nicholas pecked her fondly on the cheek then made his way along the now-dark corridor.

At Lysette's door he paused. The yearning that weighed so heavily upon him rode him sorely tonight. Thoughts of Lysette consumed him. He felt as though no risk would be too great to simply touch her—no sacrifice too much to make if only he could hold her, savor the soft femininity of her that tantalized him beyond bearing.

Sighing, he took his hand away. She had been so pleased tonight when he'd agreed to the portrait. Perhaps he would wait. This was a beginning—she had come willingly into his arms in the carriage. She had cuddled in his arms like a pampered child. Perhaps he should court her; woo her.

He shook his head and wished he had brought a snifter of brandy up with him. To think that he would find himself gawking outside his own wife's bedchamber like a stripling afraid to go in, devising plots to win his own wife's favors. What had he come to?

He left her door and went on to his own room where his lonely bed awaited him. Had he opened Lysette's door, he might have heard the heart-rending sobs she muffled in the downy softness of her pillows. Had he simply entered her room, he might have discovered that his longing for her was no greater than the aching need that gnawed at Lysette's tender heart.

# CHAPTER 18

To the annoyance of several grand ladies of New Orleans society, Kit Stratton agreed to begin preliminary sketches for Lysette's portrait the day after Nicholas commissioned the work. Ecstatic at the thought of finally being allowed to draw her from life, Kit arrived at the Callaways' before Nicholas had ever left for his office.

Lysette, not yet dressed, was summoned and Nicholas kept Kit company while he waited for his subject to appear.

"It's hardly necessary for you to arrive at the crack of dawn," Nicholas snarled as Kit arranged his pads and pencils on a table in the sun-filled morning room.

"I was anxious to begin," Kit admitted, brushing back his sandy forelock. Though he tried valiantly to hide it, Nicholas's looming presence made him exceedingly nervous.

"Were you?" Nicholas's tone implied his belief that painting was not all that might be on the painter's mind. Unlike Kit, he felt not in the least compelled to hide his dislike for the man sitting opposite him. "My wife is pregnant, you know, Stratton. Did it never occur to you that she might need more rest than some of your other subjects? Did you never stop to think that she may be in the habit of sleeping later in the mornings?"

Kit busied himself with his pencils to avoid Nicholas's eyes. He knew Lysette was pregnant—how could he help knowing it? While painting Elizabeth's portrait he'd had to watch while Lysette and Leigh Scofield worked at delicate garments fit for some European princeling. That she carried a child, h owever, troubled him less than the knowledge that it was Nicholas's child she carried. The thought of her, his angel, his essence of innocence, bedding with a man he considered a vulgar, rutting womanizer sickened him.

"Perhaps I used poor judgment," he admitted grudgingly. He chose his words carefully, always aware that even as Nicholas had given him this opportunity, he could as easily snatch it away. He began gathering his belongings. "Perhaps I should leave. I'd be grateful, sir, if you would be so kind as to advise me as to the most convenient time for Madame Callaway's sittings."

"Perhaps that would be best," Nicholas agreed, a smirk playing about his lips. He disliked the entire notion of Stratton's painting Lysette and was not in the least adverse to postponing the start of her sittings.

He was thwarted, however, when Lysette swept into the room. Both men caught their breath. Her gown was Italian, of fine pink silk, with a low square neck and a high waist. The mameluke sleeves were tied with white lace ribbons and lace trimmed the edge of the neckline. In it she looked impossibly fragile and incredibly alluring.

She paused in the doorway as both men rose. She saw Nicholas hold out a hand to her and quickly took it knowing that to have acknowledged Kit first would have hardly endeared him to Nicholas.

"Good morning, darling," Nicholas murmured. He slipped an arm about her waist and drew her closer.

"Good morning," she answered dutifully. She hated his blatant display of possession staged, she knew, solely for Kit's benefit, but raised her lips willingly to his as he bent to kiss her.

"I've told Mr. Stratton that he needn't arrive so early; that you need your rest now more than ever. If you're too tired to sit for him, you've only to say so."

Lysette stiffened in his arms. Out of the corner of her eye, she saw Kit pale and avert his eyes. How dare Nicholas infer that they had . . . that they were still. . . She felt the angry flush stain her cheeks and cursed herself knowing that Kit would take it for a maidenly blush.

"Nonsense, cherie," she murmured, gently but firmly extricating herself from his too-tight embrace. "I'm hardly an invalid. We can begin immediately, Kit."

Putting the table between Nicholas and herself, she glared at him. "You are going to the office, aren't you, darling?"

Nicholas lowered himself into the wing chair he'd occupied when Lysette appeared. "Perhaps I'll stay at home this morning, cherie. I've never watched an artist at work."

Lysette seethed, knowing that the last thing Kit needed or wanted was to be supervised by a jealous husband. She herself wished to be left alone with Kit though hardly for the reasons Nicholas would have supposed. With Kit she could relax, she could revel in being a beautiful woman fawned over by an admiring man. It was not necessary to be on her toes all the time with her tongue sharpened to parry hostile barbs.

Still, she knew that if she protested, Nicholas would decide she had some ulterior motive for wanting the portrait and revoke the commission. She forced herself to smile sweetly.

"As you wish, cheri. Kit? Where do you wish me to sit?"

With exquisite care, Kit situated her in a delicate French armchair so that the morning sunlight bathed her in its golden warmth. It shimmered amidst the folds of her skirt, glowed in the rich, chestnut depths of her hair, and highlighted the warm, porcelain translucence of her skin. Even Nicholas, watching with open skepticism, had to admit to himself that there could have been no more perfect place for her.

He scowled as Kit carefully—lovingly, it seemed to him—draped a fat curl over Lysette's shoulder and down onto her breast. He stiffened, torn between maintaining a stoic silence and clouting the overbold painter with the nearest heavy object, but then Lysette herself indicated her unease by drawing away and Kit instantly obeyed, returning to his armless chair and taking up his pencil and pad.

"Must I sit perfectly still?" she asked, not daring to move a muscle.

"Not at all," Kit hastened to assure her. "These are only preliminary sketches. I am only making myself familiar with your features. You may move as much as you wish."

Relaxing, Lysette shot a challenging look at Nicholas. "Aren't you bored, cheri? There isn't anything to see."

Sitting there, Nicholas had already begun to feel foolish. His suspicions seemed silly to him now. The house was filled with servants. Leigh was there. It was broad daylight. Even were they so inclined, it seemed hardly likely that left alone Kit and Lysette would rush into one another's arms. After all, he reminded himself, Lysette had not taken a lover in all her seven loveless years of marriage to Jules Ravaisson.

But that was before, a treacherous voice reminded him. That was before her slumbering passions had been awakened. That was before the sensual side of her nature had been fully aroused.

He looked into her eyes. They seemed to be issuing a challenge. Trust me, Nicholas, if you dare, her russet eyes cried. I can prove to you that I am not like you—let me show you.

"Perhaps you're right," he allowed, rising. "I do have business waiting." He cast a disdainful look at Kit who worked feverishly over his pads trying to capture the changing expressions as they flitted across Lysette's beautiful face. "I hadn't realized what boring work art can be. Henceforth, instead of envying those men who turn paint and canvas into objects of beauty, I shall pity them."

Lysette felt a pang of embarrassment for Kit. "It must certainly seem dull to you, sir," she hissed, "since you have the more difficult task of turning greedy men into Midases."

"And widows and orphans into the street," Nicholas added genially. With a shallow bow, he left them and they heard him whistling softly as he strode out to the carriage waiting in the drive.

"I'm sorry, Kit," Lysette apologized. "Nicholas can be harsh with people."

"Don't think of it," he told her, sketching the way her pretty mouth turned down at the mention of her husband's name and the endearing sadness in her beautiful eyes. "Many men do not understand how a man can dedicate himself to beauty rather than the more lucrative pursuit of wealth and position. Do you think you could move to the settee? I should like to sketch you in a different light."

Lysette complied with his wishes taking the arm he offered her with a shy smile.

Throughout the morning and into the afternoon, Kit filled page after page with Lysette. Her eyes, her nose, her mouth; smiling, frowning, laughing. His pencils, worn to nubbins, were quickly discarded only to be replaced with another from a seemingly endless supply, flew over the paper.

As the time passed, Lysette grew less and less conscious of Kit's eyes upon her. She relaxed and went about her daily chores talking to Leigh, going over the household accounts with Mrs. Jonelle, stitching on a lace-trimmed baby blanket. Only occasionally, when she happened to glance his way, did she notice Kit and remember that her every movement, her every expression, was being recorded in one of his numberless sketchbooks.

By the time Nicholas returned home, Kit had gone. He questioned her and she answered, honestly but with a minimum of detail. The next day was a repetition of the first and the next the same until they fell into a pattern from which there seemed little hope of escape. At last, one morning when Lysette arrived downstairs too early and, it seemed to Nicholas, too eager, he demanded, "How many more damned sketches is this cursed artist going to need?"

"I don't know," she replied icily. "I'm not an artist."

"An artist," he repeated, mocking the irritating note of admiration in her voice. "You're enjoying this, aren't you?"

"I am," she admitted defiantly, bridling at the veiled accusation in his tone. "And why shouldn't I? A woman needs—"

His black eyes flashed. "What does a woman need, madame? To be fawned over? Flattered?"

"Appreciated!"

Nicholas rose, drawing himself up to his

full, towering height. "It is not his place to salve the egos of neglected women! He is a painter, no more! I will not have him worming his way into your good graces with a lot of worthless pandering." Lysette tilted her chin haughtily at him but he went on. "Tell him to make an end, madame. He either starts this portrait tomorrow morning or I withdraw my permission."

"You wouldn't!"

Her obvious distress aggravated him far more than her scornful indifference ever could.

"Are you so afraid of losing your little toady, Lysette?" he asked tightly. "Does his lickspittle flattery mean so very much to you?"

"Why must you drag everything down to your level, Nicholas?" she whispered, tears glimmering in her eyes.

"He is that important to you?"

She turned her back but he seized her shoulders and swung her toward him.

"Answer me!"

"He means nothing to me," she murmured brokenly.

It was not true. She had come to look forward to spending hours basking in the warmth of Kit's unflagging admiration. If she realized, if she had any inkling that his regard was turning into something more, she refused to admit it even in the deepest corners of her own mind for she knew if that proved to be the case, propriety would demand an end to their daily tête à têtes.

Mrs. Jonelle appeared in the doorway. She hesitated, realizing that she had intruded at a delicate moment, but then announced that Mr. Stratton had arrived.

"If I told you to," Nicholas said, waving a dismissal to the housekeeper, "would you send him away?"

Lysette knew there was only one possible reply. "Yes," she answered instantly.

"Send him away."

He saw the glimmer of pain in her eyes but it vanished in an instant as she straightened her back, squared her shoulders, and went with stately grace to the foyer where Kit waited.

Kit knew immediately that there was something wrong. Her eyes—those magnificent eyes—still shimmered with unshed tears. She was pale, strained, maintaining calm with the greatest of efforts.

"Lysette," he whispered, "what has hap—" A movement behind her stilled his words. Nicholas filled the parlor doorway and the look on his swarthy face was unmistakably triumphant.

"I'm sorry, Kit," Lysette said softly, her eyes never quite meeting his. "I cannot sit for you today. Perhaps tomorrow."

A single glance at Nicholas told him that this was none of Lysette's doing. His heart bled for her, his delicate, fragile angel. At that moment he would have given everything to sweep her out of Nicholas Callaway's life, out of that smirking bastard's possession, to the safety of his rooms where he would protect her from all the ugliness her husband forced her to face.

"I hope you're not feeling badly," he

managed.

"No, it's nothing, truly, Kit."

Her eyes pleaded with him to withdraw quietly and he had no choice but to comply. It tortured him to murmur polite good-byes and take his leave but he knew there was nothing else he could do. In his heart, however, a black fury raged and vowed before all he held sacred to make Nicholas pay for every tear that wet those rose-kissed, satin cheeks.

"Are you satisfied?" Lysette demanded brokenly as Kit's carriage rolled down the drive toward the street.

Nicholas watched as she hurried past him and up the stairs without waiting to hear his reply. In truth, he was far from satisfied. He knew he had been a fool—that his had been a hollow, spiteful victory. He didn't know himself why his pride demanded such a childish show of possession—why it had seemed so important for him to prove to Kit that Lysette belonged to him, that she was his and his alone and Kit's access to her was entirely dependent upon Nicholas's whim.

He watched her disappear around the landing and knew she was going to her room to weep away her anger and humiliation. He took a step toward the stairs but the futility of the gesture stayed his further progress. Not only would she refuse to let him in, he hadn't the vaguest idea of any words he could say that would atone for his actions nor lessen her pain.

Snatching up the sheaf of papers he was taking to his office, he bellowed for a carriage and left the house.

# CHAPTER 19

Her angry tears passed, Lysette was lying listlessly across her bed when Leigh appeared in the doorway.

"Am I intruding?" she asked gently.

"Only if you intend to defend Nicholas's actions to me," she answered honestly.

"No, I don't. What he did was reprehensible. I've never known him to act out of pure spite before."

"Is that what it was?"

"Don't you think so?"

Sitting up, Lysette dangled her stockinged feet over the side of the bed. With one hand she pushed back the disheveled curls of her ruined coiffure and smoothed the deep creases in her rumpled skirts.

"I don't know, Leigh. Sometimes it's as though we are strangers. I simply can't predict what he will or won't do—what will please him or anger him. Whether when he comes through the door at night he will be cruel or kind. It's impossible."

"Perhaps he's jealous."

"Jealous!" Lysette was incredulous. "Why on earth should he be jealous? I don't give Kit the least bit of encouragement, you know that. Oh, he flirts, of course, but he flirts with every woman. It means nothing." She shook her head disbelievingly. "No, I can't think that's the case. Nicholas doesn't care enough to be jealous."

Leigh sighed, astonished by the supreme blindness of the two people with whom she lived. Neither could see that each was in a torment for love of the other. Neither could begin to understand the pain they were unwittingly causing the other by their shortsightedness and pig-headedness.

"As you will, dear," she surrendered. "In any case, I did not come up here to discuss Nicholas. I wanted to know if you'd like to come shopping with me."

"Thank you, Leigh, but no. I really don't feel up to it. I hope you don't mind."

"Not at all." She kissed Lysette's cheek. "Why don't you have Mimette come and undress you. A nap will do you the world of good."

"Perhaps I will," Lysette agreed.

But once Leigh had gone, Lysette lay back down and inevitably relived the humiliation of the morning's confrontation between Nicholas and Kit. An hour passed, then two. The afternoon was just commencing when the plan formed in her mind. She slid off the bed and tugged the rope to summon Mrs. Jonelle.

"Madame?" The housekeeper appeared in answer to Lysette's call.

"Please order a carriage for me," Lysette instructed.

"Mrs. Scofield has left, madame. Surely you're not thinking of going out alone."

"If Mrs. Scofield can go out alone, why not I?"

Mrs. Jonelle studied the floor. It was one thing for a guest in the house to do as she pleased—Mrs. Scofield's husband was half a continent away and so she was more or less free to run rampant. But for Mr. Callaway's lady, well, there would be hell to pay if he came home and learned that she had been gallivanting about New Orleans on her own.

"Please, madame, at least take Mimette."

Lysette rolled her eyes in exasperation. "Oh, very well. In the meantime, please order that carriage and send Mimette up here. I shall need a fresh gown and my hair arranged presentably."

"Are you going calling, madame?" the housekeeper ventured. If she was not back before the master returned, Mrs. Jonelle wanted at least to be able to give him some idea of where she had gone.

But Lysette had no intention of confiding her plans to anyone least of all Nicholas's trusted and oh, so loyal, housekeeper.

"That will be all, Mrs. Jonelle," she said imperiously.

Not believing in contradicting one's masters, the housekeeper had little recourse save to cursty and go about her mistress's bidding. There was nothing Lysette could do, however, that would wipe the expression of open disapproval off Anne Jonelle's round face.

Though she'd been more than a little annoyed by the coachman's reluctance to take her to the address she'd given him, Lysette understood better once she saw the run-down neighborhood in which Kit Stratton made his home. When the carriage drew up before a shabby mansion she hesitated before refusing Mimette's offers to accompany her.

The front door creaked as she opened it, and noises emanating from the flats of the converted mansion lent a sinister air to the ramshackle interior. She climbed the stairs nervously, her imagination running amuck, her eyes darting to and fro as though expecting to be attacked at any moment by a horde of pirates bent on murder and mayhem.

When she finally found herself before Kit's door, she breathed a little, shaky sigh of relief. She tapped timidly on the panels as though afraid to knock loudly and risk attracting unwanted attention.

"Come in!" a voice that was unmistakably Kit's called from within.

To her surprise, Lysette found that the door was not locked. Had she lived in this place, she told herself, she would certainly have had bars on the doors that would have held back the hordes of the Hun!

"Who is it?" Kit called from the depths of the apartment as his astonished guest paused in the cluttered parlor.

"Lysette Callaway," she called back.

There was a long moment of silence, then

the sound of scurrying footsteps. In an open doorway, Kit appeared. His hair was disheveled and he was tugging on a wrinkled coat with more than a little difficulty because the long sleeves of his shirt were still rolled to the elbows.

"Lysette," he breathed, at last succeeding in donning the coat. He made a hurried search of his pockets and, when it turned up no comb, ran his long, paint-spattered fingers through his hair. "What are you doing . . . I'm sorry. Come in. I hope you didn't come alone. This district. . ."

"My maid is down in the carriage," she told him, relinquishing her bonnet and ruffled paletot.

He conducted her through the parlor, for once ashamed by the bohemian style of life he led. For the first time he wished he had an apartment, no, a grand house, in which he could entertain her.

Lysette followed him into his studio where the afternoon light spilled across the polished wood floor. Having once been the ballroom of the mansion in its days of glory, the parquet floor and crystal-draped chandeliers lent a melancholy air of faded elegance to the lofty room. At one end, in a curved bay, a faded Louis XV sofa waited for a model to grace it. Before it stood an easel and table. Across the room stood a second easel but, unlike the first, this held a canvas.

"I've interrupted you," she murmured apologetically.

"Not at all," he hastened to assure her. Still, he went to the canvas and picked up a cloth to drape over it.

"May I look?"

Kit paused before the easel. His eyes swept over the canvas upon which a nymph rose from a flower-bedecked bower as though from a century's slumber. She was beautiful, her unashamed nudity draped only with the cascading glory of her hair in which soft flower petals clung. She was Lysette.

"I'm sorry. It isn't nearly ready to be seen," he declined, draping the work.

"I understand. I shan't take too much of your time. It's only that. . ."

"Sit down, please," Kit urged. "Let me get you something." He thought of the bottle of wine standing in the kitchen and wished desperately he had two unbroken glasses that matched. If only he had something delicate, exquisite to offer her. He cursed himself for his thoughtlessness.

"I cannot stay long," she told him, even as he led her to the burgundy velvet sofa near the windows.

Kit winced at this unspoken reminder that she belonged to someone else. "Of course," he acknowledged wanly.

Lysette sat beside him, her fingers toying with the top ruffle of her layered skirt. "I had to come, Kit, and apologize for this morning. It was horrendous of Nicholas to treat you so callously." Her chin quivered with remembered humiliation. "Please forgive. . ."

"Shhh." He touched her cheek, moved by the tears that shimmered in her great brown eyes. "You mustn't apologize. I won't hear of it."

"Oh, Kit," she murmured. "I didn't want to send you away, but. . ."

Somehow his arm slipped about her, the gentle, comforting touch of his hand on her cheek became a caress. He bent toward her and his lips found the tantalizing corner of her delicious mouth.

"Well, well, well," a feline voice purred from the doorway. "What have we here?"

Kit and Lysette jumped to their feet and gaped as Rosalyn D'Everaux glided into the room. Behind her a nearly hysterical Mimette hovered in the doorway.

"I'm sorry, madame," she whimpered, appalled that she had not managed to warn her mistress. "I tried to hurry."

"It's all right, Mimette," Lysette assured her, reaching for her bonnet and paletot. "There was no reason for you to warn me."

"Wasn't there?" Rosalyn asked skeptically. "I should think that there was every reason. I can't imagine that Nicholas would approve of your little tête à tête."

"Hardly that," Lysette retorted coldly. "Kit is painting my portrait. I had to discuss. . ."

"You don't owe her an explanation," Kit interrupted. "Get out, Ros."

"Oh, I will, I will," she agreed readily. "And you can well imagine where I'm going now, can't you?"

"To Nicholas, I suppose?" Lysette asked, with a defiance that belied the quaking within her.

"But of course, darling. Really, you should have been more discreet."

She turned and with a swish of her pearl colored velvet skirts, was gone.

Lysette fumbled with the ribbons of her bonnet. "I must go," she said unnecessarily.

"Don't," Kit said suddenly. His hand closed about her arm. "Don't go back. Rosalyn wasn't joking. She will go to Nicholas."

"And he will come home and I must be there," she countered.

"Will he hurt you?"

She could not but be touched by the very real concern on his handsome face.

"No," she answered flatly, without emotion. "He will not want to risk harming his child."

A flicker of distaste crossed Kit's face. Much as he loathed Nicholas, he could not quite believe that the only thing that would keep him from doing real harm to this delicate, exquisite creature was the presence of his child in her womb.

"I wish you would stay," he said again.

She shook her head, a tremulous smile on her lips. "I can't." She averted her eyes. "Perhaps . . . perhaps if would be better if you did not come tomorrow, Kit. I will send a message when the sittings may resume."

She turned to leave but Kit caught her wrist. "Send a message anyway," he entreated. "Let me know you're all right."

She nodded. "If I can."

At the same time that Lysette's carriage rolled away from the front of Kit's townhouse, Rosalyn's drew to a rocking halt before the building that housed Nicholas's office. It was with a sense of excited apprehension that Rosalyn climbed the stairs and entered the waiting room.

"I must see Nicholas," she told the clerk. "And—" she interrupted as he was about to protest. "I must see him now. It is a matter of the utmost urgency."

The clerk hesitated. Nicholas had given strict orders that Madame D'Everaux was not to be admitted to his presence but he would have been equally annoyed with the scene she was fully capable of creating in the outer office. Already several distinguished clients were eyeing her with open curiosity.

The office door opened and Nicholas conducted a client out. His black eyes flashed angrily as he saw her there.

"Madame," he said coldly.

"I must speak to you, Nicholas," she insisted.

"If it is a business matter, I suggest you have Edouard make an appointment and. . ."

"It is not business. At least not Edouard's business."

"Then we have nothing to dis—"

"It is business concerning your wife—your wife and Kit Stratton."

Nicholas's face flushed with outrage. How dare she link Lysette's name and Stratton's in public. How dare she insinuate that there was anything between them! Whatever the woman's grievances, she should have had the good breeding to keep her mouth shut.

Seizing her arm, he dragged her into his office and slammed the door.

"You sicken me, madame," he snarled. "I once thought you a lady but I am beginning to believe that you are little more than a bitch masquerading as a lady."

"Bitch, am I?" she hissed. "Heigh ho! And I suppose your precious Lysette is an angel! Well, I have just come from Kit's flat and your angel was there, Nicholas, alone. He was kissing her, Nicholas. Kit was kissing your wife!"

Nicholas's body shook with rage. "You're lying!"

"Am I? Why don't you ask her? And then we'll see who is the bitch!"

Spinning on her heel, she stalked out of the office confident that Nicholas would do the rest.

In that, if nothing else, Rosalyn proved that she knew the workings of Nicholas Callaway's mind. With a few terse orders he cancelled his appointments for the rest of the day and dismissed the disappointed clients who were waiting in his outer office. Then, his face set in a grim scowl, he strode out of the office and down to his waiting carriage.

Having been warned to expect Nicholas's imminent arrival, Mrs. Jonelle was nonetheless seized with a dreadful sense of trepidation when he stormed through the door.

"Where is Lysette?" he demanded sternly as he doffed his topcoat and hat and all but threw them at the hapless butler.

"In her room, monsieur," Mrs. Jonelle replied timidly.

"Has she been there all day?"

A part of him wished desperately that the housekeeper would say yes even if it were a lie concocted to protect her mistress.

Anne dropped her gaze. "No, monsieur," she whispered, dashing Nicholas's last tenuous hopes. "She went out this afternoon."

"Alone?"

"Mimette was with her."

"Mimette!" His disgusted tone conveyed his opinion of the flighty maid's protection. "Did she say where she was going?"

"No, monsieur. But she did tell me to expect you."

Sighing, Nicholas felt as though the weight of the world had dropped squarely onto his shoulders. If Lysette were expecting him to arrive, she must have known that Rosalyn would run to him with her tale. It followed, then, that what he'd been told was the truth or at least some version of it. She had been with Stratton. Stratton! She had gone to him—been alone with him—perhaps allowed him to—

Without dismissing Mrs. Jonelle, he turned and took the stairs two at a time. He strode up the corridor, each step seeming to fuel his rage until by the time he reached Lysette's door he could easily have killed her, or Kit, or both.

Propelled by his fist, the door flew back and crashed against the fine pink silk that covered the wall. He loomed in the doorway, massive, terrifying, his black eyes twin furnaces of blazing fury.

Across the room, Lysette rose from the armchair in which she had fatalistically awaited his arrival. She tilted her chin upward, determined not to cower before him even though her heart seemed to beat so hard she thought it must surely burst.

For a long time they stood there, a tableau vivant, then Nicholas entered the room and kicked the door closed behind him. Despite her bravado, Lysette trembled as the distance between them narrowed. She wanted to run, to hide, to seek protection from the murderous fury burning in his ebony eyes. Instead she stood her ground and waited.

# CHAPTER 20

He stopped when they were but inches apart.

"Rosalyn went to see you?" Lysette asked, her tone surprisingly calm.

"Did you think she wouldn't?" he snarled, towering over her.

"I was quite sure she would."

"Then it's true?"

Lysette started to turn away but he seized her arm and swung her back to face him. Lysette winched, knowing that come the morning her arm would bear the livid purple imprints of his fingers, but she made no attempt to pull away.

"I don't know what she told you, mon. . ."

"She told me," Nicholas growled, "that she found you with Kit Stratton. That he was kissing you."

"I was with Kit." She sighed. "I suppose he was kissing me."

"You suppose!"

"It was innocent, Nicholas!"

"Innocent! You were alone with him, kissing him!"

"He was kissing me!"

Nicholas trembled. He forced himself to

move away from her for in that moment he wanted desperately to shake her until her teeth rattled.

"What the hell game are you playing, madame?"

"I'm not playing a game!"

"How long has this been going on? How many times have you gone to him!"

"Never!" She drew herself up indignantly.

"Never?" His sneer told her what he thought of that.

"Never before today!" she amended angrily. "And I wouldn't have gone to him today had it not been for you!"

His black eyes glittered. "For me! How the hell can you always manage to blame me for what you do! As I recall, madame, the last time I found you with Stratton, you managed to blame me. And now this. . ."

"Well, it was your fault! I went to apologize to Kit for your behavior this morning."

"You did what!" A vein throbbed in his forehead. "Don't you ever—ever—apologize for me to anyone! Do you hear me!"

"Do you want people to think you a rude boor, then?" she challenged.

"I don't give a good goddamn what people think of me and I won't have my decisions questioned nor my actions apologized for by you or anyone else!"

"Well, no one would have to if you behaved like . . . like. . ."

"Like whom?" he sneered. "Like Stratton? Like your lover?"

"He's not my lover!"

"No? But why not? Did Rosalyn arrive too soon?"

"You foul-minded bastard! You condemn me because of some lie your whore told you!"

"At least she's an honest whore, madame. She doesn't masquerade as an ice-blooded virgin."

Outraged, Lysette slashed her fist through the air. She wanted to hit him, hurt him, tear that handsome, sneering face to ribbons.

Nicholas caught her wrist and forced it behind her back. He ignored Lysette's cries as he shoved her back sending her sprawling like a broken doll across the bed.

As he approached, Lysette tried to kick him but he deftly dodged her feet entangled as they were in her skirts.

"Stay away from me," she hissed.

Pinioning her wrists to the bed on either side of her head, he knelt over her.

"Don't touch me!" she snarled.

"I wouldn't touch you, Lysette," he sneered. "By God, I wouldn't touch you tonight if you begged me. But I want to tell you smething and I want to make sure you listen. If ever I discover you've let Stratton, or any man, touch you, I'll kill him." The deadly calm on his face, in his voice, was terrifying to behold. "And before God I'll make you wish I had killed you as well. Do you hear me?" He shook her savagely. "Do you!"

"Yes, I hear you!" she ground out. "I hate you!"

"I know, oh yes, I know, madame. But the

fact remains that you belong to me. To me!"

He pushed her back into the enveloping softness of the feather bed and stormed from the room. He was barely out the door when Lysette slid off the bed and ran after him.

"Where are you going!" she screamed down the hall at his retreating back. "To your bitch, Rosalyn?"

"One bitch or another," he snarled from the head of the stairs. "What difference does it make? Oh, and madame? I am giving instructions that you are not to be given assistance in leaving this house. If necessary, I will give orders that you be forcibly restrained."

"I am not your prisoner!" The prospect of being a captive in her own home appalled her.

"I am your husband, my dear," he reminded her, revealing a horrifyingly diabolical smile on his handsome face. "I am your master. You will . . . you . . . will . . . obey me!"

With a scream of pure rage, Lysette seized a priceless Sevres vase from a marquetry table and hurled it at him. He watched, unperturbed, as it sailed past him and smashed somewhere near the bottom of the stairs.

Glancing down the stairs, he eyed the wreckage dispassionately. "That came from Saint-Cloud," he told her calmly. "I was under the impression that you were quite fond of it."

Too late, Lysette realized that the vase had been a wedding gift to her and Jules—a family heirloom, the single object of value salvaged from her father's ruined fortunes. Her scream of fury and dismay all but drowned Nicholas's disdaining laugh as he descended the stairs and left the house.

In the privacy of her room, Lysette nursed her hatred of Nicholas long into the night. She kept her doors securely locked but even so each noise made her jump skittishly. She was certain that Nicholas would never let her off so easily. He would be back to torment her. Of that, if nothing else, she had no doubt.

The clock chimed one in the morning, then two, then three. Heavy-eyed, Lysette looked at the windows. Soon dawn would streak the sky but still Nicholas had not returned.

Turning the key in the dressing room door, she slipped through the armoire-lined chamber to Nicholas's door. Through the keyhole she could see his bed turned down and a low fire kindled in the fireplace in readiness for his arrival. But the bed had not been slept in and both the fire and the lamps were burning low. It was obvious that the man for whom the preparations had been made had not been in the room all night.

"Where is he?" she mused aloud, returning to her room. Her mouth twisted with bitterness. "With Rosalyn!" came the undesired reply.

Sighing, she sat heavily in an armchair. Though barely into her fifth month of pregnancy, she felt monstrously unattractive and Rosalyn's beauty seemed all the more overwhelming. It isn't surprising, a treacherous voice murmured in the back of her mind, that he wants to be with Rosalyn. Why should he bother with you when he can have her? He was hers long before you came to know him—came to love him. He'll be hers long after your usefulness to him is at an end. You're a convenience to him, nothing more. If he could have had a child without you, he would simply have taken Saint-Cloud and thrown you into the street.

Her chin quivered and she felt the ache of tears threatening to well into her eyes.

"No!" Resolutely she pushed herself out of the chair. "I won't cry for him! I won't! He's a miserable bastard and I hate him! I'll give him what he wants—I'll give him his child—then I'll go away, far away, where I'll never have to see his face again!"

Suddenly the emptiness of her room seemed to press on her, stifle her. She had to get out. Letting herself out of the room, she went downstairs where she found Leigh sitting in the burgundy parlor eating rolls left over from dinner and drinking hot chocolate.

"You couldn't sleep either?" she asked, turning over another cup and filling it with the steaming, fragrant chocolate.

"No, but why couldn't you? Surely you're not worried about Nicholas."

"Actually, I am. He was furious when he stormed out. You know he left orders that you are not to be allowed out without an entourage that would do credit to royalty."

"I know," Lysette acknowledged ruefully. She laughed bitterly. "Ironic, isn't it? I'm to be punished because he fancies I may be taking a lover but it is perfectly acceptable for him to be out all night with his mistress."

"You think he's with Rosalyn?"

Lysette's russet eyes met Leigh's blue ones. "Don't you?"

Leigh shrugged. "I suppose so." She noted the flicker of pain that crossed Lysette's face. "If it hurts you to know that Nicholas is with her, why don't you tell him so? Perhaps he doesn't know you care."

"He knows," Lysette muttered. "He doesn't give a damn."

"Lysette!"

"Well? He doesn't."

"Then why should he fly into such a jealous rage over Kit?"

Lysette's smile was wistful. "It wasn't jealousy. It was merely possessiveness. He owns me in the same way he owns this house, or Saint-Cloud. I belong to him and he can't bear the thought of anyone else touching what belongs to him." She shook her head sadly. "It's Rosalyn he loves. So be it. Let them have one another. I hate him!"

"No, you don't," Leigh contradicted gently. "If you hated him, you wouldn't be down here awake at four in the morning worrying about him."

"I'm not worried," Lysette maintained stubbornly.

But even as the words left her mouth, they heard the crunch of the gravel on the drive. Both leapt to their feet and ran to the hall.

They heard Nicholas long before they saw

him. He roared as he tried to leap from the carriage and instead nearly sprawled on the front steps.

"He's drunk," Lysette observed, awed.

"Drunk hell," Leigh laughed. "He's pissed as a newt!"

"Ah, here they are!" Nicholas cried, balanced precariously against the aged butler's narrow shoulder. "My shrew of a wife and her crony, once my friend."

"I am still your friend, Nicholas," Leigh told him patiently as she took the burden from the grateful old butler.

"No, you're not," he disagreed chidingly. "You've gone over to the enemy. Traitor."

Leigh winced at the full impact of his breath on her face. "Never that, Nick. But Lysette needs friends too, you know."

"Lysette?" He squinted at his wife and found, to his regret, that even through the haze of too much drink she was still breathtaking. "She doesn't need friends. She doesn't need a husband or a lover. She has her virtue to keep her warm." He gave Lysette a lopsided grin. "Don't you, m'love?"

"You're disgusting," she spat.

He sighed. "As always."

With Leigh supporting him and Lysette following, he tried to make it up the stairs. More than once the three of them made more progress backward than forward but at last they managed with Leigh leading him and Lysette pushing at his broad back. Together the women got him to his room and pushed him down across the bed.

"Go to bed, Leigh," Lysette told her. "It's nearly dawn. I'll pull his shoes off and then he's on his own."

"Will he be all right?" Leigh asked, moving reluctantly toward the door.

"I suppose, providing he doesn't fall off the bed and hit his head on the floor."

Laughing, Leigh left the room and Lysette bent to remove Nicholas's shoes. When they were discarded, she knelt on the edge of the bed and untied his cravat.

"I'm helpless," he murmured ruefully. "You can have your way with me, my beauty."

"If I had my way," Lysette told him sternly, "I'd throw you in a cold bath and let you drown."

"Cruel woman," he chided.

"Drunken lout," she countered.

"Why are you still up? Did you worry about me?"

"Don't flatter yourself."

He caught her hand as she deftly removed the studs from his shirt.

"Love me a little, Lysette. Only a little."

"How can I when you scorn me, punish me, mock me? You accuse me of crimes of which you are the guilty one. You curse me as an adultress then leave me to meet with your mistress."

"I have no mistress," he murmured sleepily.

Lysette sighed as she dropped the last of his shirtstuds into the palm of one hand. Even dead drunk he couldn't tell her the truth. Why did she harbor any tenuous hopes that he might come to love her? He was a liar and a cheat. And she was a fool.

Still, her heart could not but melt a little at the sight of him, sound asleep, his face devoid of the cynical harshness that mistrust had etched there, seemingly as innocent as a child. His black lashes lay across his cheeks in feathery crescents. In sleep, even drink-induced sleep, he was still handsome beyond imagining. Lysette could not but wish to Heaven that the soul that dwelt inside him was as beautiful as the rest of him.

"If only. . ." she began, then laughed a bitter laugh filled with self-mockery. If only—if only—her world, it seemed, was filled with "if only." The only purpose served was to remind her of what was missing in her life.

Leaving the bed, she dropped the studs onto his table and blew out the lone remaining lamp that had not already guttered out. With a last look at Nicholas as he slept, still half-dressed in his evening clothes, she retired to her room and whatever sleep she could snatch from the few hours remaining of the night.

Behind her, in the shadowy bedroom, Nicholas stirred and in his restless slumber called out to the elusive, chestnut-haired woman who seemed forever just out of his grasp. And if he called her name, and if he told her that he loved her, his words fell on deaf ears for she had once more eluded his grasp as he feared, in his secret heart, she might well do forever.

# CHAPTER 21

It was mid-afternoon by the time Nicholas tiptoed down the stairs. The house was hushed as if the very walls were afraid to make the slightest noise and risk aggravating the pounding in his head.

"Good afternoon!" Lysette called cheerily as she passed him at the foot of the stairs.

"Don't shout," he moaned. His face was alarmingly pale for one generally so swarthy. He reached out a steadying hand toward the newel post.

"Why, Nicholas, you look suspiciously green."

"Enjoy yourself, my pet," he hissed, though there was an amused gleam in his red-rimmed eyes.

"I assure you, I am not enjoying myself in the least. I can concerned as any wife should be."

"Concerned my ass, madame, you're loving every moment of this."

She gave him a coy little shrug. "Well, perhaps just a little."

"More than a little," he contradicted.

"Be that as it may, I should tell Cook you're down. Perhaps you'd like some of the delicious gumbo she made for dinner. It was wonderful! She put shrimp and oysters in it and a bit of sausage too, I think." She widened her eyes in innocent surprise. "Why, Nicholas! Are you going to be ill?"

"Damn you, Lysette," he moaned through gritted teeth. "Is this your revenge?"

"Revenge? How can you say such a thing?" She fluttered her eyes at him, inordinately pleased with herself. "May I assume, then, that you're not interested in the gumbo?" He snarled an unintelligible reply and she thought it prudent not to ask for a translation. "As you wish. Cook will be disappointed."

With a little, self-satisfied smile, she disappeared into the front parlor.

Nicholas followed and found her sitting at one end of the long velvet sofa. He watched as her needle moved in and out of a piece of fine silk embroidering an intricate border on what would soon be a tiny shirt.

"I'm going to lie down," he announced abruptly.

"Fine."

Before she knew what was happening, Nicholas had stretched full length on the sofa and lain his head in the comforting pillow of her skirts.

"Nicholas!" she protested.

"Shhh," he hushed. "In sickness and in health, remember?"

"You're not sick," she argued. "You brought this upon yourself."

"Gently, cherie. Whatever the cause, I assure you I am truly sick and in need of comfort."

Lysette's tongue burned to ask him why he did not go to his mistress if he were so in need of comfort. But then, she told herself, hadn't she wept time and again because he was with someone else instead of her? Hadn't she told Leigh that she would live with Nicholas's terms if only to be near him? Was she, then, so great a fool as to send him away on one of the rare occasions when he came to her?

She looked down and found his eyes upon her beseechingly.

"There's no need to act the invalid," she chided softly, charmed in spite of herself. "You're being punished for your own foolishness."

"Cruel chit," he chided, pouting like a child. "How can you be so heartless?"

"Nicholas. . ."

"Shhh. Sit still," he ordered sharply, suddenly serious.

Lysette held her breath, wondering what was wrong, but then a brilliant smile lit Nicholas's face.

"The baby is moving," he told her softly.

Lysette's cheeks pinkened. The tenderness in his face seemed to blot out every grievance she'd borne against him.

She brushed back a lock of black hair that had fallen over his forehead. He sighed and closed his eyes.

"That's good," he murmured. "Don't stop."

"But, Nicholas. . .

"Shhh." Taking her cool hand, he kissed it then placed it back on his brow. "Don't stop."

Softly, tenderly, she stroked his brow as his head rested on her lap. His eyes were closed; a tiny smile played about his mouth. In a few moments she realized that he was fast asleep.

"Lysette?" Leigh appeared in the doorway.

"Shhh." She pressed a finger to her lips.

"Is he asleep?" Leigh seemed stunned by the picture of blissful domesticity before her.

Lysette nodded happily. She twined a black curl about her finger feeling absurdly content.

"I thought we were going to visit Elizabeth."

"After Nicholas wakes up."

"Perhaps if you were careful, you could slide out from under. . ." Leigh stopped, seeing the stricken look on Lysette's face at the thought of leaving. "All right, after Nicholas wakes up."

It was long into the evening by the time Leigh and Lysette made their way to the grand entrance of Nicholas's parents' house. Lysette, still alight with the euphoria of having spent the afternoon in such close and gentle company with Nicholas, returned Elizabeth's hug enthusiastically and chattered happily as she was led into the parlor where tea awaited them.

"You're positively glowing," her mother-in-law told her.

"Am I?"

"Oh, dear, look at that smile." Elizabeth winked at Leigh.

Lysette giggled but her humor quickly faded as the Callaways' stern butler appeared and announced that Kit Stratton had arrived.

Lysette rose immediately. "I'm sorry. I must go, Elizabeth." She looked at Leigh. "Are you coming or shall I send the carriage back for you?"

"Oh, darling," Elizabeth cajoled. "Don't rush off. You know how I enjoy your company and, of course, Kit is always delighted to see you."

Lysette had no wish to drag Elizabeth into the middle of the ugly situation that had developed between herself, Nicholas, and Kit. At the same time, however, Nicholas had so disarmed her by his charm during the afternoon that the last thing she wanted was to risk another quarrel by spending the evening in Kit's company, even in such innocent surroundings as his own mother's parlor.

"No, truly, I must be going."

"Going?" Kit appeared in the parlor doorway. "But you can't!"

He was stunned by the icy haunter in the look Lysette turned upon him.

"I assure you, monsieur, I can and I will."

"But . . . but . . . why?"

The frank curiosity with which Elizabeth was watching her made Lysette uncomfortable. She had no desire to apprise her mother-in-law of her troubles with Nicholas, yet she knew this abrupt change of attitude toward Kit must inevitably cause questions to arise.

"Monsieur," she began. "Kit," she amended when she saw the anguish in his azure eyes. "Nicholas has decided that the time is not right after all for my portrait to be painted. Perhaps later, after our child is born. . ."

"But the sketches, the studies; I have given up all my other commissions to devote myself to you!"

"I'm very sorry, Kit. I'm sure Nicholas will pay you whatever you think. . ."

"I don't want the money! Your portrait would have been my masterpiece!"

"Kit," Elizabeth intervened, growing weary of the pointless confrontation and more than a little embarrassed for both Kit and Lysette, who was obviously distressed. "Lysette is with child. It is a trying time for her. You must be patient."

Kit seemed to pull himself together. "You're right, of course, madame," he agreed. "My apologies," he offered Lysette.

"Think nothing of it," she forgave. "But now I really must be going."

She and Leigh went to the door but Kit could not resist following.

"Lysette?"

She turned and regarded him calmly and so impersonally that he dared not reach out a hand to touch her.

"We will finish your portrait at some point, won't we?"

"I imagine we will," she allowed, believing that in time Nicholas's temper would cool. If nothing else, she thought, a hint of bitterness creeping into the aura of happiness that had surrounded her all afternoon, Rosalyn would convince Nicholas that Kit needed the commission. "After the child comes."

Kit's eyes could not help but glance toward her midsection where her pregnancy was only just beginning to be distinguishable from the fullness of her skirts. 'After the child comes' seemed like years away. Still, there was little he could do but yield gracefully.

"As you wish. I am at your service whenever you are ready to resume your sittings."

"Thank you, Kit."

Though he would have gone on, Kit's next words were abruptly silenced by the unexpected appearance of Nicholas who suddenly loomed up behind Lysette.

Kit glared at him with unveiled hostility, resenting Nicholas's unruffled calm that conveyed a supreme confidence in himself and his ability to control the world around him.

He hated him even more when he saw the unabashed adoration in Lysette's beautiful face as she turned and saw him there.

"Nicholas!" she cried, delighted. "We were just leaving for home. Monsieur Stratton has arrived to visit with Elizabeth."

"I see. Stratton," Nicholas snapped by way of greeting.

"Monsieur," Kit replied, not daring to show him disrespect since it could not only cost him Lysette's portrait but Elizabeth's friendship as well.

Nicholas looked away and it was as though Kit simply ceased to exist for him. Never in his life had Kit felt so superfluous.

Instead, Nicholas's black eyes were resting with extraordinary tenderness on his wife who returned his look with equal fervor. Watching, Kit wanted to scream with the sheer injustice of it all. Why should—how could—Lysette love such a man as she had been forced to marry? What had he done to enslave her? When had it happened? Kit had seen her fear when Rosalyn found them together. He knew Nicholas mistreated her.

"Darling," Nicholas said softly, one finger lifting back one of Lysette's curls. (Kit saw the little shiver course through Lysette at her husband's touch. He wanted to leap between them, shield her from Nicholas's wiles, but he knew he could do nothing.) "I thought perhaps we could go for a late supper. At Antoine's, if you like?"

"Oh, yes, please," Lysette breathed.

"Nicholas," Leigh interrupted. "Why don't you and Lysette go alone? I think I'd like to stay here and visit with Elizabeth and Kit."

"Are you sure?" Nicholas asked, not displeased.

"Yes, quite sure."

"Thank you, Leigh," Lysette whispered as Nicholas turned away to take Lysette's paletot from the butler.

"Enjoy, dear," Leigh returned, giving her a quick hug.

Together they took their leave from Elizabeth who could not contain her delight at seeing them together. No one seemed to notice that Kit had gone on into the parlor. None of them would have guessed the anguish that wracked him at the thought of Nicholas and Lysette together sharing an intimate tête à tête in a restaurant and then going home alone to an empty house.

"He has done something to her," Kit told himself spitefully. "Perhaps he's threatened her—beaten her—"

But even with all his hatred and all his vengeful spite boiling inside him a part of his mind—albeit a small part—had to recognize that Lysette looked neither like a woman who had been threatened into submission nor a wife who'd fallen victim to a brutal husband. She looked, Kit admitted bitterly, like a young bride completely and unashamedly in love with her husband.

In that instant all the hatred, all the grievances, all the spite inside Kit redoubled. He would have his revenge, he vowed, someday, in some way, and Rosalyn would help him. Lysette would be his. . . .

# CHAPTER 22

Having reached a manageable—if tentative—truce with Nicholas, Lysette plunged into the business of decorating a nursery for their child and filling it with the best New Orleans had to offer. No matter was too trivial, no shopping expedition too tedious to merit her full attention. The happiest moments of her days were spent in that large, sunny chamber overlooking the courtyard where, by the time the child was born, the flowers of spring would be in full, fragrant bloom.

On occasion Nicholas would join her there. Together they examined new purchases, discussed what else they might need, and found, to their mutual surprise, that they not only enjoyed one another's company, they looked forward to sharing those gentle, intimate moments.

But if they were finding a new peace together, Leigh was feeling cross and neglected. Not that she would have seriously expected them to eschew one another's companionship to be with her, but she could see the bonds forming between them—bonds that had not, and never would, form between herself and Michael.

That they loved one another, she already knew. Now, she could see, they were on the verge of discovering that their love was not the hopeless, one-sided disaster each had thought. They were about to make a miraculous discovery that would change their lives. A discovery that Leigh knew she and Michael would never make.

"If only I could have given Michael a child," she sighed one day in early March as she sat in what would soon be the baby's nurse's room.

Lysette looked up from the samples of fabric from which she was trying to choose upholstery patterns.

"It must have been very difficult for you."

Leigh shrugged. "Michael has never thrown it up to me. He's never made me suffer for it. Some men would not have been so understanding."

"Nicholas would not have been so patient, I'm sure," Lysette commented. She didn't believe a word of it—in her new mood she would scarcely have believed a harsh word about Nicholas had she heard it from his own lips.

"Nicholas," Leigh murmured. "When I think of how bitter I was when I learned I was bethrothed to Michael; that our parents had come to the agreement when I was barely out of the cradle. . ."

Lysette shifted uncomfortably as Leigh's voice trailed off. "Were you so in love with Nicholas then, Leigh?"

Leigh's smile was wistful. "I shouldn't answer that—not to you. But yes, I loved him madly. I'm very jealous of you, you know. Sometimes I . . . sometimes I hate you."

Lysette stared at her, stunned into silence. "Hate me?" she managed at last. "Hate me, Leigh?"

Leigh pressed her hands to her lips. "I'm sorry, Lysette! That was an idiotic thing to say. Forgive me, please, forgive me!"

Tossing aside her samples, Lysette went to kneel beside Leigh's chair. She gathered the weeping woman into her arms and held her as she sobbed.

"There's nothing to forgive," she murmured, rocking her gently. "You can't dictate to your heart; it, above all else, does as it wills."

Gradually Leigh's tears gave way to a kind of gentle melancholy. Though she professed to be comforted, though she assured Lysette that she meant none of what she had said—that her words were merely the foolishness of a moment of madness, she had felt while in Lysette's arms the movement of Nicholas's child and she loathed Lysette for having captured for herself that most elusive of all prizes—Nicholas Callaway's heart.

"Lysette," she said casually as they sat in Lysette's sewing room a week later. "When are you going to resume your sittings for Kit Stratton?"

Lysette shrugged. "I don't know. It's odd, isn't it? Not so long ago that portrait was so important to me. Now I simply don't care if it is ever painted."

"But Nicholas did commission Kit to paint it," Leigh pointed out.

"Don't worry about Kit, cherie. Like a cat, Kit Stratton will always land on his feet. I've no doubt he has patrons lined up to give him commissions. He won't starve if he loses mine." She chuckled and it had a curious, smug sound that grated on Leigh's nerves. "Of course, if nothing else, he can always appeal to his cousin for funds."

"Ah, Rosalyn. What have you heard of her lately?"

Lysette lifted her shoulders. "Nothing."

"Nicholas is no longer. . ?"

"I don't see how he could be. When he is not attending to business, he is with me. Rosalyn is like Kit. For them there will always be another commission, another lover."

"That doesn't sound like you; it seems so callous, so uncaring."

"Did Rosalyn ever give me a reason to be concerned for her?" Lysette demanded.

"And Kit?"

A frown creased Lysette's brow. "Kit wanted more than I could give him."

"He loves you."

"I don't believe that." Stretching, Lysette arched her back easing the ache that came of bending over her sewing for hours at a time. "I think he saw me as someone other than myself. I don't know, an ideal he had created in his mind. He's a romantic. I suppose it comes of his being an artist. He lives in a fantasy world of his own creation. It's not fair of him to expect others to join him there."

"He will be terribly hurt if you simply turn your back on him."

"Leigh," Lysette sighed, weary of the subject, "I know you found Kit terribly attractive. But you cannot expect me to rearrange my life—possibly ruin what happiness I am beginning to find with Nicholas—merely to fuel Kit's fantasies. It's not fair of you to expect that."

"I suppose you're right," Leigh admitted grudgingly. "Well, I'll leave you to your decorating."

Leaving Lysette, Leigh sought out Nicholas who was at work in his study. He was spending more and more time at home now, a fact that had not escaped either Elizabeth's delighted observation or Leigh's envious one.

"Am I disturbing you?" she asked, peering around the door.

Nicholas leaned back in his chair. "No, I was about to stop for a while. What are you doing this afternoon, Leigh?"

She entered the room and perched on the edge of his desk. "I was just up talking to Lysette."

"In the nursery, I suppose?" His smile was fondly indulgent.

"In the nurse's room, actually. I was asking her when she was going to resume her sittings with Kit."

The humor faded from Nicholas's dark face. Rising, he crossed the room and poured himself a drink.

"I wish you hadn't brought it up," he told her. "Lysette hasn't mentioned Kit for weeks. I don't think she's even thought of him."

"But shouldn't the portrait be finished?"

"I don't give a damn if it ever is, to be frank. You know perfectly well that the portrait was not my idea. I was against it. It was only that my mother and Lysette wanted it so badly. If Lysette is no longer interested. . ." He shrugged.

Exasperated, Leigh left the study and went up to her room where she summoned a maid to help her change into a gown suitable for paying calls. Nicholas and Lysette's indifference toward Kit's well-being annoyed her. Kit was a darling, sensitive man and if Lysette didn't give a tinker's damn about him, Leigh did. She remembered the day when she had vowed that Lysette would not have both Nicholas and Kit. As far as Leigh was concerned, Lysette had forfeited her right to a place in Kit's affections. Leigh would be more than happy to fill that void.

"Kit?" she called as she entered the appallingly cluttered parlor of the small apartment. "Kit, are you here?"

"Who is that?" came his voice from the depths of the studio.

"Leigh Scofield."

Receiving no reply, Leigh went in the

direction of the voice and found Kit in his studio busily draping a large canvas.

"I'm sorry. I've disturbed you at work," Leigh apologized.

"Not at all." Though it wasn't true—he had been absorbed by his painting—Kit hoped against hope that Leigh had brought him word of Lysette's intention to return to her sittings. He'd been despondent when they had been so abruptly terminated. "Sit down. Let met get you something."

"No, thank you."

Leigh smiled her most engaging smile as Kit stripped off his paint-spattered smock and sat beside her on the sofa.

"How have you been?" she asked. "Has Nicholas's decision to rescind the commission hurt your—"

Kit's naturally pale complexion took on an even starker pallor. "Rescind? Then Lysette won't come back?"

Leigh wished she could take back the words. "I'm sorry. I thought you knew. I've spoken to them both but. . ." She shook her head. "It's no use." Reaching out, she took his hand. She realized suddenly that if she couldn't compete with Lysette in his affections, she might be able to win him through sympathy. "I am sorry, Kit. Truly, I have tried."

Kit raised her hand and kissed her fingers. "You're kindness itself," he murmured. "Let me go to the kitchen and get us some wine."

Smiling to herself, Leigh watched him

leave. Alone in the studio, she glanced around fascinated by the paraphernalia of the artist at work. Again and again her eyes went to the draped canvas on the easel. She longed to see what he was at work on now and yet she knew he would never agree to her inspecting it.

Cautiously, holding her breath, she eased off the sofa and scurried across the room on tiptoe. Her fingers trembled as she lifted back the canvas and gazed at the nearly completed work beneath.

"My God!" she breathed.

Before her in glorious detail, the color breathtakingly lifelike, Lysette Callaway stood bathed in the mauve light of an exquisite sunrise. Her chestnut hair streamed about her yet hid none of her naked beauty. All about her the plump, rosy cherubs who attended her gazed at her with rapt adoration.

"Kit, darling, I'm glad I caught you before you left."

Leigh dropped the canvas back into place when she heard Rosalyn's D'Everaux's voice from the kitchen. She hurried back to the sofa, reaching it just in time as Kit and Rosalyn entered the studio.

"Why, Mrs. Scofield," Rosalyn purred. "Kit didn't say he had company." Her green eyes scanned the room. "Is Lysette here as well?"

"No," Kit answered shortly, handing Leigh a glass of wine.

"What a pity." She gave Leigh a wan half-smile. "Kit's been absolutely despondent since Nicholas stopped Lysette's sittings. You really should speak to him about it."

"I have," Leigh replied. "He's against it."

"How tedious of him." Rosalyn accepted a chair and a glass of wine. She nodded toward the covered painting. "Still at work on your masterpiece, I see. When will you let me look?"

"When it's finished," Kit snapped.

Rosalyn sighed. "He's being so secretive. You'd think it was a state secret. Has he let you look?"

"Oh, no," Leigh assured her quickly. "I hadn't thought to ask."

"Then you're less curious than I am, dear. Kit, be a darling and get me something else to drink, won't you? This wine is dreadful."

Rising, Kit snatched her glass out of her hand and left the studio. Rosalyn sat silently until he had left then leaned forward and spoke in hushed tones.

"Tell me, my dear, how fares that paragon, Lysette Callaway?"

Leigh smiled. At that moment she felt a venomous jealousy of Lysette that matched Rosalyn's exactly.

"She and Nicholas have been billing and cooing like lovebirds."

Rosalyn made a sour face. "Are they . . . sleeping together?"

"No. They still have separate bedrooms. But they gaze at one another as though they could devour each other at a moment's notice."

"Don't you find it difficult to live with them?"

"Why should I?"

Rosalyn laughed shortly. "You may fool Lysette and Nicholas, darling, but you can't fool me. You're in love with Nicholas, aren't you?"

"I'm married. . ."

"So am I," Rosalyn interrupted. "That is not the issue here. Admit it or not, you do love him. I commiserate with you. I love him too, you know. Tell me frankly, wouldn't you like to see this farce of a marriage ended once and for all? After all, it has served its purpose, has it not? Nicholas has an heir, or he will within a reasonable length of time."

Leigh shook her head. "It's impossible. They love one another."

"Ah, but they don't trust one another. Where there is the kernel of suspicion, my dear, you will also find fertile ground for discord to grow. All that is required is a proper planting of the seed."

"And you know that method?"

"Perhaps. But it is not something I can do alone. Nicholas—" She hesitated, hating to have to reveal too much. "—Nicholas will not see me. What I have in mind would require help by someone who has access to their home."

Though she was fast losing her taste for watching Nicholas and Lysette make calf's eyes at one another, Leigh was not sure she was ready to take such drastic action to separate them.

"I don't know," she hedged.

"Let me know when you decide," Rosalyn told her.

"If I do. . ." Leigh began, but Rosalyn silenced her with a gesture as Kit returned to the room.

"Tell me, Kit," Rosalyn said as he returned to his place beside Leigh, "when do you plan to leave for Baton Rouge?"

"Next week," Kit replied.

"Kit is going to Fairhaven, which belongs to my brother-in-law, William Crozier, and my sister Rebecca," Rosalyn explained to Leigh. "Their eldest daughter, Jocelyn, is to be married and Kit is painting their wedding portrait."

"How lovely," Leigh commented. She rose abruptly. "I really must be going."

"So soon?" Rosalyn murmured. She caught Leigh's wrist as she would have passed her. "Why don't you come to visit me, my dear? I'm sure we have much in common."

Leigh's eyes and Rosalyn's met and held for a long moment. "Perhaps I will," Leigh allowed, feeling guilty and yet strangely exhilarated. She was dying of curiosity to hear Rosalyn's plan. "Yes, perhaps I will."

Rosalyn smiled, already confident that Leigh Scofield would prove an invaluable ally. "Good," she sighed. "Very good."

If Leigh seemed troubled as Kit conducted

her to the door and thanked her for her visit, he was mercifully too involved in his own worries to notice.

# CHAPTER 23

Leigh bided her time as the days passed. Though she could not deny that it pained her to see the growing intimacy between Lysette and Nicholas, she could not quite bring herself to take the step that would send them hurtling to the brink of a total dissolution of their marriage.

Still, it seemed inevitable that she would one day take that step. It was only the what and the when of the matter that was in question.

As it happened, the when turned out to be two weeks after the day Leigh had gone to visit Kit. The what was the discovery on a fine late March morning, that Nicholas's bed had not been slept in.

She went to his room intending to ask if he had heard any word from Michael. That he had not written to her was not, in itself, a cause for alarm. He was often gone for months at a time writing only to settle some matter concerning the running of Buckland. But he regularly corresponded with Nicholas who acted as his chief financial advisor.

She rapped at Nicholas's door wondering why he had not appeared downstairs as he generally did before leaving for the office.

"Nicholas?" she called through the thick door. "Nicholas, are you awake?"

There was no reply. She knocked again. Nothing. She hesitated then pressed the latch, hesitated again then entered the sun-filled room. It was empty. The bed, neatly made, had obviously not been used. A dreadful certainty swept over Leigh. There was, suddenly, no doubt in her mind where Nicholas could be found.

Her eyes went to the dressing room door—that same dressing room that adjoined Lysette's bedroom. In that room, Leigh knew without question, she would find Nicholas.

She thought of the evening before. Nicholas and Lysette had gone out to dinner—something they'd been doing with increasing frequency. Though they were always careful to insist on Leigh's accompanying them, she always declined. It was obvious to anyone that they wanted to be alone; to Leigh it was painfully apparent that she would merely be in the way for they spent these evenings out gazing into one another's eyes, smiling softly. For them it was heaven, sheer paradise; for Leigh, it was only hour after hour of torment. If they wished to believe that she refused to accompany them out of consideration for their privacy, so be it. The truth of the matter was that she was simply unequal to the task of watching their love blossom into something rare and beautiful—of watching Nicholas become the kind of husband she'd always known he could be and dreamed of his being to her.

There had been a kind of comfort in Nicholas's seemingly perpetual bachelorhood. Though she'd never believed he could ever be hers—her parents' betrothal of their infant daughter to their best friends' son had long ago put Nicholas far beyond her reach—she had come to believe that no other woman would ever win him either. And now here was Lysette doing precisely that, effortlessly, undeservingly winning his adoration.

Though one part of her knew it was folly, a perverse curiosity propelled her through the dressing room to Lysette's bedroom door. Her pent-up breath ached in her lungs as she listened at the door for some sign of whether the occupants of the room were awake. She heard nothing. Tentatively her shaking hand pressed the latch and the door swung inward on silent hinges.

The pink silk walls of Lysette's room reflected the morning sunshine that streamed through the pair of tall, white-draped windows bathing the room in its warm, rosy glow. Leigh squinted; the windowless dressing room had been dark and it was a moment before her eyes could adjust to the light.

Her eyes sought out the silk-testered bed at the far end of the room. The lace baire had been drawn down and it lent the scene a gauzy, ethereal air that somehow added to its beauty.

Lysette and Nicholas slept. Her hand,

fragile and white, lay on his chest. Her cheek rested on the warm curve of his shoulder. Her cascading chestnut curls fanned out over them both as they lay clasped in one another's arms. It was, Leigh realized with a pang of envy bordering on hatred, the most beautiful sight she'd ever seen.

As silently as she'd come, Leigh left the room and retraced her steps to the hallway. The decision with which she'd been struggling for a week was suddenly made for her. Her stride filled with new decisiveness, she went to her room and summoned her maid.

An hour later she was ushered into Rosalyn's D'Everaux's boudoir. Rosalyn rose from her delicate gilded desk and came to welcome her, a saccharine smile on her rosebud lips. She was casual, as if Leigh were simply another acquaintance, but in truth she had been expecting her. Leigh's appearance now, combined with the wary, furtive look in her sky-blue eyes, evoked a flutter of excitement in Rosalyn's breast. Leigh had made her choice: she was casting in her lot with Rosalyn. Separately, neither had the power to come between Nicholas and Lysette. Together, they would crush Lysette like one of the bothersome mosquitoes that plagued New Orleans's sultry summers.

After ordering tea, Rosalyn waved Leigh into one of the chairs grouped around the chaise-longue where she habitually held court for the legion of admirers from whose ranks she sought in vain to find a replacement for Nicholas.

"How kind of you to call," she said cordially as a maid placed a small lacquered table between them.

"You know why—" Leigh began but Rosalyn cautioned her to silence until the maid brought their tea and they were once more alone.

"Yes, I do." Rosalyn answered Leigh's abbreviated question. "I know why you've come. I've been expecting you."

"But how—"

Rosalyn smiled. "I told you, my dear, we're more alike than you may imagine. We have the same goals, the same ambitions."

Leigh tasted her tea and found it contained a healthy dollop of whiskey. The burning seemed somehow soothing as she drained her cup.

"Lysette and Nicholas slept together last night," she announced bluntly.

Rosalyn smiled weakly. "Yes. I rather suspected that would be the catalyst to spur you into action. I'd heard that they've been seen acting like lovesick newlyweds. I expected this would be the next logical development."

"You mentioned a plan at Kit's that day. Can you still do it?"

"Not I . . . we," Rosalyn corrected. "And yes, I do believe I can nip this little affaire de coeur of theirs in the bud most effectively."

Leigh was openly skeptical. "But they're mad about one another."

"Oh, yes, I'm quite sure they are."

"If you're thinking of trying to seduce Nicholas away from Lysette. . ."

"Not at all. I'm afraid that particular avenue is closed, perhaps indefinitely."

"Then I don't see how you can hope to destroy him in her eyes."

Rosalyn laughed. "Darling, I've no intention of trying to destroy him in her eyes. In fact, I hope she remains madly in love with him. That will only make our vengeance the sweeter."

Leigh shook her head, hopelessly confused. "Then how can you come between them?"

"By destroying her in his eyes. If, after giving her a taste of what it is to be loved by him, Nicholas were to suddenly loathe her, how would Lysette react?"

"Nicholas? Loathe Lysette? Impossible! She'd never do anything to cross him."

"Doubtless she wouldn't," Rosalyn allowed with a gentle curl of her lip. "But if he thought she had, wouldn't that be just as effective?"

"If there was evidence."

"Tell me, dear, that day at Kit's studio. You did steal a glance at that portrait he's working so feverishly upon, didn't you?"

"The portrait!" Leigh breathed. "My God, I'd almost forgotten! But Lysette never posed for it. Kit created it from his sketches."

"How would Nicholas know that? How would Lysette prove otherwise?"

"Kit would be forced to admit. . ."

"Kit is in Baton Rouge. He will be there for some weeks to come. He has given up all his other commissions save for this one for my sister because he could not bear to be parted from his masterwork. Now that it's finished, he's left the city. And no one, save you and I, know where he's gone. He has been all but incommunicado since he began work on his—" She had to force herself to choke out the words. "—Essence of Innocence."

"Essence of Innocence?" Leigh repeated.

"Nauseating, isn't it? Still, the details are so lovingly drawn, don't you think? The painting is like a hymn; a paean from a lover to his beloved."

She smiled slyly and Leigh felt a bubble of excitement expanding in her chest.

"But how can Nicholas see the painting? He'd never go near Kit's studio unless I told him about the painting and if I did, I'd put myself under suspicion—"

"Darling, darling!" Rosalyn interrupted. "You're making all this far too complicated. All we have to do is make sure Nicholas and the painting are in the same place at the same time."

"And how can we do that?"

"Haven't the illustrious Callaways received their invitations to the charity ball at the St. Louis Hotel?"

"Yes."

"They are going to attend?"

"Of course."

"Have you read the invitation?" Leigh

shook her head and Rosalyn went to her desk and retrieved her own invitation. "There is to be a showing by New Orleans's premier artists. Naturally, Kit was asked to contribute a sample of his work. He ignored the request since the only painting he had finished of late was—"

"The Essence of Innocence!" Leigh breathed.

"Precisely."

"But how can we get it? Surely he's locked his door now."

"Of course, but I have a key. If I take the painting to Collier Shaw and explain that Kit was called away but asked that I, his loving cousin, bring the painting at my first opportunity, who is to say it is not the truth?"

"Then Shaw will take the painting to the ball. . ."

"Where Nicholas, Lysette, and the cream of New Orleans society will see it." Rosalyn laughed, delighted. "There she will be in all her radiant beauty; that paragon of virtue, Lysette Callaway, as painted by the loving hand of her most ardent admirer. Naked as the proverbial jaybird, darling, and totally unashamed."

"Nicholas will kill Kit," Leigh murmured, suddenly afraid for the charming artist.

"First he has to find him," Rosalyn pointed out. "And in his fury, he is more than likely going to turn his attention to. . ."

"Lysette!"

"Exactly."

"God, it's so devious! It's so wicked."

"It's so perfect," Rosalyn sighed.

She rose from the chaise and tugged the bell rope.

"And so, my dear Mrs. Scofield, are you with me?"

The image of Lysette clasped in Nicholas's embrace, their naked bodies intertwined, flashed in Leigh's mind and a searing arrow of malicious envy shot through the very heart of her.

"I am," she affirmed.

"Good." Rosalyn turned to the maid who had answered her summons. "Clarisse, order my carriage immediately."

The girl scurried away and Rosalyn turned to Leigh with a malicious smile that somehow never reached her glittering green eyes. "Shall we, dear? We have work to do."

A faint misgiving stirred in Leigh's heart, but the pain of what she saw as Nicholas's betrayal of the life-long passion she'd nurtured was far too strong to be quelled now—especially now—when vengeance lay within her grasp.

The stench of rotting food met Rosalyn and Leigh at the door as they entered Kit's apartment.

"How that man can paint like an angel and still live like a pig is beyond me! I'd send my housekeeper over with some of the maids to clean this hovel, but I'm afraid I'd never see them again!"

She shuddered as she passed the molded

remains of a wedge of cheese.

"Come along, Leigh, the sooner we are gone the sooner I can breathe again."

They went to the studio where Rosalyn carefully wrapped Kit's beloved Essence of Innocence in a cloth. Handing the canvas to Leigh, she led her to the bedroom which was still papered with hundreds of sketches; of Lysette at home and of his ideas for translating those innocuous little drawings into his masterpiece.

After browsing among them for a considerable time, she selected one that was unmistakably a study for his masterwork. With exquisite care, she rolled the sketch into a narrow tube and slipped it into Leigh's reticule.

"What am I to do with that?" Leigh asked, perplexed.

"Take it home. When Nicholas and Lysette are out, take it to Lysette's room and hide it somewhere—somewhere where it is not too easily found yet somewhere where one could come across it given the right set of circumstances."

Leigh was both repelled and fascinated by the devious workings of Rosalyn's diabolical mind.

"If Nicholas were to find the sketch among Lysette's things. . ." she mused.

"He would naturally leap to the conclusion that Lysette had known about it all along."

"He'll be insane."

"No doubt. Above all else, Nicholas is an

extremely possessive man. And what would a possessive man think if he were to find such a sketch of his wife done by a man he knows to adore her—a man he has found mooning over her more than once."

"He would think the man was his wife's lover," Leigh concluded wonderingly.

"Yes, he would, wouldn't he?" Rosalyn agreed, leading the way out of the stale-aired apartment.

"But, Rosalyn," Leigh objected as they paused in the hall and Rosalyn twisted the key in Kit's front door. "You must know that Nicholas has a violent temper. Pushed to the brink, he could—he really could—fly into such a fury that he would harm Lysette."

"So he could," Rosalyn agreed cheerfully.

"He could even kill her."

Rosalyn's smile held a touch of wistfulness as she took up Kit's canvas and started toward the stairs.

"So he could," she repeated, and Leigh felt a quiver of revulsion at the hopeful note in Rosalyn's purring voice.

# CHAPTER 24

"It's magnificent," Collier Shaw breathed as he stepped back and gazed at Kit's painting in the back room of his gallery. "Really, it's far and away his finest work."

"Then you'll take it for display at the charity ball?" Rosalyn's question was phrased so casually that only Leigh noticed the undercurrent of excitement in her voice.

"Absolutely." He studied the painting more closely. "It seems to me I have seen this woman before."

Leigh held her breath and marveled at Rosalyn's serene facade. If Shaw remembered having seen Lysette in his shop—if for a moment he realized who she was—there was no way in the world he would agree to display the painting in public.

"Is she a professional artists' model?" he asked.

"Not really," Rosalyn replied. "She's a special friend of Kit's, if you understand me."

"Ah, I see. Well, one can see by the way he's portrayed her that she is more than simply a face and figure to him. One has merely to look at this painting to see it was painted by a lover for his—inamorata, shall we say?"

Rosalyn's eyes glittered maliciously. That was precisely the reaction she wanted the painting to evoke in Nicholas; in all of New Orleans society. She had gone beyond wanting to destroy Nicholas's love for Lysette; she wanted to destroy Lysette herself.

"Well, then, Mr. Shaw. I'll leave the painting with you. You'll frame it, of course, and see it's taken to the hotel gallery?"

"I will," he promised. "I'll see that it's displayed prominently as it deserves to be."

"Wonderful." She smiled at Leigh. "Shall we go, darling? We still have so much to do."

With Leigh trailing in her wake, Rosalyn left the gallery. Behind them, Collier Shaw stood gazing at Kit's Essence of Innocence wondering where it was he could have seen that glorious creature and why he hadn't paid more attention to her.

"So," Rosalyn said, stripping off her kid gloves as their carriage rolled away from Shaw's shop, "the first step is complete."

"It seems so simple," Leigh marveled.

"Why shouldn't it be? After all, much as I dislike Lysette even I must admit that she is beautiful and Kit's painting of her is actually quite extraordinary. It deserves a place of honor at the showing."

"When Nicholas sees it. . ." Leigh whispered.

"When Nicholas sees it," Rosalyn took up with undisguised satisfaction, "Lysette will be fortunate to escape with her life. Particularly when he sees it while surrounded by a mob of his colleagues and clients."

"Perhaps this isn't so wise after all," Leigh mused. "Perhaps. . ."

Rosalyn seized her wrist and dug her nails into Leigh's tender flesh. "It's too late for misgivings now," she hissed. "You've thrown in your lot with me and there's no way out. You may as well do your part because as easily as you see me destroying Lysette, I can destroy you!"

Leigh shivered, recognizing Rosalyn for the dangerous foe she had already proven she could be.

"I wil do my part," she promised.

"See that you do. Take the sketch I gave you. Slip it among Lysette's things but not until the night of the ball. We don't want her finding it before Nicholas has a chance to see it and we don't want him to see it before he sees the painting. Its purpose is to confirm all his suspicions. It will prove that Lysette knew about the painting."

"I'll see to it," Leigh promised.

"Good."

Rosalyn smiled as they turned into the courtyard of the D'Everaux's townhouse. Nicholas had come to her once after vowing that their affair was over. Who was to say it couldn't happen again?

When Leigh returned to the Callaways', she found Lysette in the rear parlor studying sketches brought by Madame Coquillon, a fashionable, exclusive, and expensive modiste.

"But exactly what color is wisteria?" Lysette was asking.

"It is lavender, madame," the dressmaker replied. "Well, perhaps it is not quite lavender. Let me see. It is almost orchid but not quite lilac. It is—well—it is wisteria."

Lysette sighed. "If you say so, madame. But please, this gown must be perfect. This ball is to be a very grand occasion and I must look as well as I can."

"You will be beautiful, madame," the dressmaker promised. "Eh, bien, how could you help it, non?"

Lysette glanced ruefully at the bulge in her gown. "How indeed," she agreed self-mockingly.

"Ah, madame," the modiste murmured slyly. "Do not think the other ladies will peer down their noses at you because you are with child. Non, non. They will look at your husband and envy you." She rolled her eyes comically. "What a man!"

In spite of herself, Lysette had to giggle. Though more recently than she cared to remember she would have angrily denounced such a statement or, at best, met it with cool disdain. Now she had to agree with all her heart. And particularly after last night.

Last night. Her eyes grew distant, dreamy. There had never been a night like that. No two people could possibly have shared the ecstasies she and Nicholas had found together. It was impossible—unthinkable.

She sighed, not realizing that Madame Coquillon watched the emotions flitting so plainly across her face.

How in love she is, the dressmaker thought enviously. It shines in her eyes. What must it be to share a love with a man like Nicholas Callaway? She is a fortunate woman, this fillette.

Realizing that she had been daydreaming, Lysette flushed.

"Pardonnez, madame. My thoughts were off in the clouds."

Up in the bedchamber, more likely, Madame Coquillon mused, though she knew better than to say so.

"Quite all right, madame," she assured Lysette. "I imagine you were thinking of how beautiful your new gown will look at the ball."

"Of course. You're exactly right," Lysette agreed, too quickly.

Tactfully hiding her amusement, the dressmaker gathered her sketches and left amidst the promises that Lysette's gown would be far more beautiful than any other woman's at the gala. Though Lysette did not believe a word of the woman's flattery, she was far too happy that afternoon to care.

Humming softly to herself, she went to her sewing room where she found Leigh busily stitching at an exquisite nightshirt for the baby.

"I had no idea you'd come back," she told

Leigh. "You should have come into the back parlor. Madame Coquillon had the sketches for my gown. It's quite lovely, or at least it will be. When we go to the charity ball, I—Oh! You've stabbed yourself!"

She hurried to press a handkerchief to the bloody puncture on Leigh's finger but not before an ugly splotch had marred the creamy perfection of the tiny nightshirt.

"I'm sorry," Lysette apologized. "Did I startle you?"

"No, I was clumsy," Leigh disagreed.

Lysette sadly examined the bloody silk. "Perhaps Mrs. Jonelle can get the stain out."

"Never mind." Leigh snatched it roughly out of her hands. "I'll make another."

"Nonsense. You've put so much work into that one; don't even think of. . ."

"Dammit, I said I'd make another!" Leigh shouted.

Lysette jumped back, startled, and watched as the other woman stalked to the fireplace where a low fire burned. Viciously, Leigh cast the tiny garment into the flames and watched as it blackened and crumbled.

"There!" she shrieked, her blue eyes blazing as she glared at Lysette. "Now it's gone. Forget it!"

"Leigh? Leigh!"

Lysette called out as Leigh stormed out of the room and disappeared in the direction of the stairs.

"Leave me alone!" came her reply echoing down the stairwell.

"But what . . . why. . ."

Lysette noticed Leigh's reticule lying on the table beside the settee. Picking it up, she felt the stiffness of the rolled up paper inside. For a moment she debated opening the purse and looking at the page—perhaps it was a letter from Michael. It might contain something that had upset her and there might be something she or Nicholas could do to help.

But no. It was not her place. What was in Leigh's reticule was Leigh's to share or not and it was not for her to pry where she had no business prying.

She tugged a bell rope and handed the purse to the maid who answered.

"Take this up to Mrs. Scofield," she directed. "Tell her she left it in the sewing room."

The maid curtsied and turned to leave but Lysette called her back. "Oh, and Kate? Tell her that if there is anything troubling her, I'd like to help if I can."

The maid left and Lysette sank onto the settee. She wanted to help Leigh—Leigh's violent outburst had both confused and upset her. Still, she could do nothing if Leigh refused her help.

Shrugging, she leaned back and pondered the problem, but the much more pleasant subject of Nicholas and their newfound happiness soon replaced all thoughts of Leigh and whatever might be bothering her. She felt a growing excitement at the thought of attending the charity ball on Nicholas's arm. For the first time they would be entering society as a real couple. For the first time she felt she was truly Nicholas's wife, the mother of his child. For the first time she could think of him as her husband, her lover, her friend. For the first time since her marriage over six months before, she was utterly and inexpressibly happy.

The night of the ball arrived and Lysette twirled delightedly before the cheval glass in the bedchamber she was once again sharing with Nicholas.

Her gown, despite Madame Coquillon's vacillating between orchid and lilac, was a breathtaking shade of lavender that, in some lights, seemed to take on a pink luster. The raised waistline was encircled by a wide silk sash and the skirt was wonderfully full. It hid Lysette's pregnancy but at the same time its very styling proclaimed it. In it she felt delicate and very beautiful.

"How lovely it is," Mimette breathed, lifting aside the hanging cascade of curls to slide an amethyst eardrop into Lysette's lobe. Around Lysette's neck she clasped a necklace of amethysts set in silver.

"Madame Coquillon should have a bonus," Lysette agreed. "I confess when she first told me her plan for the gown I was skeptical. But she is truly, truly a wizard with her needles and threads."

"That she is, my dear," Nicholas said from the doorway.

Slowly, seductively, Lysette turned before

him. She did not need to have him tell her how beautiful she looked; it was there for her to see in his eyes.

She went to him and slid her hands up the satin revers of his coat.

"Oh, Nicholas, you are magnifique, as always."

He threw back his head and laughed. "Little flirt," he chided gently. "Stop looking at me that way or we'll never make it to the ball."

"I don't care if we don't go," she whispered. She caressed his cheek. "Let's stay at home."

"Shameless hussy," he teased, but his voice was husky and his eyes glowed with the warmth of his quicksilver passion. "We cannot disappoint Leigh. She wants very much to go."

Lysette pouted prettily. "Oh, very well. If you don't want to be alone with me."

"Cherie, I always want to be alone with you. But mon dieu! In these past weeks you have grown into an insatiable vixen. Where has my demure Lysette gone? Where is the shy little girl I married?"

"She has changed, Nicholas, into a woman who loves you. Who desires you. Would you rather I didn't?"

"Good God, no! But duty calls, darling. We must save our pleasures for later."

Sighing, Lysette slipped her arm through his and they left the bedchamber. As they went down the hall, Nicholas rapped his knuckles against Leigh's door.

"Almost ready?" he called.

"Almost," came the muffled reply from within.

Lysette and Nicholas went downstairs to wait for her and it was not until she heard the sound of their footsteps on the stairs that Leigh slipped out of her room and scurried up the hall to their chamber.

She opened the door and slipped inside.

"Pardon, madame," Mimette said, startled by Leigh's unexpected appearance. "The madame and monsieur have already left."

"I see," Leigh said nervously, disarmed by Mimette's presence in what she thought to be a deserted room. "Thank you, Mimette."

Cursing beneath her breath, she left the room and went downstairs. Kit's sketch was concealed in a fold of her cloak but she knew she couldn't wait to conceal it in Lysette's room. She didn't dare take it to the ball—there was too much risk of discovery and too little chance that she would be able to plant it in Lysette's room upon their return.

At the bottom of the stairs, she made a show of searching for something.

"Anything wrong, Leigh?" Nicholas asked, appearing at the salon door.

"I've forgotten something," she replied distractedly, one eye and one ear cocked toward the stairs.

"What?"

"Oh, just my . . ." She paused, praying

for Mimette to finish tidying up after Lysette and leave the room. At last, from above, came the sound of a door closing and footsteps retreating toward the backstairs.

She flashed Nicholas an apologetic smile. "Never mind, I'll just run up and get it."

He gave the tall case clock a pointed look. "Better hurry. We're late as it is."

"Be right back," she promised, scurrying up the stairs.

At the end of the stairs she paused to be sure he hadn't decided to follow. When she was certain, she ran to their room and let herself inside. Mercifully, the chamber was empty this time. Only a single lamp burned on a table before the windows.

Leigh glanced around the room trying to decide upon the best place to conceal the sketch. It had to be someplace entirely Lysette's. Someplace Nicholas would not have had occasion to look before.

She slid open the large center drawer of Lysette's dressing table. Perfect! It held only Lyste's belongings. Nicholas would have had neither the interest nor the inclination to look there. Unless—

Lysette's vinaigrette lay there. It was unused; she was not prone to fainting spells. After the ball, however, she might find a use for the smelling salts.

Smiling to herself, Leigh slid the sketch into the drawer and laid the vinaigrette atop it. Her heart pounding with apprehension, she let herself out of the room and went down to join Nicholas and Lysette as they left for the ball.

# CHAPTER 25

The Royal Street entrance of the St. Louis Hotel was aswarm with carriages as Nicholas reached up to help Lysette and Leigh descend. The cream of New Orleans society was there and the distinguished men in their dashing evening dress and beautiful women in their swaying silk skirts and glittering jewels moved in a body toward the staircase that would take them up to the magnificent ballroom with its soaring painted ceiling—the masterwork of Domenica Canova.

"Nicholas, wait, we've lost Leigh!" Lysette cried as they were propelled forward by the irresistible force of the surging crowd.

Nicholas glanced back over the heads of most of the people around him. "She's there. She's coming. We'll see her once we reach the top."

"Shouldn't you go back for her?"

"Darling, in the first place, there's no going back in this mob. In the second, I'm afraid if I left you alone, you might be crushed."

By the time they'd reached the top, Lysette felt as though she'd been squeezed like an orange. She paused to shake out her skirts and noticed that more than one grand old dowager strolling on the landing was staring at her. More than one man was openly ogling her.

It's only because we appear in public so seldom, she told herself. Still, it was annoying to be treated like a sideshow curiosity.

"Perhaps I should go back and try to find her," Nicholas mused aloud.

"What? Oh, Leigh. Whatever you think best, Nicholas."

She noticed, with a growing sense of bewilderment, that a few of the ladies were giving her wide berth as they passed. One, forced to pass quite closely, actually drew in her skirts to avoid their touching Lysette's. Across the landing, a gentleman clamped his pince-nez onto his nose and stared until his dour-faced wife swatted him with her fan.

What in the world is going on? Lysette wondered.

"Here you are," Nicholas said, drawing Lysette's attention back to Leigh who had at last appeared. "I was about to mount a rescue attempt."

Leigh smiled wanly. "I thought you'd have already gone inside."

"What? And leave you defenseless?" Nicholas tugged one of her curls playfully. He offered each lady an arm. "Shall we?"

They were nearly to the door when Elizabeth appeared. Her face was starkly pale and she trembled visibly.

"Mother?" Nicholas was instantly filled with concern. His first thought, and

Lysette's, was that his father had been again taken ill.

"Take me home, Nicholas," she asked, her voice quavering.

"Home? But why? What's wrong?"

"Just take me home. And Lysette as well. She must come."

"Mother, please, tell me what it is? Is it father?"

"No, no, he's fine. He's at home. I came with the Fosters."

"Then what. . ?"

"Why, Nicholas, darling!"

Seemingly from nowhere, Rosalyn appeared. Instinctively, Lysette drew closer to her husband. Rosalyn had never looked more beautiful, it seemed to her, nor more dangerous.

She tapped his arm with her fan, her green eyes glittering. "Why are you tarrying out here? I should have thought you'd want to go right in. The art showing is in there, just outside the ballroom."

"Nicholas—" Elizabeth entreated, grasping his arm.

Rosalyn spared her a single, disdainful glance. "I thought you'd be eager to see Lysette's portrait."

"Portrait?" Lysette repeated, confused.

"What portrait?" Nicholas demanded.

"Why Kit's portrait, of course."

"I canceled that commission."

"Well, this isn't that portrait." She widened her eyes. "Oh, Lysette, I am sorry. Was it supposed to be a surprise? Or perhaps a secret?"

"What the hell are you talking about, Rosalyn?"

She pointed a delicate finger over her shoulder. "In there, darling. See for yourself."

Leaving Lysette, Leigh, and Elizabeth to trail in his wake, Nicholas strode away intent upon discovering what portrait that damned Stratton had had the colossal nerve to paint after he had withdrawn his permission.

He entered the long, wide corridor that had been turned into a gallery for the evening. The crowd milling about parted as he passed as though knowing without being told what it was he sought. They watched, spellbound, not wanting to miss the moment when he found what he was looking for.

It didn't take long. The canvas, its engraved brass plaque reading, "The Essence of Innocence—K. Stratton" had been mounted in a magnificent gold frame and hung at the far end of the corridor all alone, bathed in the glowing light of a crystal-draped chandelier.

Nicholas stopped and stared. Had the subject been anyone else, he would have been struck by the breathtaking beauty of the work, entranced by it as had been so many others that night. As it was, all he could see was his wife, his Lysette, displayed there for all and sundry to ogle. All he could picture in his mind's eye, was Lysette posing for Stratton in that god-forsaken, filthy sty he called a studio.

Twenty yards behind him, Lysette stopped.

Flanked by Elizabeth and Leigh, she saw the portrait at the same time as Nicholas. Unlike him, she saw neither its beauty nor its tawdriness—she saw in it only the betrayal of a friendship offered in innocence.

Then she saw something else—she saw the shudder of outrage course through Nicholas's body. He turned toward her and his face was the face of a stranger—a stranger gone mad with fury.

"You bitch!"

Though the words were hissed through gritted teeth, they may as well have been shouted, so silent had the throng crowding the gallery fallen.

"Nicholas. . ." She raised trembling hands entreatingly toward him.

"I'll kill you. By God, I'll kill you!"

He moved toward her, stalking her like a great killer cat. She fell back a step, then two. She couldn't breathe; it was as if his powerful hands were already about her throat. Tears stung her eyes. She shook her head in mute, terrified denial.

As if cued by some unheard signal, several of the men came forward and seized Nicholas. He struggled, cursing them, cursing Lysette and Kit.

"Get her out of here!" one of the men shouted.

Lysette stood frozen watching as Nicholas fought to throw off the restraining hands that were all that stood between her and the bloodlust that burned in his black eyes. She cried out as Leigh and Elizabeth seized her arms and pulled her backward toward the staircase.

Elizabeth shouted for her carriage as they stumbled down the stairs. They were oblivious to the eyes—the startled, curious, sneering eyes—that followed them as they went.

"Where should we go?" Leigh asked as they bundled Lysette into the carriage.

"Home," Lysette said softly, sadly. "Take me home."

"Lysette," Elizabeth reasoned. "When they let Nicholas go. . ."

"He'll come for me," Lysette acknowledged. "He'd find me wherever I went." She took her mother-in-law's hand between her two. "But, Elizabeth, I am innocent! I did not pose for that portrait. I swear it!"

"I believe you," Elizabeth vowed. "But Nicholas. . ."

"Nicholas. . ." Lysette repeated, resigned to the fact that even if she could get him to listen to her, she could not hope to make him believe.

She sat back against the seat, her head cradled on the tufted velvet. She longed to be home, in her room, in her bed.

Leigh, watching, wondered what she would think if she knew that at home, waiting in that room, was the evidence that would seal her doom.

Undressed and tucked into bed, Lysette lay in the shadowy bedroom listening to the soft rain that had begun to fall shortly after they had reached home. A lamp burned before the window and in its glow she could see the rivulets that ran down the panes. Usually rain comforted her; its steady beating on the roof and the windows soothed her. But tonight it seemed merely a reflection of the tears she could not quite seem to shed. She was waiting . . . waiting . . . listening in the darkness for the sound of the carriage wheels, the horses' hooves, the sound of Nicholas's voice calling her down to face her punishment.

It came.

"Lysette!"

She stiffened beneath the quilts. Her heart leapt; her blood raced. She lay still, unable to move.

"Lysette!"

His thunderous voice echoed up the stairwell and reverberated along the corridor. Obediently, resignedly, she pushed back the quilts and slid from the bed. Barefoot, her billowing gown flowing about her, she padded down the hall and down the first flight of stairs.

"Leave her alone, Nicholas," Elizabeth's voice as saying. "Give the matter time."

"Time? Time! Time for what, pray? How many lovers should a husband tolerate before he takes his bitch-wife to task?"

"There's been a hideous mistake. . ."

"Indeed there has, madame! And it happened the day I married that little French slut!"

"Nicholas! I will not hear. . ."

Elizabeth's words were cut off as Lysette appeared on the landing. In her demure, lace-trimmed gown of pristene white, her chestnut curls twining about her shoulders and spilling down her back, she looked like a child, a mere girl—the phrase leapt to Nicholas's tortured mind—the Essence of Innocence.

Leigh and Elizabeth grabbed his arms as he moved toward the stairs but he shook them off as though they were but bothersome puppies. He mounted the stairs slowly, deliberately, but Lysette stood her ground.

"I did not pose for that painting, Nicholas," she said at last, her voice surprisingly steady considering the wild fluttering of her heart within her breast.

"Liar!" he hissed. "How many times did you go to Stratton before Rosalyn caught you together?"

"Never!"

"How many times did you stand before him that way letting him feast his eyes on you? Bitch!"

"Never!"

"How many times did he throw down his brushes and come to you there in that filthy hole he calls a studio? How long were you his whore!"

"Never!" She screamed in his face as he mounted the last step. "Never!"

"Liar!"

Raising his arm, he backhanded her viciously sending her reeling into the settee that stood on the landing. Below, both Elizabeth and Leigh screamed but neither Lysette nor Nicholas heard them.

A red haze seemed to cloud Lysette's vision as she slid to the floor, dazed. The great dark shape that was Nicholas loomed over her. A sharp, searing pain shot through her and she curled in agony.

"I didn't pose for it, Nicholas," she breathed, as he forced her onto her back. "I didn't!"

"He'll never touch you again," Nicholas hissed, his face close to hers. "He'll never see you again."

His hands were caressing as they moved over her throat, but then they tightened—tightened—and the world seemed to whirl around her.

"Oh, God!" Elizabeth moaned. "He's going to kill her!"

She started up the stairs unaware that Leigh had backed away. The horror of what she'd been a party to was just beginning to dawn on Leigh. She'd thought to destroy a love—a marriage—she had never taken Nicholas's violent temper fully into account.

She came back to herself and saw Elizabeth on the landing, her small fists pounding Nicholas's broad back. He seemed unaware that she was there—unaware that there was anyone in the world save him and the woman he loved; the woman he now sought to kill.

"Nicholas!" Leigh shrieked.

Bounding up the stairs, she clawed at his hands as they tightened on Lysette's throat.

"Let her go, Nicholas," she wept. "Stop this; stop it! She didn't pose for the painting. She didn't! It was all my doing—mine and Rosalyn's. Nicholas, please, listen to me! We did it! We stole the painting from Kit. Lysette never saw it before tonight!"

It seemed an eternity passed before Nicholas's black eyes turned on her.

"We did it!" Leigh repeated. "She's innocent—innocent! Let her go, Nicholas, for the love of God!"

Nicholas's fingers slackened on Lysette's bruised throat. She lay before him half-conscious, her face mottled, her throat red as fire with the livid marks of Nicholas's fingers.

"You—" he breathed, gazing at Leigh, stunned.

Tears of shame and fright spilled down Leigh's cheeks. "Yes, we did it. She had no part in it—none."

"Good God," he breathed. He looked down at his hands as though they belonged to a stranger. He heard Lysette's ragged, painful gasps, saw the spasmodic jerkings of her body as she fought for every breath. The enormity of his action dawned on him and the rage drained out of him, leaving him limp with shock at the force of his own fury.

"Why?" he demanded of Leigh. "Why, in heaven's name. . ."

A soft, anguished moan from Lysette halted his words. He looked down and found her shuddering with pain, her knees drawn up, her arms clasped about herself.

"Mother. . ." he asked helplessly.

Elizabeth looked up at him and her pale, porcelain cheeks were wet with tears.

"Send for the doctor, Nicholas," she ordered, weeping. "She's losing the baby."

# CHAPTER 26

As he had for the greater part of the three days since Lysette's miscarriage, Nicholas sat sprawled across the sofa in the burgundy parlor. A glass of bourbon, never allowed to remain empty for long, was loosely clasped in one hand. With the other hand, he rubbed at the prickly three-day growth of beard he had not bothered to shave off.

There was a movement in the doorway and he turned red-rimmed eyes toward Leigh. They narrowed and the glitter of hatred in them—the only outward trace of emotion in his face—was terrifying to Leigh who had loved him too dearly for all their sakes.

"I'm leaving now," she announced, not daring to meet his eyes.

"You'll excuse me if I don't see you off," he snarled.

"Nicholas, I. . ." she began, but he turned his head away. Elizabeth appeared at Leigh's elbow.

"The carriage is waiting."

Though she could have expected nothing more, Leigh was wounded by the undisguised disgust in Elizabeth's voice. They'd been there together in that house for the past three days—three days in which Lysette had fought for her baby's life and, failing that, now fought for her own. In all those three days, Leigh had not allowed herself to forget her own part in the tragedy, nor had Elizabeth and Nicholas allowed her to forget.

Not once had she been allowed into Lysette's room—not once had either Elizabeth or Nicholas looked at her with anything less than contempt.

Turning away from the parlor door, Leigh went with Elizabeth through the entrance hall to the door which already stood open.

They're so anxious to see me leave, she thought to herself. She glanced back at the house she knew she would never enter again. How Michael was going to view her disgrace she couldn't begin to imagine, but she knew it would spell the end of any semblance of a real marriage between them.

"Elizabeth," she said softly, knowing there was no point in concealing anything from this woman who already loathed her. "There is a sketch in Lysette's dressing table. I put. . ."

"I found it," Elizabeth told her curtly. "I burned it."

"I need to tell you. . ."

"Good-bye, Leigh," Elizabeth interrupted icily.

With a swish of her skirts, she told the butler to see Mrs. Scofield to her carriage, then left Leigh standing forlorn in the entrance hall.

She returned to the parlor and found Nicholas, his elbows propped on his knees, his head in his hands.

"I don't know why I'm punishing Leigh," he said miserably. "I was the one who tried to kill her—I was the one who murdered my child—my son."

There was little Elizabeth could offer by way of comfort—too much of what he said was true. But even if it was Nicholas who had actually precipitated Lysette's miscarriage, she would always hold Leigh responsible for helping to set the wheels in motion. It was on Leigh's shoulders that the blame for the loss of her grandson would always and forever rest.

"Mr. Callaway?"

Nicholas and Elizabeth turned to find the doctor, Richard Veret, standing in the doorway. Nicholas rose.

"I think you'd better come up, sir."

Nicholas pressed his glass into his mother's hand. "She's better?" he asked anxiously. In the past three days Lysette had had but a few moments of half-consciousness.

The doctor's bushy white brows drew downward. "She's dying," he said bluntly.

Nicholas's mind reeled. "Dying! She can't be! Why can't you help her!"

The doctor led the way to the stairs. "Because there's nothing really wrong with her. There were no complications following the miscarriage."

"Then why is she dying?"

At the head of the stairs, the doctor removed his pince-nez and shrugged. "Because, sir, she doesn't want to live."

"But why?"

"I think you're the one who had best discover that for yourself and, if you can, convince her to survive."

Running a hand through his hair, Nicholas let himself into the sun-filled chamber where Lysette lay. The bright, cheerful glow of the afternoon sun made her seem all the more pitiful as she lay on snowy satin pillows that were no whiter than her drawn face. Her hair, once so glowing and filled with vibrant life, hung lank and lusterless about her shoulders. Her hands, the skin bloodless and translucent, lay limp on the pink satin coverlet which was mercifully drawn up to her chin hiding the hideous purple and yellow bruises on her throat.

"Lysette?" Nicholas said softly as he approached the bed. He didn't notice the nurse who rose and left the room with a whispering of her rustling silk skirts.

He sat on the edge of the bed and took one of Lysette's cool, limp hands in his. "Lysette?"

Her eyelids fluttered, then lifted. She squinted in the bright sunlight. Nicholas went to the windows and drew the draperies plunging the room into shadowy twilight.

"Nicholas?" she breathed, her voice weak, hushed, hoarse.

"I'm here." He sat gingerly on the edge of the bed, determined not to jar her any more than necessary.

She raised a hand to him and he lifted it to his lips.

"Nicholas, where is the baby?"

"The ba—" He caught his breath, realizing that she believed she had given birth safely.

"Is he handsome?"

"Very handsome, my love," he lied softly.

She smiled weakly. "Will you take care of him, Nicholas? Will you love him?"

"We both will, once you're well," he whispered.

A frown touched her brow. "Promise me, Nicholas. . ."

"Anything."

She reached up and touched his face and he could not suppress a shiver at the death-like chill of her fingers.

"When you marry again, make sure she will be kind to him."

"Oh, God," he moaned, guilt and sorrow overwhelming him.

"Nicholas?" she prompted. "Promise."

"You are my wife," he told her. "The only wife I'll ever have—the only wife I'll ever want."

"Promise me, Nicholas," she persisted stubbornly.

"I love you, Lysette," he told her fiercely. "You must get well. You will! Do you hear me!"

"But, Nicholas, why should you want. . ."

"Promise me, Lysette, that you'll try!"

Disbelief and wonder shone in her eyes as she gazed up at him. "Do you mean it? Do you actually want me to. . ."

"Yes, I do! Say you will!"

"I will," she breathed.

The nurse, having returned, touched Nicholas's shoulder.

"She must rest now," she told him. "She's very weak."

Nicholas nodded. He kissed Lysette's fingers and stared hard into her eyes one last time. "You will!" he insisted.

"I will," she agreed. She watched, hovering on the edge of unconsciousness, as he went to the door. She felt the nurse's soothing hand on her brow and, sighing, slid into oblivion.

Nicholas and Doctor Veret passed one another in the bedroom doorway. At the foot of the stairs, Elizabeth waited anxiously.

"She was awake," Nicholas told her.

"What did she say?"

Together they went into the parlor. Nicholas sat heavily on the sofa emotionally drained.

"She thinks she's borne the baby," he told his mother wearily. "She asked me to make sure my next wife is kind to him."

"Oh, Nicholas." Tears glimmered in Elizabeth's eyes. "Did you tell her the truth?"

"About the baby? Of course not. She'll learn the truth soon enough anyway. But I told her I want her to live. I told her I love her."

"Will she try now?"

"I think so."

"Thank God." Elizabeth's fingers unconsciously rolled the mother-of-pearl beads of her rosary. "The doctor says it may be difficult for her to conceive another child."

Nicholas laughed mournfully. "What makes you think she'd even want to try? Right now she doesn't know the baby is dead. She doesn't remember that I tried to kill her—that I killed our child." He swallowed hard. "When she does, she'll hate me and with reason. What on earth makes you think she'd ever want me within arm's reach of her again?"

Worn out by the sorrow and the horror of the past three days, Elizabeth put her head into her hands and wept. Nicholas watched her, helpless to comfort her. He started when Mrs. Jonelle entered and handed him a message that had just been delivered to the front door.

"What is it?" Elizabeth asked, wiping her tears.

Nicholas sighed and tossed the paper onto the table beside the sofa. "Edouard E'Everaux died of a heart attack this morning."

The ornate tomb of the D'Everauxs was located in Saint Louis Number One, one of the oldest cemeteries in the city. Among its inhabitants were numbered many of New Orleans's most illustrious residents. Not least among them was the D'Everauxs, whose iron-railed tomb, though only large enough to accommodate two members of the family at any one time, had served as a final resting place for eight generations. Like other tombs of its type, theirs had a hidden crypt into which the bones were pushed when it came time to inter another body. The coffin was taken out and burned just as the new one would be when its occupant had to make way for a new arrival.

Nicholas attended Edouard D'Everaux's funeral out of a sense of duty and respect for the deceased. But he could not—he would not—play the hypocrite to the point of offering condolences to the grieving widow.

Rosalyn cringed in the face of his unconcealed repulsion as their eyes met in the mortuary chapel. She knew, indeed it seemed as if all of New Orleans knew, that Lysette had lost her child and nearly her life as a result of the beating given her by her husband. That in itself they could have forgiven Nicholas if the rumors that Lysette and Kit Stratton were lovers had been proven to be true. But when it became known that Lysette was innocent—that her husband's jealousy had been whipped to a fever pitch through a lie concocted by his former mistress, Rosalyn had found herself shunned.

That husbands had mistresses and wives lovers was a fact of life among the sophisticated society of New Orleans. That a woman, supposedly a lady of sense and breeding, would deliberately goad a former lover into jeopardizing his wife's life and destroying his unborn heir was unheard of. She was a dangerous, unbalanced woman, they whispered behind their fans. She was not fit company for ladies of refinement. Despite her beauty and accomplishments she was far too dangerous for any man to consider as a mistress. In spite of the wealth Edouard had left her, she was much too unsound for any man to risk taking as a wife.

Even Edouard's death was being laid by many at his wife's door. Rosalyn had nagged him to take his business away from Nicholas—had tried to cajole him into doing everything in his power to ruin Nicholas. She had, so they said, pushed the old man into an early grave.

Needless to say, the black-clad widow received little in the way of sympathy from those who appeared at her husband's funeral. Still fewer agreed to appear at the D'Everaux's house afterward. It was, Rosalyn realized with a burgeoning fear, the harbinger of things to come.

The moment the ceremony had ended, Nicholas turned and strode toward his waiting carriage. Few present were surprised when Rosalyn lifted her black, crepe-trimmed, bombazine skirts and followed.

"Nicholas!"

He stopped just within the door and swung toward her. His swarthy face was so filled with disgust that she quailed at the sight of it.

"Have you no shame at all?" he demanded,

not caring who heard. "I know you have no scruples. I know you have no heart. But you could at least have a little respect for the man who gave you the means to masquerade as a lady."

Beneath the heavy veil that fell from her black bonnet, Rosalyn blushed for the first time in years.

"I only wanted to ask," she murmured, "if Lysette is. . ."

"She'll live," he snapped.

"Thank God."

His mocking laughter was spine-chilling in that place of death.

"Don't bother," he snarled. "Hypocrisy doesn't become you, madame. You're a bitch par excellence. Act the part you play the best. And I will tell you one thing more since I do not expect to speak to you again. Tell your cousin that neither you nor he is to approach me or any member of my family in any way at any time in the future. You have both done enough harm. Do you understand?"

"Yes," she whispered.

"Good. Good-bye, madame. I trust we'll not be meeting again."

Forlorn, Rosalyn watched him climb into his carriage and drive away. She had lost him, even in her befuddled mind she knew with awful certainty that he would never be able to bear the sight of her much less return to any semblance of their former relationship. But even though she knew she'd lost him, even though she knew she had put

Lysette through the agony of losing the child she had cherished, it wasn't enough. She would make Lysette pay and pay and pay for the sin of winning Nicholas's love. And she would make Lysette pay and pay and pay for of ceasing to love her.

Weary, depressed, Nicholas stepped out of his carriage and climbed the steps to his front door. He entered the hall and handed his hat and coat to the butler. Elizabeth had gone home. With Lysette's newfound will to live, she was well enough for Mrs. Jonelle to care for. The nurse had been dismissed and Dr. Veret called once a day rather than spending hours at her bedside.

Now Nicholas looked up as Mrs. Jonelle appeared at his side.

"How is she?" he asked.

The housekeeper couldn't seem to meet his eyes. "Well, monsieur," she replied. "She asked that you come up as soon as you returned."

"Is anything wrong?" He remembered her hysterics upon realizing she'd lost the child she'd thought she'd borne. He'd held her all night, rocking her gently, soothing her. She'd quieted at last near dawn and had seemed to accept her loss as well as could be expected. But the doctor had warned him to expect bouts of melancholia which could occur at any time.

"It's not the baby," the housekeeper assured him, reading his thoughts in his eyes.

"Then what?"

"She wouldn't tell me. She just asked to see you."

Nicholas climbed the stairs and went to Lysette's room. The draperies were drawn back and the sun-filled room seemed cheerier than it had for many days, owing to the vases of flowers he'd had placed there.

Amidst it all, Lysette, pale and delicately beautiful in a lace-frothed nightdress, lay propped on satin pillows in the middle of the wide testor bed.

"Cherie," Nicholas murmured, sitting on the edge of the bed. He took her hand in his and raised it to his lips but she firmly drew it away. He frowned. "Anne said you wanted to see me as soon as I returned."

"I did," she confirmed coolly.

"What's wrong?"

"Nothing. I want you to give me something, Nicholas."

He smiled fondly. "Anything; you know that you have only to ask. What is it you want, darling?"

Her russet eyes glinted with a hint of their old fire. "A divorce."

# CHAPTER 27

"You want what!"

"You heard me." She eyed him as though he were a none-too-bright child. "A divorce, Nicholas. That means. . ."

"I know what it means," he snarled. "You must be crazy to even ask such a thing."

"I assure you I am not mad nor delirious. In fact, I have never been more rational in my life. I want a divorce."

"It's out of the question." Turning his back on her, he went and stood at the windows. Outside, the courtyard garden bloomed with riotous color but neither it nor the warming spring sunshine gave him an instant's pleasure.

"I should think you would be willing to at least discuss the matter."

He swung toward her, his body blotting out the sunlight and throwing her into shadow. "Should you? And just why in the hell should you think a thing like that?"

Lysette shrugged. She had pondered this move long and hard until she'd made her decision. Once made, however, she'd managed to convince herself that Nicholas would undoubtedly desire the end of their marriage as fervently as she did. His refusal was as irritating as it was unexpected.

"After all," she reminded him, "Rosalyn is a widow now. If you and I were divorced—"

"Rosalyn!" he spat. "Sweet Jesus, Lysette! I gave you credit for more sense than that! You can't truly imagine for one instant that I'd have anything more to do with that bitch after what she did."

"What did she do?" Lysette's eyes were wide with innocence.

"What did she. . ." Nicholas was plainly flabbergasted. "She cost us our son! She caused your miscarriage."

"No, Nicholas," Lysette disagreed bluntly, cruelly. "You caused my miscarriage."

Nicholas drew a deep, pained breath. His guilt over what he'd done still rode him sorely and would, he had no doubt, for the rest of his life. His only consolation was that he'd been goaded into doing what he'd done by Rosalyn and Leigh.

"I did what I did, Lysette," he ground out, "because I believed that you and Stratton—"

"I told you I hadn't posed for that portrait," Lysette snarled. "If you had believed me . . . if, for a moment, you had trusted me. . ."

"All right! I admit my guilt! Does that make you happy? I murdered my son, is that what you wanted to hear?"

They both fell silent, staring at one another, both consumed by grief and misgivings. At last, Nicholas waved a dismissing hand.

"This name-calling and bickering is getting

us nowhere. Let me just say, once and for all, that I will not give you a divorce. You are my wife; you will always be my wife. Don't ask me again."

Lysette opened her mouth to argue with him but he turned his back and wearily left the room.

The days passed and slowly, surely, Lysette's strength returned. Gratefully she left her bed and descended the stairs to the parlors that had seemed so inviting to her while she'd been confined to her room above.

Though she was nearly well and in no further danger, Mrs. Jonelle, Elizabeth, and the entire staff of Nicholas's house seemed determined to pamper her as if she were an invalid. That a great part of their concern came not out of worry for her health but out of sympathy for her loss was understood though the baby was never mentioned.

If there was one person beneath Nicholas's roof who was less than cosseting with Lysette, it was Nicholas himself. Though he had forbidden her to mention the subject of divorce again, she made her point in subtle ways that irritated him far more than any outright discussion ever could.

"I think I should go to Saint-Cloud for a while, Nicholas," she announced one evening at dinner.

"I can't possibly get away just now," he told her absently, never lifting his eyes from the papers he brought to the table to fill the void caused by their frequent, and lengthy, silences.

"I didn't say you should try," she pointed out. "I want to go—alone."

He glanced at her over the tops of the papers. "Why?"

"After all, it's my property. I should see how the season's planting has progressed. I should have been. . ."

"The planting has gone well," he told her. "I had a report from the overseer last week."

"Why didn't you tell me? It's my plantation, Nicholas."

"It is mine," he disagreed, his jaw set stubbornly.

"Mine!"

"According to the terms of our marriage contract. . ."

"Do you know what you can do with that damned marriage contract?" she demanded, bringing a flush to the cheeks of the maids who had entered the room with a fresh course.

"Will you shut up!" he shouted. "Saint-Cloud reverts to you after you give me a son!"

"I did give you a son, damn you! And what did you do to him!"

"You're a spiteful little bitch," he growled.

"And you're an arrogant, lying bastard," she snarled back. "And I'll never give you another son because you'll never touch me again."

"And you'll never own Saint-Cloud!"

She rose and the maids scurried to get out of her way. "So be it! You can put Saint-Cloud in the same place as that damned contract of yours!"

She stalked out of the room but Nicholas was after her in an instant. He caught her wrist as they passed through the parlor and jerked her backward.

Lysette kicked and scratched, clawing him like a wildcat.

"Let me go, damn you!" she shrieked. "Take your hands off me!"

"Listen to me!" he demanded, shaking her. "I said listen!"

Lysette ceased her struggles and stood quietly in his grasp but her bosom heaved and her eyes sparkled with the fires of her anger. She glared at Nicholas with undisguised hatred as he spoke in clipped, furious tones.

"The women in this house might cosset you, madame. My mother may pamper and spoil you. But to me you are a grown woman and my wife and as such you have certain responsibilities. You're going to accept those responsibilities and stop acting like an obnoxious brat."

"And if I don't?" she hissed, chin raised defiantly.

"If you don't, I'll treat you as I would treat any obnoxious brat; I'll turn you over my knee and paddle your backside until you can't sit!"

"You wouldn't dare!"

Nicholas's slow-growing grin was somehow predatory. "Oh, now you've said the wrong thing, my dear," he murmured softly.

Pulling her by the wrist, he dragged her over to the sofa and sat down. Lysette struggled against him but his was by far the superior strength. In a flurry of skirts and lacy petticoats, he pulled her down across his knees.

Lysette shut her eyes tight and tensed, waiting for the first blow to fall. Instead, she heard Mrs. Jonelle's soft, shocked gasp.

"I beg your pardon," she murmured.

Lysette struggled to rise from her undignified position but Nicholas held her fast.

"What is it, Mrs. Jonelle?" he asked so casually that one would never know he held his furious wife across his knees primed for a paddling.

"Dr. Veret has arrived for madame's examination."

"Thank you. Take him upstairs and tell him we'll be along in a moment."

The housekeeper left and Nicholas let Lysette go.

"Don't think of this as a rescue, my dear," he said, not yet releasing his hold on her wrist. "Think of it as a temporary reprieve. I've no doubt you'll get your spanking sooner or later."

Yanking her wrist out of his grasp, Lysette whirled away and stalked out of the room. She was halfway up the stairs when she heard Nicholas's footsteps following her.

"Where do you think you're going?" she demanded, arms akimbo.

"Why, to your room, of course, cherie," he answered matter-of-factly.

"Dr. Veret is going to examine me," she reminded him.

"Precisely. Your condition is of more than passing interest to me as well, you know."

"But you can't . . . you mustn't. . ."

He lifted a black brow and eyed her questioningly. Lysette flushed. It was perfectly acceptable for a lady's husband to be present while she was being examined by a male doctor; in fact, it was the exception for any man to allow his female relatives to be alone in the company of a physician. If the lady were not his wife, then a maid generally remained during the examination.

With a gnashing of her teeth, Lysette turned and led an amused Nicholas up the stairs and down to her room.

For what seemed an excrutiatingly long time, Lysette submitted to Dr. Veret's poking and prodding. It would have been bad enough at any time, but beneath Nicholas's watchful eyes it made her want to scream.

When at last the doctor was led away to wash, Lysette pulled her dressing gown around her and glared at her husband.

"I hope you enjoyed yourself, monsieur," she snapped.

"Don't be ridiculous," he snarled. "Contrary to what you believe, I did not choose to be here merely to annoy you. It is, after all, to my advantage to have a healthy wife. I am concerned for your welfare, you know."

"Are you?" She was frankly skeptical. "To be quite honest with you, I don't believe you give a tinker's. . ."

The door opened and Dr. Veret appeared. Lysette glared at Nicholas but said no more as the doctor took a seat opposite the bed.

"So far as I can tell, madame, you have suffered no permanent damage as a result of your losing your child. I must tell you, however, that it may be difficult for you to conceive again."

"But she could bear another child," Nicholas insisted.

"Oh, yes. I say it might be difficult—not impossible. There is always the chance. In any case, there is no real reason why you cannot try again right away . . ." He gave Nicholas a meaningful look over his spectacles. " . . . providing you use a little common sense."

Lysette blushed but Nicholas merely looked relieved. He turned a glimmering glance toward her but she averted her eyes.

"Thank you, doctor," she murmured as the men rose to leave the room.

"You're welcome, madame." The doctor smiled encouragingly as Nicholas escorted him from the room.

Lysette stayed where she was having neither the energy nor the inclination to get dressed and go back downstairs where there was every possibility of resuming her argument with Nicholas.

Why couldn't he simply give her the divorce she wanted? Their marriage was an unqualified disaster; wouldn't it make more sense to end it now? Have another child, the doctor said. No. No! The memories of her baby moving inside her, the love she had borne for the child were too recent. The pain of losing him was still too raw.

And having another child would entail going back to Nicholas's bed—something she had vowed never to do. She felt strong now; she was the mistress of her body, of her senses. She never wanted to put herself in Nicholas's hands again. He too easily overcame her defenses and held her senses in thrall.

She looked up, startled, as someone knocked at her door.

"Entrez?"

The door swung open and Mrs. Jonelle appeared with two maids. Immediately they went to work gathering her things from the dressing table and the chest of drawers.

"Wait! What are you doing?" Lysette demanded.

"Mr. Callaway has ordered your belongings taken back to his room;" the housekeeper explained.

"He did what! When?"

"Just now, madame. After the doctor left."

"Well, I won't have it! Here now!" She called back a maid who was about to disappear through the dressing room with her toiletries. "Bring those back this instant!"

"But, madame," the girl protested. "The monsieur said. . ."

"Bring them back now!" Lysette slid off the bed and tied the sash of her robe. "Don't touch anything else. I'm going to have a talk with 'the monsieur'!"

Furious, she stalked out of the room and down the stairs. After demanding to know where Nicholas had gone, she was directed to the study where he sat at his desk.

"Nicholas!"

He sat back in his chair apparently not in the least surprised to see her.

"My dear?"

"What is the meaning of telling Mrs. Jonelle to take my things into your room?"

He lifted his broad shoulders. "The doctor said we may . . . how shall I put this delicately . . . be intimate again."

"And if I don't wish to 'be intimate'?"

"You have no choice."

"I have no. . ." She suddenly found it difficult to breathe. "How dare you!"

He rose and came to her. His black gaze bore twin holes into her as he stared down from his far greater height.

"You are going to give me a child, Lysette. That was our agreement."

Lysette shivered, swallowing hard. "Dr. Veret said it might be difficult for me to conceive again."

A wolfish grin crept over Nicholas's face. "Then we'll have to try doubly hard, won't we, love?"

"I won't," she whispered. "I won't!"

His eyes narrowed, his mouth hardened. His hand caressed her cheek then gripped her chin painfully. When he spoke, his voice was low and filled with grim determination.

"Oh, yes, my love," he murmured, his lips against her ear, his breath hot on her cheek, "you will!"

# CHAPTER 28

"Do you know what you've done to me!" Kit roared, his normally placid features contorted with rage. "You've ruined me! Ruined me! My name is anathema to every one of my former patrons! They act as though I were carrying the plague! When I appear at their doors, it's as if they're planning to salt the earth behind me as I'm leaving!"

Rosalyn, pale and fragile in black silk, waved a languid hand. She was far too sunk in her own troubles to spare a care for her cousin's difficulties.

"If it's any consolation, Kit," she muttered, "there isn't a door in New Orleans open to me at this point either."

"Well, you deserve it."

"How dare you! I'm not the one who painted that disgusting portrait! I'll thank you to remember that!"

"No! But you're the one who put it on display! I never intended for anyone to see that painting! It was for me—me alone!"

Kit sank into a chair and glared at his cousin. "Didn't you even suspect what the public reaction would be to that painting? Nicholas Callaway's anger aside, you must have known that everyone else would be horrified!" He ran a shaking hand through his hair. "My God, every one of my former patrons has canceled their sittings. They all seem certain I'll turn out some embarrassing picture of their wives or daughters." He laughed hollowly. "Even Martin Ormsby. He said to me, 'I don't want no pitcher of my Adele buck nekked showin' up nowheres, sonny'."

In spite of her oppression, Rosalyn laughed at Kit's cruelly accurate impression.

"Adele Ormsby looks like one of Martin's beef cattle," she sneered.

"Exactly. But that doesn't seem to matter. They can't see that I painted Lysette out of love. The portrait was a celebration of her beauty—hers! It wasn't merely the act of a deranged painter choosing a random victim to humiliate."

They fell silent, each pondering their myriad troubles. At last Kit gathered the ambition to ask:

"What has become of the painting?"

Rosalyn lifted her narrow shoulders listlessly. "I don't know. You'd have to ask Collier Shaw. I hope I never lay eyes on the damned thing again."

"I want it back," he insisted, a glint of steel in his cerulean eyes.

"As I said, you'd have to ask Shaw. Perhaps someone bought it."

Kit leapt to his feet. "It wasn't for sale!"

"Darling, all the paintings at the exhibit

were for sale. The proceeds were to go to charity, you knew that." She laughed maliciously. "Perhaps your fair Lysette is even now gracing the barroom in some bordello. How fitting."

"I'll get her back!"

"Doubtless you'll give it your best attempt, Kit," she sighed, her momentary good humor having faded. "And I hope the two of you will live happily ever after in that slum you call home. In any case, there's no use worrying about it tonight." She glanced toward the window. Night had fallen. "Shaw's gallery is closed and he probably wouldn't welcome you at his home. No one does these days."

Kit wandered to Rosalyn's desk and sat down. Taking up a pen, he began doodling on one sheet of her black-bordered stationery.

"Have you heard how Lysette is?" he asked.

Bored, Rosalyn tugged the bell-rope and ordered brandy. "Lysette's health is scarcely a matter with which I concern myself, darling."

"Was she at Edouard's funeral?"

"Of course not. I'm surprised Nicholas came. As you might expect, he was hideously rude to me in front of everyone."

"Which you richly deserved."

"Oh, please! Let's not let this generosity of spirit become nauseating, dear! When you begin sympathizing with Nicholas. . !"

"I commiserate with him for what you did to his wife. I have no sympathy for him."

"What I did to his wife! I'm not the one who tried to kill her and almost succeeded! I'm not the one who threw her across the landing and brought on her miscarriage!"

Kit winced. He couldn't bear to think of Lysette being harmed. "All right! I simply asked if you'd heard how she was."

Rosalyn snatched her brandy from the maid's hands and snarled for her to leave the decanter within reach. She gulped down a snifter-full and poured herself another.

"I'll tell you what I know, if you promise to let the subject drop afterward."

"I promise," Kit agreed, sulking.

"Victoria Rendell has been having a lot of trouble with her gout. Dr. Veret has been attending her; he has also been attending Lysette. She asked him how Lysette was faring and he said she was up and about now, recovering very well." She sipped her brandy and waited a moment to give her next words more impact. "He said they are going to try for another child right away."

"Lysette and Nicholas?" Kit whispered, appalled.

"Well, hardly Victoria and Bernard Rendell, Kit. My God, Victoria must be at least. . ."

Kit ignored her sarcasm. "She can't!"

"She's his wife," Rosalyn purred. "He's determined to have a child."

"He can't put her through that again!"

"Calm yourself, Kit. It's really none of your affair, if you'll pardon the expression."

Leaving the desk, he began prowling the room restlessly. "She can't stay with him! Ros, she isn't safe with him! What if he turns on her again?"

"He wouldn't have 'turned on her' as you put it, at all if they had been left alone. From what Leigh Scofield said, they were on the edge of living happily ever after just before all this exploded in our faces."

"Leigh!" Kit's scowl faded a bit. "If I can talk to Leigh, perhaps she can help me. . ."

"Save your energy," Rosalyn warned. "Leigh has been packed off in disgrace to Buckland, there to wait her husband's wrath when he returns from Washington and discovers how she betrayed his best friend and his best friend's wife."

Kit jammed his hands into his pockets. "Then she's there alone. She's in that house with that man without a friend . . . a protector."

Rosalyn rolled her eyes. "Oh spare me! She's a woman, Kit. Nothing more. Don't romanticize everything. You make her sound like some fairy princess locked in a haunted castle with an ogre. Why don't you face the truth? You're not her knight in shining armor and she's not waiting for you to rescue her and carry her off to your enchanted palace."

"But I can't believe she's happy with him!"

"For sweet Christ's sake, will you let it go!" Rosalyn thrust herself to her feet and faced him, eyes blazing. "She is beyond your reach just as Nicholas is beyond mine! Haven't you learned that lesson yet! Nicholas would rather see her dead than with you or any other man!"

"I don't give a damn for Nicholas Callaway or what he wants!" Kit shouted back. "I'm going to get her out of there. The two of us, working together. . ."

"Oh, no!" Rosalyn shook her head vehemently. "You're not dragging me into this! I've had enough of Lysette Callaway and your gallantry!"

"It's your fault all this has happened!" he reminded her. "You owe it to me to help. . ."

"I owe you nothing!" she hissed. "I helped you establish yourself in New Orleans and you ruined it with your ridiculous painting. Now you're on your own!"

Kit started to speak but Rosalyn cut him off.

"I mean it, Kit! I'm leaving New Orleans tomorrow. I'm going to Fairhaven for Jocelyn's wedding and I intend to stay there a good, long time. You're welcome to come along if you like."

"I just came from there," he reminded her. "Your dear sister, Becca, gets on my nerves and a little of that boring husband of hers goes a long way." He shook his head. "Your precious niece, Jocelyn, is turning out to be a real little Tartar, by the bye. I pity the fool she's marrying."

"Then go somewhere else," she snapped. "But leave New Orleans." Something akin to compassion crept into her eyes as she reached out and touched his sleeve. "There's nothing for us here anymore, Kit. We, neither of us, have anything to keep us here anymore."

"I can't leave, Ros, not yet."

"Let her go. She'll never be yours."

Shrugging cryptically, Kit took his leave. But Rosalyn knew he hadn't heard a word. She knew he would never give up his dream of one day possessing Lysette.

She went to the desk and gazed down at the sheet of notepaper on which he'd been sketching. It was no surprise to see Lysette's face, faintly smiling, gazing back at her.

Though they quarreled; though it seemed they were forever at odds over something or other, Rosalyn bore a genuine affection for her cousin. When she thought of him trying to take Lysette from Nicholas, she knew a very real fear. Kit was not, had never been, and would never be, any match for Nicholas Callaway. In any real battle between them, Nicholas would crush Kit in the twinkling of an eye.

Determined to discover the whereabouts of his masterpiece, Kit made his way to Collier Shaw's elegant house on Esplanade Avenue. Though he fully expected to be turned away, the butler led him to the darkly-paneled study where Collier Shaw was examining a set of French prints he intended to display in his gallery.

"Come in, Kit," he invited cordially. "I would say you're a sight for sore eyes but the plain truth is that you're a sight, period."

Kit brushed ineffectually at his creased coat. "I've been running all over the city all day," he explained. "All of my patrons have taken their commissions away. I'm ruined."

Collier handed him a glass of wine which Kit accepted gladly though he would have preferred something stronger.

"I rather expected that they would, didn't you?" he remarked, sitting at his desk.

Kit nodded mournfully. "I did. Once I'd heard what had happened." He smiled weakly. "Quite frankly, I expected to be turned away from your door as well."

Collier stroked his grey moustache thoughtfully. "Well, my boy, I take some of the responsibility for your downfall. I should have realized that you never meant for that painting to be publicly displayed."

"I shouldn't have painted it," Kit muttered.

"Nonsense. It's the best thing you've ever done. You've finally found a way to release some emotion into your work. This could be the turning point in your career. Surely you must realize that."

"I realize nothing! Don't you understand? There is not a family in New Orleans who will commission. . ."

"New Orleans is not the world. You've a great talent. Go to London, better yet, Paris. Once you've become the rage in Europe, these small-minded cretins will hang their "Stratton's" over the front parlor mantel and brag to their friends that you were once in their employ."

"I don't want to leave New Orleans."

"That's tantamount to saying that you don't want to paint."

Kit shrugged. "I can paint. I can paint every moment of every day if I want to."

"You realize that the market for your work here—unless the piece was really extraordinary. . ."

"I'm well aware of my limitations here."

"Then why stay?"

Kit looked away and his silence spoke more eloquently than any words he might have uttered.

"Give it up, Kit." Collier's tone was surprisingly gentle. He had dealt with too many temperamental artists not to know how to coddle genius. "Callaway will never allow you near her again. From what I hear, she's a virtual prisoner in his house. When she does leave, she has an escort the likes of which hasn't been seen in this town since the days of the Spanish duennas."

Kit sighed. "I know your intentions are good, Collier, but I have already heard this lecture once tonight."

"By someone, no doubt, with your best interest at heart."

"By my cousin, Rosalyn."

Collier laughed. "Forgive me for saying so, but she's hardly the one to be giving advice."

"My thoughts exactly. But none of this is getting us anywhere. I had a reason for coming here tonight beside to garner sympathy from a graciously-lent ear."

"And that is?"

"My Essence of Innocence. I want to know what became of her."

Collier made a steeple of his fingers. "Regretably, she was sold."

"Sold!"

"Now, hear me out. Though I realized, unfortunately too late, that the model for your painting was not some ordinary girl you discovered somewhere on your travels, I had no notion that the portrait was there entirely by mistake. After all, I had dealt with your cousin before. More than once she's acted as your intermediary when you've been out of town. How was I to know this was not one of those times?"

"Who bought it?"

Collier spread his hands. "I can't tell you."

"Collier!" Kit half rose in his chair.

"I'm sorry, Kit. I am. But the buyer insisted upon anonymity and my reputation is at stake here." He sighed. "Forgive my saying so, but this entire episode has damaged my good name—to reveal the name of a client, to betray a confidence, could well spell the end of my business in this city."

"But she's mine, Collier, mine!"

"I'm sorry, Kit. There's nothing I can do."

Kit slumped in his chair, dejected. A stranger had her, his Lysette, his Essence of Innocence. He had put his heart into that work; it was as though his lifeblood had mixed with the paint to translate the vision in his mind into perfection on canvas. Even now, as he sat there, someone could be looking at her, seeing her not as he'd meant her to be seen but as something lascivious. They would not see the innocent purity of her beauty but merely the tawdry display of her naked flesh.

In fact, Kit was partly right. Not so far away, in another softly-lit study in another French Quarter mansion, a man sat gazing at Kit's masterpiece. But contrary to Kit's belief; he recognized the purity of spirit in which the portrait had been painted. And, perhaps unfortunately, he felt the adoration which Kit had poured into each and every stroke of the brush.

Nicholas stood before the painting, a knife in his hand. A part of him wanted to destroy the work, slash it into ribbons and cast it into the fire. Another part could not bear the thought of mutilating such a magnificent rendering of the woman who had enslaved his senses to the point of obsession.

The knife wavered, glinting in the lamplight. He had sent a representative back to the ball while waiting for the doctor to tell him if Lysette would live. It had seemed so important for him to possess the portrait—he'd had to prevent its falling into other hands. He had, from the first, planned to destroy it. But something had prevented him. This was not the first time he had locked himself in the study intending to destroy the painting.

With a groan of self-disgust, he cast away

the knife and returned the portrait to its place in the cabinet against the wall. No, tonight was not the first night he had stood before the painting knife in hand. Nor, it seemed, would it be the last.

# CHAPTER 29

"Going out?"

Lysette started, grasping the railing as she descended the stairs. At the foot of the staircase, maddeningly handsome in chocolate brown, Nicholas leaned indolently against the newel post.

"As a matter of fact, I am," she informed him coolly, drawing on the gloves of ivory kid that matched the ivory trimming on her hunter green day dress.

Coming down the stairs, she passed him with a haughty tip of her chin. "You needn't worry, Nicholas. My cadre of guards awaits."

She nodded in the direction of Mrs. Jonelle and Mimette who waited near the carriage outside the open door.

"I wouldn't have worried in any case, my love," he told her lightly. "I am merely concerned as to whether or not you are well enough to undertake the strains of a shopping expedition."

"Of course I'm well enough. You needn't act as though I were undertaking to explore darkest Africa. I'm only going to the bookshop."

"I'm glad to know you're regaining your strength, my dear."

Lysette stiffened as he drew too near. His hand touched her cheek—he drew his fingertips along her jaw teasingly.

"What do you want, Nicholas?" she demanded.

His arm snaked about her waist as he pulled her against him. His lips were but a kiss away.

"I thought you knew what I wanted, cherie," he murmured as his mouth captured hers.

"No!" she protested against his punishing lips. She wriggled in his arms. "Let me go!"

His arms held her fast, her struggles were but the flutterings of a fragile bird against his far greater strength. His mouth was teasing, savage, caressing, crushing. Lysette trembled, buffeted by an onslaught of emotions she had thought buried irretrievably beneath the avalanche of pain she'd suffered since the fateful night of the charity ball.

Nicholas felt her resistance lessening. He felt the first, tentative stirrings of a response as her lips trembled beneath his. He touched her lower lip with the tip of his tongue and her lips parted invitingly.

"Nicholas," she breathed, her hands roving hungrily over his broad back.

She was rudely jarred back to her senses as he released her and stepped away.

"Enjoy yourself, enfant," he said coolly, even as he turned and disappeared into his study.

Standing in the middle of the entrance hall, Lysette gaped after him. He had proven his point—damned if he hadn't! He could still make her dance to his tune—tremble at his touch.

"You bastard!" she shouted after him.

His only response was a deep rumble of laughter that wafted back to her from the depths of the mansion.

Stalking out to the carriage, she climbed in and threw herself down on the seat facing Anne Jonelle and Mimette.

"Anything wrong, madame?" the housekeeper asked.

"Only that I hope a plague takes that son of a whore!" she muttered.

"Which son of a—that is—which person would that be, madame?"

"Your master! May God damn him to hell for all eternity!"

She scowled, first out the window then at her two companions as they hurriedly crossed themselves and silently asked God to forgive her for uttering such a foul curse against her own husband.

As she lost herself amidst the rows of shelves of Arnaud Rivleau's bookshop, Lysette gradually forgot her anger against Nicholas. She would deal with him later—he needn't be so sure of himself just yet. He had given her fair warning that this was to be a fight to the end with the winner taking everything including the vanquished's pride and self-respect. She would find a way to beat him at his own game.

"Lysette?"

In the shadows of a tall bookcase that blocked the light of the hanging lamp, Lysette stiffened. She knew that voice. She glanced to the right and left certain that Mrs. Jonelle or Mimette could not fail to materialize like guardian angels. She saw no one.

"Lysette?"

Above the books on the shelf at her eye level, Lysette met the fervent stare of a pair of all too familiar sky-blue eyes.

"Kit!" she hissed. "Go away!"

He scooted around the end of the bookcase and sidled close to her all the while pretending to study the goldlettered, tooled leather spines of the books before him.

"I saw your carriage outside," he explained.

"I'm not alone!"

"I know. But your companions are on the other side of the shop. They didn't see me come in."

Her voice seemed to flutter with fear. "Please go away! This is too dangerous—for both of us!"

"I must speak to you!"

"We have nothing to say to one another!"

Monsieur Rivleau appeared at the end of the row. "Is there a problem, madame?" he asked.

Kit averted his face and Lysette flashed the bookseller a blinding smile.

"Nothing at all, monsieur," she assured him cheerily. "Everything is fine."

The elderly man eyed them suspiciously but went about his business. As his footsteps faded, Lysette turned on Kit.

"There! You see! He'll likely warn Mrs. Jonelle! Now leave me alone!"

"First you must tell me you believe that I had nothing to do with what happened! You must believe me, Lysette!"

"I do, truly I do. I know it was Rosalyn and Leigh's doing. Now go, quickly!"

"Is Nicholas being cruel to you?" Abandoning all pretense of discretion, Kit turned to her, his eyes drinking in the sight of her of which he had been too long deprived.

Lysette felt a fear akin to terror at the thought of being found here with him. Would Mrs. Jonelle think she had arranged this meeting? Would Nicholas!

"Kit, please," she begged. "I am watched."

She turned to leave but he seized her wrist.

"Wait! Tell me first that you know how I love you!"

"My God, Kit. . !"

"You know you can come to me whenever you wish, don't you? I'll keep you safe. Protect you."

"Yes, yes, I know!" she cried. "Now let me go!"

He released her and she hurried away, darting among the stacks of books trying to put as much distance as possible between them. Snatching a book from the shelf at random, she paid for it then left the shop before Kit had a chance to accost her in some other deserted corner.

"Are you all right, madame?" Mrs. Jonelle asked.

Lysette was pale, her hands shook, she had chosen a volume of German philosophy and Mrs. Jonelle knew she neither read nor spoke German nor knew anyone who did.

"I'm fine," Lysette assured her.

Mimette, facing backward in the two-seater carriage saw Kit step into the street and gaze after them. For a moment she thought of the promise Nicholas had exacted from her—a promise to tell him whenever Kit tried to make contact with Lysette. But, looking at Lysette, it was easy to see that she had neither planned their meeting nor enjoyed it. Having seen Lysette nearly swooning in Nicholas's arms in the entrance hall that morning, Mimette decided to keep her mouth shut and let nature take its course between her mistress and master.

From the moment Nicholas arrived home from work ("Early, wouldn't you know it!" Lysette had groused as she heard him whistling in the hall.) Lysette was jumpy as the canary about whose cage the hungry cat prowls. In his every glance she thought she saw a glimmer of suspicion; his every look seemed filled with knowing. But he said nothing and his silence seemed to hold more threat than any epithets he could have hurled at her.

Unable to bear any more, she retired to the comparative safety of her room as soon as possible. There, dressed in her summer gown of gossamer silk, Lysette sat on the window seat overlooking the garden. Mimette, brush in hand, sat behind her.

"You saw him, didn't you, Mimette?" she asked abruptly. She had been intercepting meaningful glances from the maid all afternoon and knew the cause.

"Madame?" the maid asked, vainly attempting to feign innocence of Lysette's meaning.

"Kit Stratton. You saw him at Rivleau's bookshop didn't you?"

"I saw him after we had left, madame," Mimette admitted. "He came out the door and watched us go."

"I didn't know he was there, I swear it. I didn't even know he'd returned to New Orleans. You believe me, don't you?"

"I do," Mimette assured her solemnly. "I saw the look on your face when we left. I knew you were afraid."

"Did you tell Nicholas?" she shook her head as Mimette averted her eyes. "Come now, Mimette, don't imagine I don't know you're to report on everything I do and everyone I see on our outings. I'm not so great a fool as to think that Nicholas would not make use of you."

"I didn't tell him," Mimette confessed. "It seemed to me that'd be making a fuss over nothing."

Impulsively, Lysette swiveled on the silken cushions and hugged the maid.

"Thank you, Mimette! Thank you!"

"It wasn't anything, madame," Mimette protested self-consciously.

"You believed me! You trust me! That is a great deal, Mimette. Particularly now."

There was a click of the latch and the squeak of hinges and Lysette and Mimette looked up to see Nicholas standing in the doorway. In the flickering light of the single lamp burning on the dressing table, he looked handsome as a god—and wicked as a devil.

"You may go, Mimette," he said quietly.

"No, Mimette, wait," Lysette contradicted. She rose, unaware of the way her gown clung to her for she wore nothing else on these sultry early summer nights.

"Go," Nicholas repeated firmly.

"No!" Lysette clasped Mimette's wrist as she would have beat a tactful retreat. "She hasn't turned down the bed yet, Nicholas."

"We are capable of that, cherie," he told her. "Out—now!"

Yanking her arm out of Lysette's hand, Mimette scurried from the room. The slamming of the bedroom door seemed deafening in the silent bedchamber.

"What do you want, Nicholas?" Lysette demanded, her voice quavering, betraying her nervousness.

He moved toward her, his purple damask robe swirling sensually about him.

"Nothing more than any man wants from

his wife, ma chere," he replied, his voice husky.

"No!"

He arched a coal-black brow. "No?"

"Not yet! I'm not well enough!"

"This afternoon you said you were fine."

"I said I was well enough to go shopping."

He laughed and a chill coursed down her spine. "Cherie, shopping can hardly be less strenuous than making love. If you're worried, however, you may feel free to leave everything to me."

She held her hands out protectively but he came to her, pushed them aside, and swept her into his arms.

Lysette struggled as he carried her to the bed and lay her across it. His mouth found her throat, her shoulders, her breasts. His hands explored her, caressed her. She clenched her teeth against the probings of his mouth but her furious scream slid into an anguished moan as his hands found their way beneath her gown and moved hotly, insistently, over her skin.

Her fingers dug into the rich damask that covered his broad shoulders and back. Her kisses grew as fevered as his, her caresses grew more insistent, her body arched to meet his—imploring him to love her, to end this tormenting ravishment of her senses.

"Nicholas . . . Nicholas, please," she hissed as he parted her gown and lovingly kissed the ivory softness of her breasts. Her fingers buried themselves in the ebony silk of his hair as she wordlessly pleaded with him to continue.

She squirmed restlessly beneath him. Her hands slid to his waist and drew him closer. "Nicholas, now!"

She could not believe it when he drew away. His eyes were smoky with passion, sweat sheened his face, his chest. His breaths were short, raspy, harsh. His smile was terrible . . . triumphant.

"You see my dear?" he asked, moving off the bed and standing over her as she lay sprawled across the silk counterpane. "You are mine. Mine! Every part of you belongs to me. At a touch I can bring you alive. I can make you beg for me as once I begged for you. Only I can satisfy this hunger inside you. No one else—no one! Whenever I want you, I'll take you, and you'll come willingly, eagerly, to me."

"Nicholas. . ." she whispered, stunned, furious, aching with the pain of thwarted passion.

He steeled himself against the sight of her there. She was so beautiful. No other woman he'd ever seen could compare with her. He wanted her desperately; even the thought of taking her, loving her, threatened to rob him of his self-control.

But no, cruel as it was—cruel to him as well as to her—it was a lesson that needed to be learned. He'd had enough of her haughty ways, enough of her thinking he would be dictated to like some lovesick schoolboy (like Kit Stratton, a malicious voice whispered inside his head). He was her master and she would obey him in body as well as in mind and spirit.

"Good-night, my dear," he said as icily as he could manage.

Turning, he strode out of the room before he lost his fragile hold upon his own emotions and took her even as he had vowed not to.

Her fast-cooling passion giving way to fury, Lysette slid off the bed and ran through the dressing room to his door. She seized the latch with both hands and yanked it with all her strength. It was locked.

Doubling her fists, she pounded on the stout panels. "Open this door, damn you!" she screamed.

"Is that you, my love?" he asked innocently from the opposite side.

"You know damned well it is! Open this door!"

"But why?"

"I'm going to kill you!"

Nicholas's laughter only fanned her fury. "That's hardly incentive, sweeting," he murmured mockingly.

"Damn you, Nicholas!"

"Oh, and don't bother trying the hall door, darling," he said as she would have turned away. "It's locked as well."

"I hate you!" she hissed. "I hate you! I loathe you! I despise you!"

"Go to bed, enfant. You'll feel better in the morning."

Listening, Lysette could hear his footsteps

crossing the floor. She knelt and peered through the keyhole and saw him extinguish the lamps one by one. In the moonlight that streamed through the window, he went to the bed and discarded his robe. Lysette caught her breath at the sight of him as he stood for a moment at the bedside before slipping nude beneath the sheet.

Trembling with rage, she sat heavily on the floor. "I'll kill him for this," she muttered. "I'll kill him!"

It was only the muffled chuckle from the next room that warned her he could hear her rantings. Thrusting herself to her feet, she stormed into her own room and slammed the door with an ear-shattering, but somehow less than satisfying, crash.

Blowing out her own lamp, she climbed into bed. But sleep eluded her and when it finally came it was filled with dreams of gorgeous men with flashing black eyes and gleaming black hair who taunted her from just without her reach.

# CHAPTER 30

Still furious at Nicholas for what had happened the night before, Lysette pointedly ignored him as they sat at breakfast the next morning. Her lack of resistance, and the ease with which Nicholas had overcome what little there had been, humiliated her.

"I can't abide women who hold a grudge," Nicholas sighed, not looking up from his paper.

"I don't hold a grudge!" Lysette snapped.

He glanced across the table at her. "Did I say anything about you, my love?" he asked, ever so innocently. "I merely mentioned the fact that. . ."

"Oh, shut up!" she snarled, her cheeks reddening.

His paper hid his smirk but did nothing to smother the chuckle that accompanied it.

"Do you enjoy baiting me?" she demanded.

"As a matter of fact, I do," he admitted blithely. "I find you adorable when you're angry."

"You're hateful!"

"Just one of my many virtues, cherie." His coal-black eyes twinkled merrily over the edge of the paper. "I have several others which I'm sure you would find far more enjoyable."

"I'm not interested in your so-called virtues!"

"No? In that case, I have a rather impressive set of vices I'd be happy to show you."

"You're disgusting!"

"And you're delectable. Why don't we go back upstairs."

Flouncing out of her chair, Lysette stalked from the dining room. Nicholas followed and grabbed her wrist as they passed through the downstairs hall.

"Leave me alone!" she snarled. But a shiver ran through her as he pulled her against him.

"All I want, for now, is a good-bye kiss, my love."

His hand cupped her chin and held her face immobile. "Is that too much for a husband to ask?"

His mouth slanted across hers and his kiss, contrary to her expectations, was soft and exquisitely tender. A lover's kiss. She trembled and felt herself responding in a way she'd vowed she never would again.

Though she'd expected to see a triumphant smirk on his handsome face when he released her, she found him smiling softly, gently, his eyes shining with an affection that was disquietingly close to love.

She pushed out of his arms and turned away, desperate to keep him from seeing the havoc he wreaked on her all too susceptible senses.

"Good-bye, Lysette," he said softly.

"Good-bye," she murmured.

Before he left her, his hand came up unbidden and caressed the nape of her neck where her upswept hair laid it bare. Lysette caught her breath but refused to look at him.

She heard his departing footsteps, then the opening and closing of the door. Still she did not move. It was not until the sound of the horses and carriage on the drive could no longer be heard that she dared turn and gaze down the length of the hall toward the front door.

Sighing, she leaned against the wall. "Oh, Nicholas, Nicholas," she whispered. "What have we done to one another? From the moment we first saw one another on that deserted veranda it seems we have loved and loathed one another almost as though the two emotions were one."

"I beg your pardon, madame?" Kate, one of the maids sent to clear away the breakfast dishes, appeared at the dining room door.

Lysette pushed herself away from the wall. "Nothing, Kate. I was just thinking aloud."

"Yes, madame," the girl agreed uncertainly. She watched until Lysette had disappeared into the sewing room then, with a shrug, she went back to her chores.

In the sewing room, Lysette busied herself mending one of Nicholas's shirts. But her mind seemed busier than her needle. She could not help remembering the enchanted fortnight before the charity ball. The memories made her want to cry. How happy they had been then, how blissfully, innocently happy. How foolish to have thought it could go on that way. Could anything so beautiful possibly last?

Her hand moved to her taut, corsetted abdomen and a pain gnawed at her heart as she remembered the living roundness that had been her child but a few short weeks ago. How she had wanted her child—Nicholas's child! Perhaps Nicholas was right—perhaps they should try to have another baby right away.

She jerked her hand away and clenched her fist. "No!" she muttered. "I will not be his wife again—not that way! He destroyed our marriage the night he destroyed our child. I'll never forgive him. Never!"

But at the same time she remembered the feeling of his lips on hers, his body against hers, and a flickering of desire curled inside her. She wondered if he would come to her again tonight as he had last night. If he did, she knew he could as easily overcome her resistance as he had then—as he had only this morning. A part of her trembled in apprehension.

"What's wrong with me?" she demanded angrily. "I must be mad to want him this way!"

And yet, in the darkest recesses of her mind where the secrets of her heart lay hidden, she knew she had always wanted him, from the moment she'd first seen him, and she would continue to want him until the day one of them was dead. The knowledge weighed heavily upon her for she knew that in the end it would be her own desire that would defeat her.

"Madame?"

Lysette started as Mimette's voice shattered the silence of the sewing room. She looked around and was amazed to see that the sun was now streaming into the west-facing windows. She had daydreamed the whole of the morning away.

"What is it, Mimette?" she asked, folding away the shirt she had scarcely touched.

"Nothing, madame." The girl fidgeted with the folds of her cotton dress. "Only. . ."

"Only?"

"I thought perhaps you might like to go out. You haven't been out in ever so long. I hear there's a new shipment of bonnets all the way from Paris at Mrs. Archer's."

"Thank you, Mimette, but I don't think so."

The maid looked so downcast that Lysette patted the sofa beside her.

"Come, sit down," she invited.

When Mimette was sitting beside her, Lysette took one of her hands and gave it a gentle squeeze.

"I know this has been hard for you," she told her. "You've been as much a prisoner in this house as I have these past weeks."

"But you can go out if you want to,"

Mimette pointed out. "The monsieur did not forbid you. . ."

"I know, Mimette. It's just . . . well . . . perhaps you haven't noticed. . ." She smiled wanly and gave a little lift of her shoulders. "Perhaps it's all in my mind, but it seems that each time I set foot out the door, I see Kit Stratton. If I'm in the carriage, he's in a hired carriage following. If I'm in a shop, he's outside peering in the window." She sighed. "I even thought I saw him in church last Sunday."

"Why don't you tell the monsieur?"

"Nicholas?" Lysette grimaced. "He's too touchy where Kit is concerned. And, as I said, I have no proof. For all I know I'm imagining it all. There's no point in getting Nicholas upset for nothing. Kit has already caused so much trouble; I don't want to even mention his name to Nicholas."

She smiled apologetically at the maid. "Still, I do think it best if we stay here for the most part; at least for a while."

Rising, Lysette went to the French windows that opened onto the upper gallery. Throwing open the doors, she stepped out into the fine, warm sunshine.

Crossing the gallery, she leaned on the iron railing. She lifted her face toward the sun. It felt so soothing, so warm, so. . .

The impatient neighing of a horse caught her attention. She shaded her eyes and peered across the street toward a carriage standing at the road's edge. A driver sat holding the reins. There was a movement behind him. A face appeared at the window. Kit Stratton.

Gasping, Lysette drew back. He was staring at her, watching her; he lifted his hand toward her entreatingly.

Lysette fled back into the house and out of the sewing room leaving Mimette to stare after her bewildered.

That night, Lysette went to Nicholas's study.

"And so, my love, to what do I owe this honor?"

"Nicholas, I want to go to Saint-Cloud."

He sighed and leaned back in his chair. "We've been through this before, Lysette. You're not getting a div. . ."

"No, no," she interrupted, "I know that. Couldn't you come away with me? Even for a few weeks? I know you're busy, but . . ."

Her fear was plain in her voice, in the way her hands gripped the arms of her chair, in the haunted, hunted look in her wide, russet eyes.

"What's wrong?" he asked.

Rising, she flitted about the room trying in vain to affect an air of unconcern.

"Nothing is wrong. We haven't been to Saint-Cloud since our marriage. I haven't seen Tess. . ."

Tears welled into her eyes and she hurriedly brushed them away. "Never mind," she murmured.

Nicholas rose as she fled from the room. She was behaving so strangely. Could it be she was actually homesick for Saint-Cloud or was there something else? Was it still a reaction to losing the baby?

Sitting down at his desk, Nicholas flipped through his appointment book. He frowned, rubbing his forehead. There was nothing he could do. There was no way for him to simply cancel so many appointments. It would be impossible for him to leave New Orleans for at least a month.

He rang for Mrs. Jonelle.

"Yes, monsieur?" She appeared in the doorway.

"Anne, has Lysette said anything to make you believe. . ." He frowned. "That is to say, do you know of anything that's happened lately that might have upset her?"

The housekeeper shrugged. "No, monsieur. She hasn't been out of the house except with you for quite some time. To my knowledge, nothing has happened here."

"Thank you." He dismissed her and sat back in his chair pondering the matter.

Outside the door, Mimette overheard his question and Mrs. Jonelle's reply. She wondered if she should tell him what Lysette had told her earlier. But no, she couldn't. Her first loyalty was to her mistress and she could not betray a confidence. And besides, there was nothing Kit Stratton could do while Lysette was surrounded by Nicholas's servants. No matter how obsessed with her Kit might be, Lysette was safe among those who cared for her and for Nicholas.

# CHAPTER 31

Though she tried to convince herself that there was no reason for her to be afraid, Lysette couldn't help being aware that Kit was outside, waiting, watching, lurking in the shadows. He loved her, she knew; she couldn't truly believe he meant to do her harm. But his kind of love frightened her. It was too obsessive, too smothering. Nicholas might want to dominate her but Kit wanted to control her every waking moment.

"Lysette?"

She cried out in alarm and swung away from the window. She had taken to peering out into the street to spot Kit, whom she was certain was always there.

"Yes, Nicholas?"

He reached for her and she forced herself to stand still while he caressed her arm.

"What's wrong?" he asked, genuinely worried by her constant nervousness of late. "I know there's something bothering you. You've been nervous as a cat for weeks."

"Nothing is bothering me," she insisted, pulling away from him. "I need a change of scenery. I told you that."

"And I told you that it was impossible for

me to get away just now. Perhaps in a month or so."

"A month!" Lysette wanted to cry. Another month of Kit and his vigil and she'd be stark-raving mad.

"I'm sorry, cherie. That's the best I can do."

He came to her and pulled her into his arms. Lysette leaned against him. He was so strong. She felt so secure with his arms about her this way.

He stroked her hair. "Are you certain it's only a change of scenery that you need?" he asked softly.

"What?"

She looked up at him and he smiled. His fingers grazed her cheek, her throat, and trailed down to the neck of her gown.

"Damn you, Nicholas!" She pushed out of his arms. "I come to you for comfort and you insist on misunderstanding!"

His black eyes glinted angrily. "Forgive me, my dear," he snarled. "Perhaps you've forgotten, but I am merely a man and you are, after all, my wife. It's hardly an unforgiveable sin for a man to wish to make love to his wife!"

"I told you I would not. . ."

"And I told you you would. I've been patient with you, Lysette. More patient than many other men would be. More patient than you deserve."

"What do you want me to do?" she snapped. "Fall to my knees and sing your praises for having had the good taste not to force yourself. . ."

"Force myself! By damn, Lysette! Let me remind you that as your husband, I have every right to enter your bed whenever I wish!"

"You may enter my bed, as you put it, whenever you wish, Nicholas," she agreed tightly. "Whenever you wish to resort to rape!"

His laugh was filled with bitter mockery. "How chaste—how very upright you are, my darling. But why don't you admit the truth to yourself if only this once. If I wanted you—if I truly wanted you at this very moment—I wouldn't have to resort to rape. You're not the ice-maiden you'd like to believe. You know it and I know it."

"Leave me alone, Nicholas!" It was half-demand, half-plea.

"I will," he agreed. "For now. But the time will come, and come soon, when we will put it to the test. We both know what the result will be, don't we?"

Lysette refused to reply, but in her troubled eyes Nicholas had his answer.

Behind the creamy lace baire that draped her bed, Lysette tossed restlessly. She was tormented, haunted by visions of Nicholas, but the knowledge, galling as it was to admit, that everything he had said to her—every hateful, self-satisfied syllable—was perfectly true. But though she might have to admit it to herself in the private recesses of her own conscience, in the darkness of her own night-shrouded bed, she vowed she would never, never admit it to him.

She forced her mind off Nicholas. Kit's face swam before her. Kit. She'd thought him so gentle—so kind. She'd known he adored her—had taken comfort in his love when she'd found none with Nicholas. But now. How did one rid oneself of an unhealthy love? An obsession? How far would Kit go to 'protect' her as he believed she needed protecting?

A shadow passed before her windows. She recoiled in the darkness. Was it Kit? Had he dared trespass onto the very gallery of Nicholas's home?

Her eyes went to the dressing room door. She should go to Nicholas, warn him. He would deal with Kit once and for all.

She slid out of bed and padded through the dressing room. A light glimmered beneath Nicholas's door. She hesitated for a moment before opening it.

"Nicholas?" The long, green-walled chamber was filled with shadows. "Nicholas?"

He was gone. Leaving the room by the hall door, she saw that the French doors at the end of the hall were opened onto the upper gallery. A wave of giddiness assailed her. It was Nicholas on the gallery! It had been Nicholas who had passed her windows, not Kit. What a fool she was becoming. She was skittish as a schoolgirl.

Cursing herself for a coward and worse, she went to the doors. The night air was cool, refreshingly so after the heat of the day, and perfumed with the fragrance of the last, fast-fading lilacs. For a few peaceful moments she stood framed in the doorway. She debated going to Nicholas—telling him of her foolish fantasy. But then, she reasoned, he might mistake her meaning. Coming to him this way, in the night, in her whisper-thin gown. . .

She started to turn away when the glimmer of moonlight on steel caught her eye. She peered into the darkness and for the first time saw the carriage standing at the edge of the road. Someone sat inside, their features disguised by a low-drawn hat. Not that she would have recognized anyone at that distance and with the moon throwing them into silhouette. What she did recognize was the rifle they held to their shoulder. The telltale moonlight illuminated the rifle barrel thrust through the carriage window.

It took Lysette but a moment to realize that Nicholas, standing on the gallery, his cigar glowing in the darkness, was the target.

"Nicholas!" she cried, taking to her heels.

She did not venture another glance across the street. Had she, she would have seen the glimmer of the moon on the rifle as Nicholas's would-be assailant pulled the weapon up even as their finger tightened on the trigger.

Nicholas saw her coming and flicked his half-smoked cigar off into the darkness of the lawn.

"Enfant! What are you doing up? Bad dream?"

"A nightmare!" she whispered.

"Poor cherie. Come here."

She stepped into his arms, her back carefully toward the street, shielding Nicholas. Standing together in the darkness, they were a single shadow on the gallery. It was impossible for the watcher in the shadows across the street to distinguish one from the other, and equally impossible for them to fire at Nicholas without the risk of hitting Lysette.

"Come inside," she asked him urgently.

"Ah, ma chere," he teased lightly. "If only you meant that in the way I'd like you to. But I think I'll stay out here a few minutes longer."

"No!" she disagreed. "Come inside now!"

"Lysette. If it's more bad dreams you're afraid of, I'm sure you'll be fine."

She wanted to punch him. "Nicholas!"

He laughed, perplexed by her stubbornness. "What is it? Is there a monster hiding in your chiffonier? Shall I chase him away?"

Lysette blew out her cheeks in exasperation. She had to get him inside. The carriage still stood across the street and she knew that once she had gone back there was nothing to prevent the person inside from trying again. But it was plain that the nightmare ruse was not going to work. There was one certain way . . . one method sure to get him to go into the house. But should she? Could she?

She didn't dare leave him out here no matter what the risk to herself if she lured him inside.

"Nicholas. . ." She trailed her fingertips along the deep vee of his robe where the cool, rich damask and the warm, living flesh met. "Come into the house."

"Lysette. . ." The word contained as much a warning as a question.

Steeling herself, she rose on tiptoe and slipped her arms about his neck. Twining her fingers in his hair, she pulled his head down and pressed her lips to his.

His arms went about her; his hands caressed her back through the tissue-thin silk of her gown.

"If this is what nightmares do to you, cherie," he breathed into her cascading hair. "I'll never wish you sweet dreams again!"

She clung to him and he slipped a hand behind her knees and swept her into his arms. He carried her into the mansion and over his shoulder Lysette caught a glimpse of the carriage. The rifle barrel had disappeared. In the window there was only the silhouette of someone watching . . . watching. . .

Letting himself into Lysette's room, Nicholas lay her across her bed. As he breathed deeply of the sweet scent of her hair, his fingers worked at the ribbons fastening the front of her gown.

"Nicholas? Nicholas!"

She pushed at his shoulders. His robe hung askew and he paused long enough to shrug it off. Lysette trembled as she felt his lips moving against her throat; she gasped as his fingers freed her gown and his hands slipped inside to savor the silken warmth of her skin.

"Nicholas, no!"

He paused; his head came up. His black eyes were narrowed with suspicion.

"What did you say?" he asked tightly.

"No! Don't! Please!" She bit her lip to smother a moan as his hands continued their leisurely explorations. "I've changed my mind!"

His smile began as a faint quivering at the corners of his mouth and built until he tossed back is head and laughed aloud.

"By God, Lysette! This marriage may put me into an early grave but at least it won't be from boredom!"

Then his smile faded. He made no attempt to leave her bed, in fact, his hands found their way to her wrists and pinioned them to the soft feather mattress. He leaned over her blocking any hope of escape.

"You may have changed your mind, m'love," he murmured. "But I haven't. I don't believe in turnabout being fair play."

"But you can't!" Lysette cried.

"Oh, I assure you I can."

His eyes glittered as he moved over her. Lysette gasped as their bodies touched—the hard, sleek heat of his flesh seared her tender skin.

"Oh, Nicholas, no. . ." she moaned, but one glance into the smoky depths of her glowing, red-brown eyes revealed all Nicholas needed to know.

He chuckled and Lysette thought she'd never heard anything so wicked—so exciting.

"No. . ." she begged, whether to him or to her own weakening reserve, even she wasn't sure.

"Give it up, ma petite," he breathed, his lips against the corner of her trembling mouth.

With a sigh made of equal parts anguish and ecstacy, Lysette's arms slid about him. Her hands moved over his body lovingly, lingeringly, hungrily. She pulled him closer, closer, aching for him, demanding his love.

A shudder coursed through her and she raised her eyes to him half expecting that cynical, triumphant light that mocked her for her weakness. What she found was a reflection of the burning, urgent desire that filled her with an all-consuming need.

Her body opened to welcome him as he entered her slowly, gently, savoring this, the moment each had longed for in their secret hearts. Lysette moaned and arched against him helplessly, surrendering completely to the raptures he was only too willing—only too uniquely able—to give her.

# CHAPTER 38

[illegible]

# CHAPTER 32

Morning came and Lysette awoke in Nicholas's arms. Even as she lay there, the heat of his body warming her, the smooth hardness of his shoulder cradling her head, the steady pounding of his heartbeat soothing her, she knew she had to leave him.

The incident of the night before had frightened her. Though she had seen nothing that proved, even in her own mind, that Nicholas's would-be assailant was Kit Stratton, she couldn't imagine who else it could have been. Strange, only minutes before she had been wondering how far Kit would go to keep her from Nicholas. Was that her answer?

If it was—and she believed wholeheartedly that it was—how much more jealous, how much more vengeful, might he be now having seen the trick she'd been forced to resort to in order to save Nicholas?

Kit had seen her kiss Nicholas, had seen Nicholas carry her into the house. . . Surely there could be no doubt in his mind that they had made love.

Nicholas stirred and Lysette was jarred back to the present. Taking care not to wake him, she slid out of bed and hurried to the bathroom to begin her morning ablutions. She wanted to take no chances on Nicholas's waking up and finding her still in his arms.

Waiting for her bath water, she couldn't help reliving the ecstacies of the night before. Why, oh why did it always have to be so glorious when she and Nicholas made love? If he were brutal, if he were cold, it would be so easy to hate him. It would be so simple not to have the least desire for him. But each time seemed more magnificent than the last.

The thought haunted her all through her bath, all through the long ritual of her dressing and toilette. It was still haunting her when Nicholas joined her in the parlor just before he left for his office.

"I wish you had been with me when I woke up this morning, enfant," he said softly, his eyes alight with remembered passion.

"I'm sorry," she murmured.

"Don't apologize, I wasn't scolding." He caressed her cheek. "Why don't we go out to dinner tonight?"

"If you like," she agreed. "Perhaps. . ."

"Perhaps?"

"Mimette said she'd heard Mrs. Archer, the milliner, had gotten in a new shipment of bonnets. Perhaps I'll go and buy one."

"Why don't you? The outing might do you good. Mrs. Jonelle said you hadn't been out in quite a while."

"Mrs. Jonelle?"

"You've been so nervous lately. I asked her if anything had upset you."

"And what did she say?"

"She couldn't think of anything."

Lysette breathed a little sigh of relief. So Anne hadn't noticed Kit following them, lurking outside. So much the better. It helped with what she had to do next.

She went into Nicholas's arms willingly, eagerly surprising him with the fervency of her good-bye kiss. But it was more than that, Lysette knew. She was not merely seeing Nicholas off for the day. It would, she knew, be weeks, possibly months, before she was likely to see him again.

Once Nicholas had left, she put her plan into motion. Going to his study, she took up pen and paper and wrote a letter explaining that for reasons best kept to herself, she thought it best if she went to Saint-Cloud for a while. She begged him not to follow—pleaded with him for patience and understanding—assured him she would be in no danger. She reminded him that he had said that in a month he might be free and able to leave New Orleans and suggested that if he wished to join her he might consider doing so then. At that time, she promised, she would explain why she had fled to the country.

Sealing the letter, she left it for him and then went upstairs to prepare for her flight.

She would, of course, be unable to pack any clothes. The clothes on her back would have to suffice for the trip to Saint-Cloud. She had nothing there and what she didn't have she could go to Natchez to purchase with Tess.

Tess. . . Lysette felt a pang of guilt at the way she'd neglected Saint-Cloud's housekeeper in the past months. Oh, they had written, of course, but when she'd lost the baby and Tess had entreated her to let her come and care for her, she had refused. She could not have borne seeing the way Tess blamed Nicholas for the loss of their child. Of course, it had been his fault in a very real way, but there were extenuating circumstances that had to be taken into account.

Lysette paused as she was about to stuff her brush and comb into an unfashionably large reticule. What was she doing? Making excuses for Nicholas? Rationalizing his actions? Was she mad? Had she taken leave of her senses at long last? Or was she merely in love with him and eager to forgive?

She didn't want to leave him. She wanted to stay, oh, how she wanted to stay with him. She wanted to sleep in his protective embrace, awaken in his arms, gaze into his black eyes as they made glorious love. . .

"Some day," she promised herself softly. "Some day all this with Kit will be over. We'll be happy together one day, I know we will."

The words took her breath away. It was the first time she had ever truly allowed herself to believe that she had a future in Nicholas's life—as Nicholas's wife—in every way.

"Madame?"

Mimette stood in the dressing room doorway. She was bewildered for she had not been summoned to help Lysette dress nor had she been told to make herself ready to accompany Lysette on her outing.

"Yes, Mimette?" Lysette asked coolly.

"Pardonnez, madame, but I thought you might need me."

"No, I would have rung for you."

Mimette fidgeted with her apron. "Yes, madame, only Mrs. Jonelle said you were going out."

"That's right. I remembered you mentioning that Mrs. Archer had a shipment of bonnets. I've decided to go and look at them. I may buy one or two. I have a sudden craving for a new bonnet."

"Mrs. Jonelle is going with you?"

"That's right."

She turned away and busied herself with the buttons of her brown silk paletot. She hated hurting Mimette this way—the girl had so fancied a trip to the milliner's and it had been a long time since she'd been out. She had shared Lysette's immurment with scarcely a murmur of protest. And now to be left behind. . .

Still, Lysette had a plan and while it might be possible to elude Mrs. Jonelle and make good her escape, she very much doubted that she could slip away unnoticed beneath the very eyes of both the housekeeper and the vigilant maid.

There seemed little else to be said on the subject, indeed, had Mimette said anything more she would be skirting the edges of insolence. Hiding her hurt beneath a facade of servile humility, she bobbed a little curtsy and disappeared into the dressing room.

Through the closed door, Lysette could hear the sobs she muffled in the thickness of her skirts.

"Forgive me, Mimette," she whispered, longing to say some word of reassurance but knowing she could not. "I'll explain it all to you soon, I promise."

Avoiding the dressing room, she went to Nicholas's room by way of the hall door. In his desk, she knew, he kept a small cache of gold in case of emergencies. Well, as far as she could see, this certainly qualified.

She poured the gold into her already bulging reticule and left the room.

"Are you ready?" she asked Mrs. Jonelle as she descended the stairs.

"Yes, madame." The housekeeper peered into a mirror to tie the ribbons of her bonnet. "Mimette isn't coming?"

"No. I gave Mimette some chores to do. You don't think we need her, do you?"

"I'm sure we don't."

Buoyed by Lysette's apparently high spirits, Mrs. Jonelle dismissed the thought that they might be wiser to take the maid as a precaution if nothing else. It had been so long since Lysette had expressed any interest in even leaving the house without Nicholas at her side that Anne Jonelle was not about to go about inventing reasons for canceling an outing.

Mrs. Archer's millinery shop was located in

a deceptively shabby building in the fashionable district of Chartres Street. Inside the shop where the latest bonnets from the East and from Europe were displayed, the haggling was fierce and often deafening. Ladies of impeccable breeding who normally would not raise their voices above a polite murmur, argued with the clerks, with their companions, and often with themselves over the relative worth of a scrap of silk or cobweb of lace. For Lysette's purposes, it was perfect.

She moved through the crowded shop stopping here, pausing there, admiring this bonnet, dismissing that one. Behind her, often lost in the crowd, Mrs. Jonelle struggled to keep her in her sights. That it was a lost cause was apparent from the beginning. Not only was it often impossible to move through the shoving, surging, hoop-skirted throng, Mrs. Jonelle had a well-known weakness for pretty bonnets. No sooner had she nearly caught up with Lysette than her all too susceptible eye was captured by some French confection and she was powerless to prevent herself from stopping to try it on.

It was this quality in her more than any other that had helped Lysette to decide upon her as her companion. She waited until Mrs. Jonelle was engrossed in a particularly delectible arrangement of blonde straw covered with myriad satin and lace flounces and ruffles. Then, as quickly as she could, she made her way to the door.

Outside in the street, she stepped to the curb and fluttered her hand to try and attract a hired carriage.

Obligingly, a nondescript black carriage drew to the curb. Lysette opened the door and climbed inside wrestling with her skirts and clumsy reticule.

"To the docks," she called to the driver. He made no sound—there was nothing to indicate that he had heard but she assumed he must have.

She heard the slap of the reins and was jerked against the worn leather seat as the carriage lurched away from the curb. Lysette sat back and, straightening her bonnet, drew a deep breath.

It was only then that she realized she was not alone.

"Lysette."

Kit sat in the far corner of the carriage. He was alarmingly pale and his suit was creased from many days wearing, but otherwise he had not, as far as she could see, changed.

"Kit. . ." Lysette breathed.

"Don't look frightened," he pleaded. "Please, don't! The last thing I want is for you to be frightened of me."

"Shouldn't I be?" she demanded. "You've been following me for weeks! Watching me! Spying on me!"

"I worry about. . ."

"Why don't you begin worrying about my sanity! My God! Do you know what it is like to spend your every waking moment knowing you're being watched?"

"I meant no harm."

"No? Not even last night when you were going to kill Nicholas?"

"Kill. . ."

"Don't bother to deny it, Kit! I know it was you!"

"But, Lysette. . ."

"Don't, Kit! After everything, now you lie. . ."

Anger glinted in his eyes. How could she accuse him so callously? Callaway, it was clear, was corrupting her. He was turning her into his creature as surely as he corrupted everything he touched.

"Take me home, Kit," Lysette ordered.

"No."

She was taken aback at the firmness of his refusal.

"No?"

"No!"

"Where do you think you're taking me?"

"To the country."

"The countr. . ."

Lysette wondered how to handle Kit in this mood. Should she be firm and demanding or soft and pleading? He seemed so unpredictable.

"Kit," she said softly, laying a hand on his arm. "You know I can't go off with you like this. Nicholas will come looking for me. He will find us. . ."

"Not where we're going," Kit murmured,

smiling slyly.

For the first time, Lysette felt a flicker of fear. They were heading out of town moving in the opposite direction from that she should have taken had she been going to Saint-Cloud. Even if Nicholas found the letter she'd left him and came after her, he would begin by going in the wrong direction.

"I don't want to go with you," she told him frankly.

"Nicholas has turned you against me," Kit answered gently, as though breaking particularly unpleasant news to a child. "Some time alone will restore what was between us."

"There was never anything between us!" she reminded him, fear beginning to show in her voice.

"There could have been . . . there would have been . . . if only we'd been left alone." He smiled beatifically. "Now we will be alone."

The carriage rolled on, moving too fast for Lysette to even think of leaping to freedom. Though she argued and cajoled and pleaded, Kit was firmly convinced that once they were alone at his country retreat Lysette would come to her senses and realize that he was the man she loved. Out of the corrupting shadow of Nicholas Callaway, their love would blossom into the splendid flower he'd always known it could be.

Nicholas arrived home, summoned by an

hysterical Mrs. Jonelle who'd returned home when it had become apparent that Lysette had disappeared from the shop and, as it turned out, from the district.

"She simply vanished!" she told Nicholas as the butler took his coat. "I looked everywhere, sir, everywhere! Someone said they'd seen her getting into a carriage but I don't know. . ." Her voice choked and she daubed at her eyes with a bedraggled handkerchief. "If anything's happened to her. . ."

"We'll find her, Anne," he said confidently. "I doubt anything's happened to her. Very likely she simply decided to go visit my mother or perhaps wanted to go to some other shops."

"In a hired carriage?"

"She might have left the carriage for you. If she—"

"Pardon, monsieur?"

One of the housemaids stood at Nicholas's elbow.

"Marie?"

She handed him Lysette's note. "I was dusting in the study just now, monsieur, and I found this on the desk. It is the madame's hand. . ."

Nicholas took the letter and tore it open. His black eyes skimmed the page once, then again.

"This explains it," he said thoughtfully. "That stubborn little hellion."

"Monsieur?" Mrs. Jonelle eyed him with undisguised curiosity.

"She's run away to Saint-Cloud. She's been badgering me to take her for weeks. Apparently she simply got tired of waiting for me and went alone."

"Alone!" Anne was scandalized. "She's going to travel on the river all alone?"

Nicholas sighed. "Lack of determination was never one of her faults, Anne. If she took the idea into her head, wild horses couldn't drag it out of her."

"You'll go after her, won't you, sir?"

Nicholas frowned. "All in good time. Perhaps I'll let her stew awhile."

"Stew, sir?"

"She wants some time alone—some time away from New Orleans, from this house, from me. So be it. At the end of the month I'll go to Saint-Cloud and fetch her back. In the meantime, I'll let her have her way." He shrugged and smiled fondly. "Perhaps she's earned it just this once."

As Nicholas spoke, a carriage left the city and traveled into the countryside toward the ramshackle plantation Kit had purchased with just this trip in mind. In it, Lysette prayed that Nicholas would decide to follow her to Saint-Cloud for the sooner he did, the sooner he would discover that she was not there. The sooner that happened, the sooner he would launch the search for her that would release her from Kit's too-loving captivity.

# CHAPTER 33

Burr Oak may well have been beautiful once, but by the time Kit Stratton bought it from the pair of ancient spinsters who were the last survivors of the proud family who built it, it was hard to see its beauty amidst the decay that was quickly claiming it. As the carriage rolled up the overgrown drive and circled before the mansion, Lysette was reminded of a once-beautiful old woman who hopes beyond hope that the world will see the beauty she once was, all the while knowing those around her view only the sad proof of the ravages of unkind time.

The mansion was long and low, ringed by a colonnade of pillars each four feet square. The plaster covering the pillars had broken away in huge chunks exposing the brick beneath. The once-grand gallery was collapsing at both front corners. The railings of the gallery were hung with clinging vines and Lysette wondered, not unreasonably, if they were all that was holding the delicately turned posts in place.

As they circled toward the front of the mansion, Lysette noticed a patch of bright yellow-green inside the curve of the drive. She wondered at its unusual coloring and then, as a long, lime-colored green snake slithered across it, she realized it was originally a reflecting pool, its surface choked now with duckweed and pennywort.

Reluctantly, Lysette let Kit swing her down before the broken steps that led to the sagging front door above which shards of glass that were all that remained of a shattered fanlight glittered in the sunshine.

"Kit," she said softly as he would have led her up the two tilting steps, "I don't want to stay here."

"I know it's hardly Saint-Cloud or Montcalm," he snapped, growing impatient with her haughtiness. "But one day it will be restored to its former beauty. If you were an artist, you would be able to see. . ."

"I'm not an artist," she reminded him, stumbling up the steps. "I don't see any beauty here."

"It's Nicholas!" he hissed. "Can't you see that! He's blinded you to all that's beautiful in life by showing you only ugliness!"

"That's not true, Kit. I—"

"Don't ever defend him to me! Not ever! Do you hear?"

"Yes," she whispered, intimidated by the fanatical light in his blue eyes.

"Now come along!"

Her wrist clasped in his surprisingly powerful grip, Kit led Lysette into a foyer, then into a parlor where they stepped over a pile of shattered crystal and twisted brass dusted with chips of plaster. The medallion which had been the centerpiece of the high, coved ceiling had fallen along with the exquisite French chandelier that had once lighted the chamber.

Lysette stumbled and Kit glanced back anxiously. But once he decided she was unhurt, he pulled her ruthlessly through musty rooms whose walls were dark with the mold that comes of perpetually damp plaster and rotting lathe. The ceilings sagged, many of them dangerously cracked, nearly all stained by the torrential rains pounding on the rotten roof, leaving Lysette to wonder how in heaven's name any of the upstairs rooms could possibly be habitable.

"We can't live here, Kit," she objected.

Noticing a movement from the corner of her eye, she caught a last, fleeting glimpse of some unidentified rodent as it disappeared into a gaping hole where once a marble fireplace had stood. She shivered. Kit had apparently bought the property barely in time to save it from the scavengers, both animal and human.

"We can live here," he contradicted tightly. "And we will!"

"Who's there!"

The voice, so completely unexpected, brought a little scream out of Lysette and startled even Kit to whom it came as no great surprise.

"It's me!" Kit called back. To Lysette, he explained "It's only Jesse, the caretaker."

"Caretaker?"

Looking at the ruin around her, Lysette found the notion of a caretaker ludicrous. A giggle welled up in her throat but she stubbornly suppressed it for she realized that it had its beginnings not in humor but in despair. She had to keep hold of herself, be rational, stay calm. Getting hysterical would do her no good nor would it endear her to Kit in whose good graces she knew she had to stay.

"That you, Mr. Stratton?"

"Yes, Jesse, in here."

Lysette drew closer to Kit as an old man appeared in a doorway whose ornately carved double doors hung crazily on broken hinges. Dressed in dirty rags that may once have been a fashionable suit, albeit a decade earlier, his grey hair stuck out wildly and his tattered, patchy beard was stained with the juice of the tobacco he constantly chewed.

"Well, now, what've you got there? Purty little thing."

"This is madame. . ." Kit thought a moment. "Madamoiselle Ravaisson," he amended. "She will be my guest for some time to come."

The old man's dark eyes swept slowly from Lysette's beruffled bonnet to the toes of her slippers peeking from beneath her flounced hem. They returned to her face and the predatory glitter in them belied his ancient appearance. He was, she realized suddenly and with a glimmering of fear that seemed to arise out of some primeval instinct, nowhere near as decrepit nor as humble as he at first appeared.

In an instant her plan of action was revised. She would have to be sweet to Kit—she would have to cater to him, pander to him—for she could not bear to be left to the mercies of this filthy man who ogled her openly in Kit's presence.

Incredibly, Kit did not seem to notice. He drew Lysette forward proudly.

"Darling, this is Mr. Harris—Jesse—the caretaker of Burr Oak. He has most obligingly helped me to create a studio where I can paint and chambers fit for use while the rest of the house is being made habitable." Kit smiled at the dirty man. "Is your charming wife about?"

"She is." Turning his head, the man let out a bellow that made Lysette nearly jump out of her skin.

"Valina!"

"What the hell d'ye want?" came the snarled reply.

"Git your lazy arse out here. Himself's back and he's brought his lady with him."

Lysette's eyes glittered with anger at hearing the sarcastic tone he used when speaking of Kit's 'lady.' It was obvious that the man bore no love for the man who had purchased the abandoned plantation of which Jesse had long considered himself lord and master.

"Well, now." The woman's voice appeared before she did but the image it evoked in Lysette's mind proved all too accurate. "Ain't she a fine little madame?"

Lysette slipped her hand into Kit's as the woman entered through the broken door behind her husband. Dressed in a ragged gown that may once have been black but now was a rusty brown, she raised a hand and pushed back a lifeless strand of lank grey hair that had strayed from the meagre bun at the back of her neck. Her face was pasty white and her features were sharp and hard. Her mouth was pinched with jealous spite as her small, close-set eyes skimmed over Lysette with no less interest than had her husband's lascivious gaze.

"Kit," Lysette whispered, frightened.

"Mrs. Harris," Kit reproved. "I will not have Madamoiselle Ravaisson treated with anything less than the utmost respect."

"No, indeed, sir," the woman agreed, hostility oozing from her every pore. "Such a pretty, finebred lady should be treated like a princess."

Kit seemed not to notice the sarcasm dripping from the woman's words.

"Precisely. Now, I want you to take her up to the room I chose for her. Jesse, come with me. I'll need your help bringing in some supplies I brought with me."

Kit and the caretaker left and Lysette turned wary eyes toward the woman who glared at her with open antagonism.

"This way, yer highness," she snarled.

With a twitch of her ragged skirts, Mrs. Harris moved off leaving Lysette to follow in her wake.

They climbed the creaking staircase whose broken balustrade was like the grim, toothless smile of old age. At the head of the stairs a moth-eaten, mildewed runner stretched along the upstairs corridor covering a warped floor betraying the weakened condition of the beams supporting it.

"Here y'are," Mrs. Harris snapped, thrusting open a door. Without another word, she turned and stalked off leaving Lysette to explore her new accommodations alone.

To her surprise, the room showed evidence of having been thoroughly cleaned recently. There was a fine coating of dust on the tables and a network of cobwebs stretched between the tall, fluted posts of the old four-poster, but beneath the dust the tables had obviously been waxed and the cobwebs were the only ones in the big, square room.

The draperies at the windows and on the bed were of floral-printed cotton and though their colors had long since faded into nearly indistinguishable shades of brown and gray, and they had been patched and worn and patched again, they at least showed signs of a recent cleaning.

Lysette closed the door behind herself. She was disappointed but not surprised to find no key in the lock. No doubt Mrs. Harris kept the keys like some medieval gaoler. The thought of the woman's having access to her in any part of the house at any hour of the day or night did nothing to allay her unease.

Her first thought was of the gold in her reticule. She would have need of it if she ever managed to escape this nightmare. Moreover, both Mr. Harris and his redoubtable wife seemed quite capable of slitting a person's throat for a small fortune in gold. She had to hide it. She had to put it somewhere where it wasn't likely to be found even by someone as familiar with the house as Mrs. Harris. She truly believed that for its safety, and her own, neither of the Harrises must suspect that the money was in the house.

But where? There might well be secret cavities behind the elaborately carved over-mantel or a storage box beneath the window seat. There could easily be a loose bottom on one of the chairs or a false bottom in one of the drawers of the secretary or chest. But both the Harrises were certain to be familiar with them. What could she do?

Going to the bed, she tore a hole in the worn ticking of one of the thick feather pillows. It would have to do, she told herself, shoving handsful of the coins in among the feathers. Mrs. Harris did not look the type who would be overly conscientious about changing the bed linen. The gold should be safe there until she found another place to put it.

The knock at the door took her by surprise. She gave a little, high-pitched scream and frantically plumped the pillows. The knock came again, more insistently, and she nearly cried with relief when she heard Kit's voice call out:

"Lysette? Are you all right? What are you doing?"

"Kit!"

The door flew open and he entered, alarmed by the fear in her voice. He was stunned when he found her in his arms, her face buried in his shoulder, her arms wound about him.

"Cherie, cherie," he murmured. "What is

this? What's happened?"

"Take me away from here, Kit," she begged tearfully. "I don't want to stay!"

He stiffened as she clung to him. "I told you, Lysette," he began sternly. "Nicholas has turned you against me, but. . ."

"No!" She shook her head, wiping her cheeks with the back of one hand. "It's not you, Kit. It's not even this house. It's those people! They frighten me, Kit! Please, take me away from them!"

"Those people?" he repeated, nonplussed. "The Harrises?"

"Yes! The Harrises! I'm afraid of them!"

Kit was genuinely surprised. Having given little thought to his surroundings, he had often lived among people like the Harrises—people who scrounged for their bread and had no time nor patience for the niceties of life. They were crude people, vulgar and rude, but theirs was not an easy existence. To them virtues like delicacy and fastidiousness were the prerogative of those with more time than sense—the leisured class with little else to do than worry about the proper tone of voice or their place in society.

"But, darling. You needn't be frightened. They're strange to you, I've no doubt. But they won't harm you—they wouldn't dare. One incident and I'd turn them out. They'd have no place to go and they know it."

"Oh, God, Kit," she moaned.

Why was he so blind? Couldn't he see that it would be all too possible for the Harrises to dispose of Kit and his unwelcome guest and go on about their daily lives just as they had in the years since Burr Oak had been abandoned?

There were swamps nearby. Lysette had caught glimpses of them as they had driven to Burr Oak along the narrow, rutted roads. In the swamps alligators glided in their ceaseless pursuit of prey. If a body, living or dead, were to be tossed to those creatures. . .

A shudder of revulsion coursed through her and she cuddled closer to Kit.

"Hold me, Kit," she whispered. "Just hold me. Say you'll watch over me."

Elated, Kit clung to her. Could it be . . . could it truly be that Nicholas's spell was already beginning to weaken? It was more than he could have wished for.

Held in his arms, Lysette felt a little of her fear fading away—fading, that is, until she happened to glance over Kit's shoulder.

In the doorway, Jesse Harris watched as Kit held Lysette, caressed her, murmured soft words of comfort to her. Knowing that Lysette saw him there, the man smiled. Gasping, Lysette buried her eyes in Kit's shoulder. She had never in her life beheld a smile that was so terrifying, so dreadful, so filled with malevolent glee.

When she dared risk another glance toward the open doorway, the man had gone. But how long would it be before he returned? And if he found her alone, what might he not dare to possess her and the gold she had no doubt he would soon discover she had in her possession?

# CHAPTER 34

The days passed and Lysette chafed to be free. She had ceased to believe that Nicholas would appear as if by magic and rescue her. In all likelihood, she had to admit, he hadn't even discovered that she was not at Saint-Cloud. Stubborn as she could be, he was more than a match for her. It would, no doubt, be some time before he recovered from his anger enough to even make inquiries as to her safe arrival. She had to face the fact that her stay at Burr Oak would be a long one. Perhaps, she thought with a shudder, a permanent one.

On the morning of the fifth day, Lysette stretched and stared up at the patched canopy that draped her bed. She slept better now than she had on those first tortuous nights. She had taken to wedging chairs beneath the doorlatches—a precaution she might not have taken with Kit but one she considered more than necessary with Jesse Harris prowling the old house at all hours.

Jesse. Her nose wrinkled in disgust at the thought of him. What a loathsome creature he was. Though he never approached her, hardly directed a word to her, his eyes followed her everywhere with disturbing persistence. It was not only his attitude that troubled her, his manners disgusted her. He chewed tobacco constantly and sent a stream of brown juice spewing at random whenever he desired. His language would shame a Mississippi River bargeman. If Kit reproved him for it, he simply nodded in Lysette's direction and mumbled something that sounded only remotely like an apology.

Lysette started as Kit knocked on her door.

"Who is it?" she called, wondering if this was the morning when Jesse would attempt to force his way into her room.

"Kit," he shouted. "It's half after eleven. When are you getting up?"

"I'm not!" She looked at her gown which she'd spread out on the window seat to air, not that that could help it much.

"What do you mean, you're not?"

"Kit, I came here with the clothes on my back. My gown is filthy. I won't wear it anymore."

"Give it to Mrs. Harris. She can sponge it."

"And in the meantime?"

"In the meantime, you can wear one of my shirts and a pair of breeches."

"Kit!"

"Well? It's better than lying in bed all day, isn't it?"

She hesitated. What he said might be true, but she wasn't sure she wanted to strut around in a shirt and breeches in front of. . .

"Where's Jesse?" she demanded.

"He's gone out hunting. He'll be gone most of the day."

Sighing, she threw back the covers. "Oh, all right. Get me something to wear and I'll give my clothes to Mrs. Harris."

In the cloudy mirror of the sagging dressing table, Lysette turned and peered over her shoulder at her reflection. Kit's breeches were too loose in the waist and too tight in the hips. The former was easily corrected by the use of the belt he'd given her. But the latter. . .

She smoothed her hands over her backside. It was positively indecent. With a sigh, she pulled out the neatly-tucked shirt and let it fall nearly to her knees. It was hardly fashionable but not quite so provocative.

Hoping that for once Mrs. Harris would bestir herself to do her work quickly, Lysette left her room and went down stairs to the sunlit parlor that served as Kit's studio.

"Lysette!" Kit breathed. He immediately took up a pencil and pad and began to sketch.

"Oh, Kit, no, please," she moaned. In the past five days he had never stopped drawing her. Much as she tried to ignore him, the eternal scratching of pencil on paper was driving her mad.

"But you look adorable," he protested.

She lifted a self-conscious hand to her hair which she'd left cascading loosely about her shoulders. "I look a fright."

"Never!"

Sighing, Lysette dropped into a chair and

gazed out at the ruined garden that had once bloomed with radiant life. Now it resembled nothing so much as a jungle of the native vines and growth of the swampland, creeping over the once carefully manicured lawns and borders, choking the life from the delicately nurtured plants transplanted here and then abandoned—as all of Burr Oak had been abandoned.

"How long are we to remain here?" she asked.

Kit's pencil never wavered. She had asked him that same question every morning and every night since their arrival and he had given up trying to avoid answering it.

"Until you forget Nicholas," he said softly.

"That will never happen."

He scowled and glared at her from beneath lowered brows. "It's been a week. Only a week. After a month, two months, a year. . ."

"A lifetime?" she suggested.

He shrugged. "If necessary."

"Kit, how many times must I remind you that Nicholas is my husband. He will always be my husband."

"There are ways. . ."

"He would never agree. I. . ." She frowned, not wanting to remember those painful days just after her miscarriage. "I asked him for a divorce."

"You did?" Kit was plainly astonished.

"Yes." Her voice dropped to a breathy hush. "He refused, not surprisingly. He will always refuse. He is determined that I will always be his."

"But you are not his now."

Lysette looked away. But I am, Kit, she thought. I am. Just because we are apart, does not mean I am not his.

She knew that to prolong the argument would be useless. "Why must we stay inside all the time?" she demanded petulantly. "There are horses in the stable. Why can't we go riding?"

"Would you like that?"

She waved a languid hand. "I'd like anything that would get us out of this wretched ruin for a change."

Kit compressed his lips. In his dreams, Lysette was a paragon. She never complained, she accepted his will demurely, amenably. He was finding the real Lysette far less compliant.

"We can't go riding," he announced sullenly.

"But why not?"

"There's no sidesaddle."

"I'll ride astride."

"Ride astride! Good God, Lysette!"

She thrust herself out of her chair. "Damn it all, Kit!" she shouted, unconsciously using Nicholas's favorite oath. "I'm not made of glass! I won't break! I'm bored sitting here all day while you fill page after page with drawings of me. I want to go back to New Orleans!"

"We'll go when and if I say we will!" Kit shouted back, throwing his pad and pencils aside. "I don't know what Nicholas has done to make you this way. . ."

"He's done nothing! Nothing! This is the way I am, Kit! I'm not some saint! I'm no 'Essence of Innocence.' I'm only a woman and I want to go home!"

"For the last time, we will go when I say, not before!"

"Well, I won't be a prisoner in this house! If I want to go outside, I will!"

Stalking out of the studio, she stormed through the house to the back door which opened onto the crumbling gallery and then into the overgrown garden. As she wrenched open the warped door on its rusted hinges and stepped outside, a long stream of tobacco juice streaked the peeling floorboards just missing the toes of her cashmere boots.

"For Christ's sake, will you stop that!" she shouted at Jesse. "It turns my stomach to see you chewing all day like a damned cow!"

"Yer pardon, mada'm," he said politely.

"I'll pardon you," she muttered, marching off the gallery and down into the garden where the flagstone paths were only barely visible. Stooping to examine a yellow Carolina mallow that bloomed amidst the tangle of vines, she glanced back and saw that the caretaker remained where she'd left him—watching her.

She straightened and tugged down the tails of Kit's shirt.

"What the hell are you staring at?" she demanded crossly.

She got no answer but Jesse shrugged and turned away, disappearing into the house.

"Filthy old bastard," she muttered.

Inside the mansion, Jesse went to the kitchen where his wife was busily wringing out Lysette's petticoats.

He fingered the delicate lace that frothed the garments. They seemed as fragile as spiderwebs against his rough, calloused fingers.

His wife slapped his hand away.

"There's no use in gettin' yerself all riled up over her, Jesse," Valina told him, a sneer in her voice. "She wouldn't suffer you within ten feet of her precious little self. High-nosed, that one. Thinks she's fit for some planter's son. Makes you wonder how that one got hold of her."

She nodded in the direction of Kit's studio. Jess thoughtfully chomped the wad of tobacco he kept stored in his cheek.

"There's somethin' that ain't right 'bout those two," he speculated softly. "They don't git alone, that's one thing. You'd think with her bein' here, they'd be friendlier. Hell, he don't even sleep with her."

"Humph." Valina fished Lysette's pantalettes out of the cauldron of soapy water. "I might've known you'd notice that."

"It's true, ain't it?"

"I guess so. But it still don't matter. She wouldn't have you and her beau in there would as soon slit yer throat as have you touch her."

Jesse laughed disdainfully. "I could take care of that one."

"Jesse, no. This is the same thing that happened with. . ."

"I know, I know." He scowled, annoyed by the sudden fear in his wife's voice. "I told you it ain't gonna happen no more. Didn't I tell you that?"

"You did," she admitted.

"Well, listen when I tell you something. I said it wouldn't happen again and it won't!"

Turning on his heel, he stalked out the door and it was only moments later that Valina heard the back door creaking open as he left the mansion.

Twisting the water out of Lysette's pantalettes, she could not help remembering the reason she and Jesse had first come to this god-forsaken spot. It was not because they liked the smelly, foggy swamplands that they had immured themselves in this broken-down ruin. It was not for their health that they agreed to stay here as caretakers for little more than enough money to keep them from starving. Oh, no. It was because they were hiding—hiding from the law and, more importantly, hiding from a man named Pierre Laroux upon which plantation Jesse had once been overseer and she had been cook.

It had begun just this way, she remembered, a feeling of foreboding growing inside her. The mistress of Laroux's plantation, his wife, Eugenie, had been just such a beauty as Kit Stratton's lady, and Jess had admired her —admired her so much that finally he could contain his admiration no longer.

But Eugenie Laroux had not had Lysette's spirit. She had been delicately raised, cosseted, protected from the cruelties of life. She had gone from the marble halls of her father's Loire valley chateau to the equally sumptuous chambers of Pierre Laroux's magnificent plantation as if floating on a cotton wool cloud, never suspecting that there was anything in the world save the genteel adoration of everyone about her.

And so Jesse's attack had come as a two-fold shock to one so unknowing. That a servant should dare touch her was beyond her comprehension—that he should force himself upon her had so ravaged her senses that she'd withdrawn into herself. She became a mere shadow of the gay, vivacious, if ever so childish, woman-child she had once been.

It was this withdrawing that Jesse had counted upon to keep his secret. He had known that she would never admit to her husband the shame that had befallen her. Had she gone to Pierre, he might have been able to comfort her, to tell her it was not her fault, that the shame was not hers. But in her eyes, she was forever sullied. She could never go to her husband for comfort for she knew that there was nothing he could say, nothing he could do, that would ever purify her.

When they found her body in the stream that ran across the elegant, French garden, Jesse had thought his secret forever safe. He had not suspected that one so frivolous as Eugenie would have fallen into the habit of keeping a journal in which she faithfully recorded the happenings of her idyllic life. Her grief-stricken maid had brought the journal to Pierre's attention.

The Harrises had escaped, but only barely. Now their safety depended upon keeping a low profile and staying buried in the tangled swamplands. But now—now it was beginning again. Valina fingered the delicate lace of Lysette's petticoats which had so fascinated Jesse.

"God help me," she breathed, taking the clothing out to dry in the afternoon sunshine. "Don't let it happen again—don't let this one be the same as Eugenie Laroux!"

But even as she stepped out onto the back gallery, she saw Lysette wandering among the tangled undergrowth. Not so far away, nearly hidden by the grey-green Spanish moss festooning a fallen cypress, Jesse was watching.

# CHAPTER 35

Nicholas sat late in his study as had become his habit in the week since Lysette had fled to Saint-Cloud. Kit's portrait of her, propped on a chair, faced him.

Lysette, beautiful Lysette. Whatever Stratton's failings, not even Nicholas could fault his art. The depiction was flawless. He had captured the porcelain perfection of her skin, the delicate bloom in her cheeks, the lush, glowing richness of her hair, the mischievous sparkle of her eyes. . .

Nicholas sighed. Much as he hated to admit as much, her failure to write him and let him know she had arrived safely wounded him. Surely she must know he would be concerned. Common courtesy would seem to dictate that she should at least write him a note detailing the time of her arrival and the welcome she'd received.

He debated going after her. She had pleaded with him not to and his pride quailed at the thought of chasing like some lovesick puppy who cannot exist outside the shining radiance of his beloved. Still, it had been a week. Even Lysette in a snit should not be quite so callous as to deliberately ignore the barest social amenities.

He scowled, wracked by indecision. If he went after her, would she be touched by his concern or angered by his disregard of her requests in her letter? Would she welcome him or make him feel an intruder in a home that, after all, had been hers long before he had come into her life. He had treated her badly during the months of their marriage. The portrait, much as the beauty of its subject enthralled him, served as a reminder of his moment of greatest folly when he had allowed rash emotion to rob him of his son and, nearly, of Lysette herself. Had he been patient then, had he taken the time to consider the possibilities, the child might not have been lost. In fact, it would have been nearly time for the birth. Tonight, yes, even this very night, he might be somewhere else—upstairs in the nursery holding his son in his arms. He thought of the nursery which had been hurriedly stripped of the decor Lysette had labored so lovingly to create. He should have left it—he should have forced himself to sit in it every day as a reminder to keep his temper, his supsicious nature in check.

"I'll give her time," he decided at long last. "But perhaps there is something. . ."

It was late and the staff had long since been dismissed to go to their rest. But Nicholas could not wait—having decided upon a course of action, he was impatient to put it into motion.

He climbed the stairs to the servants'

quarters beneath the eaves. Letting himself into the long, narrow room where the housemaids slept, he moved down the aisle between the rows of beds until he found Mimette's.

She started as he shook her awake. Yanking the blanket up to her chin, she stared at him horrified as he pressed a hand over her mouth to keep her from awakening the other girls.

"Come with me," he ordered softly.

As he left the chamber, Mimette climbed out of bed and followed, pulling her cotton wrapper about her as she did.

"Yes, monsieur?" she asked when they stood in the corridor outside the room.

"Tomorrow I want you to go to Saint-Cloud," he told her. "I will not go—your mistress prefers to be alone for a while. But she may need you and you are to go. I will send someone with you if you prefer not to travel alone."

"Whatever you think best, monsieur," she acquiesced.

"All right." He ran his fingers through his hair ruffling it. "Go back to sleep, Mimette. You are to pack first thing in the morning. And pack whatever you think your mistress will need as well."

"Yes, monsieur."

She watched as he turned and strode off down the dimly lit corridor. A flurry of excitement fluttered in her breast. She was going to Saint-Cloud! She was going to travel again on one of the magnificent floating palaces that plied the river!

"And Mimette?" he said from halfway down the long dark hall.

"Yes, monsieur?"

"You are to send back word of how your mistress is faring, do you understand?"

"Oui, monsieur, only. . ." She cast down her eyes, embarrassed.

"Only?"

"I cannot write, monsieur."

"Never mind. I'll send someone with you who can."

"As you wish, monsieur."

He left her then and she returned to her room. She was relieved, despite her earlier bravado, not to be making the journey alone. That might be fine for such a one as her mistress who never let fear stand in the way of her actions once she was determined to do something, but the Mimettes of the world were not quite so brave.

Climbing back into her now cold bed, she stared up at the shelf above her head where her few personal belongings were stored. She had a busy day ahead of her—packing for herself and for her mistress. But in spite of that knowledge, she doubted she would get much sleep.

The day dawned bright and warm and Mimette, despite the occasional yawn, went about her packing with a light heart. She was eager to leave, eager to ride the river, eager to see Saint-Cloud and Lysette again. She was far from unhappy when it came time to climb into the carriage and ride to the docks.

The steamboat upon which Nicholas booked passage for Mimette and her companion, Judah, the butler's son, was the Belle Helene. Impossible as it seemed, it was even more sumptuous than the Bienville which had brought Mimette and Lysette to New Orleans in the first place. Though their accommodations were less than grand, the sort of modest cabins normally assigned to servants such as they, they were free to spend their days wandering the decks mixing with the beautiful, elegant travelers who rode the river with every expectation of enjoying each and every luxury they would have found in their own homes.

"Isn't it exciting, Judah?" Mimette asked as they leaned on the railing and watched the scenery passing on the near bank of the river.

Judah Baker, fifteen-year-old son of Benjamin Baker, Nicholas's longtime butler, shrugged. He was feeling terribly wise and terribly grown up, far superior to the chattering girl he had been asked to escort upriver.

"It's well enough, I suppose," he allowed haughtily.

Mimette shot him a disgusted glance. "You needn't give yourself airs, Judah Baker," she snapped. "You're no better than I am even if Monsieur Callaway has given you schooling."

Judah drew himself up indignantly. In the

past year he had grown immensely and now fell short of six feet by a mere inch. In addition, his fair good looks caught the eyes of more than one New Orleans belle when he ventured to and from the academy where Nicholas Callaway had sent him as a gesture of gratitude for his father's many years of service. He felt very grand and very proud; he was terribly vain, a failing that greatly vexed his father who believed implicitly in keeping to one's place; a notion Judah dismissed with bitter disdain.

"Maybe not yet," he grudgingly admitted, a sparkle of resentment in his heavily-lashed brown eyes, "but one day! Mr. Callaway has promised to make me his clerk when I have finished my studies. Someday, I'll be one of them. . ."

He nodded toward the elegant gentlemen who squired their beautiful ladies along the deck.

"One of them?" Mimette scoffed. "How can you be? No matter what pretty feathers you think you may wear, monsieur peacock, you are still and will always be, the butler's son!"

Judah's eyes flashed. His hands curled into fists. He raised one of them and would have struck her, but his wrist was seized and held in a powerful, and painful, grip.

He turned and found himself gazing into the chisled, aristocratic features of a grand and forbidding man in fawn and brown.

"Never, sirrah," the man said in a low, stern tone, "never lift your hand in violence to a woman."

"I beg your pardon, sir," Judah apologized quickly, recognizing power and influence when he found himself face to face with it.

"Do not apologize to me; apologize to the lady. It is she you have offended."

Dropping Judah's hand, the man strode away leaving Mimette to gaze raptly after him.

"How kind he is; how gallant," she sighed.

"You deserved a slapping," Judah snarled, not in the least contrite. "You would have gotten it, too, had it not been for that old popinjay."

"That old popinjay is a gentleman," Mimette sniffed, "and if you want to be one, you'd do well to take his advice."

With a twitch of her skirts, she stalked away, her nose raised indignantly.

Entering the main salon, she spotted her rescuer sitting on a green velvet, gold-braided ottoman. In his hands he held a hinged leather picture frame and he gazed at it with an expression of almost unutterable sadness.

Mimette hesitated, not knowing if she dared intrude upon him. But then he folded the frame and tucked it into his pocket. Gathering her courage, Mimette approached him and curtsied.

"My dear?" he said, and the tiny smile that curved his mouth seemed to transform him.

His face was narrow and heavily lined but Mimette could see he was not nearly as old as he at first appeared. He was tall and thin but to judge from Judah's reaction, his strength belied the air of cultivated gentility about him. His hair was more grey than brown but it was thick and waving if one could judge by the portions visible beneath the brim of his hat. His clothing, though of obviously good quality, was plain, but a diamond solitaire sparkled on the little finger of his left hand implying wealth one might not have at first suspected he possessed.

"I wanted to thank you, monsieur," Mimette said. "You were kind to help me."

"Not at all." His eyes traveled over her and he immediately ascertained her position. "You should not stray from your mistress's side, my dear. She may need you and you will not be there."

"I am traveling to join my mistress, monsieur," she told him, not quite sure why he seemed to invite confidences. "She has gone for a visit to her plantation and my master has sent me to be with her." She nodded toward Judah who had just appeared in the salon. "The young man is my companion; the son of my master's butler."

"I see. But surely your mistress did not travel to her home alone?"

"She did, monsieur. She is a headstrong lady." Not wishing him to think she was criticizing her mistress, she added quickly, "but I'm sure she knows what she is doing."

"Apparently she does not," he disagreed gently. "A woman alone invites danger. She was very foolish to go off on her own. You must not allow her to do it again."

The urge to defend Lysette rose up in Mimette but secretly she agreed with the gentleman. It had been foolish for Lysette to go off by herself. And then, too, there was still a bit of resentment inside Mimette for Lysette's refusal to take her into her confidence. She had been with Lysette a long time—if she didn't trust her, of what use was she to her?

"As you say, monsieur," she murmured. "If you will pardon me, I have disturbed you long enough."

"Not at all, my dear," he smiled. "I hope you find your mistress well and safe."

"Merci, monsieur."

With another bobbed curtsy, she left him and sallied past Judah who, having been reproved by the grand gentleman, did not dare approach him much as he would have liked to.

The Belle Helene drew up to the docks of Saint-Cloud to let Judah and Mimette disembark in the middle of the following afternoon. Leaving their baggage on the dock to be brought up by servants, they climbed the hill to the beautiful mansion that was far more beautiful than Mimette remembered.

"Lord!" Judah breathed, never having seen anything half so grand. "All this belongs to Mr. Callaway!"

"All this belongs to Madame Callaway," Mimette corrected pettishly. "Her first husband, Monsieur Ravaisson, built it."

"With Mr. Callaway's money," Judah reminded her smugly.

"That's not true!" Mimette pouted knowing it was in fact the truth. "And anyway, he's going to give it back to the madame once they have a child."

Judah made a face at the ludicrousness of handing such a magnificent piece of property over to a woman. Had he ever managed to get hold of such a place, he wouldn't have relinquished it to anyone, ever!

Judah pounded on the door and they were admitted by a housemaid. She showed them into the parlor where the furniture was still covered with dustcloths and the chandelier was covered and tied and resembled nothing so much as an enormous coccoon ready to disgorge its butterfly.

"Mimette?"

Judah and Mimette turned and found Tess standing in the doorway. The old housekeeper, impossible as it seemed, was even thinner than before. Her black silk gown hung loosely on her skin-and-bones body and her face was gaunt and hawkish.

"Mimette, what are you doing here?"

"What am I doing here?" Mimette repeated, puzzled. "Monsieur Callaway sent me, of course." She looked around, brows drawn downward. "Why hasn't the house been opened?"

"Opened? Why should it have been opened?"

"I should have thought the madame would want the rooms aired and the furniture uncovered and. . ."

"The madame?" The older woman could hardly contain her excitement. "Lysette? Lysette is coming home?"

Mimette and Judah looked at one another. In both their stomachs a knot of fear formed.

"What's wrong?" Tess demanded. The smile left her face. She frowned. "He's coming as well, isn't he? The monsieur!" Her nose wrinkled.

"No. . ." Mimette murmured. "No, he's not coming."

"Then what is it?"

"She isn't here? The madame is not here?"

"What are you babbling about? Of course she's not here. You just said she was coming."

"No!" Mimette had begun to tremble. "Tess, Tess! You don't understand! She's supposed to be here. Oh, God! Sweet Jesus!"

Tess, alarmed by the tears of fright welling into Mimette's eyes, seized her arms and shook her.

"What are you talking about! Tell me!"

"Oh, Tess!" Tears spilled unheeded down Mimette's cheeks. "The madame! She left for Saint-Cloud over a week ago!"

"No!" Tess breathed.

"The monsieur sent me here to join her!" She shook her head, openly sobbing now. "She never got here, did she?"

Shaking, Tess weaved and Judah guided

her into a chair heedless of the sheeting that covered it.

"No," Tess whispered, mortally afraid. "She never got here."

# CHAPTER 36

With all possible haste, Tess, Mimette, and Judah departed Saint-Cloud for New Orleans. Lysette was uppermost in their minds and though each had his or her own private theories on what had happened to her, not one of the three wanted to worry the others by revealing their fears.

Aboard the Belle Helene once more, the three of them stalked the decks and salons unable to settle down, eager for the trip to be over, anxious to tell Nicholas their horrifying news.

"It's all his fault!" Tess muttered. "That vile man! He drove her to run away and now look what's happened!"

"Don't say such things," Mimette chided, not so in awe of Tess as she had once been. "The madame loves him. And he loves her."

"Love! Bah! What can an animal like Nicholas Callaway know of love! And how could you ever think that Lysette could love him after what he has done to her! He killed their child and nearly killed her!"

"That was not his fault!" Judah defended hotly. "He was driven to it by Madame D'Everaux and Mrs. Scofield!"

"He was!" Mimette chimed in, herself almost surprised by her defense of Nicholas. "They made him believe that she was unfaithful! He is madly jealous and afraid—"

"Afraid?" Tess scoffed.

"Yes! Afraid that she does not love him! That she will not forgive him for what happened between them!"

"And why should she forgive him? If he were any kind of a man, he would let her go back to Saint-Cloud to live in peace!"

"She would find no peace without him, can't you see that Tess? She loves him!"

"Then why was she running away? Answer me that!"

Mimette frowned, troubled. That same question had been on her mind since Mrs. Jonelle had come home from the millinery shop with the astonishing news that Lysette had disappeared. Why had Lysette run away? Mimette remembered her skittishness in the past weeks. She recalled Lysette's vigils at the window, her telling her that Kit was forever watching, always following. . .

"Kit Stratton!" she whispered, finally understanding.

"What?" Tess demanded.

"Kit Stratton! The artist who painted the portrait that so enraged Monsieur Callaway. He'd been following her wherever she went for weeks! Perhaps he took her off somewhere!"

"How dare you suggest that Lysette would run off with any. . ."

"No, Tess, listen!" Mimette leaned toward

her, excited. "I know she meant to go to Saint-Cloud. That is why she wouldn't let me come to the milliner's—she knew it would be easier to slip away from Mrs. Jonelle. But what if, once she got outside. . ."

"He was waiting for her?" Judah supplied.

"Yes! Don't you see? He'd been following her; he'd been sitting outside the house in a carriage trying to catch a glimpse of her. . ." She spread her hands. "It only makes sense that he was there when she went to Mrs. Archer's millinery as well. If she came out suddenly, alone, unguarded. . ."

The three of them stared at one another in uneasy thought.

"Where would he take her?" Judah wondered aloud.

"To his apartment?" Mimette ventured.

"No." Judah shook his head. "I don't think he'd risk keeping her in the city."

"Then where?" Tess demanded impatiently.

"I don't know. We'll have to wait and ask Mr. Callaway. He'll know what to do."

They fell silent, each lost in thought, each wondering where Lysette was at that moment. Whether she was safe; whether Stratton could be trusted to keep her safe until Nicholas managed to find and rescue her. They said nothing to one another as they strolled the decks. It was not until they entered the grand main salon that Mimette caught Tess's arm bringing her to an abrupt halt.

"See that man?" she asked, nodding in the

direction of the handsome, thin man with the greying brown hair.

Tess squinted toward him. Her eyes were not what they had once been but she would have been the last to admit it.

The man in question was seated in an armchair near a bank of windows. His legs were crossed and in his hands he held the same leather covered hinged frame Mimette had seen him with before.

"What about him?" Tess asked.

Mimette related the story of how, during their trip to Saint-Cloud, the man had kept Judah from striking her. Judah rolled his eyes but it was obvious that Mimette relished the tale of how the dapper man had come to her rescue.

"Perhaps I should thank him again," she mused at the end of her tale.

"You'll do no such thing," Tess decreed. "You should be ashamed of yourself, miss. You've grown very forward during your stay in New Orleans!"

"I have not!" Mimette argued hotly. She sulked when she glanced back toward the man and saw that another woman had joined him thus destroying her chance to speak to him again.

"He was very nice," she finished lamely.

"Yes, well, you may depend upon it that he would not be so nice if you showed yourself to be a pushy littly hussy!" Tess sniffed.

"Hussy!" Mimette gasped. "How dare. . ."

"Oh, stop!" Judah groused. "It doesn't

matter. The man is gone now. We have more important things to worry about."

The thought sobered them all and they settled into a pensive silence that lasted the rest of the trip.

Arriving in New Orleans, they took a hired carriage home but none of them was really eager to tell Nicholas their news. Under protest, Mimette agreed to act as their spokesman and break the bad news to their master.

He scowled when he saw Tess. "What in blazes are you doing back so quickly?" he demanded. He glared at Tess. "And what in blazes are you doing here at all?"

"Let me explain, monsieur," Mimette begged.

"Please do."

Quickly, with as little emotion as possible, Mimette told him what she'd learned upon her arrival at Saint-Cloud. Stunned, Nicholas listened. When she'd finished, he clenched his fists with rage.

"Stratton!" he snarled. "It has to be Stratton who is behind this!"

"I agree," monsieur," Mimette said quickly. "Monsieur Stratton has been following the madame for weeks."

"He what!"

Tess, Judah, and Mimette flinched as his words echoed up the soaring stairwell.

"Do you mean to tell me," Nicholas ground out, each word like the cracking of a whip.

"Do you actually mean to tell me that this bastard's been following Lysette for weeks and no one told me! Didn't it occur to you that I might be the least bit interested!"

"I wanted to tell you," Mimette protested. "I pleaded with the madame to tell you, She refused!"

"Why didn't you tell me!"

Mimette lowered her eyes. "She is my mistress, monsieur."

"And I am your master!"

Covering her eyes with her hands, the maid began to sob. An awkward silence fell over the rest until Nicholas went to the girl and patted her comfortingly.

"Come now, none of that," he soothed impatiently.

"I'm sorry, monsieur," Mimette wept, scrubbing at her wet cheeks with the backs of her hands. "I know I should have told you but she asked me not to. Oh! I'll never forgive myself if anything happens to her."

"Nor should you, you stupid girl!" Tess spat.

"That's enough of that!" Nicholas growled "I'll tolerate your presence, Tess, because I know you are concerned for Lysette. But if you begin causing trouble, I'll pack you back to Saint-Cloud so fast you won't know what's happening to you!"

Tess returned his glare defiantly for several moments but then, realizing that he had not only the authority but the willingness to carry out his threat, she acquisced.

"As you wish, monsieur," she murmured.

"Now, I want the three of you to begin unpacking. I am going to Stratton's."

Ordering a carriage, Nicholas set out for Kit Stratton's apartment. He took the rickety stairs two at a time and, reaching the top, pounded on the door until the corridor resounded with the thunderous pounding.

A door down the hall creaked open and a slovenly woman in a torn gown of raggedy cotton glared at him.

"He ain't there!" she shouted over the ear-splitting noise.

"He what?" Nicholas demanded.

"I said, he ain't there. He left. Moved out."

"When?"

She shrugged. "I dunno. Mebbe a week—a week and a half ago. No, wait, closer to two weeks now."

"Where did he go?"

"How should I know? He never talked to me. Never talked much to anybody here. We weren't good enough for the likes of him what with him paintin' society women an' all."

Scowling, Nicholas turned and started down the stairs.

"What's 'e done?" the woman called after him.

Nicholas ignored her and, with a muttered oath against high-nosed snobs without the manners God gave mules, she slammed back into her own apartment.

Leaving Kit's, Nicholas went next to

Rosalyn's where he was told that she had gone to Baton Rouge but was expected back any day. Angry and frustrated, Nicholas climbed back into his carriage and set out for Collier Shaw's gallery.

Shaw saw him as he strode through the door. Leaving his clerk to see to the patrons then browsing among the paintings and sculpture, he led Nicholas into the privacy of his office at the rear of the shop.

"If this has to do with Kit Stratton," he said quickly, "I want you to know I'm not handling his work any longer. I haven't seen him in some time."

"Damn!" Nicholas ran a hand through his hair. "No one has seen him! How the devil can the man disappear like this?"

"May I ask why you're looking for him?"

Nicholas glared at him. "My wife."

Collier groaned. "He hasn't painted another portrait, has he?"

"Worse than that, I'm afraid."

"Worse?"

"He's abducted her."

Collier was stunned. "Abducted. . . You can't be serious!"

But the unrelenting hatred in Nicholas's eyes quashed any notions Collier might have had as to the seriousness of Nicholas's accusations. "When did this happen?"

Nicholas lifted his shoulders. "Apparently nearly two weeks ago."

"Apparently, sir? Forgive me, but. . ."

"She was going on a trip, Mr. Shaw. It was

not until I got concerned at not hearing from her and sent some of my servants after her that I discovered she had never reached her destination."

"And you have reason to suspect Kit is behind all this?"

"I have."

"May I ask what they are?"

Nicholas shot the man an impatient glare. "I don't really see where my reasons are at issue here, Mr. Shaw. Suffice to say that are sound reasons."

"I see." Collier's mind raced. If possible, he had to prevent a direct confrontation between the furious Callaway and Kit, who was no match for him in any way. He stroked his moustache thoughtfully. "I'm afraid I can't help you, sir. I'm told that Kit has left New Orleans."

"I know that much already. I went to his apartment and was told he had moved some time ago."

"Yes. I am afraid that all I can do just now is promise to keep you informed in the event that I discover anything about Kit's whereabouts."

Nicholas scowled. How had that man so completely covered his tracks? "I suppose that will have to do for now, Mr. Shaw. I would appreciate anything you should learn."

"Of course. You may depend upon me."

Conducting Nicholas back out to the street, Collier Shaw beckoned his clerk to his office.

"I'm going out of town for a few days, Marcus. You will be in charge. If, that is, you think you can manage without making a muddle of things."

"I can, Mr. Shaw!" the sandy-haired boy assured him. "I know I can!"

"Very well, see that you do."

"Where can you be reached, sir?"

"I can't. That is why you must proceed on your own, my boy." He treated the young man to a baleful glare. "If you think you are not up to the task. . ."

"I am, sir. I am!" the boy assured him.

"Humph. Well, we shall see; we shall see."

Dismissing the boy with a wave of his hand, he began gathering the papers he would take home. Within hours, he would be on his way to Burr Oak. Someone had to talk some sense into Kit Stratton before this asinine obsession of his got him killed!

# CHAPTER 37

As Lysette had always known it would, the time came when she could no longer bear to spend another moment amidst the crumbling decay that was Burr Oak, beneath the watchful eyes of Kit and the lecherous gaze of Jesse Harris.

Donning Kit's breeches and shirt, she took a fistful of the gold she still kept hidden in the feathers of her pillow and stuffed them in her pockets. She was determined to escape. And if she could make it out of the swamps and find help, she might well need the money to pay for her transportation back to New Orleans.

She slipped out the back door and ran through the tangled gardens. She was going to follow the road as best she could, depending upon it to lead her back to civilization. But she could not walk on the road itself for should Kit discover her missing, he was certain to ride along the twisting lane in search of her.

From the moment she plowed into the dense undergrowth the marshes that surrounded the grounds of Burr Oak, she was beset by doubts. It would be easy, so easy, to get lost. Even if she tried to stay in sight of the road there might well be places where it forked and then her life could depend upon her choosing the right road. Then too, there were natural hazards in the swamp. The marshlands teemed with life but for every charming rabbit, black-masked raccoon, or playful otter, there was a deadly predator like the venomous copperhead, the black bear, the ever-vigilant alligator gliding in the shallows.

And there were other dangers . . . Lysette was not certain exactly when she became aware that she was being followed. It might have been the crackling of a dead limb beneath a boot or the startled cry of a bird as it fluttered into the treetops. But she knew he was there, in the shadows behind her, as stealthy and as deadly as the alligators whose piercing eyes rode just above the algae-green surface of the water—Jesse Harris.

She walked faster. Her feet, in her soft boots, were bruised by sharp branches and stones. The vines winding their clinging tendrils about everything in their path entangled her time and again. She pushed a strand of damp hair off her forehead with a dirty hand as she broke into a run. Without venturing a glance over her shoulder, she knew her pursuer had done the same.

"God, help me!" she whispered, desperation making her clumsy. She stumbled, nearly falling, then, righting herself, ran on.

Over the harsh wheezing of her own

breaths, she heard the sound of hoofbeats on the road off to her left. Without stopping to consider alternatives, she changed her direction. She didn't know what she was running toward, but she knew what she was running from. In her mind, the choice was clear.

The two horses shied as she broke from the undergrowth and emerged onto the narrow dirt lane. Their riders, a thin man with grey-brown hair and another, reined in their mounts as Lysette stumbled toward them.

"Please, help me?" she cried, grasping the bridle of the sorrel mare. "There's a man! He's following me! He wants to . . ."

Jesse Harris had been so intent upon his pursuit of Lysette that he had not even heard the hoofbeats of the approaching horses. It was not until he, too, broke from the underbrush and found himself in the road that he saw the men to whom his intended victim had run for help.

His eyes seemed to pop with shock and fear. He seemed paralyzed as he stood in the middle of the lane staring into a pair of hate-filled grey eyes he had thought never to see again.

A muscle in the horseman's lean cheek quivered. In an instant he remembered all the pain this man had caused him—the torment Harris had inflicted upon the woman he had loved more than his own life—the anguish that had caused her to seek her own death.

From that day to this, he had searched for Jesse Harris. He had not spent a day or a night without thinking of him and of the vengeance that would someday be his. Without bothering to take out the frame, he remembered every beloved detail of the woman's face in the picture he carried with him at all times—the same picture Mimette had seen him gazing at aboard the Belle Helene when he was traveling to meet the detective he'd hired to find Harris—the detective who now rode beside him.

Pierre Laroux drew a gun from his pocket.

"I'm going to kill you, Harris," he said, so softly that Lysette, standing beside his horse, could hardly believe she'd heard him correctly. "For Eugenie."

Jesse lifted his hands and held them in front of him as though they could protect him.

The deep lines in Laroux's prematurely aged face deepened as he forced a wan smile. "You cannot escape my justice. You were the cause of her death—you preyed upon her as ruthlessly as any animal preys upon its victim—as mercilessly as you would have preyed upon this woman had we not stopped you."

He raised the gun and steadied it to shoot, but Jesse suddenly bolted. Wheeling, he ran back into the undergrowth. Lysette was left standing alone in the road as the two men set off in pursuit.

She moved slowly, warily, up the lane, not

knowing which way to go. She was turned around, lost. She was confused, frightened. When Jesse's high, despairing wail drowned the noise of the swamp creatures and the five shots rang out heralding the end of his miserable existence, she screamed and slid heavily to the ground in the shade of a towering, gnarled oak.

When at last she awoke, it was not softly but with a shriek of pure terror. She fought as Kit ran into the room and wrapped her in his arms.

"Jesse!" she cried. "He's after me! Nicholas! Nicholas! Help me!"

Kit winced, hurt that it should be Nicholas she called out to for comfort. It should have been him! Him! A small voice inside him whispered that his was a hopeless quest but by now he had convinced himself that his life would have no meaning without her. If Lysette would never be his, there was no point in his existence.

"Hush, now, hush," he soothed, rocking her in his arms. "He's dead. Jesse's dead."

"Dead?" She frowned, confused, then remembered. "Yes! Oh, yes! Oh, Kit! They shot him! Those men!"

"They were here. They brought you back to me."

"But why did they kill him? One man said something about a woman—a woman named Eugenie."

"He was Pierre Laroux. Eugenie was his wife. She killed herself after their overseer forced himself upon her. Jesse was their overseer."

"Oh, God." Lysette covered her face with her hands. "He was chasing me, Kit. Through the swamp. He wanted to . . . to. . ."

"I know. I've been blind to him. Thank God Laroux and his man found you in time. The man was a detective from Baton Rouge whom Laroux had hired to find Harris and his wife. Valina was the cook at Laroux's plantation."

"Where is Valina? Did they take her with them?"

Kit frowned. "She's dead, Lysette."

"Dead?" Lysette paled. "They shot her as well?"

"No. She'd done nothing, really. Oh, she knew what Jesse had done but she kept his secret—he was her husband, after all. Laroux only wanted to talk to her. But when she saw him, she ran out the back door. They followed her into the marshes."

"What happened to her?"

"It's not important, Lysette," he hedged.

"Tell me, Kit, I've a right to know."

"Darling, please. . ."

"Kit! Tell me!"

He sighed. "She was running. Her skirts became entangled as she was trying to cross a pond on a fallen cypress. She fell into the water."

"She drowned?" Lysette prompted when he fell silent for too long.

Kit looked away. "No. There . . . there are a

lot of alligators in those marshes, Lysette."

She pressed a hand to her mouth. "Oh, God, Kit! An alligator!"

"Now you're upset. Let me give you something to help you rest."

"I don't want anything."

"Don't argue with me, Lysette. You'll need to be well rested for the trip back to New Orleans."

"New Orleans?" Lysette couldn't believe she'd heard him. "Kit?"

The desperate hope in her eyes and her voice sealed the fate of all Kit's dreams. He knew he could never win her heart—she would forever belong to Nicholas Callaway no matter how many miles might separate them. But he was determined to keep her with him as long as possible. A dream, even a futile dream, was better than no dream at all.

"In three days," he told her. "I will take you back to New Orleans in three days."

Lysette was disappointed but at least he had agreed to take her back. Nicholas! She would be with Nicholas again in three days' time.

"If," Kit went on, "if you will take this and sleep. You need your rest."

He held out a glass to her and she took it, obeying without question, perhaps foolishly, but nevertheless trusting in Kit's love enough to believe he would not hurt her although knowing she would never be his.

Drinking the laudanum-laced tea, she lay back on the pillows which were soft now, since the gold she had hidden inside had gone to the bottom of the pond with what remained of Valina Harris, and let the drug take effect.

Kit stood by the bed watching her. His heart ached with love and the pain seemed harsher now, searing, piercing. He knew that once he returned her to Nicholas's side, he would never see her again. He would take Collier Shaw's advice and go away to Europe. But unlike Collier's prophecy, he would never return to New Orleans in triumph; he would never return at all.

He heard a carriage turn into the drive before the house and looked out. Collier Shaw!

"Speak of the Devil," he muttered, leaving the room.

Lysette was sleeping soundly; he need have no worries on that score. No one, not Collier, not Callaway, not the Devil himself was going to cheat him out of these three last precious days with Lysette.

He opened the front door as Collier stepped down from his carriage.

"Kit." The art dealer's eyes skimmed the darkened hallway behind Kit for some sign of Lysette.

"What are you doing here, Collier?" Kit demanded.

"I think you know. I want you to let me take her back with me."

"Who?"

"Come now, don't fence with me. Nicholas

Callaway came to my gallery the other day. His wife is missing. Let me take her back and perhaps I can keep him from killing you."

Kit's sigh was world-weary. "I don't know what you're talking about, Collier, and I haven't time for games. I think it would be best if you just got back into your carriage and went home."

"Not without Lysette."

Blue fires flashed in Kit's eyes. Why was the world conspiring to keep him from enjoying a moment's happiness? Was three days too much to ask out of a lifetime? Callaway would have her forever. All Kit wanted was three short days in her company.

"Get out of here! Now! And don't come back! In three days I'm going to Europe. I won't be back. Leave me alone, Collier, now!"

In the hard, unyielding expression on Kit's face, Collier saw clearly the futility of his task. He had no doubt that Lysette was somewhere in the mansion but there was no way he could force his way inside to search. For all he knew, Kit had servants inside who would help him repel any intruder. Still, he had to have proof to show Nicholas—to show the authorities if necessary.

"Could I at least have something to drink before I leave?" he asked. "It's a deucedly long drive and a damned hot day."

Kit's eyes gleamed with suspicion. "All right. Wait here."

Turning on his heel, he disappeared in the direction of the kitchen. Collier waited only until Kit was out of sight then, taking a chance, chose a door at random and ducked into the parlor off the entrance hall. He seized the first likely-looking object he saw, a pad lying on a table near the door, and stuffed it into his coat pocket.

By the time Kit returned to the entrance hall, a glass of water in hand, Collier was once again standing where he'd left him, apparently having waited there the entire time.

"Thank you," he muttered, drinking enough of the water to allay Kit's suspicions. "You won't change your mind?"

"There's no reason for me to change my mind," Kit maintained stubbornly. "And you can tell Callaway there's no reason for him to make the drive. He'll find nothing more here than you did."

"I've no choice but to believe you, Kit," Collier said, leaving the gallery and walking to his carriage. "But I hoped you would consider Lysette's feelings in all this."

"If Lysette were here," Kit said patiently, confident in the knowledge that it would be several hours before she even stirred in her upstairs bedroom, "I would certainly do what I believed was best for her."

"She loves Callaway, Kit, and he. . ."

"You've outstayed your welcome," Kit ground out coldly. "You'd better leave."

"As you wish. Goodbye, Kit. I doubt we'll be meeting again."

He climbed back into his carriage and with the crack of his whip the coachman took them off down the curving drive. Kit watched until they were out of sight then returned to his studio confident that he had three days in which to have Lysette to himself—three days before his dream world came to a shattering end.

Sitting back in his carriage, Collier Shaw took out the pad he had stolen from Kit's parlor and flipped through it. His fears were confirmed as he'd known they were bound to be. Page after page was filled with Lysette. Frowning, scowling, pleading, weeping, all posed against the unmistakable, decaying backdrop of Burr Oak. She was never smiling, never laughing. Here was not Lysette Callaway, the belle of New Orleans society. Here was Lysette Callaway, the captive of a man's obsessive, unhealthy love. He knew what he had to do. Once returned to New Orleans, he would go to Nicholas and tell him where Lysette was. He could protect Kit no longer; he'd given him every chance. Now it was Lysette who had his sympathy; it was Lysette who needed his help.

Slipping the pad back into his pocket, he leaned back against the seat and wished for the miles between him and New Orleans to pass quickly—he wished for the hours before he could put Lysette's rescue into effect to fly.

# CHAPTER 38

Nicholas's hands shook as he leafed through the sketchbook Collier Shaw had presented to him upon being shown into his office.

"So she is with Stratton," he muttered. "I knew it!" He glared at Shaw with hate-filled eyes. "You knew she was there. You deliberately lied to. . ."

"I suspected she was there," Collier corrected. "I had no proof. There was no way of knowing for certain that he had gone there or that he had taken her there."

"You didn't see her?"

"He wouldn't even let me in. I tricked him into allowing me the time to gain some evidence. . ." He nodded toward the pad on Nicholas's desk. "The sketchbook."

Sighing, Nicholas closed the book. He could not bear to see again the anguish in Lysette's eyes, the fear, the pleading. The drawings tore at his heart when he tried to imagine what she'd gone through since Kit had taken her away.

"If he's touched her . . ." he muttered, more to himself than to Shaw.

"No one would blame you for killing him,"

Shaw said callously. "If he's dishonored her. . ."

"If? I?" Nicholas was incredulous. "If you think for a moment I'd even consider letting Stratton walk away from all this. . ."

Shaw recognized the grim determination in Nicholas's very stance. "You are going to kill him, aren't you?"

Nicholas's black eyes smoldered with the rage that had burned inside him for what seemed like years.

"I am," he confirmed. "If not now—if he should manage to escape me this time—then someday. But one day I will kill him."

"He's an artist; he's temperamental. . ."

"He's a madman!" Nicholas shouted. "Good God, Shaw! How long are you going to make excuses for him? Even you must admit that he's gone too far? What if this were your wife? It's Lysette he's obsessed with now but if it weren't her it would be someone else. Eventually it will be someone else. And how long will it go on before he turns violent? Before he decides that he'd rather see some poor woman dead than out of his arms?"

"I don't think. . ."

"Well, I do! By God, he's not getting away with this! Yes! Yes, I plan to kill him! And if you won't tell me how to find him, I'll find someone else who will!"

He had too long dealt in art not to regret the loss of genius such as Kit Stratton possessed, but even Collier had to admit that Nicholas was right. Kit was unbalanced. It was bound to get worse. Still. . .

"You won't simply shoot him down like an animal, will you?" he asked.

Scowling, Nicholas leaned back in his chair. "I won't say he doesn't deserve it, Shaw. In my heart, I feel he's no better than a mad dog and doesn't deserve to be treated any differently. But he is a man. I will deal with him as I would with any man." He shoved a pen and paper across the desk toward Shaw. "Now, if you will, I'd like directions to Burr Oak."

Collier hesitated before picking up the pen. He felt he was being asked to sign Kit's death warrant. But he had no choice; no matter his feelings for Kit, there was Lysette to be considered. She'd been hurt enough. He would not stand in the way of her being delivered from her tormentor.

He took up the pen and began to write.

It was nearly half an hour later that he let himself into his gallery. There were a few customers being attended to by his clerk who had, apparently, kept the business running with some degree of efficiency during his master's absence.

"Mr. Shaw!" the pudgy, freckle-faced clerk left his customers and hurried to Collier's side. "There is a lady waiting in your office. Apparently she'd seen your carriage and came here to wait for you to return. I tried to tell her that. . ."

"Who is it?" Collier interrupted impatiently.

"Madame D'Everaux."

Sighing, Collier went to his office. He'd had

enough of the Strattons for one lifetime. Now that he'd dealt with Kit, he had to find himself face-to-face with Kit's equally devious cousin.

"Madame," he said politely as he hung his hat on the stand and shrugged off his coat. "What can I do for you?"

Dressed completely in widow's black, Rosalyn was no less beautiful than she had ever been. But those who knew her well could detect the minute changes that the past weeks had wrought. She was thinner, paler, and there were lines around her eyes and flanking her mouth that had not been there before. Worry had etched them there; despair had deepened them; hatred had fixed them in place for all time.

"Mr. Shaw, I want to know where Kit has gone. I returned to New Orleans yesterday and went to his apartment. Some old hag there told me. . ."

She was interrupted by Collier's weary laughter.

"I fail to see what is so terribly humorous about my question, sir," she snapped.

"I imagine you do, madame," he replied. "But I can tell you that I am so sick of hearing about your cousin, I could live a happy man for the rest of my life if only I knew I never had to hear his name again!"

"What are you talking about?"

"Your cousin, madame, your damnable cousin, has committed his last folly. At this moment, Nicholas Callaway is on his way to Burr Oak to kill him."

"Kill him! No!"

"Yes!"

Rosalyn sagged back into her chair as Collier told her what had happened. When he'd finished, she rose, shaking, and took her leave. But if she looked frail, if more than one of the customers in the gallery watched in alarm as she made her unsteady way to her carriage, it was belied by the determined sparkle in her green eyes. The wheels inside her pretty head were turning. There might, there just might, be one last chance for revenge against Nicholas Callaway and that little French she-bitch who had stolen him from her!

Climbing into her carriage, she ordered it away to Burr Oak with all possible speed.

It was morning of the following day when Nicholas turned his horse into the drive of Burr Oak. The fog that rose above the marsh swirled about him. It blurred the contours of the moss-draped trees and the logs and stumps with their shrouds of resurrection fern. It lent an air of eerie calm about the marshland that made every shape and shadow into something sinister and threatening.

Burr Oak came into view. With the fog creeping along its decaying gallerys, eddying about the broken pillars, it was a deplorable sight. Nicholas's rage renewed itself at the thought of Lysette's captivity in such a grim ruin.

Lysette came awake at the sound of a

horse's neigh. Kicking away the quilt, she went to the window.

"Nicholas. . ." She scrubbed at the dirt-streaked panes with a red, roughened hand. With the death of Valina Harris, she had fallen heiress to the chores that had to be done: the cooking, the washing, the cleaning. . . Unused to such labor, her hands had grown cracked and sore. She winced as she wiped clean a window pane. "Nicholas!"

Impossible as it seemed, she knew she wasn't dreaming. It was Nicholas! It was! Even then he was dismounting; even then he stood before the broken steps of the mansion.

She tore out of her room and down the stairs heedless that she wore only the chemise that had become her nightdress.

She reached the bottom and raced across the entrance hall.

"Nicholas!" Her anguished cry cut the silence of the foggy morning. She threw herself into his arms. "Nicholas! You've come! I prayed you would!"

Nicholas looked down into her eyes. Even filled with tears they were more beautiful than anything he'd ever seen. He wrapped her in his arms; crushed her in his embrace. Lysette clung to him desperately, her hands grasping at his coat as though afraid to let go lest he vanish like some desert mirage.

Pulling off his coat, Nicholas wrapped it around her. He held her close and she gazed up at him with all the love he'd ever hoped to see in her eyes. But he was looking past her—toward the door of the mansion where Kit stood, just awakened by Lysette's cry.

"Stratton." Nicholas's voice was filled with a deadly calm that was far more frightening than any oath he could have uttered.

"So Shaw sent you," Kit surmised tonelessly.

"Did you think he wouldn't?"

"No. I knew he would. I was going to bring her back soon."

"It's too late."

Kit nodded. "I know. You mean to kill me, don't you?"

Lysette looked from one man to the other. How could they be so calm? They were discussing murder and death and yet neither seemed to have a care in the world. Each man seemed resigned to Kit's death as though it were inevitable.

"I do," Nicholas confirmed. He reached into his saddle bag and took out a long, polished wooden box. Lysette knew it contained a pair of matched, exquisitely tooled dueling pistols. "When and where?" he asked Kit.

"There," Kit replied, nodding toward the clearing at the side of the mansion near where the drive disappeared into the trees. "In an hour?"

Nicholas nodded. "In an hour."

Kit turned and walked back into the mansion. Nicholas looked down at Lysette.

"It's the only way," he told her gently. "You know that, don't you?"

"I won't question you," she told him. "I've had done with questioning you, Nicholas." Reluctantly, she stepped out of his arms. "I'll go get dressed."

Nicholas watched her reenter the mansion. It would be the last time, he told himself, that she would be parted from him. From now on . . . But no, he cautioned himself against undue optimism. He was confident of his ability as a marksman but there was danger in overconfidence. In an hour they would begin to plan their future together. In an hour. . .

The hour passed as if four, but at last Nicholas and Kit stood back to back in the center of the overgrown meadow at the edge of the drive. Birds sang in the trees, fluffy clouds scudded across a sky filled with sunshine that had burned away the morning's fog. Lysette stood at the base of a gnarled oak praying for it all to be over.

The two men paced off their distance and turned, a pistol held in their right hands. In the second before they leveled their weapons and fired, it was Kit who, facing the drive, saw the glitter of the sunshine on the barrel of the rifle as it was raised. He swung his gun wide of its mark and fired into the trees even as Nicholas's gun discharged the bullet that would end Kit's life.

Lysette screamed as the shots echoed in the forest. She saw Kit fall; she knew he was dead. She turned in astonishment in the direction toward which Kit had fired when she heard the sound of a second body falling into the crackling underbrush.

"Nicholas!" she cried. "Over there!"

Nicholas reached Rosalyn before Lysette could. The ugly wound in her breast oozed blood that stained the black mourning she wore for a husband she had never loved.

"I hated you," she whispered to Nicholas as he knelt beside her. "I hated you and I loved you."

"Rosalyn. . ."

"I wanted to kill you! I tried before but she stopped me!" Her eyes went to Lysette who had come to Nicholas's side. "Yes, you! You protected him; shielded him. I didn't want you dead. I wanted you to live without him as I had to."

"It was you!" Lysette remembered the night when she had gone to Nicholas on the gallery of their New Orleans home and kept him from being shot by the unknown assailant in the carriage across the street.

"Yes, it was me! I should have killed you! I should have! I. . ."

Her eyes glazed and the awful death rattle gurgled in her throat. Rosalyn D'Everaux was dead.

Rising, Nicholas pulled off his coat and covered her. He went to Rosalyn's coach standing in the lane and instructed her coachman to come and receive the bodies of Rosalyn and her cousin and take them to New Orleans. He and Lysette would follow in Kit's coach and make the proper reports to the proper authorities.

"Is it over?" Lysette asked as she and Nicholas walked back to the mansion. "Is it really over?"

"Nearly," he told her, an arm draped about her waist.

A gentle rain was falling, running in rivulets down the window panes of the Callaways' New Orleans townhouse as Nicholas and Lysette sat before the fireplace of the emerald-walled bedroom that they would, from that night forward, share. In the grate of the marble fireplace a fire burned, feeding hungrily on the sheaf of papers that had once been Nicholas and Lysette's marriage contract.

"Are you sure you want to burn it?" Nicholas asked softly.

"Yes! Oh, yes!" she sighed, nestling contentedly in his arms as they lay propped against a pile of down pillows on the soft carpet. "I don't need a contract to prove that I'm your wife. No signature on a piece of paper can prove that I love you."

"And do you love me?" he asked, a teasing light sparkling in his black eyes.

"Do you doubt it?" she challenged lightly. "Shall I prove it?"

"Can you?"

With a seductive smile, she pushed aside the pillows and lay back on the carpet. Her hands slid up the rich, silky damask of his robe, caressed his face, then buried themselves in the thick softness of his hair. She pulled his head down.

"I can, my love," she whispered, her lips against his as her body molded itself to his. "Indeed, I can!"